W9-AAL-401

The Civil War Stories of Harold Frederic

New York Classics
Frank Bergmann, Series Editor

The Civil War Stories of Harold Frederic

Edited by
THOMAS F. O'DONNELL

With an Introduction by
EDMUND WILSON

SYRACUSE UNIVERSITY PRESS

Copyright © 1992 by Syracuse University Press
Syracuse, New York 13244-5160

All Rights Reserved

First Paperback Edition 1992
92 93 94 95 96 97 98 99   6 5 4 3 2 1

The Civil War Stories of Harold Frederic was originally published by Syracuse University Press in 1966 under the title *Harold Frederic's Stories of
York State.*

This book is published with the assistance of a grant from the John Ben
Snow Foundation.

The paper used in this publication meets the minimum requirements of
American National Standard for Information Sciences—Permanence of
Paper for Printed Library Materials, ANSI Z39.48-1984. ∞™

Library of Congress Cataloging-in-Publication Data

Frederic, Harold, 1856–1898.
    [Harold Frederic's stories of York State]
    The Civil War stories of Harold Frederic / edited by Thomas F.
O'Donnell ; with an introduction by Edmund Wilson. —1st paperback
ed.
        p.   cm.
    Originally published: Harold Frederic's stories of York State. 1st ed.
Syracuse : Syracuse University Press, 1966.
    ISBN 0-8156-2572-3 (pbk. : alk. paper)
    1. New York (State)—History—Civil War, 1861–1865—
Fiction.   I. O'Donnell, Thomas Francis, 1915–   .   II. Title.
PS1706.036   1992
813'.4—dc20   92-4260

Manufactured in the United States of America

Editor's Foreword

ONE of the men Stephen Crane most wanted to meet when he arrived in London in 1897 was Harold Frederic, European correspondent for the *New York Times*. Frederic had come to London some thirteen years before, after editorial experience on Utica and Albany newspapers. Now, at forty, he was widely known on both sides of the Atlantic, not only as a brilliant journalist, but as the author of a recent publishing sensation, *The Damnation of Theron Ware*. Since Frederic had been abroad so long, and since his career had been so glittering, Crane was prepared, he wrote later, to meet "a cosmopolitan figure, representing many ways of many peoples." But when he found Frederic at his club, Crane recalled with delight, "behold, he was still the familiar figure, with no gilding, no varnish, a great reminiscent panorama of the Mohawk Valley!"[1]

Even as the two authors met—and became firm friends—the reading public in both America and England was still buzzing about Frederic's new novel. But Crane and Frederic both knew, if not many other people did, that *The Damnation of Theron Ware* was only the most recent in a long series of novels and short stories that perceptively mirrored a number of aspects of life in Frederic's native region in upstate New York. This series —"a great reminiscent panorama of the Mohawk Valley"— began with his first novel, *Seth's Brother's Wife* (1887) and continued with *In the Valley* and *The Lawton Girl*, both published in 1890. In the first of these, Frederic told a story against the background of political warfare in the region; in the second,

---

[1] These and subsequent quotations from Crane come from his article, "Harold Frederic," *The Chap-Book*, VIII (March 15, 1898), 358–59.

against the background of military warfare; in the third, against the background of economic warfare.

Heartened by the moderate success of these works and prompted by memories of his wartime boyhood in Utica thirty years before, Frederic turned, in 1892 and 1893, to the stories that comprise this volume. Now, in seven novelettes and short stories, he recalled—with pride in their strength and sadness for their weakness—his onetime neighbors in Mohawk Valley towns and villages and the ways in which they had reacted to the national catastrophe that shattered the stillness of their quiet lives.

As he wrote these stories, Frederic gathered the artistic and stylistic strength that was to distinguish his later work. More important, perhaps, he developed a new appreciation of the American character of his time. Competent as his early fiction had been, none of it is especially notable for its awareness of the strain of dark memory that lay deep beneath the garish surface of the Gilded Age. Until 1892, when he was thirty-six—he was born in Utica in 1856—his own career and American life itself had been pretty much of a comedy for Frederic. The black-and-white successes of Seth Fairchild, Reuben Tracy, and Douw Mauverensen—the heroes of his early novels—reflect not only Frederic's own early and easy triumphs, but an incomplete understanding of the American that he wanted desperately to portray. The early novels reveal a conviction, to be sure, that in every American's blood there must be some politics, some economics, even some revolution. But this is not enough, Frederic seemed to realize in 1892; there must also be some sense of tragedy derived from recent history.

And so, in the stories that came from his pen in rapid succession during the next two years, he called up his memories— both bright and dark—of life as he had seen it in the Mohawk Valley during the Civil War. None of the stories, to be sure, is tragic; Frederic was incapable of writing tragedy. All of them, however, are written against a background that is potentially, if not actually, tragic. In the words of Stephen Crane, they are stories of "the great country back of the line of fight—the waiting women, the lightless windows, the tables set for three instead of five . . . a land elate or forlorn, triumphant or despairing, always strained, eager, listening, tragic in attitude, trembling and quivering like a vast mass of nerves from the shock of the far away conflicts in the South."

These stories, Crane went on, breathe "the spirit of a Titanic conflict as felt and endured at the homes," and "form a most notable achievement in writing times in America." Ironically, at the very time the stories appeared, Crane observed, "the critics were making a great deal of noise in an attempt to stake the novelists down to the soil and make them write the impressive common life of the United States." Yet "there was Frederic doing his locality, doing his Mohawk Valley, with the strong trained hand of a great craftsman, and the critics were making such a din over the attempt to have a certain kind of thing done, that they did not recognize its presence."

When Frederic finished "A Day in the Wilderness" some time in 1893, he was ready to abandon the short forms of fiction and return to the novel. His style was sharper and more graceful now, his sense of character was stronger and deeper, and he knew his fellow upstate New Yorkers better now than he had ever known them before. Already he was planning *The Damnation of Theron Ware,* destined to be his best novel and his last piece of regional fiction. Two years after its publication in 1896 he was dead at forty-two.

For six decades Frederic's posthumous reputation as a writer has rested heavily on one book. But modern admirers of *The Damnation of Theron Ware*—and that there are many is attested by the recent appearance of four new editions within eighteen months—will want to know more about Frederic and his pictures of life in the Mohawk Valley. This collection is especially for them.

None of these stories has been reprinted in the twentieth century; and never before have all seven appeared within a single volume. The text of "The Deserter" and "A Day in the Wilderness" as reprinted here is from *The Deserter and Other Stories: A Book of Two Wars* (1898); the text of the other five stories is from *In the Sixties* (1897). Obvious misprints and typographical errors have been corrected, but no other changes have been made. Frederic's nineteenth-century hyphenation and occasional British spelling have been retained throughout.

The order in which the stories appear here differs somewhat from the order in which they were written. "The Copperhead," "My Aunt Susan," "The Eve of the Fourth," and "The War Widow" were written, in that order, in 1892; "The Deserter," "Marsena," and "A Day in the Wilderness" in 1893.

THOMAS F. O'DONNELL

Utica College
Utica, New York
January 1966

Contents

Introduction

THE State of New York in the Civil War played the apparently paradoxical role of supplying more soldiers for its population than any other state of the Union and at the same time putting up perhaps the strongest opposition to the Republican administration. The principal opponent of the policies of Lincoln was Horatio Seymour of Utica, who was Democratic Governor of the State from 1863 to 1865. It has become part of the mythology of the Civil War—like Lee's proferring his sword to Grant and Grant's handing it back and Jefferson Davis' fleeing in a woman's dress—that Seymour was a treacherous Copperhead, who connived at and encouraged the New York City draft riots of July, 1863, which were provoked by the federal Conscription Act. This act was decidedly unfair to the poor, since, with the intention of allowing exemption for men with large families or in responsible positions, it provided that the well-to-do could buy themselves off by hiring a substitute or paying three hundred dollars. New York City had a large foreign-born population—especially of Irish—who, from reading the Democratic press, had been prejudiced against the administration. The draft was supposed to include all able-bodied foreign males "between the ages of twenty and forty-five years" who intended to become citizens. When the names were drawn of those who were immediately drafted for three-years service, a good many of these foreign-born citizens made trouble. They were embittered against the Negroes, who had been fleeing from the South to New York and whom they believed to be competing for their jobs. They lynched several and burned down a colored orphanage as well as murdered a number of whites and burned a suburban block.

Horatio Seymour at the time was on his way to spend a weekend in Long Branch, New Jersey, but he immediately returned to New York. Seymour had never been a Copperhead in the sense of one who totally opposed the war. Though he was in favor of settling the conflict by compromise, he had loyally supported the Union and been active in raising troops. He had protested against the suspension of habeas corpus and the disregard of civil liberties, the more and more unscrupulous attacks on the freedom of press and speech. He had opposed the Emancipation Proclamation—as had a number of other people—on the quite correct constitutional grounds that such a measure could not be taken by the Executive alone without the approval of Congress. He now, incorrectly, opposed the draft on the ground that it was unconstitutional. He demanded that its constitutionality be ruled upon and its enforcement in the meantime deferred, and he insisted that unfair quotas had been required of districts known in New York to be Democratic, in comparison with the New England districts. As a result, the injustices were ironed out and the enforcement of the draft—though only very briefly—was held up. It was reported in the Republican press that Seymour had egged on the rioters from the steps of the City Hall; but this is completely untrue: the riots were a mile away from the City Hall. The people that Seymour addressed were a random crowd of passers-by. He urged his hearers to restrain themselves, and he called out the militia to keep order. There were very few troops in the city, for they were mostly in Pennsylvania, where the battle of Gettysburg had just been fought.

Governor Seymour was a victim of war fever of a kind with which we are now familiar. He was denounced as a renegade, a traitor, an agent of Jefferson Davis. He was actually a cool and independent man—a heated Republican like John Templeton Strong resented what he called Seymour's smugness— with a strong sense of moral principle, and an unperturbed Democrat in a period of Republican ascendancy. The population of New York State consisted at that time of the original more-or-less feudal Dutch and the settlers from New England who had moved that far west at the end of the eighteenth century—together with a later-arriving admixture of Germans and Irish. Even the former New Englanders, enjoying their new freedom from the constrictions of New England bigotry and of the tightness of New England towns, in the vast spaces of that sparsely peopled countryside, did not necessarily catch the contagion of the fanatical Calvinists from among whom they had come. True, Utica produced Gerrit Smith, who financed the mad homicide John Brown; but it was also the home of Seymour, who did not believe in abolition, though, believing in free speech, he had defended the abolitionists when they were being hooted down in Utica. The very looseness of the New York communities, and their remoteness from one another, made agreement and consistency difficult.

Harold Frederic, who was born in Utica and who became, first, the editor of a Utica paper; then, the London correspondent of the *New York Times;* then a novelist who dealt mainly with the Mohawk Valley and the author of that once famous and still excellent book *The Damnation of Theron Ware,* was a friend and great admirer of Horatio Seymour. The example set by Seymour, in fact, seems to have been one of the chief influences in Frederic's life. He dedicated to Seymour his second book, *In the Valley,* an historical novel of the Revolution, and the spectacle of Seymour's rectitude is said to have provided the compass by which Frederic steered himself, in his novels as well as his journalism, through the complexities and the corruptions of New York State politics. His stories of New York during the Civil War reflect the peculiar mixture of patriotism and disaffection which was characteristic of that region and for which Seymour was so forthright a spokesman. Due to this, these stories differ fundamentally from any other Civil War fiction I know, and they have thus a unique historical as well as a literary importance. The hero of the longest of them—

really a short novel—is not merely a critic of Republican policies but a real out-and-out Copperhead, an upstate farmer whose ideas are rooted in the principles of the American Revolution and who believes that the South has the right to secede. He is ostracized and persecuted by his neighbors, but then, when the conflict is over, they realize they have injured a man who ought to have commanded respect, since he has stuck to his conviction of what is right and braved the hysteria of wartime, and they rebuild the house that has been burned as a result of one of their raids on him. (It was, and still is, a custom in that part of the world that when a house or barn has been burned, the neighbors must all lend a hand to rebuilding it.)

The other stories, too, in various ways, are true reports on the place and the time. They differ from most other fiction inspired by the Civil War not only in their honest description of the mixed feelings aroused by the war but also in their realistic focusing on the civilian population at home. There are very few glimpses of the armies in the field. "A Day in the Wilderness" is the only one—and it is not one of the best—that is entirely occupied with soldiers on active service. There is in general no melodrama, no romance, and very little sentiment. The anguish and bitterness caused by the disruption of domestic life and the discordance of once quiet communities is treated with sober and ironic restraint. The call of the bugle is heard but from afar and not always irresistibly. In "The Deserter," even the deputy marshal at home sympathizes with the boy who has been hired as a substitute and run away to look after his old father, and, pretending to shoot at the fugitive, allows him to take refuge in the forest. In "Marsena," one of those lethal coquettes who play such a role in Harold Frederic's fiction sends a mild and harmless suitor to his death when she challenges him to compete with a more vigorous and dashing rival, whom she had also egged on to enlist. When she has got herself to the war as a nurse and finds them both seriously wounded, she hardly deigns to recognize them—though the weaker of the two is dying—in her snobbish preoccupation with a decorative and pretentious staff officer who has received a minor injury.

These stories are now for the first time collected in a single volume. *The Copperhead* first appeared in book form in 1893; and it was followed the next year by a volume called *Marsena and Other Stories,* which contained all the rest except "The Deserter" and "A Day in the Wilderness." These last two appeared in 1898 in a volume called *The Deserter and Other Stories: A Book of Two Wars,* together with two stories that are supposed to take place in England in the Middle Ages. Three of these latter stories first came out in the *Youth's Companion;* the second of the medieval tales had not been published before; but—though "The Deserter" has its serious significance—all sound as if they had been written for boys. In 1897, Scribner's brought out a uniform edition of Frederic's New York State fiction, for which the contents of the *Copperhead* and *Marsena* volumes were combined in one volume called *In the Sixties.* In his preface to the whole edition, Frederic says of these Civil War stories that "they are in large part my own recollections of the dreadful time—the actual things that a boy from five to nine saw or heard about him, while his own relatives were being killed, and his school-fellows orphaned, and women of his neighborhood forced into mourning and despair—and they had a right to be recorded." But good though these stories are, it is strange to find the author of *Theron Ware,* undoubtedly his most brilliant achievement, declaring that they are "closer to my heart than any other work of mine, partly because they seem to me to contain the best things I have done or ever shall do, partly because they are so closely interwoven with the personal memories and experiences of my own childhood—and a little, also, no doubt, for the reason that they have not had the treatment outside that paternal affection has desired for them." This reissue should give them the place that they deserve in American literature. Except for the juvenile element in those published in the *Youth's Companion,* they tolerate no Civil War clichés and they stand as acrid firsthand testimony to the delusions and lasting grievances implanted in American society by that fracture which, in the recent exploitation of the Civil War centenary, has been so much misinterpreted, so much melodramatized and romanticized.

EDMUND WILSON

The Copperhead

I
Abner Beech

It was on the night of my thirteenth birthday, I know, that the old farm-house was burned over our heads. By that reckoning I must have been six or seven when I went to live with Farmer Beech, because at the time he testified I had been with him half my life.

Abner Beech had often been supervisor for his town, and could have gone to the Assembly, it was said, had he chosen. He was a stalwart, thick-shouldered, big man with shaggy dark eyebrows shading stern hazel eyes, and with a long, straight nose, and a broad, firmly shut mouth. His expansive upper lip was blue from many years of shaving; all the rest was bushing beard, mounting high upon the cheeks and rolling downward in iron-gray billows over his breast. That shaven upper lip, which still may be found among the farmers of the old blood in our district, was, I dare say, a survival from the time of the Puritan protest against the mustaches of the Cavaliers. If Abner Beech, in the latter days, had been told that this shaving on Wednesday and Saturday nights was a New England rite, I feel sure he would never have touched razor again.

He was a well-to-do man in the earlier time—a tremendous worker, a "good provider," a citizen of weight and substance in the community. In all large matters the neighborhood looked to him to take the lead. He was the first farmer roundabout to set a mowing-machine to work in his meadows, and to put up lightning-rods on his buildings. At one period he was, too, the chief pillar in the church, but that was before the episode of the lightning-rods. Our little Union meeting-house was supplied in those days by an irregular procession of itinerant preachers, who came when the spirit moved and spoke with that entire

3

frankness which is induced by knowledge that the night is to be spent somewhere else. One of these strolling ministers regarded all attempts to protect property from lightning as an insolent defiance of the Divine Will, and said so very pointedly in the pulpit, and the congregation sat still and listened and grinned. Farmer Beech never forgave them.

There came in good time other causes for ill-feeling. It is beyond the power of my memory to pick out and arrange in proper sequence the events which, in the final result, separated Abner Beech from his fellows. My own recollections go with distinctness back to the reception of the news that Virginia had hanged John Brown; in a vaguer way they cover the two or three preceding years. Very likely Farmer Beech had begun to fall out of touch with his neighbors even before that.

The circumstances of my adoption into his household—an orphan without relations or other friends—were not the sort to serve this narrative. I was taken in to be raised as a farm-hand, and was no more expected to be grateful than as if I had been a young steer purchased to toil in the yoke. No suggestion was ever made that I had incurred any debt of obligation to the Beeches. In a little community where every one worked as a matter of course till there was no more work to do, and all shared alike the simple food, the tired, heavy sleep, and the infrequent spells of recreation, no one talked or thought of benefits conferred or received. My rights in the house and about the place were neither less nor more than those of Jeff Beech, the farmer's only son.

In the course of time I came, indeed, to be a more sympathetic unit in the household, so to speak, than poor Jeff himself. But that was only because he had been drawn off after strange gods.

At all times—even when nothing else good was said of him —Abner Beech was spoken of by the people of the district as a "great hand for reading." His pre-eminence in this matter remained unquestioned to the end. No other farmer for miles owned half the number of books which he had on the shelves above his writing-desk. Still less was there any one roundabout who could for a moment stand up with him in a discussion involving book-learning in general. This at first secured for him the respect of the whole country-side, and men were proud to be agreed with by such a scholar. But when affairs changed, this, oddly enough, became a formidable popular grievance against Abner Beech. They said then that his opinions were worthless because he got them from printed books, instead of from his heart.

What these opinions were may in some measure be guessed from the titles of the farmer's books. Perhaps there were some thirty of them behind the glass doors of the old mahogany bookcase. With one or two agricultural or veterinary exceptions, they related exclusively to American history and politics. There were, I recall, the first two volumes of Bancroft, and Lossing's "Lives of the Signers," and "Field Books" of the two wars with England; Thomas H. Benton's "Thirty Years' View"; the four green-black volumes of Hammond's "Political History of the State of New York"; campaign lives of Lewis Cass and Franklin Pierce, and larger biographies of Jefferson and Jackson, and, most imposing of all, a whole long row of big calf-bound volumes of the *Congressional Globe,* which carried the minutiæ of politics at Washington back into the forties.

These books constituted the entire literary side of my boyish education. I have only the faintest and haziest recollections of what happened when I went during the winter months to the school-house at the Four Corners. But I can recall the very form of the type in the farmer's books. Every one of those quaint, austere, and beardless faces, framed in high collars and stocks and waving hair—the Marcys, Calhouns, DeWitt Clintons, and Silas Wrights of the daguerreotype and Sartain's primitive graver—gives back to me now the lineaments of an old-time friend.

Whenever I could with decency escape from playing checkers with Jeff, and had no harness to grease or other indoor jobs, I spent the winter evenings in poring over some of these books

—generally with Abner Beech at the opposite side of the table immersed in another. On some rare occasion one of the hired men would take down a volume and look through it—the farmer watching him covertly the while to see that he did not wet his big thumbs to turn over the leaves—but for the most part we two had the books to ourselves. The others would sit about till bedtime, amusing themselves as best they could, the women-folk knitting or mending, the men cracking butternuts, or dallying with cider and apples and fried-cakes, as they talked over the work and gossip of the district and tempted the scorching impulses of the stovehearth with their stockinged feet.

This tacit separation of the farmer and myself from the rest of the household in the course of time begat confidences between us. He grew, from brief and casual beginnings, into a habit of speaking to me about the things we read. As it became apparent, year by year, that young Jeff was never going to read anything at all, Abner Beech more and more distinguished me with conversational favor. It cannot be said that the favoritism showed itself in other directions. I had to work as hard as ever, and got no more play-time than before. The master's eye was everywhere as keen, alert, and unsparing as if I had not known even my alphabet. But when there were breathing spells, we talked together—or rather he talked and I listened —as if we were folk quite apart from the rest.

Two fixed ideas thus arose in my boyish mind, and dominated all my little notions of the world. One was that Alexander Hamilton and John Marshall were among the most infamous characters in history. The other was that every true American ought to hold himself in daily readiness to fight with England. I gave a great deal of thought to both these matters. I had early convictions, too, I remember, with regard to Daniel Webster, who had been very bad, and then all at once became a very good man. For some obscure reason I always connected him in my imagination with Zaccheus up a tree, and clung to the

queer association of images long after I learned that the Marsh-
field statesman had been physically a large man.

Gradually the old blood-feud with the Britisher became obscured by fresher antagonisms, and there sprouted up a crop
of new sons of Belial who deserved to be hated more even than
had Hamilton and Marshall. With me the two stages of indignation glided into one another so imperceptibly that I can now
hardly distinguish between them. What I do recall is that the
farmer came in time to neglect the hereditary enemy, England,
and to seem to have quite forgotten our own historic foes to
liberty, so enraged was he over the modern Abolitionists. He
told me about them as we paced up the seed rows together in
the spring, as we drove homeward on the hay-load in the cool
of the summer evening, as we shoveled out a path for the
women to the pumps in the farm-yard through December
snows. It took me a long time to even approximately grasp the
wickedness of these new men, who desired to establish negro
sovereignty in the Republic, and to compel each white girl to
marry a black man.

The fact that I had never seen any negro "close to," and
had indeed only caught passing glimpses of one or more of the
colored race on the streets of our nearest big town, added, no
doubt, to the mystified alarm with which I contemplated these
monstrous proposals. When finally an old darky on his travels
did stroll our way, and I beheld him, incredibly ragged, dirty,
and light-hearted, shuffling through "Jump Jim Crow" down at
the Four Corners, for the ribald delectation of the village loafers, the revelation fairly made me shudder. I marvelled that the
others could laugh, with this unspeakable fate hanging over
their silly heads.

At first the Abolitionists were to me a remote and intangible
class, who lived and wrought their evil deeds in distant places—
chiefly New England way. I rarely heard mention of any names
of persons among them. They seemed to be an impersonal mass,
like a herd of buffaloes or a swarm of hornets. The first indi-

viduality in their ranks which attracted my attention, I remember, was that of Theodore Parker. The farmer one day
brought home with him from town a pamphlet composed of
anti-slavery sermons or addresses by this person. In the evening he read it, or as far into it as his temper would permit,
beating the table with his huge fist from time to time, and
snorting with wrathful amazement. At last he sprang to his
feet, marched over to the wood-stove, kicked the door open
with his boot, and thrust the offending print into the blaze.
It is vivid in my memory still—the way the red flame-light
flared over his big burly front, and sparkled on his beard, and
made his face to shine like that of Moses.

But soon I learned that there were Abolitionists everywhere
—Abolitionists right here in our own little farmland township
of northern New York! The impression which this discovery
made upon me was not unlike that produced on Robinson
Crusoe by the immortal footprint. I could think of nothing else.
Great events, which really covered a space of years, came and
went as in a bunch together, while I was still pondering upon
this. John Brown was hanged, Lincoln was elected, Sumter was
fired on, the first regiment was raised and despatched from our
rustic end of Dearborn County—and all the time it seems now
as if my mind was concentrated upon the amazing fact that
some of our neighbors were Abolitionists.

There was a certain dreamlike tricksiness of transformation
in it all. At first there was only one Abolitionist, old "Jee"
Hagadorn. Then, somehow, there came to be a number of them
—and then, all at once, lo! everybody was an Abolitionist—
that is to say, everybody but Abner Beech. The more general
and enthusiastic the conversion of the others became, the more
resolutely and doggedly he dug his heels into the ground, and
braced his broad shoulders, and pulled in the opposite direction. The skies darkened, the wind rose, the storm of angry
popular feeling burst swooping over the country-side, but Beech
only stiffened his back and never budged an inch.

At some early stage of this great change, we ceased going

to church at all. The pulpit of our rustic meeting-house had become a platform from which the farmer found himself denounced with hopeless regularity on every recurring Sabbath, and that, too, without any chance whatever of talking back. This in itself was hardly to be borne. But when others, mere laymen of the church, took up the theme, and began in class-meetings and the Sunday-school to talk about Antichrist and the Beast with Ten Horns and Seven Heads, in obvious connection with Southern sympathizers, it became frankly insufferable. The farmer did not give in without a fierce resistance. He collected all the texts he could find in the Bible, such as "Servants, obey your masters," "Cursed be Canaan," and the like, and hurled them vehemently, with strong deep voice, and sternly glowing eyes, full at their heads. But the others had many more texts—we learned afterwards that old "Jee" Hagadorn enjoyed the unfair advantage of a Cruden's Concordance —and their tongues were as forty to one, so we left off going to church altogether.

Not long after this, I should think, came the miserable affair of the cheese-factory.

The idea of doing all the dairy work of a neighborhood under a common roof, which originated not many miles from us, was now nearly ten years old. In those days it was regarded as having in it possibilities of vastly greater things than mere cheese-making. Its success among us had stirred up in men's minds big sanguine notions of co-operation as the answer to all American farm problems—as the gateway through which we were to march into the rural millennium. These high hopes one recalls now with a smile and a sigh. Farmers' wives continued to break down and die under the strain, or to be drafted off to the lunatic asylums; the farmers kept on hanging themselves in their barns, or flying off westward before the locust-like cloud of mortgages; the boys and girls turned their steps townward in an ever-increasing host. The millennium never came at all.

But at that time—in the late fifties and early sixties—the

cheese-factory was the centre of an impressive constellation of dreams and roseate promises. Its managers were the very elect of the districts; their disfavor was more to be dreaded than any condemnation of a town-meeting; their chief officers were even more important personages than the supervisor and assessor.

Abner Beech had literally been the founder of our cheese-factory. I fancy he gave the very land on which it was built, and where you will see it still, under the willows by the upper-creek bridge. He sent to it in those days the milk of the biggest herd owned by any farmer for miles around, reaching at seasons nearly one hundred cows. His voice, too, outweighed all others in its co-operative councils.

But when our church-going community had reached the conclusion that a man couldn't be a Christian and hold such views on the slave question as Beech held, it was only a very short step to the conviction that such a man would water his milk. In some parts of the world the theft of a horse is the most heinous of conceivable crimes; other sections exalt to this pinnacle of sacredness in property a sheep or a pheasant or a woman. Among our dairymen the thing of special sanctity was milk. A man in our neighborhood might almost better be accused of forgery or bigamy outright, than to fall under the dreadful suspicion of putting water into his cans.

Whether it was mere stupid prejudice or malignant invention I know not—who started the story was never to be learned —but of a sudden everybody seemed to have heard that Abner Beech's milk had been refused at the cheese-factory. This was not true, any more than it was true that there could possibly have been warrant for such a proceeding. But what did happen was that the cheese-maker took elaborate pains each morning to test our cans with such primitive appliances as preceded the lactometer, and sniffed suspiciously as he entered our figures in a separate book, and behaved generally so that our hired man knocked him head over heels into one of his whey vats. Then the managers complained to the farmer. He went down to meet them, boiling over with rage. There was an evil spirit in the air, and bitter words were exchanged. The outcome was that Abner Beech renounced the co-operative curds of his earlier manhood, so to speak, sold part of his cattle at a heavy loss, and began making butter at home with the milk of the remainder.

Then we became pariahs in good earnest.

II

Jeff's Mutiny

The farmer came in from the fields somewhat earlier than usual on this August afternoon. He walked, I remember, with a heavy step and bowed head, and, when he had come into the shade on the porch and taken off his hat, looked about him with a wearied air. The great heat, with its motionless atmosphere and sultry closeness, had well-nigh wilted everybody. But one could see that Abner was suffering more than the rest, and from something beyond the enervation of dog-days.

He sank weightily into the arm-chair by the desk, and stretched out his legs with a querulous note in his accustomed grunt of relief. On the moment Mrs. Beech came in from the kitchen, with the big china wash-bowl filled with cold water, and the towel and clean socks over her arm, and knelt before her husband. She proceeded to pull off his big, dust-baked boots and the woollen foot-gear, put his feet into the bowl, bathe and dry them, and draw on the fresh covering, all without a word.

The ceremony was one I had watched many hundreds of times. Mrs. Beech was a tall, dark, silent woman, whom I could well believe to have been handsome in her youth. She belonged to one of the old Mohawk-Dutch families, and when some of her sisters came to visit at the farm I noted that they too were all dusky as squaws, with jet-black shiny curls and eyes like the midnight hawk. I used always to be afraid of them on this account, but I dare say they were in reality most kindly women. Mrs. Beech herself represented to my boyish eyes the ideal of a saturnine and masterful queen. She performed great quantities of work with no apparent effort—as if she had merely willed it to be done. Her household was governed with a cold impassive exactitude; there were never any hitches, or even high words. The hired girls, of course, called her "M'rye," as the rest of us mostly did, but they rarely carried familiarity further, and as a rule respected her dislike for much talk. During all the years I spent under her roof I was never clear in my mind as to whether she liked me or not. Her own son, even, passed his boyhood in much the same state of dubiety.

But to her husband, Abner Beech, she was always most affectionately docile and humble. Her snapping black eyes followed him about and rested on him with an almost canine fidelity of liking. She spoke to him habitually in a voice quite different from that which others heard addressed to them. This, indeed, was measurably true of us all. By instinct the whole household deferred in tone and manner to our big, bearded chief, as if he were an Arab sheik ruling over us in a tent on the desert. The word "patriarch" still seems best to describe him, and his attitude toward us and the world in general, as I recall him sitting there in the half-darkened living-room, with his wife bending over his feet in true Oriental submission.

"Do you know where Jeff is?" the farmer suddenly asked, without turning his head to where I sat braiding a whiplash, but indicating by the volume of voice that his query was put to me.

"He went off about two o'clock," I replied, "with his fish-pole. They say they are biting like everything down in the creek."

"Well, you keep to work and they won't bite you," said Abner Beech. This was a very old joke with him, and usually the opportunity of using it once more tended to lighten his mood. Now, though mere force of habit led him to repeat the pleasantry, he had no pleasure in it. He sat with his head bent, and his huge hairy hands spread listlessly on the chair-arms.

Mrs. Beech finished her task, and rose, lifting the bowl from the floor. She paused, and looked wistfully into her husband's face.

"You ain't a bit well, Abner!" she said.

"Well as I'm likely ever to be again," he made answer, gloomily.

"Has any more of 'em been sayin' or doin' anything?" the wife asked, with diffident hesitation.

The farmer spoke with more animation. "D'ye suppose I care a picayune what *they* say or do?" he demanded. "Not I! But when a man's own kith and kin turn agin him, into the bargain—" He left the sentence unfinished, and shook his head to indicate the impossibility of such a situation.

"Has Jeff—then—" Mrs. Beech began to ask.

"Yes—Jeff!" thundered the farmer, striking his fist on the arm of the chair. "Yes—by the Eternal!—Jeff!"

When Abner Beech swore by the Eternal we knew that things were pretty bad. His wife put the bowl down on a chair, and seated herself in another. "What's Jeff been doin'?" she asked.

"Why, where d'ye suppose he was last night, 'n' the night before that? Where d'ye suppose he is this minute? They ain't no mistake about it, Lee Watkins saw 'em with his own eyes, and ta'nted me with it. He's down by the red bridge—that's where he is—hangin' round that Hagadorn gal!"

Mrs. Beech looked properly aghast at the intelligence. Even to me it was apparent that the unhappy Jeff might better have been employed in committing any other crime under the sun. It was only to be expected that his mother would be horrified.

"I never could abide that Lee Watkins," was what she said.

The farmer did not comment on the relevancy of this. "Yes," he went on, "the daughter of mine enemy, the child of that whining, backbiting old scoundrel who's been eating his way into me like a deer-tick for years—the whelp that I owe every mean and miserable thing that's ever happened to me—yes, of all living human creatures, by the Eternal! it's *his* daughter that that blamed fool of a Jeff must take a shine to, and hang around after!"

"He'll come of age the fourteenth of next month," remarked the mother, tentatively.

"Yes—and march up and vote the Woollyhead ticket. I suppose that's what'll come next!" said the farmer, bitterly. "It only needed that!"

"And it was you who got her the job of teachin' the school, too," put in Mrs. Beech.

"That's nothing to do with it," Abner continued. "I ain't blamin' her—that is, on her own account. She's a good enough gal so far's I know. But everything and everybody under that tumble-down Hagadorn roof ought to be pizen to any son of mine. *That's* what I say! And I tell you this, mother"—the farmer rose, and spread his broad chest, towering over the seated woman as he spoke—"I tell you this; if he ain't got pride enough to keep him away from that house—away from that gal—then he can keep away from *this* house—away from me!"

The wife looked up at him mutely, then bowed her head in tacit consent.

"He brings it on himself!" Abner cried, with clenched fists, beginning to pace up and down the room. "Who's the one man I've reason to curse with my dying breath? Who began the infernal Abolition cackle here? Who drove me out of the church? Who started that outrageous lie about the milk at the factory, and chased me out of that, too? Who's been a-layin' for years behind every stump and every bush, waitin' for the chance to stab me in the back, an' ruin my business, an' set my neighbors agin me, an' land me an' mine in the poorhouse or the lockup? You know as well as I do—'Jee' Hagadorn! If I'd wrung his scrawny little neck for him the first time I ever laid eyes on him, it'd 'a' been money in my pocket and years added onto my life. And then my son—*my* son! must go taggin' around —oh-h!"

He ended with an inarticulate growl of impatience and wrath.

"Mebbe, if you spoke to the boy—" Mrs. Beech began.

"Yes, I'll speak to him!" the farmer burst forth, with grim emphasis. "I'll speak to him so't he'll hear!" He turned abruptly to me. "Here, boy," he said, "you go down the creek-road an' look for Jeff. If he ain't loafin' round the school-house he'll be in the neighborhood of Hagadorn's. You tell him I say for him to get back here as quick as he can. You needn't tell him what it's about. Pick up your feet, now!"

As luck would have it, I had scarcely got out to the road before I heard the loose-spoked wheels of the local butcher's wagon rattling behind me down the hill. Looking around, I saw through the accompanying puffs of dust that young "Ni" Hagadorn was driving, and that he was alone. I stopped and waited for him to come up, questioning my mind whether it would be fair to beg a lift from him, when the purpose of my journey was so hostile to his family. Even after he had halted, and I had climbed up to the seat beside him, this consciousness of treachery disturbed me.

But no one thought long of being serious with "Ni." He was along in the teens somewhere, not large for his years but extremely wiry and muscular, and the funniest boy any of us ever knew of. How the son of such a sad-faced, gloomy, old licensed exhorter as "Jee" Hagadorn could be such a running spring of jokes and odd sayings and general deviltry as "Ni," passed all our understandings. His very face made you laugh, with its wilderness of freckles, its snub nose, and the comical curl to its mouth. He must have been a profitable investment to the butcher who hired him to drive about the country. The farmers' wives all came out to laugh and chat with him, and under the influence of his good spirits they went on buying the toughest steaks and bull-beef flanks, at more than city prices, year after year. But anybody who thought "Ni" was soft because he was full of fun made a great mistake.

"I see you ain't doin' much ditchin' this year," "Ni" remarked, glancing over our fields as he started up the horse. "I should think you'd be tickled to death."

Well, in one sense I was glad. There used to be no other such back-aching work in all the year as that picking up of stones to fill into the trenches which the hired men began digging as soon as the hay and grain were in. But, on the other hand, I knew that the present idleness meant—as everything else now seemed to mean—that the Beech farm was going to the dogs.

"No," I made rueful answer. "Our land don't need drainin' any more. It's dry as a powder-horn now."

"Ni" clucked knowingly at the old horse. "Guess it's Abner that can't stand much more drainin'," he said. "They say he's looking all round for a mortgage, and can't raise one."

"No such thing!" I replied. "His health's poorly this summer, that's all. And Jeff—he don't seem to take hold, somehow, like he used to."

My companion laughed outright. "Mustn't call him Jeff any more," he remarked with a grin. "He was telling us down at the house that he was going to have people call him Tom after this. He can't stand answerin' to the same name as Jeff Davis, he says."

"I suppose you folks put him up to that," I made bold to comment, indignantly.

The suggestion did not annoy "Ni." "Mebbe so," he said. "You know Dad lots a good deal on names. He's downright mortified that I don't get up and kill people because my name's Benaiah. 'Why' he keeps on saying to me, 'Here you are, Benaiah, the son of Jehoiada, as it was in Holy Writ, and instid of preparin' to make ready to go out and fall on the enemies of righteousness, like your namesake did, all you do is read dime novels and cut up monkey-shines generally, for all the

world as if you'd been named Pete or Steve or William Henry.'
That's what he gives me pretty nearly every day."

I was familiar enough with the quaint mysticism which the
old Abolitionist cooper wove around the Scriptural names of
himself and his son. We understood that these two appellations
had alternated among his ancestors as well, and I had often
heard him read from Samuel and Kings and Chronicles about
them, his stiff red hair standing upright, and the blue veins
swelling on his narrow temples with proud excitement. But
that, of course, was in the old days, before the trouble came,
and when I still went to church. To hear it all now again
seemed to give me a novel impression of wild fanaticism in
"Jee" Hagadorn.

His son was chuckling on his seat over something he had just
remembered. "Last time," he began, gurgling with laughter—
"last time he went for me because I wasn't measurin' up to his
idee of what a Benaiah ought to be like, I up an' said to him,
'Look a-here now, people who live in glass houses mustn't
heave rocks. If I'm Benaiah, you're Jehoiada. Well, it says in
the Bible that Jehoiada made a covenant. Do you make cove-
nants? Not a bit of it! all you make is butter-firkins, with now
n' then an odd pork barrel.' "

"What did he say to that?" I asked, as my companion's
merriment abated.

"Well, I come away just then; I seemed to have business
outside," replied "Ni," still grinning.

We had reached the Corners now, and my companion obligingly drew up to let me get down. He called out some merry
quip or other as he drove off, framed in a haze of golden dust
against the sinking sun, and I stood looking after him with the
pleasantest thoughts my mind had known for days. It was almost a shock to remember that he was one of the abhorrent and
hated Hagadorns.

And his sister, too. It was not at all easy to keep one's loathing up to the proper pitch where so nice a girl as Esther Haga-

dorn was its object. She was years and years my senior—she was even older than "Ni"—and had been my teacher for the past two winters. She had never spoken to me save across that yawning gulf which separates little barefooted urchins from tall young women, with long dresses and their hair done up in a net, and I could hardly be said to know her at all. Yet now, perversely enough, I could think of nothing but her manifest superiority to all the farm-girls roundabout. She had been to a school in some remote city, where she had relations. Her hands were fabulously white, and even on the hottest of days her dresses rustled pleasantly with starched primness. People talked about her singing at church as something remarkable; to my mind, the real music was when she just spoke to you, even if it was no more than "Good-morning, Jimmy!"

I clambered up on the window-sill of the school-house to make sure there was no one inside, and then set off down the creek-road toward the red or lower bridge. Milking-time was about over, and one or two teams passed me on the way to the cheese-factory, the handles of the cans rattling as they went, and the low sun throwing huge shadows of drivers and horses sprawling eastward over the stubble-field. I cut across lots to avoid the cheese-factory itself, with some vague feeling that it was not a fitting spectacle for any one who lived on the Beech farm.

A few moments brought me to the bank of the wandering stream below the factory, but so near that I could hear the creaking of the chain drawing up the cans over the tackle, or as we called it, the "teekle." The willows under which I walked stretched without a break from the clump by the factory bridge. And now, lo and behold! beneath still other of these willows, farther down the stream, whom should I see strolling together but my school-teacher and the delinquent Jeff!

Young Beech bore still the fish-pole I had seen him take from our shed some hours earlier, but the line twisted round it was very white and dry. He was extremely close to the girl, and kept his head bent down over her as they sauntered along the

meadow-path. They seemed not to be talking, but just idly drifting forward like the deep slow water beside them. I had never
realized before how tall Jeff was. Though the school-ma'am always seemed to me of an exceeding stature, here was Jeff
rounding his shoulders and inclining his neck in order to look
under her broad-brimmed Leghorn hat.

There could be no imaginable excuse for my not overtaking
them. Instinct prompted me to start up a whistling tune as I
advanced—a casual and indolently unobtrusive tune—at sound
of which Jeff straightened himself, and gave his companion a
little more room on the path. In a moment or two he stopped,
and looked intently over the bank into the water, as if he hoped
it might turn out to be a likely place for fish. And the school-
ma'am, too, after a few aimless steps, halted to help him look.

"Abner wants you to come right straight home!" was the
form in which my message delivered itself when I had come
close up to them.

They both shifted their gaze from the sluggish stream below
to me upon the instant. Then Esther Hagadorn looked away,
but Jeff—good, big, honest Jeff, who had been like a fond elder
brother to me since I could remember—knitted his brows and
regarded me with something like a scowl.

"Did pa send you to say that?" he demanded, holding my
eye with a glance of such stern inquiry that I could only nod
my head in confusion.

"An' he knew that you'd find me here, did he?"

"He said either at the school-house or around here somewhere," I admitted, weakly.

"An' there ain't nothin' the matter at the farm? He don't
want me for nothin' special?" pursued Jeff, still looking me
through and through.

"He didn't say," I made hesitating answer, but for the life
of me, I could not keep from throwing a tell-tale look in the
direction of his companion in the blue gingham dress.

A wink could not have told Jeff more. He gave a little bitter
laugh, and stared above my head at the willow-plumes for a

minute's meditation. Then he tossed his fish-pole over to me and laughed again.

"Keep that for yourself, if you want it," he said, in a voice not quite his own, but robustly enough. "I sha'n't need it any more. Tell pa I ain't a-comin'!"

"Oh, Tom!" Esther broke in, anxiously, "would you do that?"

He held up his hand with a quiet, masterful gesture, as if she were the pupil and he the teacher. "Tell him," he went on, the tone falling now strong and true, "tell him and ma that I'm goin' to Tecumseh to-night to enlist. If they're willin' to say good-by, they can let me know there, and I'll manage to slip back for the day. If they ain't willin'—why, they—they needn't send word; that's all."

Esther had come up to him, and held his arm now in hers.

"You're wrong to leave them like that!" she pleaded, earnestly, but Jeff shook his head.

"You don't know him!" was all he said.

In another minute I had shaken hands with Jeff, and had started on my homeward way, with his parting "Good-by, youngster!" benumbing my ears. When, after a while, I turned to look back, they were still standing where I had left them, gazing over the bank into the water.

Then, as I trudged onward once more, I began to quake at the thought of how Farmer Beech would take the news.

III

Absalom

Once, in the duck-season, as I lay hidden among the marsh-reeds with an older boy, a crow passed over us, flying low. Looking up at him, I realized for the first time how beautiful a creature was this common black thief of ours—how splendid his strength and the sheen of his coat, how proudly graceful the sweep and curves of his great slow wings. The boy beside me fired, and in a flash what I had been admiring changed— even as it stopped headlong in mid-air—into a hideous thing, an evil confusion of jumbled feathers. The awful swiftness of that transition from beauty and power to hateful carrion haunted me for a long time.

I half expected that Abner Beech would crumple up in some such distressing way, all of a sudden, when I told him that his son Jeff was in open rebellion, and intended to go off and enlist. It was incredible to the senses that any member of the household should set at defiance the patriarchal will of its head. But that the offense should come from placid, slow-witted, good-natured Jeff, and that it should involve the appearance of a Beech in a blue uniform—these things staggered the imagination. It was clear that something prodigious must happen.

As it turned out, nothing happened at all. The farmer and his wife sat out on the veranda, as was their wont of a summer evening, rarely exchanging a word, but getting a restful sort of satisfaction in together surveying their barns and haystacks and the yellow-brown stretch of fields beyond.

"Jeff says he's goin' to-night to Tecumseh, an' he's goin' to enlist, an' if you want him to run over to say good-by you're to let him know there."

I leant upon my newly-acquired fish-pole for support, as I unburdened myself of these sinister tidings. The old pair looked at me in calm-eyed silence, as if I had related the most trivial of village occurrences. Neither moved a muscle nor uttered a sound, but just gazed, till it felt as if their eyes were burning holes into me.

"That's what he said," I repeated, after a pause, to mitigate the embarrassment of that dumb steadfast stare.

The mother it was who spoke at last. "You'd better go round and get your supper," she said, quietly.

The table was spread, as usual, in the big, low-ceilinged room which during the winter was used as a kitchen. What was unusual was to discover a strange man seated alone in his shirt-sleeves at this table, eating his supper. As I took my chair, however, I saw that he was not altogether a stranger. I recognized in him the little old Irishman who had farmed at Ezra Tracy's beaver-meadow the previous year on shares, and done badly, and had since been hiring out for odd jobs at hoeing and haying. He had lately lost his wife, I recalled now, and lived alone in a tumble-down old shanty beyond Parker's saw-mill. He had come to us in the spring, I remembered, when the brindled calf was born, to beg a pail of what he called "baste-ings," and I speculated in my mind whether it was this repellent mess that had killed his wife. Above all these thoughts rose the impression that Abner must have decided to do a heap of ditching and wall-building, to have hired a new hand in this otherwise slack season—and at this my back began to ache prophetically.

"How are yeh!" the newcomer remarked, affably, as I sat down and reached for the bread. "An' did yeh see the boys march away? An' had they a drum wid 'em?"

"What boys?" I asked, in blank ignorance as to what he was at.

"I'm told there's a baker's dozen of 'em gone, more or less," he replied. "Well, glory be to the Lord, 'tis an ill wind blows nobody good. Here am I aitin' butter on my bread, an' cheese on top o' that."

I should still have been in the dark, had not one of the hired girls, Janey Wilcox, come in from the butter-room, to ask me in turn much the same thing, and to add the explanation that a whole lot of the young men of the neighborhood had privately arranged among themselves to enlist together as soon as the harvesting was over, and had this day gone off in a body. Among them, I learned now, were our two hired men, Warner Pitts and Ray Watkins. This, then, accounted for the presence of the Irishman.

As a matter of fact, there had been no secrecy about the

thing save with the contingent which our household furnished, and that was only because of the fear which Abner Beech inspired. His son and his servants alike preferred to hook it, rather than explain their patriotic impulses to him. But naturally enough, our farm-girls took it for granted that all the others had gone in the same surreptitious fashion, and this threw an air of fascinating mystery about the whole occurrence. They were deeply surprised that I should have been down past the Corners, and even beyond the cheese-factory, and seen nothing of these extraordinary martial preparations; and I myself was ashamed of it.

Opinions differed, I remember, as to the behavior of our two hired men. "Till" Babcock and the Underwood girl defended them, but Jancy took the other side, not without various unpleasant personal insinuations, and the Irishman and I were outspoken in their condemnation. But nobody said a word about Jeff, though it was plain enough that every one knew.

Dusk fell while we still talked of these astounding events— my thoughts meantime dividing themselves between efforts to realize these neighbors of ours as soldiers on the tented field, and uneasy speculation as to whether I should at last get a bed to myself or be expected to sleep with the Irishman.

Janey Wilcox had taken the lamp into the living-room. She returned now, with an uplifted hand and a face covered over with lines of surprise.

"You're to all of you come in," she whispered, impressively. "Abner's got the Bible down. We're goin' to have fam'ly prayers, or somethin'."

With one accord we looked at the Irishman. The question had never before arisen on our farm, but we all knew about other cases, in which Catholic hands held aloof from the household's devotions. There were even stories of their refusal to eat meat on some one day of the week, but this we hardly brought ourselves to credit. Our surprise at the fact that domestic religious observances were to be resumed under the Beech roof-tree—where they had completely lapsed ever since the trouble at the church—was as nothing compared with our curiosity to see what the newcomer would do.

What he did was to get up and come along with the rest of us, quite as a matter of course. I felt sure that he could not have understood what was going on.

We filed into the living-room. The Beeches had come in and shut the veranda door, and "M'rye" was seated in her rocking-chair, in the darkness beyond the bookcase. Her husband had the big book open before him on the table; the lamp-light threw the shadow of his long nose down into the gray of his beard with a strange effect of fierceness. His lips were tight-set and his shaggy brows drawn into a commanding frown, as he bent over the pages.

Abner did not look up till we had taken our seats. Then he raised his eyes toward the Irishman.

"I don't know, Hurley," he said, in a grave, deep-booming voice, "whether you feel it right for you to join us—we bein' Protestants—"

"Ah, it's all right, sir," replied Hurley, reassuringly, "I'll take no harm by it."

A minute's silence followed upon this magnanimous declaration. Then Abner, clearing his throat, began solemnly to read the story of Absalom's revolt. He had the knack, not uncommon in those primitive class-meeting days, of making his strong low-pitched voice quaver and wail in the most tear-compelling fashion when he read from the Old Testament. You could hardly listen to him going through even the genealogical tables of Chronicles dry-eyed. His Jeremiah and Ezekiel were equal to the funeral of a well-beloved relation.

This night he read as I had never heard him read before. The whole grim story of the son's treason and final misadventure, of the ferocious battle in the wood of Ephraim, of Joab's savagery, and of the rival runners, made the air vibrate about us, and took possession of our minds and kneaded them like dough, as we sat in the mute circle in the old living-room. From my chair I could see Hurley without turning my head, and the spectacle of excitement he presented—bending forward with dropped jaw and wild, glistening gray eyes, a hand behind his ear to miss no syllable of this strange new tale—only added to the effect it produced on me.

Then there came the terrible picture of the King's despair. I had trembled as we neared this part, foreseeing what heart-wringing anguish Abner, in his present mood, would give to that cry of the stricken father—"O my son Absalom, my son, my son Absalom! Would God I had died for thee, O Absalom, my son, my son!" To my great surprise, he made very little of it. The words came coldly, almost contemptuously, so that the listener could not but feel that David's lamentations were out of place, and might better have been left unuttered.

But now the farmer, leaping over into the next chapter, brought swart, stalwart, blood-stained Joab on the scene before us, and in an instant we saw why the King's outburst of mourning had fallen so flat upon our ears. Abner Beech's voice rose and filled the room with its passionate fervor as he read out Joab's speech—wherein the King is roundly told that his son was a worthless fellow, and was killed not a bit too soon, and that for the father to thus publicly lament him is to put to shame all his household and his loyal friends and servants.

While these sonorous words of protest against paternal weakness still rang in the air, Abner abruptly closed the book with a snap. We looked at him and at one another for a bewildered moment, and then "Till" Babcock stooped as if to kneel by her chair, but Janey nudged her, and we all rose and made our way silently out again into the kitchen. It had been apparent enough that no spirit of prayer abode in the farmer's breast.

" 'Twas a fine bold sinsible man, that Job!" remarked Hurley to me, when the door was closed behind us, and the women had gone off to talk the scene over among themselves in the butter-room. "Would it be him that had thim lean turkeys?"

With some difficulty I made out his meaning. "Oh, no!" I exclaimed, "the man Abner read about was Jo-ab, not Job. They were quite different people."

"I thought as much," replied the Irishman. " 'Twould not be in so grand a man's nature to let his fowls go hungry. And do we be hearing such tales every night?"

"Maybe Abner 'll keep on, now he's started again," I said. "We ain't had any Bible-reading before since he had his row down at the church, and we left off going."

Hurley displayed such a lively interest in this matter that I went over it pretty fully, setting forth Abner's position and the intolerable provocations which had been forced upon him. It took him a long time to grasp the idea that in Protestant gatherings not only the pastor spoke, but the class-leaders and all others who were conscious of a call might have their word as well, and that in this way even the lowliest and meanest of the farmer's neighbors had been able to affront him in the church itself.

"Too many cooks spoil the broth," was his comment upon this. " 'Tis far better to hearken to one man only. If he's right, you're right. If he's wrong, why, thin, there ye have him in front of ye for protection."

Bedtime came soon after, and Mrs. Beech appeared in her nightly round of the house to see that the doors were all fastened. The candle she bore threw up a flaring yellow light upon her chin, but made the face above it by contrast still darker and more saturnine. She moved about in erect impassiveness, trying the bolts and the window-catches, and went away again, having said never a word. I had planned to ask her if I might now have a bed to myself, but somehow my courage failed me, so stern and majestic was her aspect.

I took the desired boon without asking, and dreamed of her as a darkling and relentless Joab in petticoats, slaying her own son Jeff as he hung by his hay-colored hair in one of the apple-trees of our orchard.

IV

Antietam

On all the other farms roundabout, this mid-August was a slack season. The hired men and boys did a little early fruit-picking, a little berrying, a little stone-drawing, but for the most part they could be seen idling about the woods or along the river down below Juno Mills, with gun or fish-pole. Only upon the one farm whose turn it was that week to be visited by the itinerant threshing-machine, was any special activity visible.

It was well known, however, that we were not to get the threshing-machine at all. How it was managed, I never understood. Perhaps the other farmers combined in some way to over-awe or persuade the owners of the machine into refusing it to Abner Beech. More likely he scented the chance of a refusal and was too proud to put himself in its way by asking. At all events, we three—Abner, Hurley, and I—had to manage the threshing ourselves, on the matched wood floor of the carriage barn. All the fishing I did that year was in the prolific but unsubstantial waters of dreamland.

I did not work much, it is true, with the flail, but I lived all day in an atmosphere choked with dust and chaff, my ears deafened with the ceaseless whack! whack! of the hard-wood clubs, bringing on fresh shocks of grain, and acting as general helper.

By toiling late and early we got this task out of the way just when the corn was ready to cut. This great job taxed all the energies of the two men, the one cutting, the other stacking, as they went. My own share of the labor was to dig the potatoes and pick the eating-apples—a quite portentous enough under-taking for a lad of twelve. All this kept me very much to myself. There was no chance to talk during the day and at night I was glad to drag my tired limbs off to bed before the girls had fairly cleared the supper things away. A weekly newspaper —*The World*—came regularly to the post-office at the Corners for us, but we were so overworked that often it lay there for weeks at a time, and even when some one went after it, nobody but Abner cared to read it.

So far as I know, no word ever came from Jeff. His name was never mentioned among us.

It was now past the middle of September. Except for the fall ploughing on fields that were to be put to grass under the grain in the spring—which would come much later—the getting in of the root crops, and the husking, our season's labors were pretty well behind us. The women-folk had toiled like slaves as well, taking almost all the chores about the cattle-barns off our shoulders, and carrying on the butter-making without bothering us. Now that a good many cows were drying up, it was their turn to take things easy, too. But the girls, instead of being glad at this, began to borrow unhappiness over the certainty that there would be no husking-bees on the Beech farm.

One heard no other subject discussed now, as we sat of a night in the kitchen. Even when we foregathered in the living-room instead, the Babcock and the Underwood girls talked in ostentatiously low tones of the hardship of missing such opportunities for getting beaux, and having fun. They recalled to each other, with tones of longing, this and that husking-bee of other years—now one held of a moonlight night in the field itself, where the young men pulled the stacks down and dragged them to where the girls sat in a ring on big pumpkins, and merriment, songs, and chorused laughter chased the happy hours along; now of a bee held in the late wintry weather, where the men went off to the barn by themselves and husked till they were tired, and then with warning whoops came back to where the girls were waiting for them in the warm, hospitable farm-house, and the frolic began, with cider and apples and pumpkin-pies, and old Lem Hornbeck's fiddle to lead the dancing.

Alas! they shook their empty heads and mourned, there would be no more of these delightful times! Nothing definite was ever said as to the reason for our ostracism from the sports and social enjoyments of the season. There was no need for that. We all knew too well that it was Abner Beech's politics which made us outcasts, but even these two complaining girls did not venture to say so in his hearing. Their talk, however, grew at last so persistently querulous that "M'rye" bluntly told them one night to "shut up about husking-bees," following them out into the kitchen for that purpose, and speaking with unaccustomed acerbity. Thereafter we heard no more of their grumbling, but in a week or two "Till" Babcock left for her home over on the Dutch Road, and began circulating the report that we prayed every night for the success of Jeff Davis.

It was on a day in the latter half of September, perhaps the 20th or 21st—as nearly as I am able to make out from the records now—that Hurley and I started off with a double team and our big box-wagon, just after breakfast, on a long day's journey. We were taking a heavy load of potatoes into market at Octavius, twelve miles distant; thence we were to drive out an additional three miles to a cooper-shop and bring back as many butter-firkins as we could stack up behind us, not to mention a lot of groceries of which "M'rye" gave me a list.

It was a warm, sweet-aired, hazy autumn day, with a dusky red sun sauntering idly about in the sky, too indolent to cast more than the dimmest and most casual suggestion of a shadow for anything or anybody. The Irishman sat round-backed and contented on the very high seat overhanging the horses, his elbows on his knees, and a little black pipe turned upside down in his mouth. He would suck satisfiedly at this for hours after the fire had gone out, until, my patience exhausted, I begged him to light it again. He seemed almost never to put any new tobacco into this pipe, and to this day it remains a twin-mystery to me why its contents neither burned themselves to nothing nor fell out.

We talked a good deal, in a desultory fashion, as the team plodded their slow way into Octavius. Hurley told me, in answer to the questions of a curious boy, many interesting and remarkable things about the old country, as he always called it, and more particularly about his native part of it, which was on the sea-shore within sight of Skibbereen. He professed always to be filled with longing to go back, but at the same time guarded his tiny personal expenditure with the greatest solicitude, in order to save money to help one of his relations to get away. Once, when I taxed him with this inconsistency, he explained that life in Ireland was the most delicious thing on earth, but you had to get off at a distance of some thousands of miles to really appreciate it.

Naturally there was considerable talk between us, as well, about Abner Beech and his troubles. I don't know where I could have heard it, but when Hurley first came to us I at once took it for granted that the fact of his nationality made him a sympathizer with the views of our household. Perhaps I only jumped at this conclusion from the general ground that the few Irish who in those days found their way into the farm-country were held rather at arm's-length by the community, and must in the nature of things feel drawn to other outcasts. At all events, I made no mistake. Hurley could not have been more vehemently embittered against abolitionism and the war than Abner was, but he expressed his feelings with much greater vivacity and fluency of speech. It was surprising to see how much he knew about the politics and political institutions of a strange country, and how excited he grew about them when any one would listen to him. But as he was a small man, getting on in years, he did not dare air these views down at the Corners. The result was that he and Abner were driven to commune together, and mutually inflamed each other's passionate prejudices—which was not at all needful.

When at last, shortly before noon, we drove into Octavius,

I jumped off to fill one portion of the grocery errands, leaving Hurley to drive on with the potatoes. We were to meet at the little village tavern for dinner.

He was feeding the horses in the hotel shed when I rejoined him an hour or so later. I came in, bursting with the importance of the news I had picked up—scattered, incomplete, and even incoherent news, but of a most exciting sort. The awful battle of Antietam had happened two or three days before, and nobody in all Octavius was talking or thinking of anything else. Both the Dearborn County regiments had been in the thick of the fight, and I could see from afar, as I stood on the outskirts of the throng in front of the post-office, some long strips of paper posted up beside the door, which men said contained a list of our local dead and wounded. It was hopeless, however, to attempt to get anywhere near this list, and nobody whom I questioned, knew anything about the names of those young men who had marched away from our Four Corners. Some one did call out, though, that the telegraph had broken down, or gone wrong, and that not half the news had come in as yet. But they were all so deeply stirred up, so fiercely pushing and hauling to get toward the door, that I could learn little else.

This was what I began to tell Hurley, with eager volubility, as soon as I got in under the shed. He went on with his back to me, impassively measuring out the oats from the bag, and clearing aside the stale hay in the manger, the impatient horses rubbing at his shoulders with their noses the while. Then, as I was nearly done, he turned and came out to me, slapping the fodder-mess off his hands.

He had a big, fresh cut running transversely across his nose and cheek, and there were stains of blood in the gray stubble of beard on his chin. I saw too that his clothes looked as if he had been rolled on the dusty road outside.

"Sure, then, I'm after hearin' the news myself," was all he said.

He drew out from beneath the wagon seat a bag of crackers

and a hunk of cheese, and, seating himself on an overturned barrel, began to eat. By a gesture I was invited to share this meal, and did so, sitting beside him. Something had happened, apparently, to prevent our having dinner in the tavern.

I fairly yearned to ask him what this something was, and what was the matter with his face, but it did not seem quite the right thing to do, and presently he began mumbling, as much to himself as to me, a long and broken discourse, from which I picked out that he had mingled with a group of lusty young farmers in the market-place, asking for the latest intelligence, and that while they were conversing in a wholly amiable manner, one of them had suddenly knocked him down and kicked him, and that thereafter they had pursued him with curses and loud threats half-way to the tavern. This and much more he proclaimed between mouthfuls, speaking with great rapidity and in so much more marked a brogue than usual, that I understood only a fraction of what he said.

He professed entire innocence of offence in the affair, and either could not or would not tell what it was he had said to invite the blow. I dare say he did in truth richly provoke the violence he encountered, but at the time I regarded him as a martyr, and swelled with indignation every time I looked at his nose.

I remained angry, indeed, long after he himself had altogether recovered his equanimity and whimsical good spirits. He waited outside on the seat while I went in to pay for the baiting of the horses, and it was as well that he did, I fancy, because there were half a dozen brawny farm-hands and villagers standing about the bar, who were laughing in a stormy way over the episode of the "Copperhead Paddy" in the market.

We drove away, however, without incident of any sort— sagaciously turning off the main street before we reached the post-office block, where the congregated crowd seemed larger than ever. There seemed to be some fresh tidings, for several scattering outbursts of cheering reached our ears after we could no longer see the throng; but, so far from stopping to inquire what it was, Hurley put whip to the horses, and we rattled smartly along out of the excited village into the tranquil, scythe-shorn country.

The cooper to whom we now went for our butter-firkins was a long-nosed, lean, and taciturn man, whom I think of always as with his apron tucked up at the corner, and his spectacles on his forehead, close under the edge of his square brown-paper cap. He had had word that we were coming, and the firkins were ready for us. He helped us load them in dead silence, and with a gloomy air.

Hurley desired the sound of his own voice. "Well, then, sir," he said, as our task neared completion, " 'tis worth coming out of our way these fifteen miles to lay eyes on such fine, grand firkins as these same—such an elegant shape on 'em, an' put together with such nateness!"

"You could get 'em just as good at Hagadorn's," said the cooper, curtly, "within a mile of your place."

"Huh!" cried Hurley, with contempt, "Haggydorn is it? Faith, we'll not touch him or his firkins ayether! Why, man, they're not fit to mention the same day wid yours. Ah, just look at the darlin's, will ye, that nate an' clane a Christian could ate from 'em!"

The cooper was blarney-proof. "Hagadorn's are every smitch as good!" he repeated ungraciously.

The Irishman looked at him perplexedly, then shook his head as if the problem were too much for him, and slowly clambered up to the seat. He had gathered up the lines, and we were ready to start, before any suitable words came to his tongue.

"Well, then, sir," he said, "anything to be agreeable. If I hear a man speaking a good word for your firkins, I'll dispute him."

"The firkins are well enough," growled the cooper at us,

"an' they're made to sell, but I ain't so almighty tickled about takin' Copperhead money for 'em that I want to clap my wings an' crow over it."

He turned scornfully on his heel at this, and we drove away. The new revelation of our friendlessness depressed me, but Hurley did not seem to mind it at all. After a philosophic comparative remark about the manners of pigs run wild in a bog, he dismissed the affair from his thoughts altogether, and hummed cheerful words to melancholy tunes half the way home, what time he was not talking to the horses or tossing stray conversational fragments at me.

My own mind soon enough surrendered itself to harrowing speculations about the battle we had heard of. The war had been going on now, for over a year, but most of the fighting had been away off in Missouri and Tennessee, or on the lower Mississippi, and the reports had not possessed for me any keen direct interest. The idea of men from our own district—young men whom I had seen, perhaps fooled with, in the hayfield only ten weeks before—being in an actual storm of shot and shell, produced a faintness at the pit of my stomach. Both Dearborn County regiments were in it, the crowd said. Then, of course our men must have been there—our hired men, and the Phillips boys, and Byron Truax, and his cousin Alonzo, and our Jeff! And if so many others had been killed, why not they as well?

"Antietam" still has a power to arrest my eyes on the printed page, and disturb my ears in the hearing, possessed by no other battle name. It seems now as if the very word itself had a terrible meaning of its own to me, when I first heard it that September afternoon—as if I recognized it to be the label of some awful novelty, before I knew anything else. It had its fascination for Hurley, too, for presently I heard him crooning to himself, to one of his queer old Irish tunes, some doggerel lines which he had made up to rhyme with it— three lines with "cheat 'em," "beat 'em," and "Antietam," and then his pet refrain, "Says the Shan van Vocht."

This levity jarred unpleasantly upon the mood into which I had worked myself, and I turned to speak of it, but the sight of his bruised nose and cheek restrained me. He had suffered too much for the faith that was in him to be lightly questioned now. So I returned to my grisly thoughts, which now all at once resolved themselves into a conviction that Jeff had been killed outright. My fancy darted to meet this notion, and straightway pictured for me a fantastic battle-field by moon-light, such as was depicted in Lossing's books, with overturned cannon-wheels and dead horses in the foreground, and in the centre, conspicuous above all else, the inanimate form of Jeff Beech, with its face coldly radiant in the moonshine.

"I guess I'll hop off and walk a spell," I said, under the sudden impulse of this distressing visitation.

It was only when I was on the ground, trudging along by the side of the wagon, that I knew why I had got down. We were within a few rods of the Corners, where one road turned off to go to the post-office. "Perhaps it'd be a good idea for me to find out if they've heard anything more—I mean—anything about Jeff," I suggested. "I'll just look in and see, and then I can cut home cross lots."

The Irishman nodded and drove on.

I hung behind, at the Corners, till the wagon had begun the ascent of the hill, and the looming bulk of the firkins made it impossible that Hurley could see which way I went. Then, without hesitation, I turned instead down the other road which led to "Jee" Hagadorn's.

V

"Jee's" Tidings

Time was when I had known the Hagadorn house, from the outside at least, as well as any other in the whole township.

But I had avoided that road so long now, that when I came up to the place it seemed quite strange to my eyes.

For one thing, the flower garden was much bigger than it had formerly been. To state it differently, Miss Esther's marigolds and columbines, hollyhocks and peonies, had been allowed to usurp a lot of space where sweet-corn, potatoes, and other table-truck used to be raised. This not only greatly altered the aspect of the place, but it lowered my idea of the practical good-sense of its owners.

What was more striking still, was the general air of decrepitude and decay about the house itself. An eaves-trough had fallen down; half the cellar door was off its hinges, standing up against the wall; the chimney was ragged and broken at the top; the clapboards had never been painted, and now were almost black with weather-stain and dry rot. It positively appeared to me as if the house was tipping sideways, over against the little cooper-shop adjoining it—but perhaps that was a trick of the waning evening light. I said to myself that if we were not prospering on the Beech farm, at least our foe "Jee" Hagadorn did not seem to be doing much better himself.

In truth, Hagadorn had always been among the poorest members of our community, though this by no means involves what people in cities think of as poverty. He had a little place of nearly two acres, and then he had his coopering business; with the two he ought to have got on comfortably enough. But a certain contrariness in his nature seemed to be continually interfering with this.

This strain of conscientious perversity ran through all we knew of his life before he came to us, just as it dominated the remainder of his career. He had been a well-to-do man some ten years before, in a city in the western part of the State, with a big cooper-shop, and a lot of men under him, making the barrels for a large brewery. (It was in these days, I fancy, that Esther took on that urban polish which the younger Benaiah missed.) Then he got the notion in his head that it was wrong to make barrels for beer, and threw the whole thing up. He

moved into our neighborhood with only money enough to buy
the old Andrews place, and build a little shop.

It was a good opening for a cooper, and Hagadorn might
have flourished if he had been able to mind his own business.
The very first thing he did was to offend a number of our biggest butter-makers by taxing them with sinfulness in also raising hops, which went to make beer. For a long time they would
buy no firkins of him. Then, too, he made an unpleasant impression at church. As has been said, our meeting-house was a
union affair; that is to say, no one denomination being numerous enough to have an edifice of its own, all the farmers round
about—Methodists, Baptists, Presbyterians, and so on—joined
in paying the expenses. The travelling preachers who came to
us represented these great sects, with lots of minute shadings
off into Hard-shell, Soft-shell, Freewill, and other subdivided
mysteries which I never understood. Hagadorn had a denomination all to himself, as might have been expected from the
man. What the name of it was I seem never to have heard;
perhaps it had no name at all. People used to say, though, that
he behaved like a Shouting Methodist.

This was another way of saying that he made a nuisance of
himself in church. At prayer-meetings, in the slack seasons of
the year, he would pray so long, and with such tremendous
shouting and fury of gestures, that he had regularly to be
asked to stop, so that those who had taken the trouble to learn
and practise new hymns might have a chance to be heard. And
then he would out-sing all the others, not knowing the tune in
the least, and cause added confusion by yelling out shrill
"Amens!" between the bars. At one time quite a number of the
leading people ceased attending church at all, on account of
his conduct.

He added heavily to his theological unpopularity, too, by his
action in another matter. There was a wealthy and important
farmer living over on the west side of Agrippa Hill, who was a
Universalist. The expenses of our Union meeting-house were
felt to be a good deal of a burden, and our elders, conferring

together, decided that it would be a good thing to waive ordinary prejudices, and let the Universalists come in, and have their share of the preaching. It would be more neighborly, they felt, and they would get a subscription from the Agrippa Hill farmer. He assented to the project, and came over four or five Sundays with his family and hired help, listened unflinchingly to orthodox sermons full of sulphur and blue flames, and put money on the plate every time. Then a Universalist preacher occupied the pulpit one Sunday, and preached a highly inoffensive and non-committal sermon, and "Jee" Hagadorn stood up in his pew and violently denounced him as an infidel, before he had descended the pulpit steps. This created a painful scandal. The Universalist farmer, of course, never darkened that church door again. Some of our young men went so far as to discuss the ducking of the obnoxious cooper in the duck-pond. But he himself was neither frightened nor ashamed.

At the beginning, too, I suppose that his taking up Abolitionism made him enemies. Dearborn County gave Franklin Pierce a big majority in '52, and the bulk of our farmers, I know, were in that majority. But I have already dwelt upon the way in which all this changed in the years just before the war. Naturally enough, Hagadorn's position also changed. The rejected stone became the head of the corner. The tiresome fanatic of the 'fifties was the inspired prophet of the 'sixties. People still shrank from giving him undue credit for their conversion, but they felt themselves swept along under his influence none the less.

But just as his unpopularity kept him poor in the old days, it seemed that now the reversed condition was making him still poorer. The truth was, he was too excited to pay any attention to his business. He went off to Octavius three or four days a week to hear the news, and when he remained at home, he spent much more time standing out in the road discussing politics and the conduct of the war with passers-by, than he did over his staves and hoops. No wonder his place was run down.

The house was dark and silent, but there was some sort of a light in the cooper-shop beyond. My hope had been to see Esther rather than her wild old father, but there was nothing for it but to go over to the shop. I pushed the loosely fitting door back on its leathern hinges, and stepped over the threshold. The resinous scent of newly cut wood, and the rustle of the shavings under my feet, had the effect, somehow, of filling me with timidity. It required an effort to not turn and go out again.

The darkened and crowded interior of the tiny work-place smelt as well, I noted now, of smoke. On the floor before me was crouched a shapeless figure—bending in front of the little furnace, made of a section of stove-pipe, which the cooper used to dry the insides of newly fashioned barrels. A fire in this— half-blaze, half-smudge—gave forth the light I had seen from without, and the smoke which was making my nostrils tingle. Then I had to sneeze, and the kneeling figure sprang on the instant from the floor.

It was Esther who stood before me, coughing a little from the smoke and peering inquiringly at me. "Oh—is that you, Jimmy?" she asked, after a moment of puzzled inspection in the dark.

She went on, before I had time to speak, in a nervous, half-laughing way: "I've been trying to roast an ear of corn here, but it's the worst kind of a failure. I've watched 'Ni' do it a hundred times, but with me it always comes out half-scorched and half-smoked. I guess the corn is too old now, anyway. At all events, it's tougher than Pharaoh's heart."

She held out to me, in proof of her words, a blackened and unseemly roasting-ear. I took it, and turned it slowly over, looking at it with the grave scrutiny of an expert. Several torn and opened sections showed where she had been testing it with her teeth. In obedience to her "See if you don't think it's too old," I took a diffident bite, at a respectful distance from the marks of her experiments. It was the worst I had ever tasted.

"I came over to see if you'd heard anything—any news," I said, desiring to get away from the corn subject.

"You mean about Tom?" she asked, moving so that she might see me more plainly.

I had stupidly forgotten about that transformation of names. "Our Jeff, I mean," I made answer.

"His name is Thomas Jefferson. *We* call him Tom," she explained; "that other name is too horrid. Did—did his people tell you to come and ask *me*?"

I shook my head. "Oh, no!" I replied with emphasis, implying by my tone, I dare say, that they would have had themselves cut up into sausage-meat first.

The girl walked past me to the door, and out to the roadside, looking down toward the bridge with a lingering, anxious gaze. Then she came back, slowly.

"No, we have no news!" she said, with an effort at calmness. "He wasn't an officer, that's why. All we know is that the brigade his regiment is in lost 141 killed, 560 wounded, and 38 missing. That's all!" She stood in the doorway, her hands clasped tight, pressed against her bosom. *"That's all!"* she repeated, with a choking voice.

Suddenly she started forward, almost ran across the few yards of floor, and, throwing herself down in the darkest corner, where only dimly one could see an old buffalo-robe spread over a heap of staves, began sobbing as if her heart must break.

Her dress had brushed over the stove-pipe, and scattered some of the embers beyond the sheet of tin it stood on. I stamped these out, and carried the other remnants of the fire out doors. Then I returned, and stood about in the smoky little shop, quite helplessly listening to the moans and convulsive sobs which rose from the obscure corner. A bit of a candle in a bottle stood on the shelf by the window. I lighted this, but it hardly seemed to improve the situation. I could see her now, as well as hear her—huddled face downward upon the skin, her whole form shaking with the violence of her grief. I had never been so unhappy before in my life.

At last—it may not have been very long, but it seemed hours —there rose the sound of voices outside on the road. A wagon had stopped, and some words were being exchanged. One of the voices grew louder—came nearer; the other died off, ceased altogether, and the wagon could be heard driving away. On the instant the door was pushed sharply open, and "Jee" Hagadorn stood on the threshold, surveying the interior of his cooper-shop with gleaming eyes.

He looked at me; he looked at his daughter lying in the corner; he looked at the charred mess on the floor—yet seemed to see nothing of what he looked at. His face glowed with a strange excitement—which in another man I should have set down to drink.

"Glory be to God! Praise to the Most High! Mine eyes have seen the glory of the coming of the Lord!" he called out, stretching forth his hands in a rapturous sort of gesture I re-membered from class-meeting days.

Esther had leaped to her feet with squirrel-like swiftness at the sound of his voice, and now stood before him, her hands nervously clutching at each other, her reddened, tear-stained face afire with eagerness.

"Has word come?—is he safe?—have you heard?" so her excited questions tumbled over one another, as she grasped "Jee's" sleeve and shook it in feverish impatience.

"The day has come! The year of Jubilee is here!" he cried, brushing her hand aside, and staring with a fixed, ecstatic, open-mouthed smile straight ahead of him. "The words of the Prophet are fulfilled!"

"But Tom!—*Tom!*" pleaded the girl, piteously. "The list has come? You know he is safe?"

"Tom! *Tom!*" old "Jee" repeated after her, but with an emphasis contemptuous, not solicitous. "Perish a hundred Toms—yea—ten thousand! for one such day as this! 'For the Scarlet Woman of Babylon is overthrown, and bound with chains and cast into the lake of fire. Therefore, in one day shall her plagues come, death, and mourning, and famine; and she shall be utterly burned with fire: for strong is the Lord God which judged her!' "

He declaimed these words in a shrill, high-pitched voice, his face upturned, and his eyes half-closed. Esther plucked despairingly at his sleeve once more.

"But have you seen?—is *his* name?—you must have seen!" she moaned, incoherently.

"Jee" descended for the moment from his plane of exaltation. "I *didn't* see!" he said, almost peevishly. "Lincoln has signed a proclamation freeing all the slaves! What do you suppose I care for your Toms and Dicks and Harrys, on such a day as this? 'Woe! woe! the great city of Babylon, the strong city! For in one hour is thy judgment come!' "

The girl tottered back to her corner, and threw herself limply down upon the buffalo-robe again, hiding her face in her hands.

I pushed my way past the cooper, and trudged cross-lots home in the dark, tired, disturbed, and very hungry, but thinking most of all that if I had been worth my salt, I would have hit "Jee" Hagadorn with the adze that stood up against the door-stile.

VI

Ni's Talk with Abner

It must have been a fortnight before we learned that Jeff Beech and Byron Truax had been reported missing. I say "we," but I do not know when Abner Beech came to hear about it. One of the hired girls had seen the farmer get up from his chair, with the newly arrived weekly *World* in his hand, walk over to where his wife sat, and direct her attention to a line of the print with his finger. Then, still in silence, he had gone over to the bookcase, opened the drawer where he kept his account-books, and locked the journal up therein.

We took it for granted that thus the elderly couple had learned the news about their son. They said so little nowadays, either to each other or to us, that we were driven to speculate upon their dumb-show, and find meanings for ourselves in their glances and actions. No one of us could imagine himself or herself venturing to mention Jeff's name in their hearing.

Down at the Corners, though, and all about our district, people talked of very little else. Antietam had given a bloody welcome to our little group of warriors. Ray Watkins and Lon Truax had been killed outright, and Ed Phillips was in the hospital, with the chances thought to be against him. Warner Pitts, our other hired man, had been wounded in the arm, but not seriously, and thereafter behaved with such conspicuous valor that it was said he was to be promoted from being a sergeant to a lieutenancy. All these things, however, paled in interest after the first few days before the fascinating mystery of what had become of Jeff and Byron. The loungers about the grocery-store evenings took sides as to the definition of "missing." Some said it meant being taken prisoners; but it was known that at Antietam the Rebels made next to no captives. Others held that "missing" soldiers were those who had been shot, and who crawled off somewhere in the woods out of sight to die. A lumberman from Juno Mills, who was up on a horse-trade, went so far as to broach still a third theory, viz., that "missing" soldiers were those who had run away under fire, and were ashamed to show their faces again. But this malicious suggestion could not, of course, be seriously considered.

Meanwhile, what little remained of the fall farm-work went on as if nothing had happened. The root crops were dug, the fodder got in, and the late apples gathered. Abner had a cider-mill of his own, but we sold a much larger share of our winter apples than usual. Less manure was drawn out onto the fields than in other autumns, and it looked as if there was to be little or no fall ploughing. Abner went about his tasks in a heavy, spiritless way these days, doggedly enough, but with none of his old-time vim. He no longer had pleasure even in abusing Lincoln and the war with Hurley. Not Antietam itself could have broken his nerve, but at least it silenced his tongue.

Warner Pitts came home on a furlough, with a fine new uniform, shoulder-straps and sword, and his arm in a sling. I say "home," but the only roof he had ever slept under in these parts was ours, and now he stayed as a guest at Squire Avery's house, and never came near our farm. He was a tall, brown-faced, sinewy fellow, with curly hair and a pushing manner. Although he had been only a hired man he now cut a great dash down at the Corners, with his shoulder-straps and his officer's cape. It was said that he had declined several invitations to husking-bees, and that when he left the service, at the end of his time, he had a place ready for him in some city as a clerk in a drygoods-store—that is, of course, if he did not get to be colonel or general. From time to time he was seen walking out through the dry, rustling leaves with Squire Avery's oldest daughter.

This important military genius did not seem able, however, to throw much light upon the whereabouts of the two "missing" boys. From what I myself heard him say about the battle, and from what others reported of his talk, it seems that in the very early morning Hooker's line—a part of which consisted of Dearborn County men—moved forward through a big corn-field, the stalks of which were much higher than the soldiers' heads. When they came out, the Rebels opened such a hideous fire of cannon and musketry upon them from the woods close by, that those who did not fall were glad to run back again into the corn for shelter. Thus all became confusion, and the men were so mixed up that there was no getting them together again. Some went one way, some another, through the tall corn-rows, and Warner Pitts could not remember having seen either Jeff or Byron at all after the march began. Parts of the regiment formed again out on the road toward the Dunker church, but other parts found themselves half a mile away among the fragments of a Michigan regiment, and a good many more were left lying in the fatal cornfield. Our boys had not been traced among the dead, but that did not prove that they were alive. And so we were no wiser than before.

Warner Pitts only nodded in a distant way to me when he saw me first, with a cool "Hello, youngster!" I expected that he would ask after the folks at the farm which had been so long his home, but he turned to talk with some one else, and said never a word. Once, some days afterward, he called out as I passed him, "How's the old Copperhead?" and the Avery girl who was with him laughed aloud, but I went on without answering. He was already down in my black-books, in company with pretty nearly every other human being round about.

This list of enemies was indeed so full that there were times when I felt like crying over my isolation. It may be guessed, then, how rejoiced I was one afternoon to see Ni Hagadorn squeeze his way through our orchard-bars and saunter across under the trees to where I was at work sorting a heap of apples into barrels. I could have run to meet him, so grateful was the sight of any friendly, boyish face. The thought that perhaps after all he had not come to see me in particular, and that possibly he brought some news about Jeff, only flashed across my mind after I had smiled a broad welcome upon him, and he stood leaning against a barrel munching the biggest russet he had been able to pick out.

"Abner to home?" he asked, after a pause of neighborly silence. He hadn't come to see me after all.

"He's around the barns somewhere," I replied; adding, upon reflection, "Have you heard something fresh?"

Ni shook his sorrel head, and buried his teeth deep into the apple. "No, nothin'," he said, at last, with his mouth full, "only thought I'd come up an' talk it over with Abner."

The calm audacity of the proposition took my breath away.

"He'll boot you off'n the place if you try it," I warned him.

But Ni did not scare easily. "Oh, no," he said, with light confidence, "me an' Abner's all right."

As if to put this assurance to the test, the figure of the farmer was at this moment visible, coming toward us down the orchard road. He was in his shirt-sleeves, with the limp, discolored old broad-brimmed felt hat he always wore pulled down over his eyes. Though he no longer held his head so proudly erect as I could remember it, there were still suggestions of great force and mastership in his broad shoulders and big beard, and in the solid, long-gaited manner of his walk. He carried a pitchfork in his hand.

"Hello, Abner!" said Ni, as the farmer came up and halted, surveying each of us in turn with an impassive scrutiny.

"How 'r' ye?" returned Abner, with cold civility. I fancied he must be surprised to see the son of his enemy here, calmly gnawing his way through one of our apples, and acting as if the place belonged to him. But he gave no signs of astonishment, and after some words of direction to me concerning my work, started to move on again toward the barns.

Ni was not disposed to be thus cheated out of his conversation: "Seen Warner Pitts since he's got back?" he called out, and at this the farmer stopped and turned around. "You'd hardly know him now," the butcher's assistant went on, with cheerful briskness. "Why you'd think he'd never hoofed it over ploughed land in all his life. He's got his boots blacked up every day, an' his hair greased, an' a whole new suit of broadcloth, with shoulder-straps an' brass buttons, an' a sword—he brings it down to the Corners every evening, so't the boys at the store can heft it—an he's—"

"What do I care about all this?" broke in Abner. His voice was heavy, with a growling ground-note, and his eyes threw out an angry light under the shading hat-brim. "He can go to the devil, an' take his sword with him, for all o' me!"

Hostile as was his tone, the farmer did not again turn on his heel. Instead, he seemed to suspect that Ni had something more important to say, and looked him steadfastly in the face.

"That's what I say, too," replied Ni, lightly. "What's beat me is how such a fellow as that got to be an officer right from the word 'go!'—an' him the poorest shote in the whole lot. Now if it had a' ben Spencer Phillips I could understand it—or Bi Truax, or—or your Jeff—"

The farmer raised his fork menacingly, with a wrathful gesture. "Shet up!" he shouted; "shet up, I say! or I'll make ye!"

To my great amazement Ni was not at all affected by this demonstration. He leaned smilingly against the barrel, and picked out another apple—a spitzenberg this time.

"Now look a-here, Abner," he said, argumentatively, "what's the good o' gittin' mad? When I've had my say out, why, if you don't like it you needn't, an' nobody's a cent the wuss off. Of course, if you come down to hard-pan, it ain't none o' my business—"

"No," interjected Abner, in grim assent, "it ain't none o' your business!"

"But there is such a thing as being neighborly," Ni went on, undismayed, "an' meanin' things kindly, an' takin' 'em as they're meant."

"Yes, I know them kindly neighbors o' mine!" broke in the farmer with acrid irony. "I've summered 'em an' I've wintered 'em, an' the Lord deliver me from the whole caboodle of 'em! A meaner lot o' cusses never cumbered this footstool!"

"It takes all sorts o' people to make up a world," commented this freckled and sandy-headed young philosopher, testing the crimson skin of his apple with a tentative thumb-nail. "Now you ain't got anything in particular agin me, have you?"

"Nothin' except your breed," the farmer admitted. The frown with which he had been regarding Ni had softened just the least bit in the world.

"That don't count," said Ni, with easy confidence. "Why,

what does breed amount to, anyway? You ought to be the last man alive to lug *that* in—you, who've up an' soured on your own breed—your own son Jeff!"

I looked to see Abner lift his fork again, and perhaps go even further in his rage. Strangely enough, there crept into his sunburnt, massive face, at the corners of the eyes and mouth, something like the beginnings of a puzzled smile. "You're a cheeky little cuss, anyway!" was his final comment. Then his expression hardened again. "Who put you up to comin' here, an' talkin' like this to me?" he demanded, sternly.

"Nobody—hope to die!" protested Ni. "It's all my own spec. It riled me to see you mopin' round up here all alone by yourself, not knowin' what'd become of Jeff, an' makin' b'lieve to yourself you didn't care, an' so givin' yourself away to the whole neighborhood."

"Damn the neighborhood!" said Abner, fervently.

"Well, they talk about the same of you," Ni proceeded with an air of impartial candor. "But all that don't do you no good, an' don't do Jeff no good!"

"He made his own bed, and he must lay on it," said the farmer, with dogged firmness.

"I ain't sayin' he mustn't," remonstrated the other. "What I'm gittin' at is that you'd feel easier in your mind if you knew where that bed was—an so'd M'rye!"

Abner lifted his head. "His mother feels just as I do," he said. "He sneaked off behind our backs to jine Lincoln's nigger-worshippers, an' levy war on fellow-countrymen o' his'n who'd done him no harm, an' whatever happens to him it serves him right. I ain't much of a hand to lug in Scripter to back up my argyments—like some folks you know of—but my feelin' is: 'Whoso taketh up the sword shall perish by the sword!' An' so says his mother too!"

"Hm-m!" grunted Ni, with ostentatious incredulity. He bit into his apple, and there ensued a momentary silence. Then, as soon as he was able to speak, this astonishing boy said: "Guess I'll have a talk with M'rye about that herself."

The farmer's patience was running emptings. "No!" he said, severely, "I forbid ye! Don't ye dare say a word to her about it. She don't want to listen to ye—an I don't know what's possessed *me* to stand round an' gab about my private affairs with you like this, either. I don't bear ye no ill-will. If fathers can't help the kind o' sons they bring up, why, still less can ye blame sons on account o' their fathers. But it ain't a thing I want to talk about any more, either now or any other time. That's all."

Abner put the fork over his shoulder, as a sign that he was going, and that the interview was at an end. But the persistent Ni had a last word to offer—and he left his barrel and walked over to the farmer.

"See here," he said, in more urgent tones than he had used before, "I'm goin' South, an' I'm goin' to find Jeff if it takes a leg! I don't know how much it'll cost—I've got a little of my own saved up—an' I thought—p'r'aps—p'r'aps you'd like to —"

After a moment's thought the farmer shook his head. "No," he said, gravely, almost reluctantly. "It's agin my principles. You know me—Ni—you know I've never b'en a near man, let alone a mean man. An' ye know, too, that if Je—if that boy had behaved half-way decent, there ain't anything under the sun I wouldn't 'a' done for him. But this thing—I'm obleeged to ye for offrin'—but—No! it's agin my principles. Still, I'm obleeged to ye. Fill your pockets with them spitzenbergs, if they taste good to ye."

With this Abner Beech turned and walked resolutely off.

Left alone with me, Ni threw away the half-eaten apple he had held in his hand. "I don't want any of his dummed old spitzenbergs," he said, pushing his foot into the heap of fruit on the ground, in a meditative way.

"Then you ain't a-goin' South?" I queried.

"Yes, I am!" he replied, with decision. "I can work my way somehow. Only don't you whisper a word about it to any livin' soul, d'ye mind!"

Two or three days after that we heard that Ni Hagadorn had left for unknown parts. Some said he had gone to enlist—it seems that, despite his youth and small stature in my eyes, he would have been acceptable to the enlistment standards of the day—but the major opinion was that much dime-novel reading had inspired him with the notion of becoming a trapper in the mystic Far West.

I alone possessed the secret of his disappearance—unless, indeed, his sister knew—and no one will ever know what struggles I had to keep from confiding it to Hurley.

VII

The Election

Soon the fine weather was at an end. One day it was soft and warm, with a tender blue haze over the distant woods and a sun like a blood-orange in the tranquil sky, and birds twittering about among the elders and sumac along the rail-fences. And the next day everything was gray and lifeless and desolate, with fierce winds sweeping over the bare fields, and driving the cold rain in sheets before them.

Some people—among them Hurley—said it was the equinoctial that was upon us. Abner Beech ridiculed this, and proved by the dictionary that the equinoctial meant September 22d, whereas it was now well-nigh the end of October. The Irishman conceded that in books this might be so, but stuck wilfully to it that in practice the equinoctial came just before winter set in. After so long a period of saddened silence brooding over our household, it was quite a relief to hear the men argue this question of the weather.

Down at the Corners old farmers had wrangled over the identity of the equinoctial ever since I could remember. It was pretty generally agreed that each year along some time during the fall, there came a storm which was properly entitled to that name, but at this point harmony ended. Some insisted that it came before Indian Summer, some that it followed that season, and this was further complicated by the fact that no one was ever quite sure when it *was* Indian Summer. There were all sorts of rules for recognizing this delectable time of year, rules connected, I recall, with the opening of the chestnut burrs, the movement of birds, and various other incidents in nature's great processional, but these rules rarely came right in our rough latitude, and sometimes never came at all—at least did not bring with them anything remotely resembling Indian Summer, but made our autumn one prolonged and miserable succession of storms. And then it was an especially trying trick to pick out the equinoctial from the lot—and even harder still to prove to sceptical neighbors that you were right.

Whatever this particular storm may have been it came too soon. Being so short-handed on the farm, we were much behind in the matter of drawing our produce to market. And now, after the first day or two of rain, the roads were things to shudder at. It was not so bad getting to and from the Corners, for Agrippa Hill had a gravel formation, but beyond the Corners, whichever way one went over the bottom lands of the Nedahma Valley, it was a matter of lashing the panting teams through seas of mud punctuated by abysmal pitch-holes, into which the wheels slumped over their hubs, and quite generally stuck till they were pried out with fence-rails.

Abner Beech was exceptionally tender in his treatment of live-stock. The only occasion I ever heard of on which he was tempted into using his big fists upon a fellow-creature, was once, long before my time, when one of his hired men struck a refractory cow over its haunches with a shovel. He knocked this man clear through the stanchions. Often Jeff and I used to feel that he carried his solicitude for horse-flesh too far—particularly when we wanted to drive down to the creek for a summer evening swim, and he thought the teams were too tired.

So now he would not let us hitch up and drive into Octavius

with even the lightest loads, on account of the horses. It would be better to wait, he said, until there was sledding; then we could slip in in no time. He pretended that all the signs this year pointed to an early winter.

The result was that we were more than ever shut off from news of the outer world. The weekly paper which came to us was full, I remember, of political arguments and speeches—for a Congress and Governor were to be elected a few weeks hence—but there were next to no tidings from the front. The war, in fact, seemed to have almost stopped altogether, and this paper spoke of it as a confessed failure. Farmer Beech and Hurley, of course, took the same view, and their remarks quite prepared me from day to day to hear that peace had been concluded.

But down at the Corners a strikingly different spirit reigned. It quite surprised me, I know, when I went down on occasion for odds and ends of groceries which the bad roads prevented us from getting in town, to discover that the talk there was all in favor of having a great deal more war than ever.

This store at the Corners was also the post-office, and, more important still, it served as a general rallying place for the menfolks of the neighborhood after supper. Lee Watkins, who kept it, would rather have missed a meal of victuals any day than not to have the "boys" come in of an evening, and sit or lounge around discussing the situation. Many of them were very old boys now, garrulous seniors who remembered "Matty" Van Buren, as they called him, and told weird stories of the Anti-Masonry days. These had the well-worn arm-chairs nearest the stove, in cold weather, and spat tobacco-juice on its hottest parts with a precision born of long-time experience. The younger fellows accommodated themselves about the outer circle, squatting on boxes, or with one leg over a barrel, sampling the sugar and crackers and raisins in an absent-minded way each evening, till Mrs. Watkins came out and put the covers on. She was a stout, peevish woman in bloomers, and they said that her husband, Lee, couldn't have run the post-office for twenty-four hours if it hadn't been for her. We understood that she was a Woman's Rights' woman, which some held was much the same as believing in Free Love. All that was certain, however, was that she did not believe in free lunches out of her husband's barrels and cases.

The chief flaw in this village parliament was the absence of an opposition. Among all the accustomed assemblage of men who sat about, their hats well back on their heads, their mouths full of strong language and tobacco, there was none to disagree upon any essential feature of the situation with the others. To secure even the merest semblance of variety, those whose instincts were cross-grained had to go out of their way to pick up trifling points of difference, and the arguments over these had to be spun out with the greatest possible care, to be kept going at all. I should fancy, however, that this apparent concord only served to keep before their minds, with added persistency, the fact that there *was* an opposition, nursing its heretical wrath in solitude up on the Beech farm. At all events, I seemed never to go into the grocery of a night without hearing bitter remarks, or even curses, levelled at our household.

It was from these casual visits—standing about on the outskirts of the gathering, beyond the feeble ring of light thrown out by the kerosene lamp on the counter—that I learned how deeply the Corners were opposed to peace. It appeared from the talk here that there was something very like treason at the front. The victory at Antietam—so dearly bought with the blood of our own people—had been, they said, of worse than no use at all. The defeated Rebels had been allowed to take their own time in crossing the Potomac comfortably. They had not been pursued or molested since, and the Corners could only account for this on the theory of treachery at Union headquarters. Some only hinted guardedly at this. Others declared openly that the North was being sold out by its own generals. As for old "Jee" Hagadorn, who came in almost every night, and monopolized the talking all the while he was present, he made no bones of denouncing McClellan and Porter as traitors who must be hanged.

He comes before me as I write—his thin form quivering with excitement, the red stubbly hair standing up all round his drawn and livid face, his knuckles rapping out one fierce point after another on the candle-box, as he filled the little hot room with angry declamation. "Go it, Jee!" "Give 'em Hell!" "Hangin's too good for 'em!" his auditors used to exclaim in encouragement, whenever he paused for breath, and then he would start off again still more furiously, till he had to gasp after every word, and screamed "Lincoln-ah!" "Lee-ah!" "Antietam-ah!" and so on, into our perturbed ears. Then I would go home, recalling how he had formerly shouted about "Adam-ah!" and "Eve-ah!" in church, and marvelling that he had never worked himself into a fit, or broken a blood-vessel.

So between what Abner and Hurley said on the farm, and what was proclaimed at the Corners, it was pretty hard to figure out whether the war was going to stop, or go on much worse than ever.

Things were still in this doubtful state, when election Tuesday came round. I had not known or thought about it, until at the breakfast-table Abner said that he guessed he and Hurley would go down and vote before dinner. He had some days before secured a package of ballots from the organization of his party at Octavius, and these he now took from one of the bookcase drawers, and divided between himself and Hurley.

"They won't be much use, I dessay, peddlin' 'em at the polls," he said, with a grim momentary smile, "but, by the Eternal, we'll vote 'em!"

"As many of 'em as they'll be allowin' us," added Hurley, in chuckling qualification.

They were very pretty tickets in those days, with marbled and plaided backs in brilliant colors, and spreading eagles in front, over the printed captions. In other years I had shared with the urchins of the neighborhood the excitement of scrambling for a share of these ballots, after they had been counted, and tossed out of the boxes. The conditions did not seem to be favorable for a repetition of that this year, and apparently this occurred to Abner, for of his own accord he handed me over some dozen of the little packets, each tied with a thread, and labelled, "State," "Congressional," "Judiciary," and the like. He, moreover, consented—the morning chores being out of the way—that I should accompany them to the Corners. The ground had frozen stiff overnight, and the road lay in hard uncompromising ridges between the tracks of yesterday's wheels. The two men swung along down the hill ahead of me, with resolute strides and their heads proudly thrown back, as if they had been going into battle. I shuffled on behind in my new boots, also much excited. The day was cold and raw.

The polls were fixed up in a little building next to the post-office—a one-story frame structure where Lee Watkins kept his bob-sleigh and oil barrels, as a rule. These had been cleared out into the yard, and a table and some chairs put in in their place. A pane of glass had been taken out of the window. Through this aperture the voters, each in his turn, passed their ballots, to be placed by the inspectors in the several boxes ranged along the window-sill inside. A dozen or more men, mainly in army overcoats, stood about on the sidewalk or in the road outside, stamping their feet for warmth, and slapping their shoulders with their hands, between the fingers of which they held little packets of tickets like mine—that is to say, they were like mine in form and brilliancy of color, but I knew well enough that there the resemblance ended abruptly. A yard or so from the window two posts had been driven into the ground, with a board nailed across to prevent undue crowding.

Abner and Hurley marched up to the polls without a word to any one, or any sign of recognition from the bystanders. Their appearance, however, visibly awakened the interest of the Corners, and several young fellows who were standing on the grocery steps sauntered over in their wake to see what was going on. These, with the ticket-peddlers, crowded up close to the window now, behind our two men.

"Abner Beech!" called the farmer through the open pane, in a defiant voice. Standing on tiptoe, I could just see the heads of some men inside, apparently looking through the election books. No questions were asked, and in a minute or so Abner had voted and stood aside a little, to make room for his companion.

"Timothy Joseph Hurley!" shouted our hired man, standing on his toes to make himself taller, and squaring his weazened shoulders.

"Got your naturalization papers?" came out a sharp, gruff inquiry through the window-sash.

"That I have!" said the Irishman, wagging his head in satisfaction at having foreseen this trick, and winking blandly into the wall of stolid, hostile faces encircling him. "That I have!"

He drew forth an old and crumpled envelope, from his breast-pocket, and extracted some papers from its ragged folds, which he passed through to the inspector. The latter just cast his eye over the documents and handed them back.

"Them ain't no good!" he said, curtly.

"What's that you're saying?" cried the Irishman. "Sure I've voted on thim same papers every year since 1856, an' niver a man gainsaid me. No good, is it? Huh!"

"Why ain't they no good?" boomed in Abner Beech's deep, angry voice. He had moved back to the window.

"Because they ain't, that's enough!" returned the inspector. "Don't block up the window, there! Others want to vote!"

"I'll have the law on yez!" shouted Hurley. "I'll swear me vote in! I'll—I'll—"

"Aw, shut up, you Mick!" some one called out close by, and then there rose another voice farther back in the group: "Don't let him vote! One Copperhead's enough in Agrippa!"

"I'll have the law—" I heard Hurley begin again, at the top of his voice, and Abner roared out something I could not catch. Then as in a flash the whole cluster of men became one confused whirling tangle of arms and legs, sprawling and wrestling on the ground, and from it rising the repellent sound of blows upon flesh, and a discordant chorus of grunts and curses. Big chunks of icy mud flew through the air, kicked up by the boots of the men as they struggled. I saw the two posts with the board weave under the strain, then give way, some of the embattled group tumbling over them as they fell. It was wholly impossible to guess who was who in this writhing and tossing mass of fighters. I danced up and down in a frenzy of excitement, watching this wild spectacle, and, so I was told years afterward, screaming with all my might and main.

Then all at once there was a mighty upheaval, and a big man half-scrambled, half-hurled himself to his feet. It was Abner, who had wrenched one of the posts bodily from under the others, and swung it now high in air. Some one clutched it, and for the moment stayed its descent, yelling, meanwhile, "Look out! Look out!" as though life itself depended on the volume of his voice.

The ground cleared itself as if by magic. On the instant there was only Abner standing there with the post in his hands, and little Hurley beside him, the lower part of his face covered with blood, and his coat torn half from his back. The others had drawn off, and formed a semicircle just out of reach of the stake, like farm-dogs round a wounded bear at bay. Two or three of them had blood about their heads and necks.

There were cries of "Kill him!" and it was said afterward that Roselle Upman drew a pistol, but if he did others dissuaded him from using it. Abner stood with his back to the building, breathing hard, and a good deal covered with mud, but eyeing the crowd with a masterful ferocity, and from time to time shifting his hands to get a new grip on that tremendous weapon of his. He said not a word.

The Irishman, after a moment's hesitation, wiped some of the blood from his mouth and jaw, and turned to the window again. "Timothy Joseph Hurley!" he shouted in, defiantly.

This time another inspector came to the front—the owner

of the tanyard over on the Dutch road, and a man of importance in the district. Evidently there had been a discussion inside.

"We will take your vote if you want to swear it in," he said, in a pacific tone, and though there were some dissenting cries from the crowd without, he read the oath, and Hurley mumbled it after him.

Then, with some difficulty, he sorted out from his pocket some torn and mud-stained packets of tickets, picked the cleanest out from each, and voted them—all with a fine air of unconcern.

Abner Beech marched out behind him now with a resolute clutch on the stake. The crowd made reluctant way for them, not without a good many truculent remarks, but with no offer of actual violence. Some of the more boisterous ones, led by Roselle Upman, were for following them, and renewing the encounter beyond the Corners. But this, too, came to nothing, and when I at last ventured to cross the road and join Abner and Hurley, even the cries of "Copperhead" had died away.

The sun had come out, and the frosty ruts had softened to stickiness. The men's heavy boots picked up whole sections of plastic earth as they walked in the middle of the road up the hill.

"What's the matter with your mouth?" asked Abner at last, casting a sidelong glance at his companion. "It's be'n a-bleedin'."

Hurley passed an investigating hand carefully over the lower part of his face, looked at his reddened fingers, and laughed aloud.

"I'd a fine grand bite at the ear of one of them," he said in explanation. " 'Tis no blood o' mine."

Abner knitted his brows. "That ain't the way we fight in this country," he said, in tones of displeasure. "Bitin' men's ears ain't no civilized way of behavin'."

" 'Twas not much of a day for civilization," remarked Hurley, lightly; and there was no further conversation on our homeward tramp.

VIII

The Election Bonfire

The election had been on Tuesday, November 4th. Our paper, containing the news of the result, was to be expected at the Corners on Friday morning. But long before that date we had learned—I think it was Hurley who found it out—that the Abolitionists had actually been beaten in our Congressional district. It was so amazing a thing that Abner could scarcely credit it, but it was apparently beyond dispute. For that matter, one hardly needed further evidence than the dejected way in which Philo Andrews and Myron Pierce and other followers of "Jee" Hagadorn hung their heads as they drove past our place.

Of course it had all been done by the vote in the big town of Tecumseh, way at the other end of the district, and by those towns surrounding it where the Mohawk Dutch were still very numerous. But this did not at all lessen the exhilaration with which the discovery that the Radicals of our own Dearborn County had been snowed under, filled our breasts. Was it not wonderful to think of, that these heroes of remote Adams and Jay Counties should have been at work redeeming the district on the very day when the two votes of our farm marked the almost despairing low-water mark of the cause in Agrippa?

Abner could hardly keep his feet down on the ground or floor when he walked, so powerfully did the tidings of this achievement thrill his veins. He said the springs of his knees kept jerking upward, so that he wanted to kick and dance all the while. Janey Wilcox, who, though a meek and silent girl, was a wildly bitter partisan, was all eagerness to light a bonfire out on the knoll in front of the house Thursday night, so that every mother's son of them down at the Corners might see it, but Abner thought it would be better to wait until we had the printed facts before us.

I could hardly wait to finish breakfast Friday morning, so great was my zeal to be off to the post-office. It was indeed not altogether daylight when I started at quick step down the hill. Yet, early as I was, there were some twenty people inside Lee Watkins's store when I arrived, all standing clustered about the high square row of glass-faced pigeon-holes reared on the farther end of the counter, behind which could be seen Lee and his sour-faced wife sorting over the mail by lamp-light. "Jee" Hagadorn was in this group and Squire Avery, and most of the other prominent citizens of the neighborhood. All were deeply restless.

Every minute or two some one of them would shout: "Come, Lee, give us out one of the papers, anyway!" But for some reason Mrs. Watkins was inexorable. Her pursed-up lips and resolute expression told us plainly that none would be served till all were sorted. So the impatient waiters bided their time under protest, exchanging splenetic remarks under their breath. We must have stood there three-quarters of an hour.

At last Mrs. Watkins wiped her hands on the apron over her bloomers. Everybody knew the signal, and on the instant a dozen arms were stretched vehemently toward Lee, struggling for precedence. In another moment wrappers had been ripped off and sheets flung open. Then the store was alive with excited voices. "Yes, sir! It's true! The Copperheads have won!" "*Tribune* concedes Seymour's election!" "We're beaten in the district by less'n a hundred!" "Good-by, human liberty!" "Now we know how Lazarus felt when he was licked by the dogs!" and so on—a stormy warfare of wrathful ejaculations.

In my turn I crowded up, and held out my hand for the paper I saw in the box. Lee Watkins recognized me, and took the paper out to deliver to me. But at the same moment his wife, who had been hastily scanning the columns of some other journal, looked up and also saw who I was. With a lightning gesture she threw out her hand, snatched our *World* from her husband's grasp, and threw it spitefully under the counter.

"There ain't nothing for *you!*" she snapped at me. "Pesky Copperhead rag!" she muttered to herself.

Although I had plainly seen the familiar wrapper, and understood her action well enough, it never occurred to me to argue the question with Mrs. Watkins. Her bustling, determined demeanor, perhaps also her bloomers, had always filled me with awe. I hung about for a time, avoiding her range of vision, until she went out into her kitchen. Then I spoke with resolution to Lee:

"If you don't give me that paper," I said, "I'll tell Abner, an' he'll make you sweat for it!"

The postmaster stole a cautious glance kitchenward. Then he made a swift, diving movement under the counter, and furtively thrust the paper out at me.

"Scoot!" he said, briefly, and I obeyed him.

Abner was simply wild with bewildered delight over what this paper had to tell him. Even my narrative about Mrs. Watkins, which ordinarily would have thrown him into transports of rage, provoked only a passing sniff. "They've only got two more years to hold that post-office," was his only remark upon it.

Hurley and Janey Wilcox and even the Underwood girl came in, and listened to Abner reading out the news. He shirked nothing, but waded manfully through long tables of figures and meaningless catalogues of counties in other States, the names of which he scarcely knew how to pronounce: " 'Five hundred and thirty-one townships in Wisconsin give Brown 21,409, Smith 16,329, Ferguson 802, a Republican loss of 26.' Do you see that, Hurley? It's everywhere the same." " 'Kalapoosas County elects Republican Sheriff for first time in history of party.' That isn't so good, but it's only one out of ten thousand." " 'Four hundred and six townships in New Hampshire show a net Democratic loss of—' pshaw! there ain't nothing in that! Wait till the other towns are heard from!"

So Abner read on and on, slapping his thigh with his free hand whenever anything specially good turned up. And there was a great deal that we felt to be good. The State had been carried. Besides our Congressman, many others had been elected in unlooked-for places—so much so that the paper held out the hope that Congress itself might be ours. Of course Abner at once talked as if it were already ours. Resting between paragraphs, he told Hurley and the others that this settled it. The war must now surely be abandoned, and the seceding States invited to return to the Union on terms honorable to both sides.

Hurley had assented with acquiescent nods to everything else. He seemed to have a reservation on this last point. "An' what if they won't come?" he asked.

"Let 'em stay out, then," replied Abner, dogmatically. "This war—this wicked war between brothers—must stop. That's the meaning of Tuesday's votes. What did you and I go down to the Corners and cast our ballots for?—why, for peace!"

"Well, somebody else got my share of it, then," remarked Hurley with a rueful chuckle.

Abner was too intent upon his theme to notice. "Yes, peace!" he repeated, in the deep vibrating tones of his class-meeting manner. "Why, just think what's been a-goin' on! Great armies raised, hundreds of thousands of honest men taken from their work an' set to murderin' each other, whole deestricks of country torn up by the roots, homes desolated, the land filled with widows an' orphans, an' every house a house of mournin'."

Mrs. Beech had been sitting, with her mending-basket on her knee, listening to her husband like the rest of us. She shot to her feet now as these last words of his quivered in the air, paying no heed to the basket or its scattered contents on the floor, but putting her apron to her eyes, and making her way thus past us, half-blindly, into her bedroom. I thought I heard the sound of a sob as she closed the door.

That the stately, proud, self-contained mistress of our household should act like this before us all was even more surprising than Seymour's election. We stared at one another in silent astonishment.

"M'rye ain't feelin' over 'n' above well," Abner said at last, apologetically. "You girls ought to spare her all you kin."

One could see, however, that he was as puzzled as the rest of us. He rose to his feet, walked over to the stove, rubbed his boot meditatively against the hearth for a minute or two, then came back again to the table. It was with a visible effort that he finally shook off this mood, and forced a smile to his lips.

"Well, Janey," he said, with an effort at briskness, "ye kin go ahead with your bonfire, now. I guess I've got some old bar'ls for ye over 'n the cow-barn."

But having said this, he turned abruptly and followed his wife into the little chamber off the living-room.

IX

Esther's Visit

The next day, Saturday, was my birthday. I celebrated it by a heavy cold, with a bursting headache, and chills chasing each other down my back. I went out to the cow-barn with the two men before daylight, as usual, but felt so bad that I had to come back to the house before milking was half over. The moment M'rye saw me, I was ordered on to the sick-list.

The Beech homestead was a good place to be sick in. Both M'rye and Janey had a talent in the way of fixing up tasty little dishes for invalids, and otherwise ministering to their comfort, which year after year went a-begging, simply because all the men-folk kept so well. Therefore, when the rare opportunity did arrive, they made the most of it. I had my feet and legs put into a bucket of hot water, and wrapped round with burdock leaves. Janey prepared for my breakfast some soft toast—not the insipid and common milk-toast—but each golden-brown slice treated separately on a plate, first moistened with scalding water, then peppered, salted, and buttered, with a little cold milk on top of all. I ate this sumptuous breakfast at my leisure, ensconced in M'rye's big cushioned rocking-chair, with my feet and legs, well tucked up in a blanket-shawl, stretched out on another chair, comfortably near the stove.

It was taken for granted that I had caught my cold out around the bonfire the previous evening—and this conviction threw a sort of patriotic glamour about my illness, at least in my own mind.

The bonfire had been a famous success. Though there was a trifle of rain in the air, the barrels and mossy discarded old fence-rails burned like pitch-pine, and when Hurley and I threw on armfuls of brush, the sparks burst up with a roar into a flaming column which we felt must be visible all over our side of Dearborn County. At all events, there was no doubt about its being seen and understood down at the Corners, for presently our enemies there started an answering bonfire, which glowed from time to time with such a peculiarly concentrated radiance that Abner said Lee Watkins must have given them some of his kerosene-oil barrels. The thought of such a sacrifice as this on the part of the postmaster rather disturbed Abner's mind, raising, as it did, the hideous suggestion that possibly later returns might have altered the election results. But when Hurley and I dragged forward and tipped over into the blaze the whole side of an old abandoned corn-crib, and heaped dry brush on top of that, till the very sky seemed afire above us, and the stubble-fields down the hillside were all ruddy in the light, Abner confessed himself reassured. Our enthusiasm was so great that it was nearly ten o'clock before we went to bed, having first put the fire pretty well out, lest a rising wind during the night should scatter sparks and work mischief.

I had all these splendid things to think of next day, along with my headache and the shivering spine, and they tipped the balance toward satisfaction. Shortly after breakfast M'rye made a flaxseed poultice and muffled it flabbily about my neck, and brought me also some boneset-tea to drink. There was a debate in the air as between castor-oil and senna, fragments of which were borne in to me when the kitchen door was open. The Underwood girl alarmed me by steadily insisting that her sister-in-law always broke up sick-headaches with a mustard-plaster put raw on the back of the neck. Every once in a while one of them would come in and address to me the stereotyped formula: "Feel any better?" and I as invariably answered, "No." In reality, though, I was lazily comfortable all the time, with Lossing's "Field-Book of the War of 1812" lying open on my lap, to look at when I felt inclined. This book was not nearly so interesting as the one about the Revolution, but a grandfather of mine had marched as a soldier up to Sackett's Harbor in the later war, though he did not seem to have had any fighting to do after he got there, and in my serious moods I always felt it my duty to read about his war instead of the other.

So the day passed along, and dusk began to gather in the living-room. The men were off outdoors somewhere, and the girls were churning in the butter-room. M'rye had come in with her mending and sat on the opposite side of the stove, at intervals casting glances over its flat top to satisfy herself that my poultice had not sagged down from its proper place, and that I was in other respects doing as well as could be expected.

Conversation between us was hardly to be thought of, even if I had not been so drowsily indolent. M'rye was not a talker, and preferred always to sit in silence, listening to others, or, better still, going on at her work with no sounds at all to disturb her thoughts. These long periods of meditation, and the sedate gaze of her black, penetrating eyes, gave me the feeling that she must be much wiser than other women, who could not keep still at all, but gabbled everything the moment it came into their heads.

We had sat thus for a long, long time, until I began to wonder how she could sew in the waning light, when all at once, without lifting her eyes from her work, she spoke to me.

"D'you know where Ni Hagadorn's gone to?" she asked me, in a measured, impressive voice.

"He—he—told me he was a-goin' away," I made answer, with weak evasiveness.

"But where? Down South?" She looked up, as I hesitated, and flashed that darkling glance of hers at me. "Out with it!" she commanded. "Tell me the truth!"

Thus adjured, I promptly admitted that Ni had said he was going South, and could work his way somehow. "He's gone, you know," I added, after a pause, "to try and find—that is, to hunt around after—"

"Yes, I know," said M'rye, sententiously, and another long silence ensued.

She rose after a time, and went out into the kitchen, returning with the lighted lamp. She set this on the table, putting the shade down on one side so that the light should not hurt my eyes, and resumed her mending. The yellow glow thus falling upon her gave to her dark, severe, high-featured face a duskier effect than ever. It occurred to me that Molly Brant, that mysteriously fascinating and bloody Mohawk queen who left such an awful reddened mark upon the history of her native Valley, must have been like our M'rye. My mind began sleepily to clothe the farmer's wife in blankets and chains of wampum, with eagles' feathers in her raven hair, and then to drift vaguely off over the threshold of Indian dreamland, when suddenly, with a start, I became conscious that some unexpected person had entered the room by the veranda-door behind me.

The rush of cold air from without had awakened me and told me of the entrance. A glance at M'rye's face revealed the rest. She was staring at the newcomer with a dumfounded expression of countenance, her mouth half-open with sheer surprise. Still staring, she rose and tilted the lamp-shade in yet another direction, so that the light was thrown upon the stranger. At this I turned in my chair to look.

It was Esther Hagadorn who had come in!

There was a moment's awkward silence, and then the school-teacher began hurriedly to speak. "I saw you were alone from the veranda—I was so nervous it never occurred to me to rap —the curtains being up—I—I walked straight in."

As if in comment upon this statement, M'rye marched across the room, and pulled down both curtains over the veranda windows. With her hand still upon the cord of the second shade, she turned and again dumbly surveyed her visitor.

Esther flushed visibly at this reception, and had to choke down the first words that came to her lips. Then she went on better: "I hope you'll excuse my rudeness. I really did forget to rap. I came upon very special business. Is Ab—Mr. Beech at home?"

"Won't you sit down?" said M'rye, with a glum effort at civility. "I expect him in presently."

The school-ma'am, displaying some diffidence, seated herself in the nearest chair, and gazed at the wall-paper with intentness. She had never seemed to notice me at all—indeed had spoken of seeing M'rye alone, through the window—and now I coughed, and stirred to readjust my poultice, but she did not look my way. M'rye had gone back to her chair by the stove, and taken up her mending again.

"You'd better lay off your things. You won't feel 'em when you go out," she remarked, after an embarrassing period of silence, investing the formal phrases with chilling intention.

Esther made a fumbling motion at the loop of her big mink cape, but did not unfasten it.

"I—I don't know *what* you think of me," she began, at last, and then nervously halted.

"Mebbe it's just as well you don't," said M'rye, significantly, darning away with long sweeps of her arm, and bending attentively over her stocking and ball.

"I can understand your feeling hard," Esther went on, still eyeing the sprawling blue figures on the wall, and plucking with her fingers at the furry tails on her cape. "And—I *am* to blame, *some,* I can see now—but it didn't seem so, *then,* to either of us."

"It ain't no affair of mine," remarked M'rye, when the pause came, "but if that's your business with Abner, you won't make much by waitin'. Of course it's nothing to me, one way or t'other."

Not another word was exchanged for a long time. From where I sat I could see the girl's lips tremble, as she looked steadfastly into the wall. I felt certain that M'rye was darning the same place over and over again, so furiously did she keep her needle flying.

All at once she looked up angrily. "Well," she said, in loud, bitter tones: "Why not out with what you've come to say 'n' be done with it? You've heard something, *I* know!"

Esther shook her head. "No, Mrs. Beech," she said, with a piteous quaver in her voice. "I—I haven't heard anything!"

The sound of her own broken utterances seemed to affect her deeply. Her eyes filled with tears, and she hastily got out a handkerchief from her muff, and began drying them. She could not keep from sobbing aloud a little.

M'rye deliberately took another stocking from the heap in the basket, fitted it over the ball, and began a fresh task—all without a glance at the weeping girl.

Thus the two women still sat, when Janey came in to lay the table for supper. She lifted the lamp off to spread the cloth and put it on again; she brought in plates and knives and spoons, and arranged them in their accustomed places—all the while furtively regarding Miss Hagadorn with an incredulous surprise. When she had quite finished she went over to her mistress and, bending low, whispered so that we could all hear quite distinctly: "Is *she* goin' to stay for supper?"

M'rye hesitated, but Esther lifted her head and put down the handkerchief instantly. "Oh, no!" she said, eagerly: "don't think of it! I must hurry home as soon as I've seen Mr. Beech." Janey went out with an obvious air of relief.

Presently there was a sound of heavy boots out in the kitchen being thrown on to the floor, and then Abner came in. He halted in the doorway, his massive form seeming to completely fill it, and devoted a moment or so taking in the novel spectacle of a neighbor under his roof. Then he advanced, walking obliquely till he could see distinctly the face of the visitor. It stands to reason that he must have been surprised, but he gave no sign of it.

"How d' do, Miss," he said, with grave politeness, coming up and offering her his big hand.

Esther rose abruptly, peony-red with pleasurable confusion, and took the hand stretched out to her. "How d' do, Mr. Beech," she responded with some eagerness, "I—I came up to see you—a—about something that's very pressing."

"It's blowing up quite a gale outside," the farmer remarked, evidently to gain time the while he scanned her face in a solemn, thoughtful way, noting, I doubt not, the swollen eyelids and stains of tears, and trying to guess her errand. "Shouldn't wonder if we had a foot o' snow before morning."

The school-teacher seemed in doubt how best to begin what she had to say, so that Abner had time, after he lifted his inquiring gaze from her, to run a master's eye over the table.

"Have Janey lay another place!" he said, with authoritative brevity.

As M'rye rose to obey, Esther broke forth: "Oh, no, please don't! Thank you so much, Mr. Beech—but really I can't stop —truly, I mustn't think of it."

The farmer merely nodded a confirmation of his order to M'rye, who hastened out to the kitchen.

"It'll be there for ye, anyway," he said. "Now set down again, please."

It was all as if he was the one who had the news to tell, so naturally did he take command of the situation. The girl seated herself, and the farmer drew up his arm-chair and planted himself before her, keeping his stockinged feet under the rungs for politeness' sake.

"Now, Miss," he began, just making it civilly plain that he

preferred not to utter her hated paternal name, "I don't know no more'n a babe unborn what's brought you here. I'm sure, from what I know of ye, that you wouldn't come to this house jest for the sake of comin', or to argy things that can't be, an' mustn't be, argied. In one sense, we ain't friends of yours here, and there's a heap o' things that you an' me don't want to talk about, because they'd only lead to bad feelin', an' so we'll leave 'em all severely alone. But in another way, I've always had a liking for you. You're a smart girl, an' a scholar into the bargain, an' there ain't so many o' that sort knockin' around in these parts that a man like myself, who's fond o' books an' learnin', wants to be unfriendly to them there is. So now you can figure out pretty well where the chalk line lays, and we'll walk on it."

Esther nodded her head. "Yes, I understand," she remarked, and seemed not to dislike what Abner had said.

"That being so, what is it?" the farmer asked, with his hands on his knees.

"Well, Mr. Beech," the school-teacher began, noting with a swift side-glance that M'rye had returned, and was herself rearranging the table. "I don't think you can have heard it, but some important news has come in during the day. There seems to be different stories, but the gist of them is that a number of leading Union generals have been discovered to be traitors, and McClellan has been dismissed from his place at the head of the army, and ordered to return to his home in New Jersey under arrest, and they say others are to be treated in the same way, and Fath—*some* people think it will be a hanging matter, and—"

Abner waved all this aside with a motion of his hand. "It don't amount to a hill o' beans," he said, placidly. "It's jest spite, because we licked 'em at the elections. Don't you worry your head about *that!*"

Esther was not reassured. "That isn't all," she went on, nervously. "They say there's been discovered a big conspiracy, with secret sympathizers all over the North."

"Pooh!" commented Abner. "We've heer'n tell o' that before!"

"All over the North," she continued, "with the intention of bringing across infected clothes from Canada, and spreading the small-pox among us, and—"

The farmer laughed outright; a laugh embittered by contempt. "What cock-'n'-bull story'll be hatched next!" he said. "You don't mean to say you—a girl with a head on her shoulders like *you*—give ear to such tomfoolery as that! Come, now, honest Injin, do you mean to tell me *you* believe all this?"

"It don't so much matter, Mr. Beech," the girl replied, raising her face to his, and speaking more confidently—"it don't matter at all what I believe. I'm talking of what they believe down at the Corners."

"The Corners be jiggered!" exclaimed Abner, politely, but with emphasis.

Esther rose from the chair. "Mr. Beech," she declared, impressively; "they're coming up here to-night! That bonfire of yours made 'em mad. It's no matter how I learned it—it wasn't from father—I don't know that he knows anything about it, but they're coming *here!* and—and Heaven only knows what they're going to do when they get here!"

The farmer rose also, his huge figure towering above that of the girl, as he looked down at her over his beard. He no longer dissembled his stockinged feet. After a moment's pause he said: "So that's what you came to tell me, eh?"

The school-ma'am nodded her head. "I couldn't bear not to," she explained, simply.

"Well, I'm obleeged to ye!" Abner remarked, with gravity. "Whatever comes of it, I'm obleeged to ye!"

He turned at this, and walked slowly out into the kitchen, leaving the door open behind him. "Pull on your boots again!" we heard him say, presumably to Hurley. In a minute or two he returned with his own boots on, and bearing over his arm the old double-barrelled shot-gun which always hung above the kitchen mantel-piece. In his hands he had two shot-flasks, the little tobacco-bag full of buckshot, and a powder-horn. He laid these on the open shelf of the bookcase, and, after fitting fresh caps on the nipples, put the gun beside them.

"I'd be all the more sot on your stayin' to supper," he remarked, looking again at Esther, "only if there *should* be any unpleasantness, why, I'd hate like sin to have you mixed up in it. You see how I'm placed."

Esther did not hesitate a moment. She walked over to where M'rye stood by the table replenishing the butter-plate. "I'd be very glad indeed to stay, Mr. Beech," she said, with winning frankness, "if I may."

"There's the place laid for you," commented M'rye, impassively. Then, catching her husband's eye, she added the perfunctory assurance, "You're entirely welcome."

Hurley and the girls came in now, and all except me took their seats about the table. Both Abner and the Irishman had their coats on, out of compliment to the company. M'rye brought over a thick slice of fresh buttered bread with brown sugar on it, and a cup of weak tea, and put them beside me on a chair. Then the evening meal went forward, the farmer talking in a fragmentary way about the crops and the weather. Save for an occasional response from our visitor, the rest maintained silence. The Underwood girl could not keep her fearful eyes from the gun lying on the bookcase, and protested that she had no appetite, but Hurley ate vigorously, and had a smile on his wrinkled and swarthy little face.

The wind outside whistled shrilly at the windows, rattling the shutters, and trying its force in explosive blasts which seemed to rock the house on its stone foundations. Once or twice it shook the veranda door with such violence that the folk at the table instinctively lifted their heads, thinking some one was there.

Then, all at once, above the confusion of the storm's noises, we heard a voice rise, high and clear, crying:

"Smoke the damned Copperhead out!"

X

The Fire

"That was Roselle Upman that hollered," remarked Janey Wilcox, breaking the agitated silence which had fallen upon the supper table. "You can tell it's him because he's had all his front teeth pulled out."

"I wasn't born in the woods to be skeert by an owl!" replied Abner, with a great show of tranquility, helping himself to another slice of bread. "Miss, you ain't half makin' out a supper!"

But this bravado could not maintain itself. In another minute there came a loud chorus of angry yells, heightened at its finish by two or three pistol-shots. Then Abner pushed back his chair and rose slowly to his feet, and the rest sprang up all around the table.

"Hurley," said the farmer, speaking as deliberately as he knew how, doubtless with the idea of reassuring the others, "you go out into the kitchen with the women-folks, an' bar the woodshed door, an' bring in the axe with you to stan' guard over the kitchen door. I'll look out for this part o' the house myself."

"I want to stay in here with you, Abner," said M'rye.

"No, you go out with the others!" commanded the master with firmness, and so they all filed out with no hint whatever of me. The shadow of the lamp-shade had cut me off altogether from their thoughts.

Perhaps it is not surprising that my recollections of what now ensued should lack definiteness and sequence. The truth is, that my terror at my own predicament, sitting there with no covering for my feet and calves but the burdock leaves and that absurd shawl, swamped everything else in my mind. Still, I do remember some of it.

Abner strode across to the bookcase and took up the gun, his big thumb resting determinedly on the hammers. Then he marched to the door, threw it wide open, and planted himself on the threshold, looking out into the darkness.

"What's your business here, whoever you are?" he called out in deep defiant tones.

"We've come to take you an' Paddy out for a little ride on a rail!" answered the same shrill, mocking voice we had heard at first. Then others took up the hostile chorus. "We've got some pitch a-heatin' round in the back yard!" "You won't catch cold; there's plenty o' feathers!" "Tell the Irishman here's some more ears for him to chaw on!" "Come out an' take your Copperhead medicine!"

There were yet other cries which the howling wind tore up into inarticulate fragments, and then a scattering volley of cheers, again emphasized by pistol-shots. While the crack of these still chilled my blood, a more than usually violent gust swooped round Abner's burly figure, and blew out the lamp.

Terrifying as the first instant of utter darkness was, the second was recognizable as a relief. I at once threw myself out of the chair, and crept along back of the stove to where my stockings and boots had been put to dry. These I hastened, with much trembling awkwardness, to pull on, taking pains to keep the big square stove between me and that open veranda door.

"Guess we won't take no ride to-night!" I heard Abner roar out, after the shouting had for the moment died away.

"You got to have one!" came back the original voice. "It's needful for your complaint!"

"I've got somethin' here that'll fit *your* complaint!" bellowed the farmer, raising his gun. "Take warnin'—the first cuss that sets foot on this stoop, I'll bore a four-inch hole clean through him. I've got squirrel-shot, and I've got buckshot, an' there's plenty more behind—so take your choice!"

There were a good many derisive answering yells and hoots,

and some one again fired a pistol in the air, but nobody offered to come up on the veranda.

Emboldened by this, I stole across the room now to one of the windows, and lifting a corner of the shade, strove to look out. At first there was nothing whatever to be seen in the utter blackness. Then I made out some faint reddish sort of diffused light in the upper air, which barely sufficed to indicate the presence of some score or more dark figures out in the direction of the pump. Evidently they *had* built a fire around in the back yard, as they said—probably starting it there so that its light might not disclose their identity.

This looked as if they really meant to tar-and-feather Abner and Hurley. The expression was familiar enough to my ears, and, from pictures in stray illustrated weeklies that found their way to the Corners, I had gathered some general notion of the procedure involved. The victim was stripped, I knew, and daubed over with hot melted pitch; then a pillow-case of feathers was emptied over him, and he was forced astride a fence-rail, which the rabble hoisted on their shoulders and ran about with. But my fancy balked at and refused the task of imagining Abner Beech in this humiliating posture. At least it was clear to my mind that a good many fierce and bloody things would happen first.

Apparently this had become clear to the throng outside as well. Whole minutes had gone by, and still no one mounted the veranda to seek close quarters with the farmer—who stood braced with his legs wide apart, bare-headed and erect, the wind blowing his huge beard sidewise over his shoulder.

"Well! ain't none o' you a-comin'?" he called out at last, with impatient sarcasm. "Thought you was so sot on takin' me out an' havin' some fun with me!" After a brief pause, another taunt occurred to him. "Why, even the niggers you're so in love with," he shouted, "they ain't such dod-rotted cowards as you be!"

A general movement was discernible among the shadowy

forms outside. I thought for the instant that it meant a swarming attack upon the veranda. But no! suddenly it had grown much lighter, and the mob was moving away from the rear of the house. The men were shouting things to one another, but the wind for the moment was at such a turbulent pitch that all their words were drowned. The reddened light waxed brighter still—and now there was nobody to be seen at all from the window.

"Hurry here! Mr. Beech! *We're all afire!*" cried a frightened voice in the room behind me.

It may be guessed how I turned.

The kitchen door was open, and the figure of a woman stood on the threshold, indefinitely black against a strange yellowish-drab half light which framed it. This woman—one knew from the voice that it was Esther Hagadorn—seemed to be wringing her hands.

"Hurry! Hurry!" she cried again, and I could see now that the little passage was full of gray luminous smoke, which was drifting past her into the living-room. Even as I looked, it had half obscured her form, and was rolling in, in waves.

Abner had heard her, and strode across the room now, gun still in hand, into the thick of the smoke, pushing Esther before him and shutting the kitchen door with a bang as he passed through. I put in a terrified minute or two alone in the dark, amazed and half-benumbed by the confused sounds that at first came from the kitchen, and by the horrible suspense, when a still more sinister silence ensued. Then there rose a loud crackling noise, like the incessant popping of some giant variety of corn. The door burst open again, and M'rye's tall form seemed literally flung into the room by the sweeping volume of dense smoke which poured in. She pulled the door to behind her— then gave a snarl of excited emotion at seeing me by the dusky reddened radiance which began forcing its way from outside through the holland window shades.

"Light the lamp, you gump!" she commanded, breathlessly,

and fell with fierce concentration upon the task of dragging furniture out of the bedroom. I helped her in a frantic, bewildered fashion, after I had lighted the lamp, which flared and smoked without its shade, as we toiled. M'rye seemed all at once to have the strength of a dozen men. She swung the ponderous chest of drawers out end on end; she fairly lifted the still bigger bookcase, after I had hustled the books out onto the table; she swept off the bedding, slashed the cords, and jerked the bed-posts and side-pieces out of their connecting sockets with furious energy, till it seemed as if both rooms must have been dismantled in less time than I have taken to tell of it.

The crackling overhead had swollen now to a wrathful roar, rising above the gusty voices of the wind. The noise, the heat, the smoke, and terror of it all made me sick and faint. I grew dizzy, and did foolish things in an aimless way, fumbling about among the stuff M'rye was hurling forth. Then all at once her darkling, smoke-wrapped figure shot up to an enormous height, the lamp began to go round, and I felt myself with nothing but space under my feet, plunging downward with awful velocity, surrounded by whirling skies full of stars.

There was a black night-sky overhead when I came to my senses again, with flecks of snow in the cold air on my face. The wind had fallen, everything was as still as death, and some one was carrying me in his arms. I tried to lift my head.

"Aisy now!" came Hurley's admonitory voice, close to my ear. "We'll be there in a minyut."

"No—I'm all right—let me down," I urged. He set me on my feet, and I looked amazedly about me.

The red-brown front of our larger hay-barn loomed in a faint unnatural light, at close quarters, upon my first inquiring gaze. The big sliding doors were open, and the slanting wagon-bridge running down from their threshold was piled high with chairs, bedding, crockery, milk-pans, clothing—the jumbled remnants of our household goods. Turning, I looked across the yard upon what was left of the Beech homestead—a glare of cherry light glowing above a fiery hole in the ground.

Strangely enough this glare seemed to perpetuate in its outlines the shape and dimensions of the vanished house. It was as if the house were still there, but transmuted from joists and clap-boards and shingles, into an illuminated and impalpable ghost of itself. There was a weird effect of transparency about it. Through the spectral bulk of red light I could see the naked and gnarled apple-trees in the home-orchard on the further side; and I remembered at once that painful and striking parallel of Scrooge gazing through the re-edified body of Jacob Marley, and beholding the buttons at the back of his coat. It all seemed some monstrous dream.

But no, here the others were. Janey Wilcox and the Underwood girl had come out from the barn, and were carrying in more things. I perceived now that there was a candle burning inside, and presently Esther Hagadorn was to be seen. Hurley had disappeared, and so I went up the sloping platform to join the women—noting with weak surprise that my knees seemed to have acquired new double joints and behaved as if they were going in the other direction. I stumbled clumsily once I was inside the barn, and sat down with great abruptness on a milking-stool, leaning my head back against the haymow, and conscious of an entire indifference as to whether school kept or not.

Again it was like some half-waking vision—the feeble light of the candle losing itself upon the broad high walls of new hay; the huge shadows in the rafters overhead; the women-folk silently moving about, fixing up on the barn floor some pitiful imitation, poor souls, of the home that had been swept off the face of the earth, and outside, through the wide sprawling doors, the dying away effulgence of the embers of our roof-tree lingering in the air of the winter night.

Abner Beech came in presently, with the gun in one hand,

and a blackened and outlandish-looking object in the other, which turned out to be the big pink sea-shell that used to decorate the parlor mantel. He held it up for M'rye to see, with a grave, tired smile on his face.

"We got it out, after all—just by the skin of our teeth," he said, and Hurley, behind him, confirmed this by an eloquent grimace.

M'rye's black eyes snapped and sparkled as she lifted the candle and saw what this something was. Then she boldly put up her face and kissed her husband with a resounding smack. Truly it was a night of surprises.

"That's about the only thing I had to call my own when I was married," she offered in explanation of her fervor, speaking to the company at large. Then she added in a lower tone, to Esther: "*He* used to play with it for hours at a stretch—when he was a baby."

" 'Member how he used to hold it up to his ear, eh, mother?" asked Abner, softly.

M'rye nodded her head, and then put her apron up to her eyes for a brief moment. When she lowered it, we saw an unaccustomed smile mellowing her hard-set, swarthy face.

The candle-light flashed upon a tear on her cheek that the apron had missed.

"I guess I *do* remember!" she said, with a voice full of tenderness.

Then Esther's hand stole into M'rye's and the two women stood together before Abner, erect and with beaming countenances, and he smiled upon them both.

It seemed that we were all much happier in our minds, now that our house had been burned down over our heads.

XI

The Conquest of Abner

Some time during the night, I was awakened by the mice frisking through the hay about my ears. My head was aching again, and I could not get back into sleep. Besides, Hurley was snoring mercilessly.

We two had chosen for our resting-place the little mow of half a load or so, which had not been stowed away above, but lay ready for present use over by the side-door opening on the cow-yard. Temporary beds had been spread for the women with fresh straw and blankets at the further end of the central threshing-floor. Abner himself had taken one of the rescued ticks and a quilt over to the other end, and stretched his ponderous length out across the big doors, with the gun by his side. No one had, of course, dreamed of undressing.

Only a few minutes of wakefulness sufficed to throw me into a desperate state of fidgets. The hay seemed full of strange creeping noises. The whole barn echoed with the boisterous ticking of the old eight-day clock which had been saved from the wreck of the kitchen, and which M'rye had set going again on the seat of the democrat wagon. And then Hurley!

I began to be convinced, now, that I was coming down with a great spell of sickness—perhaps even "the fever." Yes, it undoubtedly was the fever. I could feel it in my bones, which now started up queer prickly sensations on novel lines, quite as if they were somebody else's bones instead. My breathing, indeed, left a good deal to be desired from the true fever standpoint. It was not nearly so rapid or convulsive as I understood that the breathing of a genuine fever victim ought to be. But that, no doubt, would come soon enough—nay! was it not already coming? I thought, upon examination, that I did breathe more swiftly than before. And oh! that Hurley!

As noiselessly as possible I made my way, half-rolling, half-sliding, off the hay, and got on my feet on the floor. It was pitch dark, but I could feel along the old disused stanchion-row to the corner; thence it was plain sailing over to where Abner was sleeping by the big front doors. I would not dream of rousing him if he was in truth asleep, but it would be something to be nigh him, in case the fever should take a fatal turn before morning. I would just cuddle down on the floor near to him, and await events.

When I had turned the corner, it surprised me greatly to see ahead of me, over at the front of the barn, the reflection of a light. Creeping along toward it, I came out upon Abner, seated with his back against one of the doors, looking over an account-book by the aid of a lantern perched on a box at his side. He had stood the frame of an old bob-sleigh on end close by, and hung a horse-blanket over it, so that the light might not disturb the women-folk at the other end of the barn. The gun lay on the floor beside him.

He looked up at my approach, and regarded me with something, I fancied, of disapprobation in his habitually grave expression.

"Well, old seventy-six, what's the matter with you?" he asked, keeping his voice down to make as little noise as possible.

I answered in the same cautious tones that I was feeling bad. Had any encouragement suggested itself in the farmer's mien, I was prepared to overwhelm him with a relation of my symptoms in detail. But he shook his head instead.

"You'll have to wait till morning, to be sick," he said— "that is, to get 'tended to. I don't know anything about such things, an' I wouldn't wake M'rye up now for a whole baker's dozen o' you chaps." Seeing my face fall at this sweeping declaration, he proceeded to modify it in a kindlier tone. "Now you just lay down again, sonny," he added, "an' you'll be to sleep in no time, an' in the morning M'rye 'll fix up something for ye. This ain't no fit time for white folks to be belly-achin' around."

"I kind o' thought I'd feel better if I was sleeping over here near you," I ventured now to explain, and his nod was my warrant for tiptoeing across to the heap of disorganized furniture, and getting out some blankets and a comforter, which I arranged in the corner a few yards away and simply rolled myself up in, with my face turned away from the light. It was better over here than with Hurley, and though that prompt sleep which the farmer had promised did not come, I at least was drowsily conscious of an improved physical condition.

Perhaps I drifted off more than half-way into dreamland, for it was with a start that all at once I heard some one close by talking with Abner.

"I saw you were up, Mr. Beech"—it was Esther Hagadorn who spoke—"and I don't seem able to sleep, and I thought, if you didn't mind, I'd come over here."

"Why, of course," the farmer responded. "Just bring up a chair there, an' sit down. That's it—wrap the shawl around you good. It's a cold night—snowin' hard outside."

Both had spoken in muffled tones, so as not to disturb the others. This same dominant notion of keeping still deterred me from turning over, in order to be able to see them. I expected to hear them discuss my illness, but they never referred to it. Instead, there was what seemed a long silence. Then the schoolma'am spoke.

"I can't begin to tell you," she said, "how glad I am that you and your wife aren't a bit cast down by the—the calamity."

"No," came back Abner's voice, buoyant even in its half-whisper, "we're all right. I've be'n sort o' figurin' up here, an' they ain't much real harm done. I'm insured pretty well. Of course, this bein' obleeged to camp out in a hay-barn might be improved on, but then it's a change—somethin' out o' the ordinary rut—an' it'll do us good. I'll have the carpenters over from Juno Mills in the forenoon, an' if they push things, we can have a roof over us again before Christmas. It could be done even sooner, p'raps, only they ain't any neighbors to help *me* with a raisin' bee. They're willin' enough to burn my house down, though. However, I don't want them not an atom more'n they want me."

There was no trace of anger in his voice. He spoke like one contemplating the unalterable conditions of life.

"Did they really, do you believe, *set* it on fire?" Esther asked, intently.

"No, *I* think it caught from that fool fire they started around back of the house, to heat their fool tar by. The wind was blowing a regular gale, you know. Janey Wilcox, she will have it that that Roselle Upman set it on purpose. But then, she don't like him—an' I can't blame her much, for that matter. Once Otis Barnum was seein' her home from singin' school, an' when he was goin' back alone this Roselle Upman waylaid him in the dark, an' pitched onto him, an' broke his collar-bone. I always thought it puffed Janey up some, this bein' fought over like that, but it made her mad to have Otis hurt on her account, an' then nothing come of it. I wouldn't a' minded pepperin' Roselle's legs a trifle, if I'd had a barrel loaded, say, with bird-shot. He's a nuisance to the whole neighborhood. He kicks up a fight at every dance he goes to, all winter long, an' hangs around the taverns day in an' day out, inducin' young men to drink an' loaf. I thought a fellow like him'd be sure to go off to the war, an' so good riddance; but no! darned if the coward don't go an' get his front teeth pulled, so't he can't bite ca'tridges, and jest stay around, a worse nuisance than ever! I'd half forgive that miserable war if it—only took off the—the right men."

"Mr. Beech," said Esther, in low fervent tones, measuring each word as it fell, "you and I, we must forgive that war together!"

I seemed to feel the farmer shaking his head. He said nothing in reply.

"I'm beginning to understand how you've felt about it all

along," the girl went on, after a pause. "I knew the fault must be in my ignorance, that our opinions of plain right and plain wrong should be such poles apart. I got a school-friend of mine whose father is your way of thinking, to send me all the papers that came to their house, and I've been going through them religiously—whenever I could be quite alone. I don't say I don't think you're wrong, because I *do,* but I am getting to understand how you should believe yourself to be right."

She paused as if expecting a reply, but Abner only said, "Go on," after some hesitation, and she went on:

"Now take the neighbors all about here—"

"Excuse *me!*" broke in the farmer. "I guess if it's all the same to you, I'd rather not. They're too rich for my blood."

"Take these very neighbors," pursued Esther, with gentle determination. "Something must be very wrong indeed when they behave to you the way they do. Why, I know that even now, right down in their hearts, they recognize that you're far and away the best man in Agrippa. Why, I remember, Mr. Beech, when I first applied, and you were school-commissioner, and you sat there through the examination—why, you were the only one whose opinion I gave a rap for. When you praised me, why, I was prouder of it than if you had been a Regent of the University. And I tell you, everybody all around here feels at bottom just as I do."

"They take a dummed curious way o' showin' it, then," commented Abner, roundly.

"It isn't *that* they're trying to show at all," said Esther. "They feel that other things are more important. They're all wrought up over the war. How could it be otherwise when almost every one of them has got a brother, or a father, or—or—*a son*—down there in the South, and every day brings news that some of these have been shot dead, and more still wounded and crippled, and others—*others, that* God only knows *what* has become of them—oh, how can they help feeling that way? I don't know that I ought to say it—" the school-ma'am stopped to catch her breath, and hesitated, then went on—"but yes, you'll understand me *now*—there was a time here, not so long ago, Mr. Beech, when I downright hated you—you and M'rye both!"

This was important enough to turn over for. I flopped as un-ostentatiously as possible, and neither of them gave any sign of having noted my presence. The farmer sat with his back against the door, the quilt drawn up to his waist, his head bent in silent meditation. His whole profile was in deep shadow from where I lay darkly massive and powerful and solemn. Esther was watching him with all her eyes, leaning forward from her chair, the lantern-light full upon her eager face.

"M'rye an' I don't lay ourselves out to be specially bad folks, as folks go," the farmer said at last, by way of deprecation. "We've got our faults, of course, like the rest, but—"

"No," interrupted Esther, with a half-tearful smile in her eyes. "You only pretend to have faults. You really haven't got any at all."

The shadowed outline of Abner's face softened.

"Why, that *is* a fault itself, ain't it?" he said, as if pleased with his logical acuteness.

The crowing of some foolish rooster, growing tired of waiting for the belated November daylight, fell upon the silence from one of the buildings near by.

Abner Beech rose to his feet with ponderous slowness, push-ing the bedclothes aside with his boot, and stood beside Esther's chair. He laid his big hand on her shoulder with a patriarchal gesture.

"Come now," he said, gently, "you go back to bed, like a good girl, an' get some sleep. It'll be all right."

The girl rose in turn, bearing her shoulder so that the fatherly hand might still remain upon it. "Truly?" she asked, with a new light upon her pale face.

"Yes—truly!" Abner replied, gravely nodding his head.

Esther took the hand from her shoulder, and shook it in both of hers. "Good-night again, then," she said, and turned to go.

Suddenly there resounded the loud rapping of a stick on the barn-door, close by my head.

Abner squared his huge shoulders and threw a downright glance at the gun on the floor.

"Well?" he called out.

"Is my da'ater inside there?"

We all knew that thin, high-pitched, querulous voice. It was old "Jee" Hagadorn who was outside.

XII

The Unwelcome Guest

Abner and Esther stood for a bewildered minute, staring at the rough unpainted boards through which this astonishing inquiry had come. I scrambled to my feet and kicked aside the tick and blankets. Whatever else happened, it did not seem likely that there was any more sleeping to be done. Then the farmer strode forward and dragged one of the doors back on its squeaking rollers. Some snow fell in upon his boots from the ridge that had formed against it over night. Save for a vaguely faint snow-light in the air, it was still dark.

"Yes, she's here," said Abner, with his hand on the open door.

"Then I'd like to know—" the invisible Jee began excitedly shouting from without.

"Sh-h! You'll wake everybody up!" the farmer interposed. "Come inside, so that I can shut the door."

"Never under your roof!" came back the shrill hostile voice. "I swore I never would, and I won't!"

"You'd have to take a crowbar to get under my roof," Abner returned, grimly conscious of a certain humor in the thought. "What's left of it is layin' over yonder in what used to be the cellar. So you needn't stand on ceremony on *that* account. I ain't got no house now, so't your oath ain't bindin'. Besides, the Bible says, 'Swear not at all!' "

A momentary silence ensued; then Abner rattled the door on its wheels. "Well, what are you goin' to do?" he asked, impatiently. "I can't keep this door open all night, freezin' everybody to death. If you won't come in, you'll have to stay out!" and again there was an ominous creaking of the rollers.

"I want my da'ater!" insisted Jehoiada, vehemently. "I stan' on a father's rights."

"A father ain't got no more right to make a fool of himself than anybody else," replied Abner, gravely. "What kind of a time o' night is this, with the snow knee-deep, for a girl to be out o' doors? She's all right here, with my women-folks, an' I'll bring her down with the cutter in the mornin'—that is, if she wants to come. An' now, once for all, will you step inside or not?"

Esther had taken up the lantern and advanced with it now to the open door. "Come in, father," she said, in tones which seemed to be authoritative. "They've been very kind to me. Come in!"

Then, to my surprise, the lean and scrawny figure of the cooper emerged from the darkness, and stepping high over the snow, entered the barn, Abner sending the door to behind him with a mighty sweep of the arm.

Old Hagadorn came in grumbling under his breath, and stamping the snow from his feet with sullen kicks. He bore a sledge-stake in one of his mittened hands. A worsted comforter was wrapped around his neck and ears and partially over his conical-peaked cap. He rubbed his long thin nose against his mitten and blinked sulkily at the lantern and the girl who held it.

"So here you be!" he said at last, in vexed tones. "An' me traipsin' around in the snow the best part of the night lookin' for you!"

"See here, father," said Esther, speaking in a measured, deliberate way, "we won't talk about that at all. If a thousand times worse things had happened to both of us than have, it still wouldn't be worth mentioning compared with what has befallen these good people here. They've been attacked by a mob of rowdies and loafers, and had their house and home burned down over their heads and been driven to take refuge here in this barn of a winter's night. They've shared their shelter with me and been kindness itself, and now that you're here, if you can't think of anything pleasant to say to them, if I were you I'd say nothing at all."

This was plain talk, but it seemed to produce a satisfactory effect upon Jehoiada. He unwound his comforter enough to liberate his straggling sandy beard and took off his mittens. After a moment or two he seated himself in the chair, with a murmured "I'm jest about tuckered out," in apology for the action. He did, in truth, present a woeful picture of fatigue and physical feebleness, now that we saw him in repose. The bones seemed ready to start through the parchment-like skin on his gaunt cheeks, and his eyes glowed with an unhealthy fire, as he sat, breathing hard and staring at the jumbled heaps of furniture on the floor.

Esther had put the lantern again on the box and drawn forward a chair for Abner, but the farmer declined it with a wave of the hand and continued to stand in the background, looking his ancient enemy over from head to foot with a meditative gaze. Jehoiada grew visibly nervous under this inspection; he fidgeted on his chair and then fell to coughing—a dry, rasping cough which had an evil sound, and which he seemed to make the worse by fumbling aimlessly at the button that held the overcoat collar round his throat.

At last Abner walked slowly over to the shadowed masses of piled-up household things and lifted out one of the drawers that had been taken from the framework of the bureau and brought over with their contents. Apparently it was not the right one, for he dragged aside a good many objects to get at another, and rummaged about in this for several minutes. Then he came out again into the small segment of the lantern's radiance with a pair of long thick woolen stockings of his own in his hand.

"You better pull off them wet boots an' draw these on," he said, addressing Hagadorn, but looking fixedly just over his head. "It won't do that cough o' yours no good, settin' around with wet feet."

The cooper looked in a puzzled way at the huge butternut-yarn stockings held out under his nose, but he seemed too much taken aback to speak or to offer to touch them.

"Yes, father!" said Esther, with quite an air of command. "You know what that cough means," and straightway Hagadorn lifted one of his feet to his knee and started tugging at the boot-heel in a desultory way. He desisted after a few half-hearted attempts, and began coughing again, this time more distressingly than ever.

His daughter sprang forward to help him, but Abner pushed her aside, put the stockings under his arm, and himself undertook the job. He did not bend his back overmuch, but hoisted Jee's foot well in the air and pulled.

"Brace you foot agin mine an' hold on to the chair!" he ordered, sharply, for the first effect of his herculean pull had been to nearly drag the cooper to the floor. He went at it more gently now, easing the soaked leather up and down over the instep until the boots were off. He looked furtively at the bottoms of these before he tossed them aside, noting, no doubt, as I did, how old and broken and run down at the heel they were. Jee himself peeled off the drenched stockings, and they too were flimsy old things, darned and mended almost out of their original color.

These facts served only to deepen my existing low opinion of Hagadorn, but they appeared to affect Abner Beech differently. He stood by and watched the cooper dry his feet and then draw on the warm dry hose over his shrunken shanks, with almost a friendly interest. Then he shoved along one of the blankets across the floor to Hagadorn's chair that he might wrap his feet in it.

"That's it," he said, approvingly. "They ain't no means o' building a fire here right now, but as luck would have it we'd jest set up an old kitchen stove in the little cow-barn to warm up gruel for the ca'aves with, an' the first thing we'll do'll be to rig it up in here to cook breakfast by, an' then we'll dry them boots o' yourn in no time. You go an' pour some oats into 'em now," Abner added, turning to me. "And you might as well call Hurley. We've got considerable to do, an' daylight's breakin'."

The Irishman lay on his back where I had left him, still snoring tempestuously. As a rule he was a light sleeper, but this time I had to shake him again and again before he understood that it was morning. I opened the side-door, and sure enough, the day had begun. The clouds had cleared away. The sky was still ashen gray overhead, but the light from the horizon, added to the whiteness of the unaccustomed snow, rendered it quite easy to see one's way about inside. I went to the oat-bin.

Hurley, sitting up and rubbing his eyes, regarded me and my task with curiosity. "An' is it a stove-pipe for a measure ye have?" he asked.

"No; it's one of Jee Hagadorn's boots," I replied. "I'm filling 'em so't they'll swell when they're dryin'."

He slid down off the hay as if some one had pushed him. "What's that ye say? Haggydorn? *Ould* Haggydorn?" he demanded.

I nodded assent. "Yes, he's inside with Abner," I explained. "An' he's got on Abner's stockin's, an' it looks like he's goin' to stay to breakfast."

Hurley opened his mouth in sheer surprise and gazed at me with hanging jaw and round eyes. "'Tis the fever that's on ye," he said, at last. "Ye're wandherin' in yer mind!"

"You just go in and see for yourself," I replied, and Hurley promptly took me at my word.

He came back presently, turning the corner of the stanchions in a depressed and rambling way, quite at variance with his accustomed swinging gait. He hung his head, too, and shook it over and over again perplexedly.

"Abner 'n' me'll be bringin' in the stove," he said. "'Tis not fit for you to go out wid that sickness on ye."

"Well, anyway," I retorted, "you see I wasn't wanderin' much in my mind."

Hurley shook his head again. "Well, then," he began lapsing into deep brogue and speaking rapidly, "I've meself seen the woman wid the head of a horse on her in the lake forninst the Three Castles, an' me sister's first man, sure he broke down the ditch round-about the Danes' fort on Dunkelly, an' a foine grand young man, small for his strength an' wid a red cap on his head, flew out an' wint up in the sky, an' whin he related it up comes Father Forrest to him in the potaties, an' says he, 'I do be surprised wid you, O'Driscoll, for to be relatin' such loies.' 'I'll take me Bible oat' on 'em!' says he. "'Tis your imagination!' says the priest. 'No imagination at all!' says O'Driscoll; 'sure, I saw it wid dese two eyes, as plain as I'm lookin' at your riverence, an' a far grander sight it was too!' An' me own mother, faith, manny's the toime I've seen her makin' up dhrops for the yellow sicknest wid woodlice an' sayin' Hail Marys over 'em, an' thim same 'ud cure annything from sore teeth to a wooden leg for moiles round. But, saints help me! I never seen the loikes o' *this!* Haggydorn is it? *Ould* Haggydorn! *Huh!*"

Then the Irishman, still with a dejected air, started off across the yards through the snow to the cow-barns, mumbling to himself as he went.

I had heard Abner's heavy tread coming along the stanchions toward me, but now all at once it stopped. The farmer's wife had followed him into the passage, and he had halted to speak with her.

"They ain't no two ways about it, mother," he expostulated. "We jest got to put the best face on it we kin, an' act civil, an' pass the time o' day as if nothing'd ever happened atween us. He'll be goin' the first thing after breakfast."

"Oh! I ain't a-goin' to sass him, or say anything uncivil," M'rye broke in, reassuringly. "What I mean is, I don't want to come into the for'ard end of the barn at all. They ain't no need of it. I kin cook the breakfast in back, and Janey kin fetch it for'ard for yeh, an' nobody need say anythin', or be any the wiser."

"Yes, I know," argued Abner, "but there's the looks o' the thing. *I* say, if you're goin' to do a thing, why, do it right up to the handle, or else don't do it at all. An' then there's the girl to consider, and *her* feelin's."

"Dunno 't her feelin's are such a pesky sight more importance than other folkses," remarked M'rye, callously.

This unaccustomed recalcitrancy seemed to take Abner aback. He moved a few steps forward, so that he became visible from where I stood, then halted again and turned, his shoulders rounded, his hands clasped behind his back. I could see him regarding M'rye from under his broad hat-brim with a gaze at once dubious and severe.

"I ain't much in the habit o' hearin' you talk this way to me, mother," he said at last, with grave depth of tones and significant deliberation.

"Well, I can't help it, Abner!" rejoined M'rye, bursting forth in vehement utterance, all the more excited from the necessity she felt of keeping it out of hearing of the unwelcome guest. "I don't want to do anything to aggravate you, or go contrary to your notions, but with even the willin'est pack-horse there is such a thing as pilin' it on too thick. I can stan' bein' burnt out o' house 'n' home, an' seein' pretty nigh every rag an' stick I had in the world go kitin' up the chimney, an' campin' out here in a barn—My Glory, yes!—an' as much more on top o' that, but, I tell you flat-footed, I can't stomach Jee Hagadorn, an' I *won't!*"

Abner continued to contemplate the revolted M'rye with displeased amazement written all over his face. Once or twice I thought he was going to speak, but nothing came of it. He only looked and looked, as if he had the greatest difficulty in crediting what he saw.

Finally, with a deep-chested sigh, he turned again. "I s'pose this is still more or less of a free country," he said. "If you're sot on it, I can't hender you," and he began walking once more toward me.

M'rye followed him out and put a hand on his arm. "Don't go off like that, Abner!" she adjured him. "You *know* there ain't nothin' in this whole wide world I wouldn't do to please you—if I *could!* But this thing jest goes agin my grain. It's the way folks are made. It's your nater to be forgivin' an' do good to them that despitefully use you."

"No, it ain't!" declared Abner, vigorously. "No, sirree! 'Hold fast' is my nater. I stan' out agin my enemies till the last cow comes home. But when they come wadin' in through the snow, with their feet soppin' wet, an' coughin' fit to turn themselves inside out, an' their daughter is there, an' you've sort o' made it up with her, an' we're all campin' out in a barn, don't you see—"

"No, I can't see it," replied M'rye, regretful but firm. "They always said we Ramswells had Injun blood in us somewhere. An' when I get an Injun streak on me, right down in the marrow o' my bones, why, you mustn't blame me—or feel hard if—if I—"

"No-o," said Abner, with reluctant conviction, "I s'pose not. I dare say you're actin' accordin' to your lights. An' besides, he'll be goin' the first thing after breakfast."

"An' you ain't mad, Abner?" pleaded M'rye, almost tremulously, as if frightened at the dimensions of the victory she had won.

"Why, bless your heart, no," answered the farmer, with a glaring simulation of easy-mindedness. "No—that's all right, mother!"

Then with long heavy-footed strides the farmer marched past me and out into the cow-yard.

XIII

The Breakfast

If there was ever a more curious meal in Dearborn County than that first breakfast of ours in the barn, I never heard of it.

The big table was among the things saved from the living-room, and Esther spread it again with the cloth which had been in use on the previous evening. There was a stain of the tea which the Underwood girl had spilled in the excitement of the supper's rough interruption; there were other marks of calamity upon it as well—the smudge of cinders, for one thing, and a general diffused effect of smokiness. But it was the only table-cloth we had. The dishes, too, were a queer lot, representing two or three sets of widely different patterns and value, other portions of which we should never see again.

When it was announced that breakfast was ready, Abner took his accustomed arm-chair at the head of the table. He only half turned his head toward Hagadorn and said in formal tones, over his shoulder, "Won't you draw up and have some breakfast?"

Jee was still sitting where he had planted himself two hours or so before. He still wore his round cap, with the tabs tied down over his ears. In addition to his overcoat, some one—probably his daughter—had wrapped a shawl about his thin shoulders. The boots had not come in, as yet, from the stove, and the blanket was drawn up over his stockinged feet to the knees. From time to time his lips moved, as if he were reciting Scripture texts to himself, but so far as I knew, he had said nothing to any one. His cough seemed rather worse than better.

"Yes, come, father!" Esther added to the farmer's invitation, and drew a chair back for him two plates away from Abner. Thus adjured he rose and hobbled stiffly over to the place indicated, bringing his foot-blanket with him. Esther stooped to arrange this for him and then seated herself next the host.

"You see, I'm going to sit beside you, Mr. Beech," she said, with a wan little smile.

"Glad to have you," remarked Abner, gravely.

The Underwood girl brought in a first plate of buckwheat cakes, set it down in front of Abner, and took her seat opposite Hagadorn and next to me. There remained three vacant places, down at the foot of the table, and though we all began eating without comment, everybody continually encountered some other's glance straying significantly toward these empty seats. Janey Wilcox, very straight and with an uppish air, came in with another plate of cakes and marched out again in tell-tale silence.

"Hurley! Come along in here an' git your breakfast!"

The farmer fairly roared out this command, then added in a lower, apologetic tone: "I 'spec' the women-folks 've got their hands full with that broken-down old stove."

We all looked toward the point, half-way down the central barn-floor, where the democrat wagon, drawn crosswise, served to divide our improvised living-room and kitchen. Through the wheels, and under its uplifted pole, we could vaguely discern two petticoated figures at the extreme other end, moving about the stove, the pipe of which was carried up and out through a little window above the door. Then Hurley appeared, ducking his head under the wagon-pole.

"I'm aitin' out here, convanient to the stove," he shouted from this dividing-line.

"No, come and take your proper place!" bawled back the farmer, and Hurley had nothing to do but obey. He advanced with obvious reluctance and halted at the foot of the table, eyeing with awkward indecision the three vacant chairs. One was M'rye's; the others would place him either next to the hated cooper or diagonally opposite, where he must look at him all the while.

"Sure, I'm better out there!" he ventured to insist, in a wheedling tone; but Abner thundered forth an angry "No, sir!" and the Irishman sank abruptly into the seat beside Hagadorn. From this place he eyed the Underwood girl with a glare of contemptuous disapproval. I learned afterward that M'rye and Janey Wilcox regarded her desertion of them as the meanest episode of the whole miserable morning, and beguiled their labors over the stove by recounting to each other all the low-down qualities illustrated by the general history of her "sap-headed tribe."

Meanwhile conversation languished.

With the third or fourth instalment of cakes, Janey Wilcox had halted long enough to deliver herself of a few remarks, sternly limited to the necessities of the occasion. "M'rye says," she declaimed, coldly, looking the while with great fixedness at the hay-wall, "if the cakes are sour she can't help it. We saved what was left over of the batter, but the Graham flour and the sody are both burnt up," and with that stalked out again.

Not even politeness could excuse the pretence on any one's part that the cakes were *not* sour, but Abner seized upon the general subject as an opening for talk.

" 'Member when I was a little shaver," he remarked, with an effort at amiability, "my sisters kicked about havin' to bake the cakes, on account of the hot stove makin' their faces red an' spoilin' their complexions, an' they wanted specially to go to some fandango or other, an' look their pootiest, an' so father sent us boys out into the kitchen to bake 'em instid. Old Lorenzo Dow, the Methodist preacher, was stoppin' overnight at our house, an' mother was jest beside herself to have everything go off ship-shape—an' then them cakes begun comin' in. Fust my brother William, he baked one the shape of a horse, an' then Josh, he made one like a jackass with ears as long as the griddle would allow of lengthwise, and I'd got jest comfortably started in on one that I begun as a pig, an' then was going to alter into a ship with sails up, when father, he come out with a hold-back strap, an'—well—mine never got finished to this day. Mother, she was mortified most to death, but old Dow, he jest lay back and laughed—laughed till you'd thought he'd split himself."

"It was from Lorenzo Dow's lips that I had my first awakening call unto righteousness," said Jee Hagadorn, speaking with solemn unction in high, quavering tones.

The fact that he should have spoken at all was enough to take even the sourness out of M'rye's cakes.

Abner took up the ball with solicitous promptitude. "A very great man, Lorenzo Dow was—in his way," he remarked.

"By grace he was spared the shame and humiliation," said Hagadorn, lifting his voice as he went on—"the humiliation of living to see one whole branch of the church separate itself from the rest—withdraw and call itself the Methodist Episcopal Church, South, in defence of human slavery!"

Esther, red-faced with embarrassment, intervened peremptorily. "How *can* you, father!" she broke in. "For all you know he might have been red-hot on that side himself! In fact, I dare say he would have been. How on earth can *you* know to the contrary, anyway?"

Jee was all excitement on the instant, at the promise of an argument. His eyes flashed; he half rose from his seat and opened his mouth to reply. So much had he to say, indeed, that the words stumbled over one another on his tongue, and produced nothing, but an incoherent stammering sound, which all at once was supplanted by a violent fit of coughing. So terrible were the paroxysms of this seizure that when they had at last spent their fury the poor man was trembling like a leaf and toppled in his chair as if about to swoon. Esther had hovered about over him from the outset of the fit, and now looked up appealing to Abner. The farmer rose, walked down the table-side, and gathered Jee's fragile form up under one big engirdling arm. Then, as the girl hastily dragged forth the tick and blankets again, and spread them into the rough semblance of a bed, Abner half led, half carried the cooper over and gently laid him down thereon. Together they fixed up some sort of pillow for him with hay under the blanket, and piled him snugly over with quilts and my comfortable.

"There—you'll be better layin' down," said Abner, soothingly. Hagadorn closed his eyes wearily and made no answer. They left him after a minute or two and returned to the table.

The rest of the breakfast was finished almost in silence. Every once in a while Abner and Esther would exchange looks, his gravely kind, hers gratefully contented, and these seemed really to render speech needless. For my own part, I foresaw with some degree of depression that there would soon be no chance whatever of my securing attention in the *rôle* of an invalid, at least in this part of the barn.

Perhaps, however, they might welcome me in the kitchen part, as a sort of home-product rival to the sick cooper. I rose and walked languidly out into M'rye's domain. But the two women were occupied with a furious scrubbing of rescued pans for the morning's milk, and they allowed me to sit feebly down on the wood-box behind the stove without so much as a glance of sympathy.

By and by we heard one of the great front doors rolled back on its shrieking wheels and then shut to again. Some one had entered, and in a moment there came some strange, inarticulate sounds of voices which showed that the arrival had created a commotion. M'rye lifted her head, and I shall never forget the wild, expectant flashing of her black eyes in that moment of suspense.

"Come in here, mother!" we heard Abner's deep voice call out from beyond the democrat wagon. "Here's somebody wants to see you!"

M'rye swiftly wiped her hands on her apron and glided rather than walked toward the forward end of the barn. Janey Wilcox and I followed close upon her heels, dodging together under the wagon-pole, and emerging, breathless and wild with curiosity, on the fringe of an excited group.

In the centre of this group, standing with a satisfied smile on his face, his general appearance considerably the worse for wear, but in demeanor, to quote M'rye's subsequent phrase, "as cool as Cuffy," was Ni Hagadorn.

XIV

Finis

"He's all right; you can look for him here right along now, any day; he *was* hurt a leetle, but he's as peart an' chipper now as a blue-jay on a hick'ry limb; yes, he's a-comin' right smack home!"

This was the gist of the assurances which Ni vouchsafed to the first rush of eager questions—to his sister, and M'rye, and Janey Wilcox.

Abner had held a little aloof, to give the weaker sex a chance. Now he reasserted himself once more: "Stan' back, now, and give the young man breathin' room. Janey, hand a chair for'ard —that's it. Now set ye down, Ni, an' take your own time, an' tell us all about it. So you reely found him, eh?"

"Pshaw! there ain't anything to that," expostulated Ni, seating himself with nonchalance, and tilting back his chair. *"That* was easy as rollin' off a log. But what's the matter *here?* That's what knocks me. We—that is to say, I—come up on a freight train to a ways beyond Juno Junction, an' got the conductor to slow up and let me drop off, an' footed it over the hill. It was jest about broad daylight when I turned the divide. Then I began lookin' for your house, an' I'm lookin' for it still. There's a hole out there, full o' snow an' smoke, but nary a house. How'd it happen?"

" 'Lection bonfire—high wind—woodshed must 'a' caught," replied Abner, sententiously. "So you reely got down South, eh?"

"An' Siss here, too," commented Ni, with provoking disregard for the farmer's suggestions; "a reg'lar family party. An', hello!"

His roving eye had fallen upon the recumbent form on the made-up bed, under the muffling blankets, and he lifted his sandy wisps of eyebrows in inquiry.

"Sh! It's father," explained Esther. "He isn't feeling very well. I think he's asleep."

The boy's freckled, whimsical face melted upon reflection into a distinct grin. "Why," he said, "you've been havin' a reg'lar old love-feast up here. I guess it was *that* that set the house on fire! An' speakin' o' feasts, if you've got a mouthful o' somethin' to eat handy—"

The women were off like a shot to the impromptu larder at the far end of the barn.

"Well, thin," put in Hurley, taking advantage of their absence, "an' had ye the luck to see anny rale fightin'?"

"Never mind that," said Abner; "when he gits around to it he'll tell us everything. But, fust of all—why, he knows what I want to hear about."

"Why, the last time I talked with you, Abner—" Ni began, squinting up one of his eyes and giving a quaint drawl to his words.

"That's a good while ago," said the farmer, quietly.

"Things have took a change, eh?" inquired Ni.

"That's neither here nor there," replied Abner, somewhat testily. "You oughtn't to need so dummed much explainin'. I've told you what I want specially to hear. An' that's what we all want to hear."

When the women had returned, and Ni, with much deliberation, had filled both hands with selected eatables, the recital at last got under way. Its progress was blocked from time to time by sheer force of tantalizing perversity on the part of the narrator, and it suffered steadily from the incidental hitches of mastication; but such as it was we listened to it with all our ears, sitting or standing about, and keeping our eyes intently upon the freckled young hero.

"It wasn't so much of a job to git down there as I'd figured on," Ni said, between mouthfuls. "I got along on freight trains —once worked my way a while on a hand-car—as far as Albany, an' on down to New York on a river-boat, cheap, an' then, after foolin' round a few days, I hitched up with the Sanitary Commission folks an' got them to let me sail on one o' their boats round to 'Napolis. I thought I was goin' to die most o' the voyage, but I didn't, you see, an' when I struck 'Napolis I hung around Camp Parole there quite a spell, talkin' with fellers that'd bin pris'ners down in Richmond an' got exchanged an' sent North. They said there was a whole slew of our fellers down there still that'd been brought in after Antietam. They didn't know none o' their names, but they said they'd all be sent North in time, in exchange for Johnny Rebs that we'd captured. An' so I waited round—"

"You *might* have written!" interrupted Esther, reproachfully.

"What'd bin the good o' writin'? I hadn't anything to tell. Besides writin' letters is for girls. Well, one day a man comes up from Libby—that's the prison at Richmond—an' he said there *was* a tall feller there from York State, a farmer, an' he died. He thought the name was Birch, but it might 'a' been Beech—or Body-Maple, for that matter. I s'pose you'd like to had me write *that* home!"

"No—oh, no!" murmured Esther, speaking the sense of all the company.

"Well, then I waited some more, an' kep' on waitin', an' then waited agin, until bimeby, one fine day, along comes Mr. Blue-jay himself. There he was, stan'in' up on the paddle-box with a face on him as long as your arm, an' I sung out, 'Way there, Agrippa Hill!' an' he come mighty nigh fallin' head over heels into the water. So then he come off, n' we shook han's, an' went up to the commissioners to see about his exchange, an'—an' as soon's that's fixed, an' the papers drawn up all correct, why, he'll come home. An' that's all there is to it."

"And even *then* you never wrote!" said Esther, plaintively.

"Hold on a minute," put in Abner. "You say he's comin' home. That wouldn't be unless he was disabled. They'd keep him to fight agin, till his time was up. Come, now, tell the truth —he's be'n hurt bad!"

Ni shook his unkempt red head. "No, no," he said. "This is how it was. Fust he was fightin' in a cornfield, an' him and Bi Truax, they got chased out, an' lost their regiment, an' got in with some other fellers, and then they all waded a creek breast-high, an' had to run up a long stretch o' slopin' ploughed ground to capture a battery they was on top o' the knoll. But they didn't see a regiment of sharp-shooters layin' hidden behind a rail-fence, an' these fellers riz up all to once an' give it to 'em straight, an' they wilted right there, an' laid down, an' there they was after dusk when the rebs come out an' started lookin' round for guns an' blankets an' prisoners. Most of 'em was dead, or badly hurt, but they was a few who'd simply lain there in the hollow because it'd have bin death to git up. An' Jeff was one o' *them*."

"You said yourself't he had been hurt—some," interposed M'rye, with snapping eyes.

"Jest a scratch on his arm," declared Ni. "Well, then they marched the well ones back to the rear of the reb line, an' there they jest skinned 'em of everything they had—watch an' jack-knife an' wallet an' everything—an' put 'em to sleep on the bare ground. Next day they started 'em out on the march toward Richmond, an' after four or five days o' that, they got to a railroad, and there was cattle cars for 'em to ride the rest o' the way in. An' that's how it was."

"No," said Abner, sternly; "you haven't told us. How badly is he hurt?"

"Well," replied Ni, "it was only a scratch, as I said, but it got worse on that march, an' I s'pose it wasn't tended to any-ways decently, an' so—an' so—"

M'rye had sprung to her feet and stood now drawn up to her full height, with her sharp nose in air as if upon some

strange scent, and her eyes fairly glowing in eager excitement.
All at once she made a bound past us and ran to the doors,
furiously digging her fingers in the crevice between them, then,
with a superb sweep of the shoulders, sending them both rattling back on their wheels with a bang.

"I knew it!" she screamed in triumph.

We who looked out beheld M'rye's black hair and brown
calico dress suddenly suffer a partial eclipse of pale blue, which
for the moment seemed in some way a part of the bright winter
sky beyond. Then we saw that it was a soldier who had his arm
about M'rye, and his cap bent down tenderly over the head
she had laid on his shoulder.

Our Jeff had come home.

A general instinct rooted us to our places and kept us silent,
the while mother and son stood there in the broad open doorway.

Then the two advanced toward us, M'rye breathing hard,
and with tears and smiles struggling together on her face under
the shadow of a wrathful frown. We noted nothing of Jeff's
appearance save that he had grown a big yellow beard, and
seemed to be smiling. It was the mother's distraught countenance at which we looked instead.

She halted in front of Abner, and lifted the blue cape from
Jeff's left shoulder, with an abrupt gesture.

"Look there!" she said, hoarsely. "See what they've done to
my boy!"

We now saw that the left sleeve of Jeff's army overcoat was
empty and hung pinned against his breast. On the instant we
were all swarming about him, shaking the hand that remained
to him and striving against one another in a babel of questions,
comments, and expressions of sympathy with his loss, satisfaction at his return. It seemed the most natural thing in the world
that he should kiss Esther Hagadorn, and that Janey Wilcox
should reach up on tiptoes and kiss him. When the Underwood
girl would have done the same, however, M'rye brusquely
shouldered her aside.

104 The Civil War Stories of Harold Frederic

So beside ourselves with excitement were we all, each in turn seeking to get in a word edgewise, that no one noticed the approach and entrance of a stranger, who paused just over the threshold of the barn and coughed in a loud perfunctory way to attract our attention. I had to nudge Abner twice before he turned from where he stood at Jeff's side, with his hand on the luckless shoulder, and surveyed the newcomer.

The sun was shining so brightly on the snow outside, that it was not for the moment easy to make out the identity of this shadowed figure. Abner took a forward step or two before he recognized his visitor. It was Squire Avery, the rich man of the Corners, and justice of the peace, who had once even run for Congress.

"How d' do?" said Abner, shading his eyes with a massive hand. "Won't you step in?"

The Squire moved forward a little and held forth his hand, which the farmer took and shook doubtfully. We others were as silent now as the grave, feeling this visit to be even stranger than all that had gone before.

"I drove up right after breakfast, Mr. Beech," said the Squire, making his accustomed slow delivery a trifle more pompous and circumspect than usual, "to express to you the feeling of such neighbors as I have, in this limited space of time, been able to foregather with. I believe, sir, that I may speak for them all when I say that we regret, deplore, and contemplate with indignation the outrage and injury to which certain thoughtless elements of the community last night, sir, subjected you and your household."

"It's right neighborly of you, Square, to come an' say so," remarked Abner. "Won't you set down? You see, my son Jeff's jest come home from the war, an' the house bein' burnt, an' so on, we're rather upset for the minute."

The Squire put on his spectacles and smiled with surprise at seeing Jeff. He shook hands with him warmly, and spoke with what we felt to be the right feeling about that missing arm; but he could not sit down, he said. The cutter was waiting for him, and he must hurry back.

"I am glad, however," he added, "to have been the first, Mr. Beech, to welcome your brave son back, and to express to you the hope, sir, that with this additional link of sympathy between us, sir, bygones may be allowed to become bygones."

"I don't bear no ill will," said Abner, guardedly. "I s'pose in the long run folks act pooty close to about what they think is right. I'm willin' to give 'em that credit—the same as I take to myself. They ain't been much disposition to give *me* that credit, but then, as our school-ma'am here was a-sayin' last night, people 've been a good deal worked up about the war—havin' them that's close to 'em right down in the thick of it—an' I dessay it was natural enough they should git hot in the collar about it. As I said afore, I don't bear no ill will—though prob'ly I'm entitled to."

The Squire shook hands with Abner again. "Your sentiments, Mr. Beech," he said, in his stateliest manner, "do credit alike to your heart and your head. There is a feeling, sir, that this would be an auspicious occasion for you to resume sending your milk to the cheese-factory."

Abner pondered the suggestion for a moment. "It would be handier," he said, slowly; "but, you know, I ain't goin' to eat no humble pie. That Rod Bidwell was downright insultin' to my man, an' me too—"

"It was all, I assure you, sir, an unfortunate misunderstanding," pursued the Squire, "and is now buried deep in oblivion. And it is further suggested, that, when you have reached that stage of preparation for your new house, if you will communicate with me, the neighbors will be glad to come up and extend their assistance to you in what is commonly known as a raising-bee. They will desire, I believe, to bring with them their own provisions. And, moreover, Mr. Beech"—here the Squire dropped his oratorical voice and stepped close to the farmer—"if this thing has cramped you any, that is to say, if you find yourself in need of—of—any accommodation—"

"No, nothin' o' that sort," said Abner. He stopped at that, and kept silence for a little, with his head down and his gaze meditatively fixed on the barn floor. At last he raised his face and spoke again, his deep voice shaking a little in spite of itself.

"What you've said, Square, an' your comin' here, has done me a lot o' good. It's pooty nigh wuth bein' burnt out for—to have this sort o' thing come on behind as an after-clap. Sometimes, I tell you, sir, I've despaired o' the republic. I admit it, though it's to my shame. I've said to myself that when American citizens, born an' raised right on the same hill-side, got to behavin' to each other in such an all-fired mean an' cantankerous way, why, the hull blamed thing wasn't worth tryin' to save. But you see I was wrong—I admit I was wrong. It was jest a passin' flurry—a kind o' snow-squall in hayin' time. All the while, right down 't the bottom, their hearts was sound an' sweet as a butternut. It fetches me—that does—it makes me prouder than ever I was before in all my born days to be an American—yes, sir—that's the way I—I feel about it."

There were actually tears in the big farmer's eyes, and he got out those finishing words of his in fragmentary gulps. None of us had ever seen him so affected before.

After the Squire had shaken hands again and started off, Abner stood at the open door, looking after him, then gazing in a contemplative general way upon all out-doors. The vivid sunlight reflected up from the melting snow made his face to shine as if from an inner radiance. He stood still and looked across the yards with their piles of wet straw smoking in the forenoon heat, and the black puddles eating into the snow as the thaw went on; over the further prospect, made weirdly unfamiliar by the disappearance of the big old farm-house; down the long broad sloping hill-side with its winding road, its checkered irregular patches of yellow stubble and stacked fodder, of deep umber ploughed land and warm gray woodland, all pushing aside their premature mantle of sparkling white, and the scattered homesteads and red barns beyond— and there was in his eyes the far-away look of one who saw still other things.

He turned at last and came in, walking over to where Jeff

and Esther stood hand in hand beside the bed on the floor. Old Jee Hagadorn was sitting up now, and had exchanged some words with the couple.

"Well, Brother Hagadorn," said the farmer, "I hope you're feelin' better."

"Yes, a good deal—B—Brother Beech, thank'ee," replied the cooper, slowly and with hesitation.

Abner laid a fatherly hand on Esther's shoulder and another on Jeff's. A smile began to steal over his big face, broadening the square which his mouth cut down into his beard, and deepening the pleasant wrinkles about his eyes. He called M'rye over to the group with beckoning nod of the head.

"It's jest occurred to me, mother," he said, with the mock gravity of tone we once had known so well and of late had heard so little—" I jest be'n thinkin' we might 'a' killed two birds with one stun while the Square was up here. He's justice o' the peace, you know—an' they say them kind o' marriages turn out better'n all the others."

"Go 'long with yeh!" said M'rye, vivaciously. But she too put a hand on Esther's other shoulder.

The school-teacher nestled against M'rye's side. "I tell you what," she said, softly, "if Jeff ever turns out to be half the man his father is, I'll just be prouder than my skin can hold."

The Deserter

I

Discoveries in the Barn

It was the coldest morning of the winter, thus far, and winter is no joke on those northern tablelands, where the streams still run black in token of their forest origin, and old men remember how the deer used to be driven to their clearings for food, when the snow had piled itself breast high through the fastnesses of the Adirondacks. The wilderness had been chopped and burned backward out of sight since their pioneer days, but this change, if anything, served only to add greater bitterness to the winter's cold.

Certainly it seemed to Job Parshall that this was the coldest morning he had ever known. It would be bad enough when daylight came, but the darkness of this early hour made it almost too much for flesh and blood to bear. There had been a stray star or two visible overhead when he first came out-of-doors at half-past four, but even these were missing now.

The crusted snow in the barnyard did throw up a wee, faint light of its own, for all the blackness of the sky, but Job carried, besides a bucket, a lantern to help him in his impending struggle with the pump. This ancient contrivance had been icebound every morning for a fortnight past, and one needn't be the son of a prophet to foresee that this morning it would be frozen as stiff as a rock.

It did not turn out to be so prolonged or so fierce a conflict as he had apprehended. He had reasoned to himself the previous day that if the pump-handle were propped upright with a stick overnight, there would be less water remaining in the cylinder to freeze, and had made the experiment just before bedtime.

It worked fairly well. There was only a good deal of ice to be

111

knocked off the spout with a sledge-stake, and then a disheartening amount of dry pumping to be done before the welcome drag of suction made itself felt in the well below, like the bite of a big fish in deep water.

Job filled his bucket and trudged back with it to the cowbarn, stamping his feet for warmth as he went.

By comparison with the numbing air outside, this place was a dream of coziness. Two long lines of cows, a score or more on a side, faced each other in double rows of stanchions. Their mere presence had filled the enclosure with a steaming warmth.

The ends of the barn and the loft above were packed close with hay, moreover, and half a dozen lantern lights were gleaming for the hired men to see by, in addition to a reflector lamp fastened against a post.

The men did not mind the cold. They had been briskly at work cleaning up the stable and getting down hay and fodder, and the exercise kept their blood running and spirits light. They talked as they plied shovel and pitchfork, guessing how near the low-mercury mark of twenty below zero the temperature outside had really fallen, and chaffing one of their number who had started out to go through the winter without wearing an overcoat.

Their cheery voices, resounding through the half-gloom above the soft, crackling undertone of the kine munching their breakfast seemed to add to the warmth of the barn.

The boy Job had begun setting about a task which had no element of comfort in it. He got out a large sponge, took up the bucket he had brought from the well, and started at the end of one of the rows to wash clean the full udder of each of the forty-odd cows in turn. In a few minutes the milkers would be ready to begin, and to keep ahead of them he must have a clear start of a dozen cows.

When he had at last reached this point of vantage, the loud din of the streams against the sides of the milkers' tin pails had commenced behind him.

He rose, straightened his shoulders, and shook his red, dripping hands with a groan of pain. The icy water had well nigh frozen them.

It was a common thing for all about the barn to warm cold hands by thrusting them deep down into one of the barrels of brewers' grains which stood in a row beyond the oat-bin. The damp, crushed malt generates within its bulk so keen a heat that even when the top is frozen there will be steam within. Job went over and plunged his cold hands to the wrist in the smoking fodder. He held them there this morning for a luxurious extra minute, wondering idly as he did so how the cows sustained that merciless infliction of ice-water without any such comforting after-resource.

Suddenly he became conscious that his fingers, into which the blood was coming back with a stinging glow, had hit upon something of an unusual character in the barrel. He felt of it vaguely for a moment, then drew the object forth, rubbed off the coating of malt, and took it over to the lamp.

It was a finger-ring carved out of a thick gutta-percha button, but with more skill than the schoolboys of those days used to possess; and in its outer rim had been set a little octagonal silver plate, bearing some roughly cut initials.

Job seemed to remember having seen the ring before, and jumped to the conclusion that some one of the hired men had unconsciously slipped it off while warming his hands in the grains. He went back with it to the milkers, and went from one to another, seeking an owner.

Each lifted his head from where it rested against the cow's flank, glanced at the trinket, and making a negative sign bent down again to his work. The last one up the row volunteered the added comment:

"You better hustle ahead with your spongin' off; I'm just about through here!"

The boy put the circlet in his pocket—it was much too large for any of his fingers—and resumed his task. The water was as terribly cold as ever, and the sudden change seemed to scald his skin; but somehow he gave less thought to his physical discomfort than before.

It was very funny to have found a ring like that. It reminded him of a story he had read somewhere, and could not now recall, save for the detail that in that case the ring contained a priceless jewel, the proceeds of which enriched the finder for life. Clearly no such result was to be looked for here. It was doubtful if anybody would give even twenty-five cents for this poor, home-made ornament. All the same it *was* a ring, and Job had a feeling that the manner of its discovery was romantic.

Working for a milkman does not open up so rich a field of romance that any hints of the curious or remarkable can be suffered to pass unnoticed. The boy pondered the mystery of how the ring got into the barrel. For a moment he dallied with the notion that it might belong to his employer, who owned the barn and almost all the land within sight, and a prosperous milk-route down in Octavius.

But no! Elisha Teachout was not a man given to rings; and even if he were, he assuredly would not have them of rubber. Besides, the grains had only been carted in from town two days before, and Mr. Teachout had been nursing his rheumatism indoors for fully a week.

It was more probable that some one down in the brewery at Octavius had lost the ring. When Job had been there for grains, he had noticed that the workers were cheerful and hearty fellows. No doubt they might be trusted to behave handsomely upon getting back a valued keepsake which had been given up as forever gone.

Perhaps—who could tell?—this humble, whittled-out piece of gutta-percha might be prized beyond rubies on account of its family associations. Such things had happened before, according to the story-books; and forthwith the lad lost himself in a maze of brilliant day-dreams, rose-tinted by this possibility.

He could almost behold himself adopted by the owner of the

brewery—the fat, red-faced Englishman with the big watch-chain, whom he had seen once walking majestically among his vats. Perhaps, in truth, Job was a trifle drowsy.

All at once he roused himself with a start, and began to listen with all his ears. The milkers behind him were talking about the ring. They had to shout to one another to overcome the fact of separation and the noise in their pails, and Job could hear every word.

"I tell you who had a ring like that—Mose Whipple," one of them called out. "Don't you remember? He made it with his jack-knife, that time he was laid up with the horse kickin' him in the knee."

"Seems's if I do," said another. "He was always whittlin' out somethin' or other—a peach-stone basket, or an ox-gad, or somethin'."

"Some one was tellin' me yesterday," put in a third, "that old man Whipple's sick abed. Nobody ain't seen him around for up'ards of a fortnight. I guess this cold snap'll about see the last o' him. He's been poorly all the fall."

"He ain't never ben the same man since Mose 'listed," remarked the first speaker; "that is if you call it 'listin' when a man takes his three hundred dollars to go out as a substitute."

"Yes, and don't even git the money at that, but jest has it applied to the interest he owes on his mortgage. *That's* payin' for a dead horse, if anything is in this world!"

"Well, Mose is the sort o' chap that *would* be workin' to pay for some kind o' dead horse all his life, anyway. If it wasn't one it'd be another. Never knew a fellow in all my born days with so little git-up-and-git about him. He might as well be shoulderin' a musket as anything else, for all the profit he'd git out of it."

"A chip of the old block, if there ever was one. The old man always wanted to do a little berryin', an' a little fishin', an' a little huntin' an' keep a dozen traps or so in the woods, an' he'd throw up the best-payin' job in the deestrict to have a loafin' spell when the fit took him—an' Mose was like him as two peas in a pod.

"I remember one year, Mose an' me hired out in the middle o' March, an' we hadn't fairly begun early ploughin' before he said he wasn't feelin' right that spring, an' give up half his month's wages to go home, an' then what do we see next day but him an' his father down by the bridge with their fishpoles, before the snow-water'd begun to git out o' the creek. What *kin* you do with men like that?"

"Make substitutes of 'em!" one of the milkers exclaimed, and at this there was a general laugh.

Every one on the farm, and for that matter on all the other farms for miles round, knew that Elisha Teachout had been drafted the previous summer, and had sent Moses Whipple to the front in his place. This relation between the rich man and the poor man was too common a thing in those war times to excite particular comment. But, as Mr. Teachout was not beloved by his hired men, they enjoyed a laugh whenever the subject came up.

Job had gone over to the lamp, during the progress of this talk, and scrutinized the ring. Surely enough, the clumsily scratched initials on the little silver plate, obviously cut down from an old three-cent piece, were an M and a W.

This made it all the more difficult to puzzle out how the ring came in the barrel. The lad turned the problem over in his mind with increasing bewilderment.

He had known Mose Whipple all his life. His own father, who died some years ago, had accounted Mose among his intimate friends, and Job's earliest recollections were of seeing the two start off together of a spring morning with shot-guns on their shoulders and powder-flasks hung round their bodies.

They had both been poor men, and if they had not cared so much for hunting—at least if one of them had not—Job reflected that probably this very morning he himself would be sleeping in a warm bed, instead of freezing his hands in the hard employ of Elisha Teachout.

It was impossible not to associate Mose with these recriminatory thoughts; yet it was equally impossible to be angry with him long. The boy, indeed, found himself dwelling upon the amiable side of Mose's shiftless nature. He remembered how Mose used to come round to their poor little place, after Job's father's death, to see if he could help the widow and her brood in their struggle.

After Mrs. Parshall had married again, and gone West, leaving Job to earn his own living on the Teachout farm, Mose had always kept a kindly if intermittent eye on the boy. Only the previous Christmas he had managed, somehow, to obtain an old pair of skates as a present for Job, and when he had gone to the war in the following August, only the fact that he had to sell his shot-gun to pay a pressing debt prevented his giving that to the boy for his own.

The news that old Asa Whipple was ill forced its way to the top of Job's thoughts. He resolved that that very day, if he could squeeze in the time for it, he would cut across lots on the crust to the Whipple house, and see how the lonely old man was.

As the milkers said, old Asa had been "poorly" since his Mose went away. It was only too probable that he had been extremely poor as well.

Even when Mose was at home, theirs was the most poverty-stricken household in the township. Left to his own resources, and failing swiftly all at once in health, the father had tried to earn something by knitting mittens and stockings.

It had looked funny enough to see this big-framed, powerfully built old man fumbling at his needles like some grandmother in her rocking-chair by the stove.

It occurred to Job now that there was something besides humor in the picture. He had been told that people were making woollen mittens and stockings now, like everything else, by machinery. Very likely old Asa couldn't sell his things after he had knit them; and that might mean starvation.

Yes, that very day, in spite of everything, he would go over and see.

He had finished his task now. The milkers had nearly

finished theirs. Two of the hired men were taking the cloth strainers off the tops of all the cans but one, and fastening on the covers instead. He could hear the bells on the harness of the horses outside, waiting with the big sleigh to rush off to town with the milk. It was still very dark out-of-doors.

Job put away his water-bucket, warmed his hands once more in the grains-barrel, and set about getting down a fresh supply of hay for the cows. Six weeks of winter had pretty well worn away the nearest haymow, and the boy had to go further back toward the end of the barn, into a darkness which was only dimly penetrated by the rays of the lantern.

Working thus, guided rather by sense of touch than of sight, the boy suddenly felt himself stepping on something big and rounded, which had no business in a haymow. It rolled from under his feet, and threw him off his balance to his hands and knees. A muttered exclamation rose from just beside him, and then suddenly he was gripped bodily in the clutch of a strong man.

Frightened and vainly struggling, Job did not cry out, but twisted his head about in the effort to see who it was that he had thus strangely encountered. There was just light enough from the distant lantern to reveal in the face so menacingly close to his—of all unlooked-for faces in the world—that of Mose Whipple!

"Why, Mose!" he began, in bewilderment.

"Sh-h! Keep still!" came in a fierce whisper, "unless you want to see me hung higher than Haman!"

II

A Sudden Departure

The man upon whose sleeping form Job had stepped in the haymow sat up and looked about him in a half-puzzled fashion, mechanically brushing the loose particles from his hair and neck.

"I s'pose it's mornin'," he whispered, after a minute's silence. "How long'll it be before daylight?"

Job, released from the other's clutch, had scrambled to his feet, and stood staring down in astonishment at his old friend, Mose Whipple. He had regained his fork, and held it up as if to repel a possible second attack.

"What did you want to pitch on to me that way for?" he asked at last in displeased tones.

"Sh-h! Talk lower!" urged Mose under his breath. "I didn't mean to hurt you, sonny. I didn't know who you was. You come tromplin' on me here when I was fast asleep, and I took hold of you when I wasn't hardly woke up, you see, that's all. I didn't hurt you, did I?"

"No," Job admitted grudgingly. "But there wasn't no need to throw me down and choke me all the same."

"I thought it was somebody comin' to catch me," explained the other, still in a whisper. "But who else is here in the barn? What time is it gettin' to be?"

"They're just through milkin'," replied the boy. "They're gettin' the cans out into the sleigh. They'll all be gone in a minute or two. Time? Oh, it ain't six yet."

"That's all right," said Mose, with a weary sigh of relief. He added, upon reflection: "Say, sonny, can you manage to get me something to eat? I've gone the best part of two days now without a mouthful."

"Mebbe I can," responded Job, doubtingly. Then a sudden thought struck him. "Say, Mose," he went on, "I bet I can tell what you did the first thing when you came into the barn here. You went and stuck your hands into the grains there—that's how it was. "

The man displayed no curiosity as to the boy's meaning. "Yes, by jiminy!" he mused aloud. "I'd 'a' liked to have got in head first. I tell you, sonny, I was about as near freezin' to death as they make 'em. I couldn't have gone another hundred rods to save my life. They'd have found me froze stiff on the road, that's all."

"But what are you doing here, anyway?" asked Job. "You ain't gone and deserted, have you?"

"Well," said the other, doggedly, "you can call it what you like. One thing's certain—I ain't down South, *be* I?"

"Something else is pretty certain, too," the boy put in. "They'll hang you, sure!"

Mose did not seem to have much doubt on this point. "Anyway, I'll see the old man first," he said. "It's pitch dark outdoors, ain't it?"

The boy nodded. "I must git along with my work," he commented, after another little silence. "What are you figgerin' on doin', anyway, Mose?" he asked gravely.

"Well, I'm goin' to sneak out while it's still dark," said the man, "and git across lots to our place, and just wake up the old man, and—and—well, see how he is, that's all. Mebbe I can manage it so that I can skip out again, and nobody be the wiser. But whether or no, that's what I'm bound to do. Prob'ly you've heard—is he—is his health pretty middlin' good?"

"Seems to me some one was saying something about his being kind o' under the weather lately," replied Job, with evasion. "I was thinkin' of goin' over this afternoon myself, if I could git the time, to see him. The fact is, Mose, I guess he *is* failing some. It's been a pretty tough winter for old folks, you know. Elisha Teachout's been laid up himself with rheumatics now for more'n a fortnight, and he ain't old exactly."

"He ain't had 'em half bad enough!" cried Mose, springing to his feet with suddenly revived energy. "If he's let the old man suffer—if he ain't kept his word by him—I'll—I'll take it out of his old hide if I have to go to jail for it!"

"You've got enough other things to go to jail for, and get hung for into the bargain, I should think," said Job. "You'd better not talk so loud, either."

Surely enough, one of the hired men seemed to have remained in the barn, and to have caught the sound of voices—

for the noise of his advancing footsteps could be heard on the floor between the stanchions. Mose threw himself flat, and rolled under the hay as best he could. Job began to sing in a low-voiced, incoherent way for a moment, and then loudly. Prying up a forkful of hay, he staggered under the burden back to the cows, singing as he came toward the intruder.

It was only Nelse Hornbeck, an elderly and extra hand who worked at starvation wages during the winter, chopping fire-wood and doing odd chores about the house and barns. When he saw Job he stopped. He was in a sociable mood, and though he leaned up against one of the stanchions and offered no sign of going farther, displayed a depressing desire for conversation.

The boy came and went, bringing in the hay and distributing it along under the double row of broad pink noses on either side. He made the task as long as he could in the hope of tiring Nelse out, but without avail.

"I dunno but I'm almost sorry I didn't enlist myself last fall," drawled Hornbeck, settling himself in an easy posture. "So far's I can make out, Mose Whipple and the rest of the boys are having a great sight better time of it down South, with nothin' to do and plenty o' help to do it, than we are here to hum. Why, Steve Trimble's brother-in-law writes him that they're havin' more fun down there than you can shake a stick at; livin' snug and warm in sort o' little houses built into the ground, and havin' horse-races and cock-fights and so on every day. They ain't been no fightin' since Thanksgivin', he says, and they're all gittin' fat as seals."

"Well, why *don't* you enlist then?" demanded Job, curtly, going on with his work.

"I dunno," said the hired man in a meditative way. "I guess I'm afeard o' gittin' homesick. I'd always be hankerin' to git back and see my folks, and they won't let you do that, nohow. A lot of 'em tries to sneak off, they say, but Steve's brother-in-law says they've got cavalry-men on horseback all around outside the camps, and they just nail everybody that tries to git out, and then they take 'em back to camp and shoot 'em.

That's what they do—lead 'em out before breakfast and shoot 'em down."

"I thought they hung deserters," said Job, pausing with his fork in air.

"Some they hang and some they shoot," replied Nelse. "I don't see as it makes much difference. I'd about as lieve be one as the other. I guess they make it a rule to hang them that gits off into the North and has to be brought way back again. That's only reasonable, because they've give 'em so much extry trouble."

Job was interested. "But suppose a man does get up North —I guess they ain't much chance of their ever findin' him after that."

"Ain't they?" exclaimed the hired man, incredulously. "Why, it's a thousand to one they catch him! They've got their detectives in every county just doin' nothin' but watchin' for deserters. They git paid for every one they catch, so much a head, and that makes 'em keep their eyes peeled."

"But how can you tell a deserter from any other man," pursued Job, "so long as he's got ordinary clothes on and minds his own business and keeps away from where he's known?"

"Oh, they always point for home—that's the thing of it. What do they desert for? Because they're homesick. So all the detectives have got to do is to watch their place, and nab 'em when they try to sneak in. It's as easy as rollin' off a log. They always git caught, every mother's son of 'em."

Tiresome Nelse Hornbeck was still talking when Job came to the end of all possible pretexts of employment in the cowbarn, and was only too obviously waiting to accompany the boy over to the house to breakfast. At last Job had to accept the situation and go.

The boy dared no more than steal for a moment back into the hay, feel about with his foot for where Mose lay hidden in the dark, and drop the furtive whisper, "Going to breakfast. If I can I'll bring you some."

Then, in company with Nelse, he left the barn, shutting and

hooking the door behind him. It occurred to him that Mose must have effected an entrance by the door at the other end, which was fastened merely by a latch. Otherwise the displacement of the outer hook would have been noticed.

It was lucky, he thought in passing, that Elisha Teachout did not have padlocks on the doors of his cow-barn, as he had on those which protected his horses and wagons and grain. If he had, there would have been the lifeless and icy body of Mose, lying on the frozen roadside, to be discovered by the daylight.

Poor Mose! he had saved his life from the bitterly cold night, but was it not only to lose it again at the hands of the hangman or the firing party?

Job remembered having seen, just a few weeks before, a picture in one of the illustrated weeklies of a deserter sitting on his own coffin, while files of soldiers were being drawn up to witness his impending punishment. Although the artist had given the doomed man a very bad face indeed, Job had been conscious at the time of feeling a certain human sympathy with him.

As his memory dwelt now on the picture, this face of the prisoner seemed to change into the freckled and happy-go-lucky lineaments of Mose Whipple.

The boy took with him into the house a heart as heavy as lead.

Breakfast was already well under way in the big, old-fashioned, low-ceilinged kitchen of the Teachout homestead. Three or four hired men were seated at one end of the long table, making stacks of hot buckwheat cakes saturated with pork fat on their plates, and then devouring them in huge mouthfuls.

They had only the light of two candles on the table. So long as there was anything before them to eat, they spoke never a word. The red-faced women over at the stove did not talk either, but worked in anxious silence at their arduous task of frying cakes fast enough to keep the plates before the hungry men supplied.

For once in his life Job was not hungry. He suffered Nelse Hornbeck to appropriate the entire contents of the first plate of cakes which the girl brought to the table, without a sign of protest. This was not what usually happened, and as soon as Nelse could spare the time he looked at his companion in surprise.

"What ails you this mornin'?" he asked, with his spoon in the grease. "Ain't you feelin' well?"

Job shook his head. "I guess I'll eat some bread 'n' butter instead," he made reply. He added after a pause, "Somehow, I kind o' spleen against cakes this mornin'."

"They ain't much good to-day, for a fact," assented Nelse, when he had eaten half-way through his pile. "I guess they want more sody. It beats me why them women can't make their cakes alike no two days in the week. First the batter's sour, and then they put in more sody; and then it's too flat, and they dump in a lot o' salt; and then they need more graham flour, and then the batter's too thick, and has to be thinned down with milk, and by that time the whole thing's wrong, and they've got to begin all over again."

Nelse chuckled, and looked up at Job, who paid no attention.

"If we men fooled around with the cows' fodder, every day different," Nelse went on, "the way the girls here do with ours, why, the whole barnful of 'em would 'a' dried up before snow blew. But that's the way with women!" Mr. Hornbeck concluded with a sigh, and began on the second heap of cakes.

The boy had not listened. A project had been gradually shaping itself in his mind, until now it seemed as if he had left the cow-barn with it definitely planned out. As soon as the other men, who for the moment were idling with their knives and forks, had been supplied with a fresh batch of cakes, he would put it into execution.

"Why, you was feelin' first rate a few minutes ago," remonstrated Nelse, between mouthfuls, "singin' away for dear life."

"Remember how Mose Whipple used to sing?" put in one of the others. "The' was one song o' his, 'The Faded Coat o'

Blue'—seems's if I could set and listen to him singin' that all day long. He sung it over at Steve Trimble's huskin', I remember, and Lib Truax let him see her home, just on account of it. She wouldn't so much as looked at him any other time. She told my sister afterward that if he'd 'a' popped the question then, with that singin' o' his in her ears, as like as not she'd 'a' said yes."

"Lucky for her he didn't, then," remarked another. "I give Mose credit for one thing, though. He had sense enough not to git married—and that's more'n most shiftless coots like him have. He always said that as long's the old man was alive, he'd keep a roof over his head, and let everything else slide. Whatever else you may say, there's no denyin' Mose was a good son to the old man."

"If I was old," said a third, "and was dependent on my son, I'd think a good deal more of him if he shinned around, and worked stiddy, and put somethin' by for a rainy day, even if he did marry into the bargain, instid o' bein' bone-lazy like Mose, and never knowin' one day where the next day's breakfast was comin' from."

"Not if you was old Asa Whipple," rejoined the first speaker. "Mose was jest after the old man's heart. I never see father and son so wrapped up in one another as them two was. Seems's if they didn't need no other company—they was company enough for themselves. That's what made it so rough on the old man when Mose 'listed."

"He couldn't help himself," said Nelse Hornbeck; "there was the interest comin' due on the mortgage, and how else—"

"Sh-h! can't ye!" muttered one of the others, kicking Nelse under the table, and giving a backward nod of the head toward the women by the stove. "Want them to tell 'Lishe Teachout you're blabbin' about his affairs, you sawney?"

Nelse bent hastily over his cakes, and the others busied themselves at making way with the steaming fresh supply which had accumulated while they talked.

Job's opportunity had come. He rose with as fine an assumption of carelessness as he could manage, and walked up to the other end of the table, where the big loaf of home-made bread and the butter-dish were.

He cut off two thick slices; the butter which he tried to spread upon them had become hard with the night's intense cold, and had not been near enough to the fire to be softened. So Job could only distribute it in lumps over the soft surface of one slice, and then put the other on top of it.

Then, watching his chance in the dim light, he conveyed the bread to his jacket pocket. Nobody at the table had observed him, he was sure.

He turned to discover that the sitting-room door close at his back had been opened wide, and that Elisha Teachout was standing in the doorway, looking at him with all his eyes.

It was Elisha Teachout's habit to look very closely at everything and everybody—and his was at the best of times a somewhat uncomfortable gaze to sustain. Job felt that this was not one of the best of times.

His employer was in all seasons an austere and exacting man, coldly suspicious of those about him, and as pitiless in his treatment of his hired help's shortcomings as he was vigilant in looking out for them. But in the winter, when rheumatism put its dread touch upon the marrow of his bones, he was irascible as well, and led his household what they used to describe outside as "a life of it."

His lean, small figure did not seem as much bent as usual this morning—probably he was better, Job thought—but his little steel-colored eyes had an abnormally piercing effect. His pallid face, hairless and wrinkled, with its sunken lips and sharply hooked nose, was of a yellower and sourer aspect than usual, too. The boy felt himself turning very red.

It turned out to be a needless alarm. Mr. Teachout diverted his gaze from Job to look at his old silver watch, which he took from his fob, and then ostentatiously held it in his hand.

"Milk late again this morning?" he demanded, raising his querulous voice with a snap.

"No, it got off in good season," replied the head hired man, nonchalantly.

He had answered the same question now every day for several years, and was at home with it. As a matter of fact the milk from the Teachout farm was never late, but this had not prevented the master's query becoming a formula.

"Then breakfast ought to 'a' been out of the way half an hour ago!" he exclaimed, in the same high, snarling tone. "If I didn't get up and come out, sick as I am, I suppose you'd be settin' here gorging yourselves till noon! And you women, you jest aid and abet 'em in their laziness and gormandizing!"

Job stayed to hear no more. Relieved from his fear of detection, he had taken advantage of the attack upon the others to get his cap and sidle unobtrusively from the room.

Once outside he scampered headlong across the frozen ruts and hummocks of the yard to the cow-barn. There was a perilous show of pink and lemon lights in the eastern sky. Very soon it would be daylight.

He groped his way past between the stanchions to the hay, and began feeling about with his feet.

"Here you are, Mose!" he called out. "It's almost daylight! Here's something to eat."

No answer came. The boy trampled foot by foot over the whole mow in vain. Mose Whipple was gone.

III

Father and Son

It is not likely that anything whatever remains standing now of the Whipple house. It must be a dozen years ago that I shot a black squirrel as it whisked its way along over the ridge-beam which had once been Asa Whipple's roof-tree; and the place then was in ruins. The rafters had fallen in; what was left of the sides were dry-rotten under a mask of microscopic silver-gray moss. Tangled masses of wild-brier and lichens surrounded its base, and pushed their way in through the open, dismantled doorway.

Even at that time, the road which once led past the house had fallen into disuse. I suppose that to-day it would be as hard to find the house under the briers as to trace the ancient highway beneath the carpet of grass and sorrel.

Even during the war, when human beings thought of it as a home, the Whipple place was a pretty poor sort of habitation. The lowliest of Elisha Teachout's live-stock were considerably better housed and better sheltered from the weather than old Asa and his son Mose.

The house, as I remember it, used to interest me because it was so obviously a remainder from the days when the district round about was still a veritable part of the Adirondacks. Whether Asa built it or inherited it from his father, a Revolutionary soldier who took up his land-patent in these primitive parts, I never knew. It looked old enough, though, to have been erected by Hendrick Hudson himself.

There must have been a sawmill on the creek at the time, however, for it was not a log house but a frame building, with broad planks nailed roughly to its sides, and the joinings of these covered over with weather-strips.

The frames of the door and the two front windows also came from this mill, wherever it was; the window on the north side was of rude construction, and was evidently the work of some person not greatly skilled in the use of carpenters' tools; perhaps it was made by old Asa himself.

There was a legend that the roof had once been shingled; in my time it was made of flattened breadths of spruce bark, which must have leaked sadly in rainy seasons. There was no cellar under the house, but a rough lean-to woodshed at the back served to shelter any overflow of possessions which might trouble the Whipples. This lean-to was given over chiefly to traps, fishpoles, netting gear, and the like.

There was a barn, but it was roofless and long since disused. I dare say the original Revolutionary Whipple aimed at being a farmer, like the rest of his neighbors. Like the others, he cleared his land, got in his crops, built a barn for his cattle and produce, and ran up rail fences. Perhaps he even prospered thus, as prosperity was measured in those lean, toilsome times.

But either in his day, or when his son Asa was a comparatively young man, the hand of fate was laid on the Whipple place. The black moss came!

Strong and intelligent farmers, with capital behind them, can successfully fight and chase off nowadays, they say, this sinister scourge of the thin-soiled northern farm lands on the forest's edges. But forty years ago, and even much later, it was a common saying that when the moss came, the man must go.

Asa Whipple did not go. He let farming go instead. When the moss had seized upon pasture and meadow alike, nothing was simpler than to sell the cows, and allow the barn to fall to pieces. Much better than taking anxious thought about the farm, it suited Asa to turn to the woods—the kindly, lazy, mysteriously tempting woods.

Here were no back-aching ploughs and scythes, no laborious hoeing of corn and grubbing for roots, and painful wrestling with rain and drought and frost—and worst of all, the moss—for pitiful coppers. Here instead were luscious trout for the hook, and otter, mink, and even an occasional beaver for the trap; here in the greenwood, to the trained hunter, was spread a never-ending banquet of rare and toothsome meats, from the game birds, the raccoon, and the squirrel, up to the fleet-heeled deer and the black bear, lounging his clumsy way through the undergrowth.

Like father, like son. Time came, indeed, when the woods were no longer what they had been, and when the influence of advancing civilization compelled Mose to eke out a scanty living for his father and himself by hiring out a week or two now and then during busy seasons on the farms roundabout.

He did this as seldom as he could, however, and he never pretended that he liked to do it at all.

Of their own land, the Whipples for years had cultivated only a garden-patch close about the house, and this in so lukewarm a fashion that the net results—some potatoes, a little sweet corn, a few pumpkins, and so on—never by any chance saw them through the winter.

Why they did not sell this unproductive land to Elisha Teachout, who evidently wanted it, instead of borrowing money from him on it to pay taxes for it, I could never understand. Very likely they did not try to explain it to themselves.

But it was the fact, nevertheless, that in July of 1863 they owed Mr. Teachout something over three hundred dollars in accrued interest upon the mortgages he held, and that to prevent his foreclosing and evicting them from the house, Mose Whipple went to the war as Teachout's substitute.

This year of 1863 had still a week of life before it on the morning in question—when Mose returned from the war.

He had made across the stiff-crusted level wastes of snow from Teachout's straight as the bee's flight, even before the dawn began to break. He had heard the talk in the barn about the certainty of his capture, but it made little impression on his mind. It did not even occur to him that the matter concerned him. What had stirred him was Job Parshall's roundabout and reluctant admission that all was not right with the old man.

He had waited only a few minutes in the haymow after Job had gone to the farm-house before the temptation to be off again toward home mastered him. It was silly to linger here for food when the goal was so close at hand.

He took a couple of English turnips from one of the fodder bins to eat on the way, and let himself cautiously out by the rear door of the cow-barn.

It was still quite dark and bitterly cold, but he started briskly off. After he had left the barnyard an idea occurred to him. His father might be perishing of hunger! He turned and bent his steps back across the yard to the hen-house, opened the door, and crept in. A cackling murmur fell upon the dark-

ened silence, rising all at once into a harsh and strident squawk-
ing, then ceasing abruptly.

Mose emerged upon the instant, shut and hooked the door,
and started to run, stuffing a big, limp and shapeless object into
his coat pocket.

When he had rapped upon and rattled vigorously for a third
time the window on the north side of the house he had jour-
neyed so far and risked so much to return to, Mose was conscious of a heavy, sudden sinking of the heart. That was the
bedroom window; how was it his father had not heard him?

He knocked once more, more loudly than before, and bent
his head to listen. No answer came.

After a minute's waiting he walked around to the front of
the house. In the broad daylight which had spread itself now
over the white landscape, he noticed something he had missed
before. There had been no path cut through from the house to
the road. The frozen drifts lay packed as they had fallen upon
the doorsill. There was no mark of footsteps save his own. The
window-panes were opaque with frost.

Mose tried the latch. It yielded readily, and he entered. The
light inside was so dim, after the morning glow on the snow
without, that it was hard at first to make out the room, familiar
as it was to him. Apparently there was no one there.

A curious change of some sort there had been, though. Mose
shut the door and walked across to the stove, instinctively holding his hands over it. So dull a semblance of warmth radiated
up from the griddles that he put a finger on the metal. It was
only blood-warm.

Some one had left a fire here an hour ago. Where was his
father? What had happened?

Then Mose saw what it was that had at the outset vaguely
puzzled him. The straw tick had been brought from the bed in
the other room and spread there on the floor behind the stove.
It was covered with bedding and old clothes, and under these—

In a flash Mose was on his knees beside the improvised bed,

and had pushed away the coverings at the top. There was disclosed before him the head of a man asleep—a head which he scarcely recognized at first sight, so profuse and dishevelled were its masses of white hair and beard, so pinched to ghastliness the waxen features.

"He is dead!" Mose heard himself say aloud, in a voice that sounded not at all his own.

But no; there was warmth, and a feeble flicker of pulse at the shrunken wrist which he instinctly fumbled for under the bedclothes.

"Father! Father!" Mose called, bending till his lips touched the white hair. "Wake up! I've come back! it's me—Mose!"

The faintest stir of life passed over the corpse-like face, and old Asa opened his eyes. It did not seem as though he saw his son, or anything else. His whitened lips moved, emitting some husky, unintelligible sounds. Mose, stooping still lower, strained his ears to piece together these terrible words:—

"Starved—many days—don't tell Mose!"

With a cry of rage and horror Mose sprang to his feet. The things to be done mapped themselves, in the stress of this awful situation, with lightning swiftness before his brain. He strode to the woodshed door and opened it. Two sides of the old lean-to were gone, and the snow was drifted thick across the floor.

Mose realized that the shed had gone for fuel, and in another minute he had torn down half the roof, and was crushing the boards to splinters under his heels.

With the same fierce haste he started the fire blazing again; got out an old frying-pan from under the snow, and put it, filled with ice to be melted into water, on one of the open griddle holes; hacked the remaining turnip into slices, and then began at the fowl, stripping the feathers off in handfuls, and dismembering it as fast as he cleared the skin from joint to joint, filling the rusty old pan to the brim.

Even as he worked thus, and after the water was steaming, and the rude stew under way, he kept an eager and apprehensive eye upon the bed behind the stove. No token of life was forthcoming.

He could not hear his father breathe, even when he bent over him; but no doubt that was on account of the prodigious spluttering and crackling which the fire kept up. Through the other griddle hole he continually thrust in fresh, dry kindlings to swell the blaze.

He had learned some new things about cooking in the army —among others the value of a pot-lid in hurrying forward the stew. He looked about for a cover for the frying-pan. There was no such thing in the house, but he found in the shed an old sheet-iron snow-shovel, and made the blade of this serve, with a nail-hole punched through it to let out the steam.

In his researches he was glad to run upon some salt, because it would help toward making the mess on the stove palatable. But it would not be easy to tell with what emotions he discovered that there was absolutely not another eatable thing in the house.

The room had grown decently warm again, under the influence of the roaring fire, and now it began to be filled with what Mose believed to be a most delicious odor.

The conviction, though to any one else it might well have seemed unwarranted, was pardonable in Mose perhaps, for he himself had tasted his last warm meal nearly sixty hours before.

He munched the turnip peelings almost contentedly as he recalled this fact. Perhaps there would be some of the stew left, after the old man had eaten his fill. If not, there were parts of the fowl which could still be utilized.

An absurd sort of fantasy—a kind of foolish day-dream— began all at once to rise before him. He seemed to see himself eating the whole of that glorious stew, lingering with all his soul over the luxury of each piping-hot mouthful, and giving his father none at all.

This visionary thing grew so upon him, so gripped and enthralled his mind, that it made him dizzy and faint to put it away from him. When, a few minutes later, the smell of burning warned him that the cooking was done, and he lifted the pan from the stove, this brutal temptation rushed savagely at him again. He set the pan on the table, and walked away, not daring to lift the cover.

There were two or three old plates on the shelf, and a tea-cup. Mose got them all down, and arrayed them on the table, with such cutlery and spoons as he could find. He made a motion then to take off the improvised lid from the frying-pan, but once more drew back. It was as if he could not trust himself.

He knelt by the bedside again, now, and putting his arm under his father's neck sought to raise him to a more upright posture. Old Asa opened his eyes as before, and made an effort to whisper something, but he lay an almost inert weight in his son's arms.

Mose swung the tick round, propped the end of it up against the wall and raised his father into a half-sitting posture.

In this position the old man's face took on a sudden expression of interest and reviving intelligence. He had begun to smell the savor of the food.

Looking upon that pallid, vacant, starved face, and wasted, helpless form, Mose, starving himself, felt strong enough to defy the most appetizing stew in the world. He took off the cover with decision, and dipped the tea-cup up half full of the smoking contents. It was too hot, evidently, to be given to the old man at once, and it was also very thick.

Mose took it out to the dismantled woodshed, and spooned in snow until it seemed of the right temperature and consistency. He dipped a little finger into it to further satisfy himself, but he would not even lick that finger afterward. It was too dangerous to think about.

Mose fed his father as a mother might a baby—watching solicitously to see that he did not eat too fast or choke himself. After the first cupful, he brought a chair to sit in, and held the tick against his knee while old Asa, leaning more lightly upon it, helped himself.

There was a little left at last for Mose, and he swallowed it gravely, with a portentous rush of sensations within, but keeping up as best he could an indifferent exterior. It left him still hungry, but he had much more important things to dwell upon than that.

The meal worked wonders upon the old man. The combined influences of food and warmth seemed for a few minutes to send him off to sleep again.

Mose sat looking down upon him in silence, and noting that something like color was stealing back into his face.

All at once, however, Asa Whipple sat upright, lifted his hands to brush back the hair from his forehead, and, turning his face up to look at his son, smiled. There was no lack of comprehension in his gaze. He had regained his tongue as well. He patted Mose's knee as he spoke.

"Mose," he said, in a voice strangely altered and aged, but clear enough, "I'm kind o' 'shamed to tell it, but I'd laid down here just to go to sleep for good. I thought for quite a spell there, after you come in, that I was dreaming—sort o' out o' my head, you know."

"How did you come to let yourself down like this, dad?" was the only reply Mose had at hand.

"Rheumatiz," Asa explained. "It laid me up—I couldn't git around, an' nobody come near me. I ain't seen a soul since the big snowfall—up'ards of a fortnight. But—but it's all right now, ain't it, Mose? An' to think o' your comin' home here like this, right in the nick o' time. How did you come to git off, Mose?"

For answer there fell the crunching sound of footsteps on the crusted snow outside, then of a loud, peremptory knock on the door.

IV

The "Meanest Word"

Mose Whipple had lifted his head in apprehensive inquiry at the sound of the footsteps outside the door of the cabin. He sprang to his feet when the sharp knock on the door followed. Holding a hand downward with outspread fingers as a warning to silence, he tiptoed out to the middle of the room, then paused and listened.

The knock came again, bolder and more peremptory still.

Vague notions of resistance were shaping themselves in Mose's mind. He glanced up at the shot-gun hanging on the chimney behind the stovepipe, and in another instant had it down, with his thumb on the hammer.

"Loaded?" he asked in a whisper, testing the percussion-cap with his nail.

The old man nodded. Then he, too, laboriously rose to his feet. Bent as his form was, he stood a taller man than his son. He rested one hand on the table for support, and stretched out the other with a masterful gesture.

"Gimme that gun!" he said, in brusque command. Then covering Mose from head to foot, he added, slowly, "I'd ruther have starved a hundred times over than had you do this sort o' thing!"

Mose had sheepishly laid the weapon on the table. He walked now with a sullen air to the door, lifted the hook, and put his hand on the latch.

"Let me in out of the cold, can't ye?" a shrill voice complained outside. "It's only me, you gump!"

Mose's face brightened. "Why, it's only young Job Parshall, after all!" he said, and threw the door wide open.

The boy pushed past Mose without a word, and marching across the room to the stove held his red fingers over the griddles. He lifted them a little for inspection after a minute's silence, and screwed his shoulders about in token of the pain they gave him.

"I couldn't run with my hands in my pockets," he said. "I shouldn't wonder if they was froze. That's just my luck."

Mose advanced to the stove, and looked at Job's hands critically. "That little finger there is a trifle tetched, I guess," he said. "It'll be sore for a day or two, that's all. The rest are all right." Then he added, noting the boy's crimson cheeks and panting breast, "Why, sonny, you must 'a' run the whole way!"

Job nodded assent, and turned his hands palm upward. "Every inch of the way," he said between heavy breaths.

Old Asa had sunk again into a chair, and sat gazing in turn at Mose and the boy. The fire which had glowed in his eyes when he had confronted his son had died away again. He was visibly striving not to tremble, and the glance he bent from one to the other was wistful and shamefaced.

"I suppose you've brought some news," he remarked at last to Job.

The boy nodded again, twisting his fingers experimentally in the heat. "When I catch my breath, I'll tell ye," he said.

There was a moment's awkward silence; then Asa Whipple, speaking in low, deliberate tones, rid his mind of some of its burden.

"My son Mose here," he said gravely, "didn't use to be a coward. I didn't bring him up to be no coward. Seems to me you can bring up a boy so't he'll be honest and straightforward and square right up to the last minute, and then lo and behold! he cuts up some low-down, mean dido or other that makes you 'shamed to look folks in the face.

"My father fit in the Revolution, and so did my mother's father and his brothers,—their name was Lapham, and they lived in Rhode Island,—and my older brother, Jason, he was killed up at Sackett's Harbor in the 1812 War before he come of age; and they ain't one of 'em but 'ud turn in his grave to think they was a coward and a deserter in the family!"

Mose stood behind the stove, stealing furtive glances at the old man during this harangue. Once or twice he opened his lips as if to speak, but either no words would come, or he thought better of it.

But Job listened with obvious impatience. He had quite regained his breath. "Mose ain't no coward!" he broke in vehemently. "It took a mighty sight more pluck to light out there, of a night, and come way off up here just to see how you were gettin' on, and have to hide for his life, than it would to have stayed right still where he was, with no fightin' and no work, and three square meals a day."

"You might say four, a'most, countin' supper," Mose suggested softly.

Old Asa Whipple seemed impressed with this view of the situation, and pondered it for a little in silence.

"What I come over to say was," remarked Job, more placidly, "That they're out lookin' for you, Mose. Two men drove up in a cutter just after breakfast—one of 'em's Norm' Hazzard, the deputy marshal down at Octavius, and the other fellow's name is Moak, I b'lieve, and they've stopped to Teachout's to breakfast. They started from Octavius before daylight, and they was about froze solid by the time they got to 'Lishe's. They took out their horse, and they've got so much thawin' out to do themselves, I reckon they ain't more'n about started now, if they have that."

"You come straight?" asked Mose.

"Well, you'd better believe I did! I scooted 'cross lots like greased lightnin' the minute they went in t' the house. It's a good hour 'round by the road, even when it's all open. It's drifted now all the way from the sash factory down to Taft's place, and it's slow work gettin' through the fields. As I figure it, you've got more'n an hour's leeway."

The two men looked at each other as they listened, and they kept up the mutual gaze after the boy had stopped.

"'Pears to me, dad," Mose finally ventured in a deferential way, "that you don't seem to take this thing quite in the right spirit. I tell you straight out, if it was the last word I ever spoke, I ain't done nothin' I'm ashamed of. A man can't say no more'n that."

"Accordin' to the way I was brought up," replied old Asa, doggedly, "they ain't no other such an all-fired, pesky mean name for a man in the dictionary as 'desarter.'"

"Well, anyway," retorted Mose, "I'd ruther be called 'desarter' myself than have you be called 'starved to death.' So far's I can make out, if it hadn't ben one, it 'ud ben t'other."

The old man's glance abruptly sought the floor, and lingered there. The others, as they watched him, could see the muscles of his down-bent face twitching.

"Besides, they didn't need me down there just now," Mose went on in more voluble self-defence, "no more'n a frog needs a tail. An' besides that, they played it monstrous low-down on me. That German fellow that used to work at the tannery, he was my sergeant, and he kept them big eyes of his skinned for me all day long. Him and me never hitched very well down at the mills, you know, and he took it out of me whenever he got a chance.

"He got all the officers down on me. One day they'd say I'd burnt the coffee, and the next day that my gun was dirty, and after that that I was a 'malingerer,'—that's officers' slang for a shirk,—and so on; and every time it meant that some of my pay got stopped. That's why I never sent you any money.

"They worked it so't I never got more'n about ten shillings out of my thirteen dollars, and that I owed twice over before I got it."

Old Asa was looking into his son's face once more, and he nodded comprehendingly as the other paused. "We never did git a fair show, like other men," he remarked.

"But I could 'a' stood all that," continued Mose. "What riled me was when Bill Rood got a letter sayin' that you was poorly, and you stopped writin'; and then I took pains and behaved extra well, so't even the Dutchman couldn't put his finger on me. And then I got a chance one day, and I asked one of the lieutenants that I'd kind o' curried favor with, doin' odd jobs for him and so on, if he couldn't git me a furlough, just to run home and see how you was gittin' on."

"I reckon *you* never got that, Mose."

"No, dad. They was givin' 'em right and left to other fellows, and the lieutenant said he guessed he could manage it. I don't know how hard he tried, but a few days after that I see the Dutchman grinnin' at me, and I felt in my bones that the jig was up. Sure enough, they wouldn't let me have a furlough because I'd been euchred out of my pay. They wa'n't no other reason."

"No," said the old man, "that was always the way. I guess me and you ought to be pretty well used to gittin' the worst of it, by this time. There's a text in the Bible that's our own private family property, as much as if it had 'Whipple' marked on it in big letters. It's that one that says that when a man ain't got anything, he gits took away from him even what he's got. That's me, Mose, and it's you, too."

Mose had quite recovered his confidence now.

"Of course, if there'd ben any fightin' goin' on, it'd ben different," he explained, "but right in the middle of our winnin' everything along in November, after we'd chased the Johnnies across the Rappahannock and the Rapidan, and was havin' it all our own way—and in spite of the rain freezin' as it fell, and no shelter and marchin' till your feet was ready to fall off, we all liked it first-rate—along come orders for us to go back again to winter quarters around Brandy Station. So far as I could see, it was all station and no brandy. And then the new drafted men, they behaved like sin in camp, and orders got stricter, and my Dutchman piled it onto me thicker and thicker, and I got to frettin' about you—and so—so I—I lit out."

"You'd better begin figgerin' on lightin' out agin," said the practical Job. "I suppose you'll take to the woods, won't you?"

Mose nodded, and reached his hand out for the gun. "Yes," he said, "five minutes' start'll be all I need. Once I get across the creek I'm all right. One thing's lucky, there's plenty of powder and shot in the cupboard there, I see. I suppose, if worst comes to worst, I could get through the woods up to Canada. But see here,—this is a good deal more important,— what are you going to do, dad, after I'm gone?"

Old Asa had hardly given this important question a thought before. As it was forced upon him now, his mind reverted mechanically to that strange awakening, when he lay in the starved half-stupor on the very threshold of death, and Mose came in, like some good angel of a dream, to bring him back to life again. A rush of tenderness, almost of pride, suddenly suffused the old man's brain.

"Mose," he said, all at once, "I guess I talked more or less like a fool, here awhile back. Perhaps some folks are entitled to blame you for turnin' up here, this mornin'—but I ain't one of 'em, and I ought to known better. I'm stronger, my boy, ever so much stronger, for seein' you and—eatin' a good meal again. You'll see—I'll be as sound again as a butternut. I bet I could walk this minute to the bridge without a break."

"But that wouldn't feed you, after you got there," objected Mose. "Of course if I could hang around in the neighborhood, and drop in every now and then to keep an eye on you, it 'ud be different. But they're sure to watch the place, and with me caught you'd be worse off than ever. I'd give myself up this minute if only I knew you'd be all right. But that's the hang of it. There's no mistake, dad," he added, with a rueful sort of grin, "the last bell was a-ringin' for you when I turned up here, this mornin'."

It was characteristic of these two men, born and bred here in the robust air of the forest's borders, that as they confronted this dilemma, not the shadow of a notion of that standing alternative, the county-house, crossed either mind. Even if Mose

could have thought of it, he would never have dared suggest
it to Asa.

"Come, you'd better be gittin' together what you're goin' to
take with you," broke in Job, peremptorily. "You've got none
too much time to spare."

"Yes, I know," said Mose, with hesitation; "but the old man
here—that worries me."

"You just 'tend to your own knittin'," was the boy's reply.
"Asa and me'll manage for ourselves all right."

Old Asa Whipple opened his eyes wide—not at surprise at
hearing his Christian name fall so glibly from the boy's tongue,
for that is the custom of the section, but with bewilderment at
his meaning.

"What on earth are you drivin' at?" demanded Mose, no
whit less puzzled.

"Well," said Job, with deliberation, "I've kind o' soured on
that Teachout job of mine. I've had it in my mind to quit all
along, when I got the chance, and I guess this is about as good
as any. I've got along toward twenty dollars saved up, and
there's three days' work a week for me at the cheese-factory
whenever I want to take it, and I could go to school the other
days, and both places are handier to git at from here than they
are from Teachout's. So I'll rig up a bed and so on here, and
I'll look out for the old man. But do you go ahead, and git out!"

It is another custom of these parts to be undemonstrative in
the face of the unexpected.

Mose merely clapped his hand on Job's shoulder, and said,
"You won't ever be sorry for it, sonny," which had much
more of loose prediction than of pledge about it, yet seemed
quite sufficient for them both.

The old man said nothing at all, but sat bending forward in
his chair, his gaze fastened upon every move his son made
about the room. For everything Mose did now spoke plainly of
another parting, more sombre and sinister than the last. A soldier may come back, but how can one hope for the return of
a deserter?

Mose's old instincts as a woodsman rose superior to the exigencies of a life and death flight. He prepared as if for a holiday camping jaunt into the wilderness—in a hurried manner, but forgetting nothing.

He made a pile of things on the table—all the powder and shot in the house, most of the salt, some old stockings, a tin cup, fork and spoon, and what matches he could find—and then stowed them away in flasks and his pockets, along with a whole tangled mass of lines, hooks and catgut fishing gear.

From under the snow in the dismantled shed he unearthed a smaller frying-pan and two steel traps, and slung these with a string through handle and chains across his shoulder. Then he took up the gun and was ready.

"I guess this'll see me through," he said lightly.

Old Asa gazed at him through dimmed eyes. "No, you must take a blanket, Mose," he said. "I won't hear no for an answer —you must! There's plenty more for us. If they ain't, we can git more. They're cheap as dirt. And Mose," the old man rose from his chair as he spoke, "I was a-goin' to ask you to sing for me afore you went, but I—I guess we'd better let that go till we meet again. You'll be all right in the woods—"

"Why, I know twenty places," put in Mose, "where I'll be as snug as a bug in a rug. I'll make straight for a deer yard. Mebbe"—he chuckled at the thought—"I'll be bringing you in some venison some o' these nights. Prob'ly I'll hang it up on a tree—the old butternut by the fork—so't Job can come out and git it in the mornin'. And in the spring—why you must come in the spring and—and be with me in the woods."

The old man's strength had waned once more, and he seated himself.

"Mebbe," was all he said, in a dubious voice, and with his head bowed on his breast.

He did not lift his head, when Mose shook hands with him; he did not raise his glance to follow him, either, when, with the traps and frying-pan clattering about his neck, Mose let himself out by the shed door and was go

He did not even seem to hear when, two or three minutes later, the reverberating crack of revolver shots—one! two! three! four! five!—set the echoes clamoring all around the Whipple house.

V

The Deputy Marshal

As soon as Job Parshall heard the sound of firearms outside the Whipple cabin, he darted to the nearer of the front windows, scratched away some of the thick frost from one of its panes, and put his eye to the aperture.

A horse and cutter had come to a halt on the road, a few rods short of the house. The animal had been frightened by the firing, and was still showing signs of excitement, with lifted ears and stiffened forelegs.

The man, whom Job understood to be Moak, stood at the horse's head, holding the bridle tightly, but looking intently the other way across the fields in the direction of his companion, the redoubtable deputy marshal, who was not in sight.

The boy stole to the other end of the room, and cautiously opened the shed door by as much as the width of his face. Here he could cover at a glance the flat, gently sloping waste of snow which stretched unbroken backward from the house to the gray fringe of woods that marked the edge of the ravine. Beyond that belt of timbered horizon, with its shadows silvery soft in the brilliant morning sunlight, lay sunken in its hollow the ice-bound brook.

If Mose passed this stream there was before him the real forest—and safety.

The black figures of two running men moved upon this broad and dazzlingly white landscape. The farther of the two was now so far away that he seemed a mere dark speck, like the object seen from the gun-line of a turkey shoot. Perhaps this simile was suggested to Job by the fact that the other, pausing now for a moment in his race, straightened an arm and sent five more shots flashing after the fugitive.

Tenfold that number of echoes came rolling in upon one another's heels through the nipping air as the second man started again to run. He seemed not to be catching up with his prey—yes! now Mose was lost to sight in the woods, and his pursuer was not half-way there. Yes! and now the marshal had stopped, hesitated, and turned about.

The deputy marshal retraced his steps over the broken crust slowly, and with an air of dejection. He hung his head as he walked, and it took him a long time to reach the house. When he came into the yard he seemed not to look toward the house at all, but made his way straight past as if bound for the road, with his attention still steadfastly fixed on the snow in front of him.

But just as Job had jumped to the conclusion that he had not been observed, the deputy marshal called in a loud, peremptory aside over his shoulder:—

"Come along out here, boy!"

The lad had no course but to obey. He stole a quick, backward glance to where old Asa still sat motionless with bowed head near the stove. Then noiselessly shutting the shed door behind him, he followed out into the road.

"It'll be all right," the deputy marshal was saying to his companion as Job came up. "He can't take a step on this crust without leavin' a mark, 'specially now that it's goin' to melt a little. I'll land him in the stone jug before night, or you can call me a Dutchman!"

Norman Hazzard, the deputy marshal, was a thin, lithe, active man, somewhere in the thirties, with a long, sun-browned face and a square jaw. Although his keen eyes were of a light, bluish gray, one thought of him as a dark-complexioned person.

Ever since Job could remember, this man had been arresting people, first as a sheriff's officer, then as an army detective.

Looking furtively at him now as he stood at the horse's head, with his sharp glance roving the distant landscape and his under lip nursing the ends of his sparse moustache in meditation, the boy felt that that was what nature intended that Norm Hazzard should be.

The whole country knew him by sight, and talked about the risky things he had done in the line of his duty, and the stern, cold-blooded pluck with which he had done them.

As the deputy marshal stood thus pondering the situation, he rattled together with his hand some heavy metallic objects in one of his overcoat pockets. The clanking sound they gave forth fascinated the boy.

"I s'pose them's handcuffs you've got there in your pocket?" he found himself suddenly impelled to remark. It was only after the words were out that he realized the boldness of speaking in this fierce presence without having been spoken to.

Hazzard turned his head obliquely downward, and regarded Job with a sort of ironical scowl.

"They ain't for you, anyway," he remarked. "I guess the horsewhip'll about suit *your* complaint."

"No, you don't!" replied Job. "You dassent lay a finger on me unless I've done something—I know that much."

The deputy marshal emitted a chuckle of amused contempt.

"Why, you blamed little runt, you!" he said. "You've done mischief enough this mornin' to git thrashed for it within an inch o' your life, and go to state's prison into the bargain. You mind your p's and q's now mighty sharp, or it'll be the end o' you!"

"I don't see, myself," put in Moak, a bearded, thickset, middle-aged man, who drawled his words lazily, but looked as if he might be a tough customer in a fight, "I don't jest make out how you're goin' to catch up with him, even if he does leave tracks. He's got a big start, and has pretty good reasons for humpin' himself, and if he can keep ahead till dark, he knows the woods in the night-time a plaguy sight better'n any of us do."

Hazzard curled his lips in a faint, momentary grin of superiority.

"Can't we get snow-shoes?" he asked.

The word had an evil sound to Job's ears. They would run Mose down, sure enough, with those terrible aids to the pursuit.

"The only question is," the deputy marshal ruminated aloud, "where'll be the nearest place to git the shoes. We'll hitch the horse here to the fence, and take a look at the house. Did you ever see such a tumble-down place in all your life? Here, you boy, mog along there in front o' me, and watch what you do! Or no, wait a minute!"

The deputy marshal had led the horse off the roadway toward the sprawling remains of a rail fence at the side. He paused now, communed with himself for an instant, then brought the horse and cutter back again, and tossed the blanket he had taken out upon the seat once more.

"No," he said briefly to Moak, "you jump in and drive to Juno Mills as fast as you can, and git two pairs of snow-shoes somewhere,—you're bound to find plenty of 'em; the hotel-keeper'll know who's got 'em,—and race back here again. Don't whisper a word to anybody—and we'll have him out in no time."

So it happened that as the cutter with its jingling bells receded from vision and hearing down the road, Job Parshall found himself marching back in embarrassed state toward the front door of the Whipple house, with the firm tread of the deputy marshal crunching on the snow close at his heels.

He could catch the sinister rattle of those handcuffs in Hazzard's pocket at every stride the man took. He tried not to dwell upon it in his mind, but it was a fact that Norm Hazzard had killed two men, one of them a member of a famous local gang of horse-thieves, whom he had shot where he was ambushed behind the grain bags in his barn, the other a wife-murderer, who had escaped from jail to the woods.

How was it, Job wondered, that he had missed all ten of his

shots at Mose? Perhaps they were not all misses. Men did run sometimes, it was said, after they had been struck by a bullet. What if Mose, after all, was lying there, somewhere in the woods, wounded and helpless in the bitter cold!

The manacles behind him ground together with a cruel, rasping noise as this picture rose in his brain.

He pushed the door wide open and went in, closely followed by the other.

Old Asa sat where he had left him, his tall frame settled down supinely in the armchair, his head bent on his breast, motionless and apparently asleep.

"Here's somebody to see you, Asa," Job said, as he heard the door close behind him; but the old man did not stir.

The deputy marshal walked forward, brusquely pushing the lad aside, and laid a heavy hand on Asa Whipple's shoulder. He paused then, as if puzzled by what his grasp felt. Then he put his other hand, not so ungently, into the old man's beard and lifted his head up.

"Say! I wasn't figurin' on this!" was his bewildered exclamation. "Here, quick, you! run and bring some water. Maybe it's only a faint."

This indeed it turned out to be—a deep swoon, the result of long privation and weakness, accented by the sudden relief and the subsequent strain of excitement.

Hazzard could not rouse the old man from his comatose lethargy, with all his rubbing and slapping of hands, and liberal use of snow upon the temple and lips. But he did satisfy himself that there was no imminent danger, and he went to work to spread out the bed again behind the stove, loosen old Asa's clothes, and stretch him out to sleep at his ease, comfortably tucked in with Hazzard's own overcoat, which the marshal had stripped off for the purpose, quite as if his mission in life had been to nurse rather than arrest people.

He had taken out of the overcoat pocket, before spreading it across the bed, a big navy revolver, a parcel or two, presumably of ammunition, and a couple of curious steel wristlets, linked together with a chain; Job looked at these latter, as they lay on the table, with profound interest.

Job had never seen handcuffs so near, and he longed to ask the great man to show him how they worked. Finally, after he had obeyed his curt instruction to put more wood on the fire, and the deputy marshal had seated himself by the stove with his feet balanced on a stick just inside the oven door, and a pipe in his mouth, Job ventured to lift the manacles from the table and inspect them.

As this passed without protest he went to the length of opening one of the bands on its hinge, and then shutting it about his wrist. The two parts went together with a clicking snap, and the boy, after a few fruitless efforts to open them or to slip his hand through, began to guess that he would have to ask the help of the deputy marshal to release him.

He would not humble himself thus, however, before it was a matter of sheer necessity; and he tugged away at the lock in dogged silence, until his wrist was red and sore. The consciousness that the official was grinning at him only made the thing worse.

"If I'd had the sense to do that myself," remarked Hazzard after a time, "when I first laid eyes on you this morning, and then nailed the chain up to the barn door-post, I'd have saved myself a heap of trouble. Leave it alone, or you'll swell your wrist out o' shape. I'll unlock it bimeby—maybe."

He smoked silently for a minute, dividing his ruminative gaze between the steaming leather in the oven, and the rueful countenance of the boy in the handcuffs.

"You're Hank Parshall's boy, ain't you?" he asked at last.

Job nodded and held his imprisoned hand forth to hint, without saying, that he had had enough of the handcuff.

The other paid no heed to the gesture. "What's the matter with the old man, here?" he inquired with a downward nod.

"He ain't had enough to eat," said Job, bluntly. "That's what's the matter with him. He told me himself he laid down there last night to starve to death."

Mr. Hazzard pointed a thumb to the greasy frying-pan, and the remains of the chicken on the table beside Job.

"People don't go to work that way to starve," he commented dryly.

"Mose brought him that—I guess I know pretty well where he got it, too. The old man allowed that that was what saved his life. They hadn't been a soul near him before since the snowfall—and he laid up. Oh, that reminds me!" Job finished by taking the two slices of bread from his pocket, and putting them on the table.

"Bring that for the old man?" queried the deputy marshal.

Job shook his head.

"No, it's my own breakfast. I was goin' to give it to Mose," he replied stoutly. "Say, take this thing off, won't you?"

Norm Hazzard laughed outright. "No!" he said. "Guess after that I'll have to put the other one onto you, too." His tone lapsed to seriousness as he went on: "Maybe you know somethin' about it—didn't I hear that this Mose Whipple went to the war as substitute for your man—Teachout?"

"Yes, sir, he did—and Teachout didn't give him not a dollar, but jest let it go on to the mortgage, and he promised to look out for old Asa here, and he didn't—and he'd begrudge him this bread here, if he knew it."

The deputy marshal nodded comprehendingly, and blew the smoke through his pipe.

"Charged me and Moak thirty-five cents apiece for our breakfasts this mornin', and twenty cents for the horse," he said, in a musing tone. "Reckon he's about the tightest old skinflint on the whole turnpike—and that's sayin' a good deal. So he got drafted, did he? Should 'a' thought he was too old."

"He ain't as old as he looks," explained Job. "He's a good deal meaner, though. I'm glad o' one thing, anyway. I ain't goin' back there any more, except to git my clothes and my money. I'm goin' to hive in here with the old man, and kind o' look after him. I promised—"

"Promised Mose, eh?" broke in the deputy marshal.

"Yes—if you want to know—I did promise Mose! You can't touch me for that!"

"Why, that's skinnin' alive, that is—jest for that alone," said Hazzard, with portentous gravity, "to say nothin' of scootin' over here to give warnin', and bringin' that bread there in your pocket, and so on. Why, it'll puzzle a Philadelphy lawyer to find punishments bad enough for you."

Job looked him searchingly in the eye for a full minute, then held up the fettered hand again.

"Say, unlock this, will you?" he said, unabashed. "I knew you was foolin' all the time," he added, as the other produced the key from his pocket and turned the lock. "I could tell it right from the start."

"Me? me foolin'?" asked Hazzard, with simulated surprise. "Why, you're crazy, boy!"

"No, I spotted it right off," Job replied, eager to put into words the idea that had suddenly come to him. "Why, anybody could tell that. A sure-enough dead shot like you wouldn't fire ten shots at a man and not hit him once, if he wasn't foolin'. It was as plain as the nose on your face—you didn't really want to catch poor Mose. That's what made me take a shine to you, right off."

Norman Hazzard blew more smoke through his pipe, and grinned to himself, and even gave an abrupt little laugh aloud, shifting on the instant to an air of grave imperturbability.

"You mustn't talk like that—that is, outside," he said. "It might give folks wrong notions. Besides, I tell you you're mistaken. I never fired more to kill in all my life. But of course— the old man here—p'r'aps that does make it a little different."

He looked down as he spoke to where old Asa lay, under the overcoat, and Job felt sure that there was a change on his face—a change toward kindliness.

"Well, anyway," the boy persisted, "you wouldn't fire to kill now, if you was to catch up to Mose, and what's more, I don't believe you're goin' to try to catch up to him, neither."

"I ain't, eh?" broke in the deputy marshal. "You wait till

Moak gets back with the snow-shoes. We'll run him down in no time. He ain't got no more chance than a lame mud-turtle."

The words sounded savage enough, and Job, scanning the lean, tanned face of the speaker, found his mind conjuring up again visions of those two other wrong-doers whom this hunter of men had shot down.

And yet, somehow, there seemed to be a sort of relenting twinkle in those sharp, cold, gray eyes of his.

VI

A Home in the Woods

The pursuit of Mose Whipple had to be postponed, as it turned out, whether the deputy marshal relented or not.

It was late, for one thing, before Moak returned from his quest after snow-shoes, and what was worse, he came back empty-handed. He had driven about, over and through the drifted roads, for miles, directed by local rumors and surmise, to one after another of the isolated farm-houses scattered over the district, but had found no snow-shoes.

He was too cold and stiff, and too much annoyed with the day's experiences, to listen to any further delay, but sat doggedly in the sleigh, out on the road in front of the Whipple house, until the deputy marshal, followed by Job, came out to him.

"No, I ain't goin' to get out again, Norm," he said querulously. "I've had enough of this fool's errand. I'm frooze solid now in one position, and I'm gittin' used to it. I don't want to climb out and limber up, and then have to freeze stiff all over again in some new shape. Just you give it up for a bad job, and come along. We can get to Octavius by supper-time if we look sharp."

"I never got beat like this before!" growled Norman Hazzard, kicking into the crust. "I hate to give up a thing this way.

But," he added after a pause, "I s'pose you're right. It *is* a fool's errand, and I guess we're the fools, sure enough."

With a reluctant sigh he knocked the snow off his boots against the runner, as he was about to step into the sleigh. He seated himself beside Moak, and drew the buffalo-robe up over his breast, and said, "All right, go ahead!"

Moak grinned, in spite of his ill-temper.

"I didn't think it'd be as bad as that, Norm," he chuckled, "drivin' you clean out of your senses. Why, man, you're goin' away without your overcoat!"

"No. You mind your own business, Moak!" rejoined the deputy marshal, getting one of his shoulders under the robe.

"Shall I run in and get it for you?" suggested Job, half-turning to hasten on the errand.

"You mind *your* business, too!" said Hazzard, with affected roughness, but with an undertone of humane meaning which both his hearers caught and comprehended. "And look here, boy, if you and the old man find yourselves in need of help, why, you know where I'm to be found. Meanwhile you'd better take this." He handed something to Job.

Mr. Moak cast a look of hostile suspicion at the urchin by the roadside.

"Guess he's more likely to know where Mose Whipple's to be found!" Moak said. Then he drew the reins tight with a jerk, gave a loud, emphatic cluck to the horse, and the sleigh went dashing southward amid a defiant jingling of bells.

The boy stood watching till the vehicle had become a mere dwindling point of blackness on the sunlit waste of snow.

Then he turned his attention to the greenback which the deputy marshal had given him, and looked meditatively at the big and significant "5" on its right-hand corner.

When he lifted his eyes again the sleigh had disappeared. The pursuit of poor Mose was at an end.

When the spring of 1864 came slowly up on the bleak tablelands skirting the Adirondacks, it found the Whipple homestead undoubtedly better off than it had been a year before. Neighbors from Juno Mills who drove by, after the road had settled into usable condition, noticed that the place had been "spruced up," and looked considerably more shipshape than it had ever done in Mose's time. There was even a report down at the Corners that old Asa was going to borrow Taft's two-horse cultivator and put in some crops!

People said "old Asa," but every one knew that this rumor, and all the other comments upon the improved appearance and prospects of the Whipple place, really referred to young Job. Even in this hard-working and tireless region, accustomed as it has always been to energetic and capable boys, men talked this spring approvingly of what the "Parshall youngster" had done, and bragged about having predicted from the start that he had the right stuff in him.

When one comes to set down in words what it was that Job had done, it does not sound very great. He had worked three days a week at the cheese-factory, and gone to school the other three days—that is all. But the outcome of this was that April found old Asa Whipple once more, to all outward appearances, a hale and strong man for his years, and revealed the young lad who had adopted him, so to speak, as an enterprising and efficient member of the sparsely settled community, who had plans for doing things, and worked like a beaver, and paid ready money at the Corner grocery store.

When the talk of the neighborhood drifted to the subject of Mose Whipple's desertion and his supposed flight to Canada, it ended usually in the conclusion that old Asa had made a good exchange in getting such an industrious and go-ahead chap as Job Parshall in Mose's place.

Asa Whipple and Job were at work in the field across the road from the Whipple house one afternoon in mid-May. Job had come back early from the factory to finish a job upon which he had expended all the spare labor of a week. There was a patch of land, some rods square, from which he had up-rooted the black moss. He had ploughed and fertilized it, and sown it with oats.

He had resolved to put this reclaimed land to grass later on, and to this end was now dragging across it a heavy tree bough, old Asa following behind him with a bag of grass seed, which he scattered over the loosened earth as he walked.

Job glanced over his shoulder from time to time to note the uneven way in which the old man cast the flying handfuls to one side.

"Seems to me I ain't ever goin' to make a good farmer of you," he said at last, good-naturedly enough, but still with a suggestion of impatience in his tone. "You'll see that grass come up all in wads and patches. Open your hand more, and try and scatter it regular like. Let me show you again."

The old man stopped, and submissively lent himself afresh to the lesson which Job sought to teach; but at the end he sighed and shook his white head.

"No, I'm too old to learn, Job," he said. "I never was cut out for a farmer, anyway. Besides, what's the use? The black moss'll be all back agin by next spring."

"By that time, if we had good luck with this, we could be keepin' a cow, and p'r'aps a horse to do the work," remonstrated the boy. "If I had a horse, I'd knock that moss endwise, or know the reason why."

A noise from the road close behind them attracted their attention. They turned, screening their eyes against the declining sun to see who was seated in the buggy which had halted there across the tumble-down rail fence. Then old Asa pointed a lean forefinger toward the newcomer.

"That's the reason why!" he said, bitterly.

Job could make out now that it was Elisha Teachout who sat in the buggy. The boy had not seen him since the eventful day of Mose's return and escape, when he had gone over to the big farm-house toward dusk and got his clothes and the money due him. This had not been so easy or pleasant a task that he was rejoiced now to see Mr. Teachout again.

The rich farmer, thinner and yellower and more like a bird of prey than ever against the reddening flare of sunlight, looked over at the pair with an ugly caricature of a smile on his hard, hairless face.

"I happened to be drivin' past," he called out at last, snapping the shrill words forth with a kind of malevolent enjoyment, "and I jest thought I'd stop and mention that I'm going to foreclose on this place in four days' time. I've entered judgment for one hundred and six dollars and seventy-three cents, countin' interest and all. I jest thought that mebbe you'd like to know. The sheriff'll be on hand here bright and early Monday mornin'. It jest occurred to me to speak of it as I was passin'."

With these mocking words still on the air, Mr. Teachout turned and drove down the road a few yards. A thought occurred to him, and he halted long enough to call out, more shrilly than before:—

"That Parshall boy needn't come back and whine around my place to be taken back! I won't hev him!" Then he put whip to his horse and was off.

The two workers in the field looked each other in the face for one dumb moment of bewilderment. Then old Asa took the seed-bag off his arm and deliberately held it upside down, till the last grain had sifted out to the little pile at his feet.

"I don't sow for Elisha Teachout to reap—not if I know myself!" he remarked, grimly.

"Can he do it? Is it as bad as all that?" demanded Job.

Asa nodded his head.

"I s'pose it is," he said. "They ain't no use tryin' to buck against a man like him. He's got the money, and that means he's got the law and the sheriff on his side. No, the jig's up. They ain't nothin' for it but for us to git out Monday."

Job had tossed the heavy bough to one side, and walked to the fence, where he was putting on his coat.

"Oh, yes, there is," said he.

"What do you mean, Job? queried the old man, advancing toward him, "what else kin we do?"

"Git out before Monday," answered the boy, laconically.

They walked in silence across the road, and through the front yard to the house, without exchanging further words. Once indoors, they began to empty drawers, clear cupboards and shelves, and gather the portable belongings of the household into a heap on the table in the living-room. It was not a long task, and they performed it in silence. It was only when they rested upon its completion that the old man said, with a little quaver in his voice:—

"Almost the last words *he* spoke before he went was, 'And in the spring you must come and be with me in the woods.' Them was his identical words. You remember 'em, don't you, Job?"

The boy nodded assent.

"We'll kill the chickens—all five of 'em, and roast 'em to-night. They'll keep that way, and they'll see us through the whole tramp. If you'll see to that, I'll sort this stuff over, and see how much of it we really need. We can burn the rest.

"His grandfather and my father," the old man went on, "started here together, both poor men. He's managed it so that he's got everything and I've got nothing. But he can't prevent my bein' an honest man, and I'll go away not beholden to him for a cent. That was one of his chickens that my boy brought me here, when I was sick and pretty nigh starved to death. Very well, I'll leave one chicken in the coop when we go. It sha'n't be on my mind that I owe Elisha Teachout so much as a pinfeather."

Almost nothing was said between them, either then or during the evening, about Mose. Though they were starting to join him in the morning,—turning their backs upon civilization and the haunts of men,—the reserve which through all these months since his disappearance they had observed about him and his offence still weighed upon their tongues.

But in the dead watches of the night—this last night to be spent under the Whipple roof—Job woke up, where he lay wrapped in his blanket, and heard old Asa's voice softly murmuring, whether in his sleep or not the boy never knew: "In the spring you must come and be with me in the woods!"

Away in the recesses of the forest primeval, in a mountain nook linked by a sparkling band of spring-fed streams and a chain of cascades to the silent thoroughfare of the Raquette water, Mose Whipple had chosen his hiding-place, and built for himself a log hut. Thither came to him now, after a toil-some·three days' journey,—by creek-bed and steep, boulder-strewn ravine, by lonely, placid, still water, and broad, reed-grown beaver-meadow, where the deer fed unalarmed on the lily pads, and the great tracks of the moose lay on the black mud,—old Asa and Job.

There was an idyllic charm in the first few weeks of this re-united life to both father and son. Mose took an excited de-light, after months of solitude, in this new companionship, and in the splendid renewal of youth and high spirits which the free life and air of the wilderness brought to his father.

Job showed his practical character in fixing up a well-built lean-to at the side of the shanty, putting a new roof of spruce bark on the whole structure, and constructing a fishing raft to float on the still water up the outlet.

One day in early July, a chance wanderer in the forest—a Canadian who was looking about with a divining rod for min-erals on the mountain range, and who stopped at the shanty overnight—left behind him a month-old copy of a New York weekly newspaper. In this paper, after breakfast, old Asa, sitting out on a log in the sunlight with his pipe, read the horrible story of the three days' fighting—one might say butchery—at Cold Harbor.

Mose and Job had already started out on a fishing excursion to new waters across the divide. When they returned, along toward four o'clock, they found awaiting them one who seemed scarcely recognizable for Asa, so old and bowed had he once more become.

The change was apparent as they entered the clearing, and beheld him seated by the doorway a full hundred yards away.

"He's had a stroke or something!" Mose exclaimed, and they both started on a run toward him.

As they came up, the old man lifted his head and looked his son in the face, with a glance which the other dimly recalled as belonging to that bitter December day when he had first come home.

"Mose," cried Asa, holding the paper out as he spoke, "it's all wrong! There's no pretendin' it ain't! We've been enjoyin' ourselves here, foolin' ourselves into forgettin', but it's all wrong! There ain't been so much as a word dropped sence the boy and me come here, about this thing, and it seemed as if the whole affair had just slipped our mem'ries—but it won't do. I've been sittin' here ever sence you went away, thinkin' it over—thinkin' hard enough every minute for the whole five months—and it's all wrong. Here, you read this for yourself."

Mose took the paper, and spelt his way through the long, blood-drenched narrative, without a word. When he had finished he returned his father's glance, with a look of mingled comprehension and assent in his eyes.

"All right," he said simply. "I feel the same as you do about it. I'll go!"

Both seemed to feel intuitively that this great resolve, thus formed, could not wait an instant for fulfilment. Hardly another word was spoken until Mose, his pockets filled for the journey and his blanket strapped, stood ready in front of the cabin, to say good-by.

"It's no good waiting till to-morrow," he said then. "The sooner it's over the better. You can get along first-rate here by yourselves. Job can take in skins and so on, and a mess of trout now and then,—he knows the way,—and bring back ammunition and your tobacco and so on. You'll be all right."

He paused a moment, and then took from his finger the little rubber ring which Job had restored to him in Teachout's cowbarn months before, and handed it to Asa.

"Here," he said, "that's a kind of keepsake. Good-by, dad. Good-by, Job."

Half an hour or more had elapsed, and Asa still sat on the log by the doorway, his head buried in thought. He could hear the strokes of Job's axe, from where the boy was cutting firewood for the evening on the edge of the clearing. As they fell on the air with their sharp, metallic ring, one after another, the old man's fancy likened them to the deadly noises of the battle-field, whither his boy was making his way.

But he regretted nothing—no, nothing, save that the act of reparation, of atonement, had not been made long before.

There came with abrupt suddenness another sound—the un-familiar sound of a stranger's voice addressing him. Asa looked up, rousing himself from his reverie with difficulty. He saw that two men with rods, and fishing baskets, and camping packs on their backs, were standing in front of him. Their faces were in the shadow, but he slowly made out the foremost one to be the deputy marshal, Norman Hazzard.

"So here's where you moved to, eh?" the deputy marshal was asking, by way of not unfriendly salutation.

Asa stared hard for a minute at this astonishing apparition. Then his bewildered tongue found words.

"If you're lookin' for my son," he said proudly, "he's gone back to jine his regiment—to do his duty!"

Hazzard stared in turn. "Gone!" he exclaimed, "when?"

"This very day," rejoined Asa, "not an hour ago. He saw it was right, and he went!"

The deputy marshal threw up his hands in a gesture of despairing amazement. "Why, man alive!" he cried, "they'll shoot him like a dog!"

VII

Another Chase after Mose

Asa Whipple and the deputy marshal gazed in a dumfounded way at each other through a cruel minute of silence, broken only by the echoing strokes of Job's axe out in the under-growth beyond. It was the third man who first found his tongue; and Asa, looking dumbly at him, saw that he was no other than Nelse Hornbeck.

"Downright cur'ous that we should 'a' happened to hit on you like this, ain't it?" Nelse began. "If we'd ben tryin' to find you, we'd never 'a' done it in this born world! Norm and me, you see, we've ben fishin' up Panther River three days, and then we followed up the South Branch outlet, and I'd ben figgerin' on makin' a camp by the lake there, an' workin' down the other branch; but the flies were pretty bad, and Norm here, he took a fancy to this 'ere outlet, and our oil of tar was about give out, and so I—"

"Oh, shut up!" broke in the deputy marshal, impatiently. "Look here, Asa Whipple, is that straight what you're telling me—that Mose has started off to give himself up?"

The old man rose from the log and stood erect. He had never seemed so tall before in his life, and he looked down upon the more lithe and sinewy figure of the deputy marshal almost haughtily.

"No, not to give himself up. 'To jine his regiment,' was what I said."

Norman Hazzard snorted out an angry laugh.

"Were there ever two such simpletons under one roof?" he cried. " 'Jine his regiment!' Why, man, I tell you, they'll simply take him and shoot him! They can't do anything else, even if they wanted to. That's the regulations. He can't jine anything, except what the newspapers call the 'silent majority.' Do you mean to tell me—a man of your age—you didn't know *that?*"

"All I know is," said Asa, doggedly, "that Mose seen his duty, and he done it. He left his regiment because there was nothin' doin', and some mean Dutchman who had a spite agin him wouldn't let him git a furlough, and he was scairt to death about me,—and you know as well as I do that if he hadn't come just as he did I'd been a gone coon,—and then he come off up in here, and we followed him, and there was so much to do, fixin' up this new place, that we hadn't time to do much thinkin' about what was right and what was wrong till only this mornin' I happened to git hold o' that paper there, and it seems the war's about ten times worse than ever, and when Mose came in and I showed it to him, and he read it through, he jest give me a look, and says he, 'You're right. I ain't got no business here. I'm off.' And off he went. That's all; and I'm proud of him."

The deputy marshal groaned. "Don't I tell you they won't have him? The minute they lay eyes on him he's a dead man. I don't believe the President himself could save him."

"Why don't you save him yourself?" put in a new voice, abruptly.

Mr. Hazzard turned and beheld Job, who had come up with his axe and a huge armful of wood. He threw these down, brushed his sleeve, and nodded to the deputy marshal.

"How'd do, Norm," he said now. "Why don't you go and stop him yourself?"

Hazzard half-closed one of his eyes, and contemplated Job with a quizzical expression. "Hello, youngster!" he remarked. "You're lookin' after these loons, heh? Well, I wonder you didn't put a veto on this tomfoolery. You're the only party in this camp that seems to have any sense."

"They wouldn't have listened to me," rejoined Job. "They were both too red-hot about the thing to listen to anybody. I thought it was foolishness myself, but they didn't ask me, and so I went and chopped wood and minded my own business. But it'd be different with you. If you could manage to overtake Mose, he'd listen to you. You can catch him if you run."

The deputy marshal on the instant had tossed aside his rod, and was hurriedly getting off his basket and pack.

"I'll have a try for it, anyway," he said. "But it'd be jest like Mose to put his back up and refuse to come, even after I'd caught him."

"Tell him his father wants him to come back," suggested Job. "That'll fetch him. Here, Asa," the boy continued, "give us that ring there. Norm can take that and show it to him as a sign that you've changed your mind. That's the way they do it in the story-books. That's all rings are for, accordin' to them."

"But I don't know as I *hev* changed my mind," old Asa began hesitatingly, but with his fingers on the ring.

"Well, you'll have time to do that while Norm's gone," commented Job.

With grave insistence he took the old rubber ornament from Asa's hand and gave it to Hazzard. "Keep on this side of the outlet," he added. "There's a clear path most of the way. You can get down the big falls by the stones if you go out close to the stream. You'll catch him easy this side of the Raquette."

The deputy marshal wheeled and started down the clearing on a long-stride, loping run, like a greyhound. Almost as they looked he was lost to sight among the trees beyond.

It occurred to Nelse Hornbeck now to relieve himself of his pack and accoutrements, and to make himself otherwise at home. He lighted his pipe, and stretched himself out comfortably on the roots of a stump by the doorway.

"Well," he remarked after a little, "I allus said I'd rather have a pack of nigger bloodhounds after me than Norm Hazzard if I'd done anything that I wanted to git away for. But of course this is different. I don't know how much good he'll be tryin' to catch a man that ain't done anything. I s'pose it would be different, wouldn't it? But then of course he could pretend to himself that Mose had done something—and for that matter, all he's got to do is to play that Mose is still a deserter; and of course if you come to that, why, he *is* a deserter."

"He ain't nothing of the kind!" roared old Asa, with vehemence.

"Well, of course, Asy, if you say so," Nelse hastened to get in, with a pacific wave of his pipe, "I don't pretend to be no jedge myself in military affairs; I dessay you're right. Of course Mose is in one place, and the army's in another, but that don't prove that it wasn't the army that deserted Mose, does it? I'm a man of peace myself, and I don't set up to be no authority on these p'ints."

"Well, then, what are you talkin' about?" interposed Job, severely. "Don't you see old Asa's upset and nervous about Mose? Tell us about things you know something about. How's old Teachout?"

"Well, now, cur'ous enough," said Nelse, thoughtfully, "that's jest one of the things I don't know about at all, and nobody else knows, either—that is, this side o' Jordan. 'Lishe Teachout's ben dead of inflamation o' the lungs now—le's see —up'ards of a month. Why, come to think of it, Asy, why, yes, he ketched his cold goin' out to attend the sheriff's sale at your old place, and that daughter of his that run away with the lightnin'-rod agent—you remember?—she's come in for the hull property, and they say she's goin' to sell it and live down in New York. I guess she'll scatter the money right and left. And 'Lishe worked hard for it, too!"

Old Asa cast a ruminant glance over the little shanty, and the clearing full of warm sunshine, and the broad belt of stately dark firs beyond rustling their boughs in soft harmony with the tinkle of the stream below, and swaying their tall tops gently against the light of bright blue overhead. Then he drew a long, restful breath.

"There's things a heap sight better than money in this world," he said.

Mose had started out on his impulsive errand buoyantly enough. He made his way down the side hill to the outlet with a light, swinging step, and pushed along on the descent of the creek-bed, leaping from boulder to boulder, and skirting the pools with the agility of a practised woodsman, almost as if his mission were a joyful one.

At the outset, indeed, his ruling sensation was one of relief. He had had four months and more of solitude here in the woods, from New Year's through till the weary winter broke at last, in which to think over his performance.

He could not bring himself to regret having come home; the thought that it had saved his father's life settled *that*. But side by side with this conclusion had grown up an intense humiliation and disgust for the necessities which had forced upon him this badge of "deserter." Granted that they were necessities, the badge was an itching and burning brand none the less.

The excitement and change involved in the coming of Asa and Job had drawn his attention away from this for a time, but the sore remained unhealed. With the chance occurrence of the newspaper, and the sight of its effect upon his father, the half-forgotten pain reasserted itself with such stinging force that the one great end in life seemed to be to escape from its intolerable burden.

In this mood of shame and self-reproach, Mose had jumped with hot eagerness at the notion of returning to the ranks, and rushed with unthinking haste to put it into effect.

As the thought came to him now that perhaps this haste had also been unfeeling, he unconsciously slackened the pace at which he was descending the ravine. His father was once more in good health and vigor, no doubt, and was as eager as he himself about having the odium of desertion washed from the family name, if not more eager than he; but Mose began to wish that they had talked it over a little more—that he had made his leave-taking longer and less abrupt.

The war seemed to have become a much bloodier and deadlier thing than he had known it. That paper had spoken of a full hundred thousand men having been lost between the Wilderness and Cold Harbor. It was quite likely that he now, as he swung along down the waterway, was going to his death. In his present mood this had no personal terrors for him, but it did cast a chill shadow over his thoughts of his father.

They two had chosen their own life together—with all the views and aims of other men's lives put quite at one side. Their happiness had not been in making money, in getting fine clothes, or houses, or lands, but just in being together, with the woods and the water and the sky about them.

Oddly enough, Mose remembered now, for the first time almost since his escape from the lines at Brandy Station, that if it had not been for that wretched Teachout mortgage, he need never have gone to the war at all. The draft would have exempted him, as the only support of an aged father. That seemed at first sight to justify him in leaving as he did, and he walked still more slowly now to think this over.

But no, nothing justified him. Perhaps his father's suffering condition excused him in some measure—gave him the right to say that under the circumstances he would do the same thing again; but that wasn't a justification.

So Mose worried his perplexed mind with the confusing moral problems until in sheer self-defence he had to shake them all off, root and branch, and say to himself, "At any rate I'm on my way back; I'm started, and I'll go."

He had halted, as he grasped this solution of the puzzle, to draw breath and look about him. He stood on a jutting spur of naked granite, overhanging the steep, shelving hillside, and commanding a vast panorama of sloping forest reaches, with broken gleams here and there of the Raquette waters way below, and with range upon range of fir-clad mountain cones rising in basins beyond.

It dawned upon him, as his glance wandered over this stupendous prospect, that he had heard at intervals a curious noise in the woods over at his left, as of some big body making its way through the underbrush in haste. If he had had a gun with him he reflected now that he might have investigated the matter.

The sounds seemed more like those made by a bear than by a deer—perhaps more like a moose than either. Mose had never had the fortune to see a moose. It would be just his luck, he thought, with a half-grin, to see one now, when he had no gun, and was quitting the woods forever.

Hark! there was the noise again, below and ahead of him now, but still to the left. He thought he almost saw a dark object push through the bushes, hardly a dozen yards away.

Mose leaped lightly down upon the moss at the base of his perch, and crept cautiously along under the ledge of rock, the cover of which would protect him quite to within a few feet of these bushes. Reaching this point, he lifted his head to look.

His astonished gaze rested upon no moose or bear, or other denizen of the wild wood, but took in at point-blank instead the lean and leathery countenance of Deputy Marshal Norman Hazzard. It in no wise lessened Mose's confusion to note that this unlooked-for countenance wore a somewhat sardonic grin.

"Well, Mose," Mr. Hazzard observed, "I learnt last winter that a stern chase was a long chase, and I thought this time I'd make a slicker job of it by headin' you off, and gittin' 'round in front. See?"

"Yes, I see," said Mose, mechanically; but in truth he felt himself quite unable to see at all. This sudden intrusion of the officer of the law between him and his patriotic resolve, this apparition of the man who had hunted him into the wintry woods with a revolver, seemed to change and confuse everything.

There rose in him the impulse to throw himself fiercely upon the deputy marshal; then, oddly enough, he was conscious of a chuckling sense of amusement instead.

"Guess I got the laugh on you this time, Norm," he said. "You've had your hull trip for nothin'. I'm on my way now, of my own motion, to jine my regiment, or enlist somewhere else, I don't care which."

Mr. Hazzard ostentatiously drew a revolver from his pocket.

"I ain't got any handcuffs with me," he remarked, "but you'll do well to bear in mind that I ain't at all shy about firin' this here, if there's any need for it."

"But I tell you I'm goin' of my own accord!" Mose expostulated. "If you had a hull battery of twelve-pounders with you, I couldn't do no more'n that, could I? You can come along down with me if you like—the hull way—only there's no use o' your bein' disagreeable and goin' round pullin' revolvers."

The deputy marshal did not put up the weapon, and the grin on his face grew deeper.

"Nobody, to look at you," said he, "would think you'd give an officer like me more trouble than any other man in the district. I had about the hottest run on record to chase you safely into the woods here. And now, by gum, here I've had to gallop myself all out of breath, barkin' my shins and skinnin' my elbows in a rough-and-tumble scoot through the underbrush, all to keep you from makin' a fool of yourself agin! It's enough to make a man resign office."

Mose stared at the speaker—puzzled by the smile even more than by this unintelligible talk.

"See here," Norman Hazzard went on, "I represent Uncle Sam, don't I? Well, then, Uncle Sam has to be pretty rough on fellows that shirk, and run away, and behave mean—but he's got a heart inside of him all the same. He knows about you, and he understands that while you did a very bad thing, you did it from first-rate motives. So he says to himself, 'Now if that fellow Mose comes around and pokes himself right under my nose, I'll be obliged to shoot him jest for the effect upon the others; but if he's only got sense enough to lay low, and keep on my blind side, why, I won't hurt a hair of his head.' *Now* do you see?"

"You mean that I'm to stay here?" asked Mose, in bewilderment.

"I mean that you're a dead man if you don't," replied Hazzard. "Of course my business is to arrest you, and take you back to be shot. But I ain't workin' at my trade this week— I'm fishin'. And so I tell you to come back with me, and cook us some trout for supper and shut up, that's all."

"But my father," stammered Mose, "he was as sot on my goin' back as I was—this 'deserter' business has been a-stickin' in his crop all winter."

"No, it's all right," said Hazzard. "I've explained it to him. Here's the ring you give him—to show that he understands it. The fact is, he and you ain't got any business to live outside the woods. You're both too green and too soft to wrastle 'round down amongst folks. They cheat you out of your eye-teeth, and tromple you underfoot, and drive you to the poorhouse or the jail. Jest you and Asa stay up here where you belong, and don't you go down any more, foolin' with that buzz-saw that they call 'civilization.' "

Then the two men turned and began together the ascent of the outlet.

That is the story. A good deal of it I heard from Mose Whipple's own lips, at different times, years after the war, when we sat around the huge fire in front of his shanty in the evening, with the big stars gleaming overhead, and the barking of the timber wolves coming to us from the distant mountain side, through the balmy night silence.

Generally Ex-Sheriff Norman Hazzard was one of our fishing party, and he never failed to joke with Mose about the time when he fired ten shots at a running target, and missed every one.

I picked up from their numerous conversations too,—for Mose, like all the old-time Adirondack guides, would rather talk any time than clean fish or chop fire-wood,—that Asa lived to be a very old Asa indeed, and that young Job Parshall, whom Hazzard took away with him, saw through school, and then set up in business, was already being talked of for supervisor in his native town.

Marsena

I

Marsena Pulford, what time the village of Octavius knew him, was a slender and tall man, apparently skirting upon the thirties, with sloping shoulders and a romantic aspect.

It was not alone his flowing black hair, and his broad shirt-collars turned down after the ascertained manner of the British poets, which stamped him in our humble minds as a living brother to "The Corsair," "The Last of the Suliotes," and other heroic personages engraved in the albums and keepsakes of the period. His face, with its darkling eyes and distinguished features, conveyed wherever it went an impression of proudly silent melancholy. In those days—that is, just before the war —one could not look so convincingly and uniformly sad as Marsena did without raising the general presumption of having been crossed in love. We had a respectful feeling, in his case, that the lady ought to have been named Iñez, or at the very least Oriana.

Although he went to the Presbyterian Church with entire regularity, was never seen in public save in a long-tailed black coat, and in winter wore gloves instead of mittens, the local conscience had always, I think, sundry reservations about the moral character of his past. It would not have been reckoned against him, then, that he was obviously poor. We had not learned in those primitive times to measure people by dollar-mark standards. Under ordinary conditions, too, the fact that he came from New England—had indeed lived in Boston— must have counted rather in his favor than otherwise. But it was known that he had been an artist, a professional painter of pictures and portraits, and we understood in Octavius that this involved acquaintanceship, if not even familiarity, with all sorts of occult and deleterious phases of city life.

Our village held all vice, and especially the vice of other and larger places, in stern reprobation. Yet, though it turned this matter of the newcomer's previous occupation over a good deal in its mind, Marsena carried himself with such a gentle picturesqueness of subdued sorrow that these suspicions were disarmed, or, at the worst, only added to the fascinated interest with which Octavius watched his spare and solitary figure upon its streets, and noted the progress of his efforts to find a footing for himself in its social economy.

It was taken for granted among us that he possessed a fine and well-cultivated mind, to match that thoughtful countenance and that dignified deportment. This assumption continued to hold its own in the face of a long series of failures in the attempt to draw him out. Almost everybody who was anybody at one time or another tried to tap Marsena's mental reservoirs—and all in vain. Beyond the barest commonplaces of civil conversation, he could never be tempted. Once, indeed, he had volunteered to the Rev. Mr. Bunce the statement that he regarded Washington Allston as in several respects superior to Copley; but as no one in Octavius knew who these men were, the remark did not help us much. It was quoted frequently, however, as indicating the lofty and recondite nature of the thoughts with which Mr. Pulford occupied his intellect. As it became more apparent, too, that his reserve must be the outgrowth of some crushing and incurable heart grief, people grew to defer to it and to avoid vexing his silent moods with talk.

Thus, when he had been a resident and neighbor for over two years, though no one knew him at all well, the whole community regarded him with kindly and even respectful emotions, and the girls in particular felt that he was a distinct acquisition to the place.

I have said that Marsena Pulford was poor. Hardly anybody in Octavius ever knew to what pathetic depths his poverty during the second winter descended. There was a period of several months, in sober truth, during which he fed himself upon six or seven cents a day. As he was too proud to dream of asking credit at the grocer's and butcher's, and walked about more primly erect than ever, meantime, in his frock-coat and gloves, no idea of these privations got abroad. And at the end of this long evil winter there came a remarkable spring, which altered in a violent way the fortunes of millions of people— among them Marsena. We have to do with events somewhat subsequent to that even, and with the period of Mr. Pulford's prosperity.

The last discredited strips of snow up in the ravines on the hill-sides were melting away; the robins had come again, and were bustling busily across between the willows, already in the leaf, and the budded elms; men were going about the village streets without their overcoats, and boys were telling exciting tales about the suckers in the creek; our old friend Homer Sage had returned from his winter's sojourn in the county poorhouse at Thessaly, and could be seen daily sitting in the sunshine on the broad stoop of the Excelsior Hotel. It was April of 1862.

A whole year had gone by since that sudden and memorable turn in Marsena Pulford's luck. So far from there being signs now of a possible adverse change, this new springtide brought such an increase of good fortune, with its attendant responsibilities, that Marsena was unable to bear the halcyon burden alone. He took in a partner to help him, and then the firm jointly hired a boy. The partner painted a signboard to mark this double event, in bold red letters of independent form upon a yellow ground:

PULFORD & SHULL.

EMPIRE STATE PORTRAIT ATHENÆUM AND
STUDIO.

War Likenesses at Peace Prices.

Marsena discouraged the idea of hanging this out on the street; and, as a compromise, it was finally placed at the end of the operating-room, where for years thereafter it served for the sitters to stare at when their skulls had been clasped in the iron head-rest and they had been adjured to look pleasant. A more modest and conventional announcement of the new firm's existence was put outside, and Octavius accepted it as proof that the liberal arts were at last established within its borders on a firm and lucrative basis.

The head of the firm was not much altered by this great wave of prosperity. He had been drilled by adversity into such careful ways with his wardrobe that he did not need to get any new clothes. Although the villagers, always kindly, sought now with cordial effusiveness to make him feel one of themselves, and although he accepted all their invitations and showed himself at every public meeting in his capacity as a representative and even prominent citizen, yet the heart of his mystery remained unplucked. Marsena was too busy in these days to be much upon the streets. When he did appear he still walked alone, slowly and with an air of settled gloom. He saluted such passers-by as he knew in stately silence. If they stopped him or joined him in his progress, at the most he would talk sparingly of the weather and the roads.

Neither at the fortnightly sociables of the Ladies' Church Mite Society, given in turn at the more important members' homes, nor in the more casual social assemblages of the place, did Marsena ever unbend. It was not that he held himself aloof, as some others did, from the simple amusements of the evening. He never shrank from bearing his part in "pillow," "clap in and clap out," "post-office," or in whatever other game was to be played, and he went through the kissing penalties and rewards involved without apparent aversion. It was also to be noted, in fairness, that, if any one smiled at him full in the face, he instantly smiled in response. But neither smile nor chaste salute served to lift for even the fleeting instant that veil of reserve which hung over him.

Those who thought that by having Marsena Pulford take their pictures they would get on more intimate terms with him fell into grievous error. He was more sententious and unapproachable in his studio, as he called it, than anywhere else. In the old days, before the partnership, when he did everything himself, his manner in the reception-room downstairs, where he showed samples, gave the prices of frames, and took orders, had no equal for formal frigidity—except his subsequent demeanor in the operating-room upstairs. The girls used to declare that they always emerged from the gallery with "cold shivers all over them." This, however, did not deter them from going again, repeatedly, after the outbreak of the war had started up the universal notion of being photographed.

When the new partner came in, in this April of 1862, Marsena was able to devote himself exclusively to the technical business of the camera and the dark-room, on the second floor. He signalled this change by wearing now every day an old russet-colored velveteen jacket, which we had never seen before. This made him look even more romantically melancholy and picturesque than ever, and revived something of the fascinating curiosity as to his hidden past; but it did nothing toward thawing the ice-bound shell which somehow came at every point between him and the good-fellowship of the community.

The partnership was scarcely a week old when something happened. The new partner, standing behind the little showcase in the reception-room, transacted some preliminary business with two customers who had come in. Then, while the sound of their ascending footsteps was still to be heard on the stairs, he hastily left his post and entered the little work-room at the back of the counter.

"You couldn't guess in a baker's dozen of tries who's gone upstairs," he said to the boy. Without waiting for even one effort, he added: "It's the Parmalee girl, and Dwight Ransom's with her, and he's got a Lootenant's uniform on, and they're goin' to be took together!"

"What of it?" asked the unimaginative boy. He was bending over a crock of nitric acid, transferring from it one by one to a tub of water a lot of spoiled glass plates. The sickening fumes from the jar, and the sting of the acid on his cracked skin, still further diminished his interest in contemporary sociology. "Well, what of it?" he repeated, sulkily.

"Oh, I don't know," said the new partner, in a listless, disappointed way. "It seemed kind o' curious, that's all. Holdin' her head up as high in the air as she does, you wouldn't think she'd so much as look at an ordinary fellow like Dwight Ransom."

"I suppose this is a free country," remarked the boy, rising to rest his back.

"Oh, my, yes," returned the other; "if she's pleased, I'm quite agreeable. And—I don't know, too—I dare say she's gettin' pretty well along. Maybe she thinks they ain't any too much time to lose, and is making a grab at what comes handiest. Still, I should 'a' thought she could 'a' done better than Dwight. I worked with him for a spell once, you know."

There seemed to be very few people with whom Newton Shull had not at one time or another worked. Apparently there was no craft or calling which he did not know something about. The old phrase, "Jack of all trades," must surely have been coined in prophecy for him. He had turned up in Octavius originally, some years before, as the general manager of a "Whaler's Life on the Rolling Deep" show, which was specially adapted for moral exhibitions in connection with church fairs. Calamity, however, had long marked this enterprise for its own, and at our village its career culminated under the auspices of a sheriff's officer. The boat, the harpoons, the panorama sheet and rollers, the whale's jaw, the music-box with its nautical tunes—these were sold and dispersed. Newton Shull remained, and began work as a mender of clocks. Incidentally, he cut out stencil-plates for farmers to label their cheese-boxes with, and painted or gilded ornamental designs on chair-backs through perforated paper patterns. For a time he was a maker of children's sleds. In slack seasons he got jobs to help the druggist, the tinsmith, the dentist, or the Town Clerk, and was equally at home with each. He was one of the founders of the Octavius Philharmonics, and offered to play any instrument they liked, though his preference was for what he called the bull fiddle. He spoke often of having travelled as a bandsman with a circus. We boys believed that he was quite capable of riding a horse bareback as well.

When Marsena Pulford, then, decided that he must have some help, Newton Shull was obviously the man. How the arrangement came to take the form of a partnership was never explained, save on the conservative village theory that Marsena must have reasoned that a partner would be safer with the cash-box downstairs, while he was taking pictures upstairs, than a mere hired man. More likely it grew out of their temperamental affinity. Shull was also a man of grave and depressed moods (as, indeed, is the case with all who play the bass viol), only his melancholy differed from Marsena's in being of a tirelessly garrulous character. This was not always an advantage. When customers came in, in the afternoon, it was his friendly impulse to engage them in conversation at such length that frequently the light would fail altogether before they got upstairs. He recognized this tendency as a fault, and manfully combated it—leaving the reception-room with abruptness at the earliest possible moment, and talking to the boy in the work-room instead.

Mr. Shull was a short, round man, with a beard which was beginning to show gray under the lip. His reception-room manners were urbane and persuasive to a degree, and he particularly excelled in convincing people that the portraits of themselves, which Marsena had sent down to him in the dummy to be dried and varnished, and which they hated vehemently at first sight, were really unique and precious works of art. He had also much success in inducing country folks to despise the cheap ferrotype which they had intended to have made, and to venture upon the costlier ambrotype, daguerreotype, or even photograph instead. If they did not go away with a family album or an assortment of frames that would come in handy as well, it was no fault of his.

He made these frames himself, on a bench which he had fitted up in the work-room. Here he constructed show cases, too, cut out mats and mounts, and did many other things as adjuncts to the business, which honest Marsena had never dreamed of.

"Yes," he went on now, "I carried a chain for Dwight the best part o' one whole summer, when he was layin' levels for that Nedahma Valley Railroad they was figurin' on buildin'. Guess they ruther let him in over that job—though he paid me fair enough. It ain't much of a business, that surveyin'. You spend about half your time in findin' out for the people the way they could do things if they only had the money to do 'em, and the other half in settlin' miserable farmers' squabbles about the boundaries of their land. You've got to pay a man day's wages for totin' round your chain and axe and stakes— and, as like as not, you never get even that money back, let alone any pay for yourself. I know something about a good many trades, and I say surveyin' is pretty nigh the poorest of 'em all."

"George Washington was a surveyor," commented the boy, stooping down to his task once more.

"Yes," admitted Mr. Shull; "so he was, for a fact. But then he had influence enough to get government jobs. I don't say there ain't money in that. If Dwight, now, could get a berth on the canal, say, it 'ud be a horse of another color. They say, there's some places there that pay as much as $3 a day. That's how George Washington got his start, and, besides, he owned his own house and lot to begin with. But you'll take notice that he dropped surveyin' like a hot potato the minute there was any soldierin' to do. He knew which side *his* bread was buttered on!"

"Well," said the boy, slapping the last plates sharply into the tub, "that's just what Dwight's doin' too, ain't it?"

"Yes," Mr. Shull conceded; "but it ain't the same thing. You won't find Dwight Ransom gettin' to be general, or much of anything else. He's a nice fellow enough, in his way, of course; but, somehow, after it's all said and done, there ain't much to him. I always sort o' felt, when I was out with him, that by good rights I ought to be working the level and him hammerin' in the stakes."

The boy sniffed audibly as he bore away the acid-jar. Mr. Shull went over to the bench, and took up a chisel with a meditative air. After a moment he lifted his head and listened, with aroused interest written all over his face.

There had been audible from the floor above, at intervals, the customary noises of the camera being wheeled about to different points under the sky-light. There came echoing downward now quite other and most unfamiliar sounds—the clatter of animated, even gay, conversation, punctuated by frank outbursts of laughter. Newton Shull could hardly believe his ears; but they certainly did tell him that there were three parties to that merriment overhead. It was so strange that he laid aside the chisel, and tiptoed out into the reception-room, with a notion of listening at the stair door. Then he even more hurriedly ran back again. They were coming downstairs.

It might have been a whole wedding-party that trooped down the resounding stairway, the voices rising above the clump of Dwight's artillery boots and sword on step after step, and overflowed into the stuffy little reception-room with a cheerful tumult of babble. The new partner and the boy looked at each other, then directed a joint stare of bewilderment toward the door.

Julia Parmalee had pushed her way behind the show-case, and stood in the entrance to the work-room, peering about her with an affectation of excited curiosity which she may have thought pretty and playful, but which the boy, at least, held to be absurd.

She had been talking thirteen to the dozen all the time. "Oh, I really must see everything!" she rattled on now. "If I could be trusted alone in the dark-room with you, Mr. Pulford, I surely may be allowed to explore all these minor mysteries. Oh, I see," she added, glancing round, and incidentally looking quite through Mr. Shull and the boy, as if they had been transparent: "here's where the frames and the washing are done. How interesting!"

What really was interesting was the face of Marsena Pulford, discernible in the shadow over her shoulder. No one in Octavius had ever seen such a beaming smile on his saturnine countenance before.

II

Next to the War, the chief topic of interest and conversation in Octavius at this time was easily Miss Julia Parmalee.

To begin with, her family had for two generations or more been the most important family in the village. When Lafayette stopped here to receive an address of welcome, on his tour through the State in 1825, it was a Parmalee who read that address, and who also, as tradition runs, made on his own account several remarks to the hero in the French language, all of which were understood. The elder son of this man has a secure place in history. He is the Judge Parmalee whose portrait hangs in the Court House, and whose learned work on "The Treaties of the Tuscarora Nation," handsomely bound in morocco, used to have a place of honor on the parlor table of every well-to-do and cultured Octavius home.

This Judge was a banker, too, and did pretty well for himself in a number of other commercial paths. He it was who built the big Parmalee house, with a stone wall in front and the great garden and orchard stretching back to the next street, and the buff-colored statues on either side of the gravelled walk, where the Second National Dearborn County Bank now stands. The Judge had no children, and, on his widow's death, the property went to his much younger brother Charles, who, from having been as a stripling on some forgotten Governor's staff, bore through life the title of Colonel in the local speech.

This Colonel Parmalee had a certain distinction, too, though not of a martial character. His home was in New York, and for many years Octavius never laid eyes on him. He was understood to occupy a respected place among American men of letters, though exactly what he wrote did not come to our knowledge. It was said that he had been at Brook Farm. I have not been able to find any one who remembers him there, but the report is of use as showing the impression of superior intellectual force which he created, even by hearsay, in his native village. When he finally came back to us, to play his part as head of the Parmalee house, we saw at intervals, when the sun was warm and the sidewalks were dry, the lean and bent figure of an old man, with a very yellow face and a sharp-edged brown wig, moving feebly about with a thick gray shawl over his shoulders. His housekeeper was an elderly maiden cousin, who seemed never to come out at all, whether the sun was shining or not.

There were three or four of the Colonel's daughters—all tall, well-made girls, with strikingly dark skins, and what we took to be gypsyish faces. Their appearance certainly bore out the rumor that their mother had been an opera-singer—some said an Italian, others a lady of Louisiana Creole extraction. No information, except that she was dead, ever came to hand about this person. Her daughters, however, were very much in evidence. They seemed always to wear white dresses, and they were always to be seen somewhere, either on their lawn playing croquet, or in the streets, or at the windows of their house. The consciousness of their existence pervaded the whole village from morning till night. To watch their goings and comings, and to speculate upon the identity and business of the friends from strange parts who were continually arriving to visit them, grew to be quite the standing occupation of the idler portion of the community.

Before such of our young people as naturally took the lead in these matters had had time to decide how best to utilize for the general good this influx of beauty, wealth, and ancestral dignity, the village was startled by an unlooked-for occurrence. A red carpet was spread one forenoon from the curb to the doorway of the Episcopal church: the old-fashioned Parmalee carriage turned out, with its driver clasping white reins in white cotton gloves; we had a confused glimpse of the dark Parmalee girls with bouquets in their hands, and dressed rather more in white than usual: and then astonished Octavius learned that two of them had been married, right there under its very eyes, and had departed with their husbands. It gave an angry twist to the discovery to find that the bridegrooms were both strangers, presumably from New York.

This episode had the figurative effect of doubling or trebling the height of that stone wall which stood between the Parmalee place and the public. Such budding hopes and projects of intimacy as our villagers may have entertained toward these polished newcomers fell nipped and lifeless on the stroke. Shortly afterward—that is to say, in the autumn of 1860—the family went away, and the big house was shut up. News came in time that the Colonel was dead: something was said about another daughter's marriage; then the war broke out, and gave us other things to think of. We forgot all about the Parmalees.

It must have been in the last weeks of 1861 that our vagrant attention was recalled to the subject by the appearance in the village of an elderly married couple of servants, who took up their quarters in the long empty mansion, and began fitting it once more for habitation. They set all the chimneys smoking, shovelled the garden paths clear of snow, laid in huge supplies of firewood, vegetables, and the like, and turned the whole place inside out in a vigorous convulsion of housecleaning. Their preparations were on such a bold, large scale that we assumed the property must have passed to some voluminous collateral branch of the family, hitherto unknown to us. It came indeed to be stated among us, with an air of certainty, that a remote relation named Amos or Erasmus Parmalee, with eight or more children and a numerous adult household, was coming to live there. The legend of this wholly mythical personage had nearly a fortnight's vogue, and reached a point of distinctness where we clearly understood that the coming stranger was a violent secessionist. This seemed to open up a troubled and sinister prospect before loyal Octavius, and there was a good deal of plain talk in the barroom of the Excelsior Hotel as to how this impending crisis should be met.

It was just after New Year's that our suspense was ended. The new Parmalees came, and Octavius noted with a sort of disappointed surprise that they turned out to be merely a shorn and trivial remnant of the old Parmalees. They were in fact only a couple of women—the elderly maiden cousin who had presided before over the Colonel's household, and the youngest of his daughters, by name Miss Julia. What was more, word was now passed round upon authority that these were the sole remaining members of the family—that there never had been any Amos or Erasmus Parmalee at all.

The discovery cast the more heroic of our village home-guards into a temporary depression. It could hardly have been otherwise, for here were all their fine and strong resolves, their publicly registered vows about scowling at the odious Southern sympathizer in the street, about a "horning" party outside his house at night, about, perhaps, actually riding him on a rail—all brought to nothing. A less earnest body of men might have suspected in the situation some elements of the ridiculous. They let themselves down gently, however, and with a certain dignified sense of consolation that they had, at all events, shown unmistakably how they would have dealt with Amos or Erasmus Parmalee if there had been such a man, and he had moved to Octavius and had ventured to flaunt his rebel sentiments in their outraged faces.

The village, as a whole, consoled itself on more tangible grounds. It has been stated that Miss Julia Parmalee arrived at the family homestead in early January. Before April had brought the buds and birds, this young woman had become President of the St. Mark's Episcopal Ladies' Aid Society; had organized a local branch of the Sanitary Commission, and assumed active control of all its executive and clerical functions; had committed the principal people of the community to holding a grand festival and fair in May for the Field Hospital and Nurse Fund; had exhibited in the chief store window on Main Street a crayon portrait of her late father, and four water-color drawings of European scenery, all her own handiwork; had published over her signature, in the Thessaly *Banner of Liberty,* an original and spirited poem on "Pale Columbia, Shriek to Arms!" which no one could read without patriotic thrills; and had been reported, on more or less warrant of appearances, to be engaged to four different young men of the place. Truly a remarkable young woman!

We were only able in a dim kind of way to identify her with one of the group of girls in white dresses whom the village had stared at and studied from a distance two years before. There was no mystery about it, however; she was the youngest of them. They had all looked so much alike, with their precocious growth, their olive skins and foreign features, that we were quite surprised to find now that this one, regarded by herself, must be a great deal younger than the others. Perhaps it was only our rustic shyness which had imputed to the sisterhood, in that earlier experience, the hauteur and icy reserve of the rich and exclusive. We recognized now that if the others were at all like Julia, we had made an absurd mistake. It was impossible that any one could be freer from arrogance or pretence than Octavius found her to be. There were some, indeed, who deemed her emancipation almost too complete.

Some there were, too, who denied that she was beautiful, or even very good-looking. There is an old daguerreotype of her as she was in those days—or rather as she seemed to be to the unskilled sunbeams of the sixties—which gives these censorious people the lie direct. It is true that her hair is confined in a net at the sides and drawn stiffly across her temples from the parting. The full throat rises sheer from a flat horizon of striped dress goods, and is offered no relief whatever by the wide fall-ing-away collar of coarse lace. And oh! the strangeness of that frock! The shoulder seams are to be looked for half-way down the upper arm, the sleeves swell themselves out into shapeless bags, the waist front might be the cover of a chair, of a guitar, of the documents in a corporation suit—of anything under the sun rather than the form of a charming girl. Yet, when you look at this thin old picture, all the same, you feel that you understand how it was that Julia Parmalee took the shine out of all the other girls in Octavius.

This is the likeness of her which always seemed to me the best, but Marsena Pulford made a great many others as well. When you reflect, indeed, that his output of portraits of Julia Parmalee was limited in time to the two months of April and May, their number suggests that he could hardly have done anything else the while.

The first of this large series of pictures was the one which Marsena liked least. It is true that Julia looked well in it, standing erect, with a proud, fine backward tilt to her dark face, and a delicately formed white hand resting gracefully on the back of a chair. But it happened that in that chair was seated Lieut. Dwight Ransom, all spick and span in his uni-form, with his big gauntlets and sword hilt brought prominently forward, and with a kind of fatuous smile on his ruddy face, as if he felt the presence of those fair fingers on the chair-back, so teasingly close to his shoulder-strap.

Marsena, in truth, had a strong impulse to run a destroying thumbnail over the seated figure on this plate, when the action of the developer began to reveal its outline under the faint yellow light in the dark-room. Of all the myriad pictures he had washed and drained and nursed in their wet growth over this tank, no other had ever stirred up in his breast such a swift and sharp hostility. He lavished the deadly cyanide upon that por-tion of the plate, too, with grim unction, and noted the results with a scornful curl on his lip. Like his partner downstairs, he was wondering what on earth possessed Miss Parmalee to take up with a Dwight Ransom. The frown was still on his brow when he opened the dark-room door. Then he started back, flushed red, and labored at an embarrassed smile. Miss Parmalee had left her place and stood right in front of him, so near that he almost ran against her. She beamed confidently and reassuringly upon him.

"Oh, I want to come in and see you do all that," she exclaimed, with vivacity. "It didn't occur to me till after you'd shut the door, or I'd have asked to come in with you. I have the greatest curiosity about all these matters. Oh, it is all done? That's too bad! But you can make another one—and that I can see from the beginning. You know, I'm something of an artist myself; I've taken lessons for years—and this all interests me so much! No, Lieutenant!"—she called out from where she was standing just inside the open door, at sound of her companion's rising—"you stay where you are! There's going to be another, and it's such trouble to get you posed properly. Try and keep exactly as you were."

Thus it happened that she stood very close to Marsena, as he took out another plate, flooded it with the sweet-smelling, pungent collodion, and, with furtive precautions against the light, lowered it down into the silver bath. Then he had to shut the door, and she was still there just beside him. He heard himself pretending to explain the processes of the films to her, but his mind was concentrated instead upon a suggestion of perfume which she had brought into the reeking little cupboard of a room, and which mingled languorously with the scents of ether and creosote in the air. He had known her by sight for a couple of months; he had been introduced to her only a week or so ago, and that in the most casual way; yet, strange enough, he could feel his hand trembling as it perfunctorily moved the plate dipper up and down in the bath.

A gentle voice fell upon the darkness. "Do you know, Mr. Pulford," it murmured, "I felt sure that you were an artist, the very first time I saw you."

Marsena heaved a long sigh—a sigh with a tremulous catch in it, as where sorrow and sweet solace should meet. "I did start out to be one," he answered, "but I—I never amounted to anything at it. I tried for years, but I wasn't any good. I had to give it up—at last—and take to this instead."

He lifted the plate with caution, bent to look obliquely across its surface, and lowered it again. Then all at once he turned abruptly and faced her. They were so close to each other that even in the obscure gloom she caught the sudden flash of resolution in his eyes.

"I'll tell you what I never told any other living soul," he said, beginning with husky eagerness, but lapsing now into grave deliberation of emphasis: "I hate—this—like pizen!"

In the silence which followed, Marsena mechanically took the plate from the bath, fastened it in the holder, and stepped to the door. Then he halted, to prolong for one little instant this tender spell of magic which had stolen over him. Here, in the close darkness beside him, was a sorceress, a siren, who had at a glance read his sore heart's deepest secret—at a word drawn the confession of his maimed and embittered pride. It was like being shut up with an angel, who was also a beautiful woman. Oh, the wonder of it! Broad sunlit landscapes with Italian skies seemed to be forming themselves before his mind's eye; his soul sang songs within him. He very nearly dropped the plateholder.

The soft, hovering, half touch of a hand upon his arm, the cool, restful tones of the voice in the darkness, came to complete the witchery.

"I know," she said, "I can sympathize with you. I also had my dreams, my aspirations. But you are wrong to think that you have failed. Why, this beautiful work of yours, it all is Art—pure Art. No person who really knows could look at it and not see that. No, Mr. Pulford, you do yourself an injustice; believe me, you do. Why, you couldn't help being an artist if you tried; it's born in you. It shows in everything you do. I saw it from the very first."

The unmistakable sound of Dwight Ransom's large artillery boots moving on the floor outside intervened here, and Marsena hurriedly opened the door. The Lieutenant glanced with good-natured raillery at the couple who stood revealed, blinking in the sharp light.

"One of my legs got asleep," he remarked, by way of explanation, "so I had to get up and stamp around. I began to think," he added, "that you folks were going to set up housekeeping in there, and not come out any more at all."

"Don't be vulgar, if you please," said Julia Parmalee, with a dash of asperity in what purported to be a bantering tone. "We were talking of matters quite beyond you—of Art, if you desire to know. Mr. Pulford and I discover that we have a great many opinions and sentiments about Art in common. It is a feeling that no one can understand unless they have it."

"It's the same with getting one's leg asleep," said Dwight, "quite the same, I assure you"; and then came the laughter which Newton Shull heard downstairs.

III

A day or two later Battery G left Octavius for the seat of war.

It was not nearly so imposing an event as a good many others which had stirred the community during the previous twelve months. There were already two regiments in the field recruited from our end of Dearborn County, and in these at least six or seven companies were made up wholly of Octavius men. There had been big crowds, with speeches and music by the band, to see them off at the old depot.

When they returned, their short term of service having expired, there were still more fervent demonstrations, to which zest was added by the knowledge that they were all to enlist again, and then we shortly celebrated their second departure.

Some there were who returned in mute and cold finality—term of enlistment and life alike cut short—and these were borne through our streets with sombre martial pageantry, the long wail of the funeral march reaching out to include the whole valley side in its note of lamentation. Besides all this, hardly a week passed that those of us who hung about the station could not see a train full of troops on their way to or from the South. A year of these experiences had left us seasoned veterans in sightseeing, by no means to be fluttered by trifles.

As a matter of fact, the village did not take Battery G very seriously. To begin with, it mustered only some dozen men, at least so far as our local contribution went, and there was a feeling that we couldn't be expected to go much out of our way for such a paltry number. Then, again, an artillery force was somewhat out of joint with our notion of what Octavius should do to help suppress the Rebellion. Infantrymen with muskets we could all understand—could all be, if necessary. Many of the farmer boys round about, too, made good cavalrymen, because they knew both how to ride and how to groom a horse. But in the name of all that was mysterious, why artillerymen? There had never been a cannon within fifty miles of Octavius; that is, since the Revolution. Certainly none of our citizens had the least idea how to fire one off. These enlisted men of Battery G were no better posted than the rest; it would take them a three days' journey to reach the point where, for the first time, they were to see their strange weapon of warfare. This seemed to us rather foolish.

Moreover, there was a government proclamation just out, it was said, discontinuing further enlistments and disbanding the recruiting offices scattered over the North. This appeared to imply that the war was about over, or at least that they had more soldiers already than they knew what to do with. There were some who questioned whether, under these circumstances, it was worth while for Battery G to go at all.

But go it did, and at the last moment quite a throng of people found themselves gathered at the station to say good-by.

A good many of these were the relations and friends of the dozen ordinary recruits, who would not even get their uniforms and swords till they reached Tecumseh. But the larger portion, I should think, had come on account of Lieutenant Ransom.

Dwight was hail-fellow-well-met with more people within a radius of twenty miles or so, probably, than any other man in the district. He was a good-looking young man, rather stocky in build and deeply sunburned. Through the decent months of the year he was always out of doors, either tramping over the country with a level over his shoulder, or improving the days with a shotgun or fishpole. At these seasons he was generally to be found of an evening at the barber's shop, where he told more new stories than any one else. When winter came his chief work was in his office, drawing maps and plans. He let his beard grow then, and spent his leisure for the most part playing checkers at the Excelsior Hotel.

His habitual free-and-easy dress and amiable laxity of manners tended to obscure in the village mind the facts that he came from one of the best families of the section, that he had been through college, and that he had some means of his own. His mother and sisters were very respectable people indeed, and had one of the most expensive pews in the Episcopal church. It was not observed, however, that Dwight ever accompanied them thither or that he devoted much of his time to their society at home. It began to be remarked, here and there, that it was getting to be about time for Dwight Ransom to steady down, if he was ever going to. Although everybody liked him and was glad to see him about, an impression was gradually shaping itself that he never would amount to much.

All at once Dwight staggered the public consciousness by putting on his best clothes one Sunday and going with his folks to church. Those who saw him on the way there could not make it out at all, except on the hypothesis that there had been a death in the family. Those who encountered him upon his return from the sacred edifice, however, found a clue to the mystery ready made. He was walking home with Julia Parmalee.

There were others whose passionate desire it was to walk home with Julia. They had been enlivening Octavius with public displays of their rivalry for something like two months when Dwight appeared on the scene as a competitor. Easy-going as he was in ordinary matters, he revealed himself now to be a hustler in the courts of love. It took him but a single day to drive the teller of the bank from the field. The Principal of the Seminary, a rising young lawyer, and the head bookkeeper at the freight-house, severally went by the board within a fortnight.

There remained old Dr. Conger's son Emory, who was of a tougher fibre and gave Dwight several added weeks of combat. He enjoyed the advantage of having nothing whatever to do. He possessed, moreover, a remarkably varied wardrobe and white hands, and loomed unique among the males of our town in his ability to play on the piano. With such aids a young man may go far in a quiet neighborhood, and for a time Emory Conger certainly seemed to be holding his own, if not more. His discomfiture, when it came, was dramatic in its swift completeness. One forenoon we saw Dwight on the street in a new and resplendent officer's uniform, and learned that he had been commissioned to raise a battery. That very evening the doctor's son left town, and the news went round that Lieutenant Ransom was engaged to Miss Parmalee.

An impression prevailed that Dwight would not have objected to let the matter rest there. He had gained his point, and might well regard the battery and the war itself as things which had served their purpose and could now be dispensed with. No one would have blamed him much for feeling that way about it.

But this was not Julia's view. She adopted the battery for her own while it was still little more than a name, and swept it forward with such a swirling rush of enthusiasm that the men were all enlisted, the organization settled, and the date of departure for the front sternly fastened, before anybody could lay a hand to the brakes. Her St. Mark's Ladies' Aid Society presented Dwight with a sword. Her branch of the Sanitary Commission voted to entertain the battery with a hot meal in the depot yard before it took the train. We have seen how she went and had herself photographed standing proudly behind the belted and martial Dwight. After these things it was impossible for Battery G to back out.

The artillerymen had a bright blue sky and a warm sunlit noontide for their departure. Even the most cynical of those who had come to see them off yielded toward the end to the genial influence of the weather and the impulse of good-fellowship, and joined in the handshaking at the car windows, and in the volley of cheers which were raised as the train drew slowly out of the yard.

At this moment the ladies of the Sanitary Commission had to bestir themselves to save the remnant of oranges and sandwiches on their tables from the swooping raid of the youth of Octavius, and, what with administering cuffs and shakings, and keeping their garments out of the way of coffee-cups overturned in the scramble, had no time to watch Julia Parmalee.

The men gathered in the yard kept her steadily in view, however, as she stood prominently in front of the throng, on the top of a baggage truck, and waved her handkerchief until the train had dwindled into nothingness down the valley. These observers had an eye also on three young men who had got as near this truck as possible. Interest in Dwight and his battery was already giving place to curiosity as to which of these three —the bank-teller, the freight-house clerk, or the rising young lawyer—would win the chance of helping Julia down off her perch.

No one was prepared for what really happened. Miss Parmalee turned and looked thoughtfully, one might say abstractedly, about her. Somehow she seemed not to see any of the hands which were eagerly uplifted toward her. Instead, her musing gaze roved lightly over the predatory scuffle among the tables, over the ancient depot building, over the assembled throng of citizens in the background, then wandered nearer, with the pretty inconsequence of a butterfly's flight. Of course it was the farewell to Dwight which had left that soft, rosy flush in her dark, round cheeks. The glance that she was sending idly fluttering here and there did not seem so obviously connected with the Lieutenant. Of a sudden it halted and went into a smile.

"Oh, Mr. Pulford! May I trouble you?" she said in very distinct tones, bending forward over the edge of the truck, and holding forth two white and most shapely hands.

Marsena was standing fully six feet away. Like the others, he had been looking at Miss Parmalee, but with no hint of expectation in his eyes. This abrupt summons seemed to surprise him even more than it did the crowd. He started, changed color, fixed a wistful, almost pleading stare upon the sunlit vacancy just above the head of the enchantress, and confusedly fumbled with his glove tips, as if to make bare his hands for this great function. Then, straightening himself, he slowly moved toward her like one in a trance.

The rivals edged out of Marsena's way in dumfounded silence, as if he had been walking in his sleep, and waking were dangerous. He came up, made a formal bow, and lifted his gloved hands in chivalrous pretence of guiding the graceful little jump which brought Miss Parmalee to the ground—all with a pale, motionless face upon which shone a solemn ecstacy.

It was Marsena's habit, when out of doors, to carry his right hand in the breast of his frock-coat. As he made an angle of his elbow now, from sheer force of custom, Julia promptly took the movement as a proffer of physical support, and availed herself of it. Marsena felt himself thrilling from top to toe at the touch of her hand upon his sleeve. If there rose in his mind an awkward consciousness that this sort of thing was unusual in Octavius by daylight, the embarrassment was only momentary. He held himself proudly erect, and marched out of the depot yard with Miss Parmalee on his arm.

As Homer Sage remarked that evening on the stoop of the Excelsior Hotel, this event made the departure of Battery G seem by comparison very small potatoes indeed.

It was impossible for the twain not to realize that everybody was looking at them, as they made their way up the shady side of the main street. But there is another language of the hands than that taught in deaf-mute schools, and Julia's hand seemed to tell Marsena's arm distinctly that she didn't care a bit. As for him, after that first nervous minute or two, the experience was all joy—joy so profound and overwhelming that he could only ponder it in dazzled silence. It is true that Julia was talking—rattling on with sprightly volubility about all sorts of things—but to Marsena her remarks no more invited answers than does so much enthralling music. When she stopped for a breath he did not remember what she had been saying. He only knew how he felt.

"I wish you'd come straight to the gallery with me," he said; "I'd like first-rate to make a real picture of you—by yourself."

"Well, I swow!" remarked Mr. Newton Shull, along in the later afternoon; "I didn't expect we'd make our salt to-day, with Marsena away pretty near the whole forenoon, and all the folks down to the depot, and here it turns out way the best day we've had yet. Actually had to send people away!"

"Guess that didn't worry him much," commented the boy, from where he sat on the work-bench swinging his legs in idleness.

Mr. Shull nodded his head suggestively. "No, I dare say not," he said. "I kind o' begrudge not bein' an operator myself, when such setters as that come in. She must have been up there a full two hours—them two all by themselves—and the countrymen loafin' around out in the reception-room there, stompin' their feet and grindin' their teeth, jest tired to death o' waitin'. It went agin my grain to tell them last two lots they'd have to come some other day; but—I dunno—perhaps it's jest as well. They'll go and tell it around that we've got more'n we can do— and that's good for business. But, all the same, it seemed to me as if he took considerable more time than was really needful.

He can turn out four farmers in fifteen minutes, if he puts on a spurt; and here he was a full two hours, and only five pictures of her to show for it."

"Six," said the boy.

"Yes, so it was—countin' the one with her hair let down," Mr. Shull admitted. "I dunno whether that one oughtn't to be a little extry. I thought o' tellin' her that it would be, on account of so much hair consumin' more chemicals; but—I dunno—somehow—she sort o' looked as if she knew better. Did you ever notice them eyes o' hern, how they look as if they could see straight through you, and out on the other side?"

The boy shook his head. "I don't bother my head about women," he said. "Got somethin' better to do."

"Guess that's a pretty good plan too," mused Mr. Shull. "Somehow you can't seem to make 'em out at all. Now, I've been around a good deal, and yet somehow I don't feel as if I knew much about women. I'm bound to say, though," he added upon reflection, "they know considerable about me."

"I suppose the first thing we know now," remarked the boy, impatiently changing the subject, "McClellan 'll be in Richmond. They say it's liable to happen now any day."

Newton Shull was but a lukewarm patriot. "They needn't hurry on my account," he said. "It would be kind o' mean to have the whole thing fizzle out now, jest when the picture business has begun to amount to something. Why, we must have took in up'ards of $11 to-day—frames and all—and two years ago we'd 'a' been lucky to get in $3. Let's see: there's two fifties and five thirty-fives, that's $2.75, and the Dutch boy with the drum, that's $3.40, counting the mat, and then there's Miss Parmalee—four daguerreotypes, and two negatives, and small frames for each, and two large frames for crayons she's going to do herself, and cord and nails—I suppose she'll think them ought to be thrown in—"

"What! didn't you make her pay in advance?" asked the boy. "I thought everybody had to."

"You got to humor some folks," explained Mr. Shull, with a

note of regret in his voice. "These big bugs with plenty o' money always have to be waited on. It ain't right, but it has to be. Besides, you can always slide on an extra quarter or so when you send in the bill. That sort o' evens the thing up. Now, in her case, for instance, where we'd charge ordinary folks a dollar for two daguerreotypes, we can send her in a bill for—"

Neither Mr. Shull nor the boy had heard Marsena's descending steps on the staircase, yet at this moment he entered the little work-room and walked across it to the bay window, where the printing was done. There was an unusual degree of abstraction in his face and mien—unusual even for him—and he drummed absent-mindedly on the panes as he stood looking out at the street or the sky, or whatever it was his listless gaze beheld.

"How much do you think it 'ud be safe to stick Miss Parmalee apiece for them daguerreotypes?" asked Newton Shull of his partner.

Marsena turned and stared for a moment as if he doubted having heard aright. Then he made curt answer: "She is not to be charged anything at all. They were made for her as presents."

It was the other partner's turn to stare.

"Well, of course—if you say it's all right," he managed to get out, "but I suppose on the frames we can—"

"The frames are presents, too," said Marsena, with decision.

IV

During the fortnight or three weeks following the departure of Battery G it became clear to every one that the war was as good as over. It had lasted already a whole year, but now the end was obviously at hand. The Union army had the Rebels cooped up in Yorktown—the identical place where the British had been compelled to surrender at the close of the Revolution —and it was impossible that they should get away. The very coincidence of locality was enough in itself to convince the most skeptical.

We read that Fitz John Porter had a balloon fastened by a rope, in which he daily went up and took a look through his field-glasses at the Rebels, all miserably huddled together in their trap, awaiting their doom. Our soldiers wrote home now that final victory could only be a matter of a few weeks, or months at the most. Some of them said they would surely be home by haying time. Their letters no longer dwelt upon battles, or the prospect of battles, but gossiped about the jealousies and quarrels among our generals, who seemed to dislike one another much more than they did the common enemy, and told us long and quite incredible tales about the mud in Virginia. No soldier's letter that spring was complete without a chapter on the mud. There were many stories about mules and their contraband drivers being bodily sunk out of sight in these weltering seas of mire, and of new boots being made for the officers to come up to their armpits, which we hardly knew whether to believe or not. But about the fact that peace was practically within view there could be no doubt.

Under the influence of this mood, Miss Parmalee's ambitious project for a grand fair and festival in aid of the Field Hospital and Nurse Fund naturally languished. If the war was coming to a close so soon, there could be no use in going to so much worry and trouble, to say nothing of the expense.

Miss Julia seemed to take this view of it herself. She ceased active preparation for the fair, and printed in the Thessaly *Banner of Liberty* a beautiful poem over her own name entitled "The Dove-like Dawn of White-winged Peace." She also got herself some new and summery dresses, of gay tints and very fashionable form, and went to be photographed in each. Her almost daily presence at the gallery came, indeed, to be a leading topic of conversation in Octavius. Some said that she was taking lessons of Marsena—learning to make photographs—

but others put a different construction on the matter and winked as they did so.

As for Marsena, he moved about the streets these days with his head among the stars, in a state of rapt and reverent exaltation. He had never been what might be called a talker, but now it was as much as the best of us could do to get any kind of word from him. He did not seem to talk to Julia any more than to the general public, but just luxuriated with a dumb solemnity of joy in her company, sitting sometimes for hours beside her on the piazza of the Parmalee house, or focusing her pretty image with silent delight on the ground glass of his best camera day after day, or walking with her, arm in arm, to the Episcopal church on Sundays. He had always been a Presbyterian before, but now he bore himself in the prominent Parmalee pew at St. Mark's with stately correctness, rising, kneeling, seating himself, just as the others did, and helping Miss Julia hold her Prayer Book with an air of having known the ritual from childhood.

No doubt a good many people felt that all this was rough on the absent Dwight Ransom, and probably some of them talked openly about it; but interest in this aspect of the case was swallowed up in the larger attention now given to Marsena Pulford himself. It began to be reported that he really came of an extraordinarily good family in New England, and that an uncle of his had been in Congress. The legend that he had means of his own did not take much root, but it was admitted that he must now be simply coining money. Some went so far as to estimate his annual profits as high as $1,500, which sounded to the average Octavian like a dream. It was commonly understood that he had abandoned an earlier intention to buy a house and lot of his own, and this clearly seemed to show that he counted upon going presently to live in the Parmalee mansion. People speculated with idle curiosity as to the likelihood of this coming to pass before the war ended and Battery G returned home.

Suddenly great and stirring news fell upon the startled North and set Octavius thrilling with excitement, along with every other community far and near. It was in the first week or so of May that the surprise came; the Rebels, whom we had supposed to be securely locked up in Yorktown, with no alternative save starvation or surrender, decided not to remain there any longer, and accordingly marched comfortably off in the direction of Richmond!

Quick upon the heels of this came tidings that the Union army was in pursuit, and that there had been savage fighting with the Confederate rear-guard at Williamsburg. The papers said that the war, so far from ending, must now be fought all over again. The marvellous story of the Monitor and Merrimac sent our men-folks into a frenzy of patriotic fervor. Our women learned with sinking hearts that the new corps which included our Dearborn County regiments was to bear the brunt of the conflict in this changed order of things. We were all off again in a hysterical whirl of emotions—now pride, now horror, now bitter wrath on top.

In the middle of all this the famous Field Hospital and Nurse Fund Fair was held. The project had slumbered the while people thought peace so near. It sprang up with renewed and vigorous life the moment the echo of those guns at Williamsburg reached our ears. And of course at its head was Julia Parmalee.

It would take a long time and a powerful ransacking of memory to catalogue the remarkable things which this active young woman did toward making that fair the success it undoubtedly was. Even more notable were the things which she coaxed, argued, or shamed other folks into doing for it. Years afterward there were old people who would tell you that Octavius had never been quite the same place since.

For one thing, instead of the Fireman's Hall, with its dingy aspect and somewhat rowdyish associations, the fair was held in the Court House, and we all understood that Miss Julia had been able to secure this favor on account of her late uncle, the Judge, when any one else would have been refused. It was under her tireless and ubiquitous supervision that this solemn old interior now took on a gay and festal face. Under the inspiration of her glance the members of the Fire Company and the Alert Baseball Club vied with each other in borrowing flags and hanging them from the most inaccessible and adventurous points. The rivalry between the local Freemasons and Odd Fellows was utilized to build contemporary booths at the sides and down the centre—on a floor laid over the benches by the Carpenters' Benevolent Association. The ladies' organizations of the various churches, out of devotion to the Union and jealousy of one another, did all the rest.

At the sides were the stalls for the sale of useful household articles, and sedate and elderly matrons found themselves now dragged from the mild obscurity of homes where they did their own work, and thrust forward to preside over the sales in these booths, while thrifty, not to say penurious, merchants came and stood around and regarded with amazement the merchandise which they had been wheedled into contributing gratis out of their own stores. The suggestion that they should now buy it back again paralyzed their faculties, and imparted a distinct restraint to the festivities at the sides of the big court-room.

In the centre was a double row of booths for the sale of articles not so strictly useful, and here the young people congregated. All the girls of Octavius seemed to have been gathered here—the pretty ones and the plain ones, the saucy ones and the shy, the maidens who were "getting along" and the damsels not yet out of their teens. Stiff, spreading crinolines brushed juvenile pantalettes, and the dark head of long, shaving-like ringlets contrasted itself with the bold waterfall of blonde hair. These girls did not know one another very well, save by little groups formed around the nucleus of a church association, and very few of them knew Miss Parmalee at all, except, of course, by sight. But now, astonishing to relate, she recognized them by name as old friends, shook hands warmly right and left, and blithely set them all to work and at their ease. The idea of selling things to young men abashed them by its weird and unmaidenly novelty. She showed them how it should be done— bringing forward for the purpose a sheepishly obstinate drug- store clerk, and publicly dragooning him into paying eighty cents for a leather dog-collar, despite his protests that he had no dog and hated the whole canine species, and could get such a strap as that anywhere for fifteen cents—all amid the greatest merriment. Her influence was so pervasive, indeed, that even the nicest girls soon got into a state of giggling familiarity with comparative strangers, which gave their elders concern, and which in some cases it took many months to straighten out again. But for the time all was sparkling gaiety. On the second and final evening, after the oyster supper, the Philharmonics played and a choir of girls sang patriotic songs. Then the gas was turned down and the stereopticon show began.

As the last concerted achievement of the firm of Pulford & Shull, this magic-latern performance is still remembered. The idea of it, of course, was Julia's. She suggested it to Marsena, and he gladly volunteered to make any number of positive plates from appropriate pictures and portraits for the purpose. Then she pressed Newton Shull into the service to get a stereopticon on hire, to rig up the platform and canvas for it, and finally to consent to quit his post among the Philharmonics when the music ceased, and to go off up into the gallery to work the slides. He also, during Marsena's absence one day, made a slide on his own account.

Mr. Shull had not taken very kindly to the idea when Miss Julia first broached it to him.

"No, I don't know as I ever worked a stereopticon," he said, striving to look with cold placidity into the winsome and beam- ing smile with which she confronted him one day out in the reception-room. She had never smiled at him before or pre- tended to know his name. "I guess you'd better hire a man up from Tecumseh to bring the machine and run it himself."

"But you can do it so much better, my dear Mr. Shull!" she urged. "You do everything so much better! Mr. Pulford often says that he never knew such a handy man in all his life. It seems that there is literally nothing that you can't do—except —perhaps—refuse a lady a great personal favor."

Miss Julia put this last so delicately, and with such a pretty little arch nod of the head and turn of the eyes, that Newton Shull surrendered at discretion. He promised everything on the spot, and he kept his word. In fact, he more than kept it.

The great evening came, as I have said, and when the lights were turned down to extinction's verge those who were nearest the front could distinguish the vacant chair which Mr. Shull had been occupying, with his bass viol leaning against it. They whispered from one to another that he had gone up in the gallery to work this new-fangled contrivance. Then came a flashing broad disk of light on the screen above the judges' bench, a spreading sibilant murmur of interest, and the show began.

It was an oddly limited collection of pictures—mainly thin and feeble copies of newspaper engravings, photographic portraits, and ideal heads from the magazines. Winfield Scott followed in the wake of Kossuth, and Garibaldi led the way for John C. Frémont and Lola Montez. There was applause for the long, homely, familiar face of Lincoln, and a derisive snicker for the likeness of Jeff Davis turned upside down. Then came local heroes from the district round about—Gen. Boyce, Col. McIntyre, and young Adjt. Heron, who had died so bravely at Ball's Bluff—mixed with some landscapes and statuary, and a comic caricature or two. The rapt assemblage murmured its recognitions, sighed its deeper emotions, chuckled over the funny plates—deeming it all a most delightful entertainment. From time to time there were long hitches, marked by a curious spluttering noise above, and the abortive flashes of meaningless light on the screen, and the explanation was passed about in undertones that Mr. Shull was having difficulties with the machine.

It was after the longest of these delays that, all at once, an extremely vivid picture was jerked suddenly upon the canvas, and, after a few preliminary twitches, settled in place to stare us out of countenance. There was no room for mistake. It was the portrait of Miss Julia Parmalee standing proudly erect in statuesque posture, with one hand resting on the back of a chair, and seated in this chair was Lieut. Dwight Ransom, smiling amiably.

There was a moment's deadly hush, while we gazed at this unlooked-for apparition. It seemed, upon examination, as if there was a certain irony in the Lieutenant's grin. Some one in the darkness emitted an abrupt snort of amusement, and a general titter arose, hung in the air for an awkward instant, and then was drowned by a generous burst of applause. While the people were still clapping their hands the picture was withdrawn from the screen, and we heard Newton Shull call down from his perch in the gallery:

"You kin turn up the lights now. They ain't no more to this."

In another minute we were sitting once again in the broad glare of the gaslight, blinking confusedly at one another, and with a dazed consciousness that something rather embarrassing had happened. The boldest of us began to steal glances across to where Miss Parmalee and Marsena sat, just in front of the steps to the bench.

What Miss Julia felt was beyond guessing, but there she was, at any rate, bending over and talking vivaciously, all smiles and collected nerves, to a lady two seats removed. But Marsena displayed no such presence of mind. He sat bolt upright, with an extraordinarily white face and a drooping jaw, staring fixedly at the empty canvas on the wall before him. Such absolute astonishment was never depicted on human visage before.

Perhaps from native inability to mind his own business, perhaps with a kindly view of saving an anxious situation, the Baptist minister rose now to his feet, coughed loudly to secure attention, and began some florid remarks about the success of the fair, the especial beauty of the lantern exhibition they had just witnessed, and the felicitous way in which it had terminated with a portrait of the beautiful and distinguished young lady to whose genius and unwearying efforts they were all so deeply indebted. In these times of national travail and distress, he said, there was a peculiar satisfaction in seeing her portrait accompanied by that of one of the courageous and noble young men who had sprung to the defence of their country. The poet had averred, he continued, that none but the brave deserved the fair, and so on, and so on.

Miss Julia listened to it all with her head on one side and a modestly deprecatory half-smile on her face. At its finish she rose, turned to face everybody, made a pert, laughing little bow, and sat down again, apparently all happiness. But it was noted that Marsena did not take his pained and fascinated gaze from that mocking white screen on the wall straight in front.

They walked in silence that evening to almost the gate of the Parmalee mansion. Julia had taken his arm, as usual; but Marsena could not but feel that the touch was different. It was in the nature of a relief to him that for once she did not talk. His heart was too sore, his brain too bewildered, for the task of even a one-sided conversation, such as theirs was wont to be. Then all at once the silence grew terrible to him—a weight to be lifted at all hazards on the instant.

"Shull must have made that last slide himself," he blurted out. "I never dreamt of its being made."

"I thought it came out very well indeed," remarked Miss Parmalee, "especially his uniform. You could quite see the eagles on the buttons. You must thank Mr. Shull for me."

"I'll speak to him in the morning about it," said Marsena, with gloomy emphasis. He sighed, bit his lip, fixed an intent gaze upon the big dark bulk of the Parmalee house looming before them, and spoke again. "There's something that I want to say to *you*, though, that won't keep till morning."

A tiny movement of the hand on his arm was the only response.

"I see now," Marsena went on, "that I ain't been making any real headway with you at all. I thought—well—I don't know as I know just what I did think—but I guess now that it was a mistake."

Yes—there was a distinct flutter of the little gloved hand. It put a wild thought into Marsena's head.

"Would you," he began boldly—"I never spoke of it before —but would you—that is, if I was to enlist and go to the war— would that make any difference?—you know what I mean."

She looked up at him with magnetic sweetness in her dusky, shadowed glance. "How can any able-bodied young patriot hesitate at such a time as this?" she made answer, and pressed his arm.

V

It was in this same May, not more than a week after the momentous episode of the Field Hospital and Nurse Fund Fair, that Marsena Pulford went off to the war.

There was no ostentation about his departure. He had indeed been gone for a day or two before it became known in Octavius that his absence from town meant that he had enlisted down at Tecumseh. We learned that he had started as a common private, but everybody made sure that a man of his distinguished appearance and deportment would speedily get a commission. Everybody, too, had a theory of some sort as to the motives for this sudden and strange behavior of his. These theories agreed in linking Miss Parmalee with the affair, but there were hopeless divergencies as to the exact part she played in it. One party held that Marsena had been driven to seek death on the tented field by despair at having been given the "mitten." Others insisted that he had not been given the "mitten" at all, but had gone because her well-known martial ardor made the sacrifice of her betrothed necessary to her peace of mind. A minority took the view which Homer Sage promulgated from his tilted-back chair on the stoop of the Excelsior Hotel.

"They ain't nothin' settled betwixt 'em," this student of human nature declared. "She jest dared him to go, and he went. And if you only give her time, she'll have the whole male un-married population of Octavius, between the ages of sixteen and sixty, down there wallerin' around in the Virginny swamps, feedin' the muskeeters and makin' a bid for glory."

But in a few days there came the terribly exciting news of Seven Pines and Fair Oaks—that first great combat of the revived war in the East—and we ceased to bother our heads about the photographer and his love. The enlisting fever sprang up again, and our young men began to make their way by dozens and scores to the recruiting office at Tecumseh. There were more farewells, more tears and prayers, not to mention several funerals of soldiers killed at Hanover Court House, where that Fifth Corps, which contained most of our volunteers, had its first spring smell of blood. And soon thereafter burst upon us the awful sustained carnage of the Seven Days' fight-ing, which drove out of our minds even the recollection that Miss Julia Parmalee herself had volunteered for active service in the Sanitary Commission, and gone South to take up her work.

And so July 3d came, bringing with it the bare tidings of that closing desperate battle of the week at Malvern Hill, and the movement of what was left of the Army of the Potomac to a safe resting place on the James River. We were beginning to get the details of local interest by the slow single wire from Thessaly, and sickening enough they were. The village streets were filled with silent, horror-stricken crowds. The whole com-munity seemed to have but a single face, repeated upon the mental vision at every step—a terrible face with distended, empty eyes, riven brows, and an open drawn mouth like the old Greek mask of tragedy.

"I swan! I don't know whether to keep open to-morrow or not," said Mr. Newton Shull, for perhaps the twentieth time, as he wandered once again from the reception-room into the little workshop behind. "In some ways it's kind of agin my principles to work on Independence Day—but, then again, if I thought there was likely to be a good many farmers comin' into town—"

"They'll be plenty of 'em comin' in," said the boy, over his shoulder, "but they'll steer clear of here."

"I'm 'fraid so," sighed Mr. Shull. He advanced a listless step or two and gazed with dejected apathy at the newspaper map tacked to the wall, on which the boy was making red and blue crosses with a colored pencil. "I don't see much good o' that," he said. "Still, of course, if it eases your mind any—"

"That's where the fightin' finished," observed the boy, pointing to a big mark on the map. "That's Malvern Hill there, and here—down where the river takes the big bend—that's Harrison's Landing, where the army's movin' to. See them seven rings? Them are the battles, one each day, as our men forced their way down through the Chickahominy swamps, beginnin' up in the corner with Beaver Dam Creek. If the map was a little higher it 'ud show the Pamunkey, where they started from. My uncle says that the whole mistake was in ever abandoning the Pamunkey."

"Pa-monkey or Ma-monkey," said Newton Shull, gloomily, "it wouldn't be no comfort to me to see it, even on a map. It's jest taken and busted me and my business here clean as a whistle. We ain't paid expenses two days in a week since Marseny went. Here I've got now so't I kin take a plain, everyday sort o' picture jest about as well as he did—a little streakid sometimes, perhaps, and more or less pinholes—but still pretty middlin' fair on an average, and then, darn my buttons if they don't all stop comin'. It positively don't seem to me as if there was a single human bein' in Dearborn County that 'ud have his picture took as a gift. All they want now is to have enlargements thrown up from little likenesses of their men-folks that have been killed, and them I don't know how to do no more'n a babe unborn."

"You knew well enough how to make the stereopticon slide," remarked the boy with severity.

"Yes," mused Mr. Shull, "that darned thing—that made a peck o' trouble, didn't it? I dunno what on earth possessed me; I kind o' seemed to git the notion o' doin' it into my head all to once't, and somehow I never dreamt of it rilin' Marseny so; you couldn't tell that a man 'ud be so blamed touchy as all that, could you?—and I dunno, like as not he'd 'a' enlisted anyhow. But I do wish he'd showed me how to make them pesky enlargements afore he went. If I'd only seen him do one, even once, I could 'a' picked the thing up, but I never did. It's just my luck!"

"Say," said the boy, looking up with a sudden thought, "do you know what my mother heard yesterday? It's all over the place that before Marseny left he went to Squire Schermerhorn's and made his will, and left everything he's got to the Parmalee girl, in case he gits killed. So, if anything happens she'd be your partner, wouldn't she?"

Newton Shull stared with surprise. "Well, now, that beats creation," he said, after a little. "Somehow you know that never occurred to me, and yet, of course, that 'ud be jest his style."

"Yes, sir," repeated the other, "they say he's left her every identical thing."

"It's allus that way in this world," reflected Mr. Shull, sadly. "Them that don't need it one solitary atom, they're eternally gettin' every mortal thing left to 'em. Why, that girl's so rich already she don't know what to do with her money. If I was her, I bet a cooky I wouldn't go pikin' off to the battlefield, doin' nursin' and tyin' on bandages, and fannin' men while they were gittin' their legs cut off. No, sirree; I'd let the Sanitary Commission scuffle along without me, I can tell you! A hoss and buggy and a fust-class two-dollar-a-day hotel, and goin' to the theatre jest when I took the notion—that'd be good enough for me."

"I suppose the sign then 'ud be 'Shull & Parmalee,' wouldn't it?" queried the boy.

"Well, now, I ain't so sure about that," said Mr. Shull, thoughtfully. "It might be that, bein' a woman, her name 'ud come first, out o' politeness. But then, of course, most prob'ly she'd want to sell out instid, and then I'd make the valuation, and she could give me time. Or she might want to stay in, only on the quiet, you know—what they call a silent partner."

"Nobody'd ever call her a silent partner," observed the boy. "She couldn't keep still if she tried."

"I wouldn't care how much she talked," said Mr. Shull, "if she only put enough more money into the business. I didn't take much to her, somehow, along at fust, but the more I've seen of her the more I like the cut of her jib. She's got 'go' in her, that gal has; she jest figures out what she wants, and then sails in and gits it. It don't matter who the man is, she jest takes and winds him round her little finger. Why, Marseny, here, he wasn't no more than so much putty in her hands. I lost all patience with him. You wouldn't catch me being run by a woman that way."

"So far's I could see," suggested the other, "she seemed to git pretty much all she wanted out of you, too. You were dancin' round, helpin' her at the fair there, like a hen on a hot griddle."

"It was all on his account," put in the partner, with emphasis. "Jest to please him; he seemed so much sot on her bein' humored in everything. I did feel kind o' foolish about it at the time—I never somehow believed much in doin' work for nothin'—but maybe it was all for the best. If what they say about his makin' a will is true, why it won't do me no harm to be on good terms with her—in case—in case—"

Mr. Shull was standing at the window, and his idle gaze had been vaguely taking in the general prospect of the street below the while he spoke. At this moment he discovered that some one on the opposite sidewalk was making vehement gestures to attract his attention. He lifted the sash and put his head out to listen, but the message came across loud enough for even the boy inside to hear.

"You'd better hurry round to the telegraph office!" this

hoarse, anonymous voice cried. "Malvern Hill list is a-comin'
in—and they say your pardner's been shot—shot bad, too!"

Newton Shull drew in his head and stood for some moments
staring blankly at the map on the wall. "Well, I swan!" he began, with confused hesitation, "I dunno—it seems to me—well,
yes, I guess prob'ly the best thing'll be for her to put more
money into the business—yes, that's the plan—and we kin hire
an operator up from Tecumseh."

But there was no one to pass an opinion on his project. The
boy had snatched his hat, and could be heard even now dashing
his way furiously down the outer stairs.

The summer dusk had begun to gather before Octavius heard
all that was to be learned of the frightful calamity which had
befallen its absent sons. The local roll of death and disaster
from Gaines's Mill earlier in the week had seemed incredibly
awful. This new budget of horrors from Malvern was far worse.

"Wa'n't the rest of the North doin' anything at all?" a wild-
eyed, dishevelled old farmer cried out in a shaking, half-fren-
zied shriek from the press of the crowd round the telegraph
office. "Do they think Dearborn County's got to suppress this
whole damned rebellion single-handed?"

It seemed to the dazed and horrified throng as if some such
idea must be in the minds of the rest of the Union. Surely no
other little community—or big community, either—could have
had such a hideous blow dealt to it as this under which Octavius
reeled. The list of the week for the county, including Gaines's
Mill, showed one hundred and eight dead outright, and very
nearly five hundred more wounded in battle. It was too shock-
ing for comprehension.

As evening drew on, men gathered the nerve to say to one
another that there was something very glorious in the way the
two regiments had been thrust into the front, and had shown
themselves heroically fit for that grim honor. They tried, too,

to extract solace from the news that the regiments in question had been mentioned by name in the general despatches as having distinguished themselves and their county above all the rest—but it was an empty and heart-sickened pretence at best, and when, about dark, the women-folks, who had waited in vain for them to come home to supper, began to appear on the skirts of the crowd, it was given up altogether. In after years Octavius got so that it could cheer those sinister names of Gaines's Mill and Malvern Hill, and swell with pride at the memories they evoked. But that evening no one cheered. It was too terrible.

There was, indeed, a single partial exception to this rule. The regular service of news had ceased—in those days, before the duplex invention, the single wire had most melancholy limitations—but the throng still lingered; and when, in the failing light, the postmaster was seen to step up again on the chair by the door with a bit of paper in his hand, a solemn hush ran over the assemblage.

"It is a private telegram sent to me personally," he explained, in the loud clear tones of one who had earned his office by years of stump speaking; "but it is intended for you all, I should presume."

The silent crowd pushed nearer, and listened with strained attention as this despatch was read:

HEADQUARTERS SANITARY COMMISSION
HARRISON'S LANDING, VA., Wednesday Morning.

TO POSTMASTER OCTAVIUS, N. Y.:

No words can describe magnificent record soldiers of Dearborn County, especially Starbuck, made past week. I bless fate which identified my poor services with such superb heroism. After second sleepless night, Col. Starbuck now reposing peacefully; doctor says crisis past; he surely recover, though process be slow. You will learn with pride he been brevetted Brigadier, fact which it was my privilege to announce to him last evening. He feebly thanked me, murmuring, "Tell them at home."

JULIA PARMALEE

In the silence which ensued the postmaster held the paper up and scanned it narrowly by the waning light. "There is something else," he said—"Oh, yes, I see; 'Franked despatch Sanitary Commission.' That's all."

Another figure was seen suddenly clambering upon the chair, with an arm around the postmaster for support. It was the teller of the bank. He waved his free arm excitedly, as he faced the crowd, and cried:

"Our women are as brave as our men! Three cheers for Miss Julia Parmalee! Hip-hip!"

The loyal teller's first "Hurrah!" fell upon the air quite by itself. Perhaps a dozen voices helped him half-heartedly with the second. The third died off again miserably, and he stepped down off the chair amid a general consciousness of failure.

"Who the hell is Starbuck?" was to be heard in whispered interrogatory passed along through the throng. Hardly anybody could answer. Boyce we knew, and McIntyre, and many others, but Starbuck was a mystery. Then it was explained that it must be the son of old Alanson Starbuck, of Juno Mills, who had gone away to Philadelphia seven or eight years before. He had not enlisted with any Dearborn County regiment, but held a staff appointment of some kind, presumably in a Pennsylvania command. We were quite unable to work up any emotion over him.

In fact, the more we thought it over, the more we were disposed to resent this planting of Starbuck upon us, in the very van of Dearborn County's heroes. His father was a rich old curmudgeon, whom no one liked. The son was nothing to us whatever.

As at last, in the deepening twilight, the people reluctantly began moving toward home, such conversation as they had the heart for seemed to be exclusively centred upon Miss Parmalee, and this queer despatch of hers. Slow-paced, strolling groups wended their way along the main street, and then up this side thoroughfare and that, passing in every block some dark and close-shuttered house of mourning and instinctively sinking still lower their muffled tones as they passed, and carrying in their breasts, heaven only knows what torturing loads of anguish and stricken despair—but finding a certain relief in dwelling, instead, upon this lighter topic.

One of these groups—an elderly lady in black attire and two younger women of sober mien—walked apart from the others and exchanged no words at all until, turning a corner, their way led them past the Parmalee house. The looming bulk of the old mansion and the fragrant spaciousness of the garden about it seemed to attract the attention of Mrs. Ransom and her daughters. They halted as by a common impulse, and fastened a hostile gaze upon the shadowy outlines of the house and its surrounding foliage.

"If Dwight dies of his wound," the mother said, in a voice all chilled to calmness, "his murderess will live in there."

"I always hated her!" said one of the daughters, with a shudder.

"But he isn't going to die, mamma," put in the other. "You mustn't think of such a thing! You know how healthy he always has been, and this is only his shoulder. For my part, we may think ourselves very fortunate. Remember how many have been killed or mortally wounded. It seems as if half the people we know are in mourning. We get off very lightly with Dwight only wounded. Did you happen to hear the details about Mr. Pulford?—you know, the photographer—some one was saying that he was mortally wounded."

"She sent him to his death, then, too," said the elder Miss Ransom, raising her clenched hand against the black shadow of the house.

"I don't care about that man," broke in the mother, icily.

"Nobody knows anything of him, or where he came from. People ran after him because he was good-looking, but he never seemed to me to know enough to come in when it rained. If she made a fool of him, it was his own lookout. But Dwight—my Dwight—!"

The mother's mannered voice broke into a gasp, and she bent her head helplessly. The daughters went to her side, and the group passed on into the darkness.

VI

It was a dark, soft, summer night in Virginia, that of the 1st of July. After the tropical heat of the day, the air was being mercifully cooled, here on the hilltop, by a gentle breeze, laden with just a moist suggestion of the mist rising from the river flats and marshes down below. It was not Mother Nature's fault that this zephyr stirring along the parched brow of the hill did not bear with it, too, the scents of fruits and flowers, of new-mown hay and the yellow grain in shock, and minister soothingly to rest and pleasant dreams.

Instead, this breeze, moving mildly in the darkness, was one vile, embodied stench of sulphur and blood, and pestilential abominations. Go where you would, there was no escaping this insufferable burden of foul smells. If they were a horror on the hilltop, they were worse below.

It was one of the occasions on which Man had expended all his powers to prove his superiority to Nature. The elements in their wildest and most savage mood could never have wrought such butchery as this. The vine-wrapped fences, stretching down from the plateau toward the meadow lands below, were buttressed by piles of dead men, some in butternut, some in blue. Clumps of stiffened bodies curled supine at the base of every stump on the fringe of the woodland to the right and among the tumbled sheaves of grain to the left. Out in the open, the broad, sloping hillside and the valley bottom lay literally hidden under ridge upon ridge of smashed and riddled human forms, and the heaped débris of human battle. The clouds hung thick and close above, as if to keep the stars from beholding this repellent sample of earth's titanic beast, Man, at his worst. An Egyptian blackness was over it all.

At intervals a lightning flash from the crest of the outermost knoll tore this evil pall of darkness asunder, and then, with a roar and a scream, a spluttering line of vivid flame would arch its sinister way across the sky. A thousand little dots of light moved and zigzagged ceaselessly on the wide expanse of obscurity underneath this crest, and when the bursts of wrathful fireworks came from overhead it could be seen that these were lanterns being borne about in and out among the winrows of maimed and slain. Above all, through all, without even an instant's lull, there arose a terrible babel of chorused groans and prayers and howls and curses. This noise could be heard for miles—almost as far as the boom of the howitzers above could carry—and at a distance sounded like the moaning of a storm through a great pine-forest. Near at hand, it sounded like nothing else this side of hell.

An hour or so after nightfall the battery on the crest of the knoll stopped firing. The wails and shrieks from the slope below went on all through the night, and the lanterns of the search parties burned till the morning sunlight put them out.

Up on the top of the hill—a broad expanse of rolling plateaus —the scene wore a different aspect. At widely separated points bonfires and glittering lights showed where some general of the victorious army held his headquarters in a farm-house; and unless one pried too curiously about these parts, there were few enough evidences on the summit of the day's barbaric doings.

The chief of these houses—a stately and ancient structure, built in colonial days of brick proudly brought from Europe —had begun the forenoon of the battle as the headquarters of

the Fifth Corps. Then the General and his staff had reduced
their needs to a couple of rooms, to leave space for wounded
men. Then they had moved out altogether, to let the whole
house be used as a hospital. Then as the backwash of calamity
from the line of conflict swelled in size and volume, the stables
and barns had been turned over to the medical staff. Later, as
the savage evening fight went on, tons of new hay had been
brought out and strewn in sheltered places under the open sky
to serve as beds for the sufferers. Before night fell, even these
impromptu hospitals were overtaxed, and rows of stricken
soldiers lay on the bare ground.

The day of intelligent and efficient hospital service had not
yet dawned for our army. The breakdown of what service we
had had, under the frightful stress of the battles culminating
in this blood-soaked Malvern Hill, is a matter of history, and
it can be viewed the more calmly now as the collapse of itself
brought about an improved condition of affairs. But at the time
it was a woful thing, with a lax and conflicting organization,
insufficient material, a ridiculous lack of nurses, a mere hand-
ful of really competent surgeons and, most of all, a great crowd
of volunteer medical students and ignorant practitioners, who
flocked southward for the mere excitement and practice of sawing, cutting, slashing right and left. So it was that army surgery
lent new terrors to death on the battle-field in the year 1862.

The sky overhead was just beginning to show the ashen
touch of twilight, when two men lying stretched on the hay in
a corner of the smaller barnyard chanced to turn on their hard
couch and to recognize each other. It was a slow and almost
scowling recognition, and at first bore no fruit of words.

One was in the dress of a lieutenant of artillery, muddy and
begrimed with smoke, and having its right shoulder torn or cut
open from collar to elbow. The man himself had now such a
waving, tangled growth of chestnut beard and so grimly blackened a face, that it would have been hard to place him as our
easy-going, smiling Dwight Ransom.

The new movement had not brought ease, and now, after a

few grunts of pain and impatience, he got himself laboriously up in a sitting posture, dragged a knapsack within reach up to support his back, and looked at his companion again.

"I heard that you were down here somewhere," he remarked, at last. "My sister wrote me."

Marsena Pulford stared up at him, made a little nodding motion of the head, and turned his glance again into the sky straight above. He also was a spectacle of dry mud and dust, and was bearded to the eyes.

"Where are you hit?" asked Dwight, after a pause.

For answer, Marsena slowly, and with an effort, put a hand to his breast—to the left, below the heart. "Here, somewhere," he said, in a low, dry-lipped murmur. He did not look at Dwight again, but presently asked, "Could you fix me—settin' up—too?"

"I guess so," responded Dwight. With the help of his unhurt arm he clambered to his feet and began moving dizzily about among the row of wounded men to his left. These groaned or snarled at him as he passed over them, but to this he paid no attention whatever. He returned from the end of the line, bringing two knapsacks and the battered frame of a drum, in which some one had been trying to carry water, and with some difficulty arranged these in a satisfactory heap. Then he knelt, pushed his arm under Marsena's shoulders, and lifted him up and backward to the support. Both men grimaced and winced under the smart of the effort, and for some minutes sat in silence, with closed eyes.

When they opened them finally it was with a sudden start at the sound of a woman's voice. Their ears had for long hours been inured to a ceaseless din of other noises—an ear-splitting confusion of cannon and musketry roar from the field less than an eighth of a mile away, of yelping shells overhead, and of screams and hoarse shouts all about them. Yet their senses caught this strange note of a woman's voice as if it had fallen upon the hush of midnight.

They looked up, and beheld Miss Julia Parmalee!

Upon such a background of heated squalor, dirt, and murderous disorder, it did not seem surprising to them that this lady should present a picture of cool, fresh neatness. She wore a snow-white nurse's cap, and broad, spotless bands of white linen were crossed over the shoulders of her pale dove-colored dress. Her dark face, dusky pink at the cheeks, glowed with a proud excitement. Her big brown eyes swept along the row of recumbent figures at her feet with the glance of a born conqueror.

"This is not a fit place for him," she said. "It is absurd to bring a gentleman—an officer of the headquarters staff—out to such a place as this!"

Then the two volunteers from Octavius saw that behind her were four men, bearing a laden stretcher, and that at her side was a regimental hospital steward, who also looked speculatively along the rows of sufferers.

"It's the best thing we can do, anyway," he replied, not overpolitely; "and for that matter, there's hardly room here."

"Oh, there'd be no trouble about that," retorted Miss Julia, calmly. "We could move any of these people here. The General told me I was always to do just what I thought best. I am sure that if I could see him now he would insist at once that Colonel Starbuck should have a bed to himself, inside the house."

"I'll bet he wouldn't!" said the hospital steward, with emphasis.

"Perhaps you don't realize," put in Miss Julia coldly, "that Colonel Starbuck is a staff officer—and a friend of mine."

"I don't care if he was on all the staffs there are," said the hospital steward, "he's got to take his chance with the rest. And it don't matter about his being a friend, either; we ain't playing favorites much just now. I don't see no room here, Miss. You'll have to take him out in the open lot there."

"Oh, never!" protested Miss Julia, vehemently. "It's disgraceful! Why, the place is under fire there. I saw them running away from a shell there only a minute ago. No, if we can't do anything better, we'll have one of these men moved."

"Well, do something pretty quick!" growled one of the men supporting the stretcher.

Miss Parmalee had looked two or three times in an absent-minded way at the two men on the ground nearest her—obviously without recognizing either of them. There was a definite purpose in the glance she now bent upon Dwight Ransom—a glance framed in the resourceful smile he remembered so well.

"You seem to be able to sit up, my man," she said, ingratiatingly, to him; "would you be so very kind as to let me have that place for Colonel Starbuck, here—he is on the headquarters staff—and I am sure we should be so very much obliged. You will easily get a nice place somewhere else for yourself. Oh, thank you so much! It is so good of you!"

Suppressing a groan at the pain the movement involved, and without a word, Dwight lifted himself slowly to his feet, and stepped aside, waving a hand toward the hay and knapsack in token of their surrender.

Then Miss Julia helped lift from the litter the object of her anxiety. Colonel Starbuck was of a slender, genteel figure, and had the top of his head swathed heavily in bandages. He wore long, curly, brown side-whiskers, and his chin had been shaved that very morning. This was enough in itself to indicate that he belonged to the headquarters staff, but the fact was proclaimed afresh by everything else about him—his speckless uniform, his spick-and-span gauntlets, his carefully polished boots, the glittering newness of his shoulder-straps, sword scabbard, buttons, and spurs. It was clear that, whatever else had happened, his line of communication with the headquarters baggage train had never been interrupted.

"It is so kind of you!" Miss Parmalee murmured again, when the staff officer had been helped off the stretcher, and in a dazed and languid way had settled himself down into the place vacated for him. "Would you"—she whispered, looking up now, and noting that the hospital steward and the litter-men had gone away—"would you mind stepping over to the house, or to one of the tents beyond—you'll find him somewhere—

and asking Dr. Willoughby to come at once? Tell him it is for
Colonel Starbuck of the headquarters staff, and you'd better
mention my name—Miss Parmalee of the Sanitary Commission. You won't forget the name—Parmalee?"

"I don't fancy I shall forget it," said Dwight, gravely. "I've
got a better memory than some."

Miss Julia caught the tone of voice on the instant, and looked
up again from where she knelt beside the Colonel, with a
swift smile.

"Why, it's Mr. Ransom, I do believe!" she exclaimed. "I
should never have known you with your beard. It's so good of
you to take this trouble—you always were so obliging! Any
one will tell you where Dr. Willoughby is. He's the surgeon of
the Eighteenth, you know. I'm sure he'll come at once—to
please me—and time is so precious, you know!"

Without further words, Dwight moved off slowly and un-
steadily toward the house.

Miss Parmalee, seating herself so that some of her mouse-
tinted draperies almost touched the face of Dwight's companion, unhooked a fan from her girdle and began softly fanning Colonel Starbuck. "The doctor won't be long," she said,
in low, cooing tones, after a little; "do you feel easier now?"

"I am rather dizzy still, and a little faint," replied the Colonel, languorously. "That fanning is so delicious though, that
I'm really very happy. At least I would be if I weren't nervous
about you. You have been through such tremendous exertions
all day—out in the sun, amid all these horrid sights and this
infernal roar—without a parasol, too. Are you quite sure it has
not been too much for you?"

"You are always so thoughtful of others, dear Colonel Starbuck," murmured Miss Julia, reducing the fanning to a gentle,
measured movement, and fixing her lustrous eyes pensively
upon the clouds above the horizon. "You never think of yourself!"

"Only to think how happy my fate is, to be rescued and
nursed by an angel," sighed the Colonel.

A smile of gentle deprecation played upon Miss Julia's red

lips, and imparted to her eyes the expression they would wear if they had been gazing upon a tenderly entrancing vision in the sky. Then, all at once; she gave a little start of aroused attention, looked puzzled, and after a moment's pause bent her head over close to the Colonel's.

"The man behind me has taken tight hold of my dress," she whispered, hurriedly. "I don't want to turn around, but can you see him? He isn't having a fit or anything, is he?"

Colonel Starbuck lifted himself a trifle, and looked across. "No," he whispered in return, "he appears to be asleep. Probably he is dreaming. He is a corporal—some infantry regiment. They do manage to get so—what shall I say—so unwashed! Shall I move his hand for you?"

Miss Julia shook her head, with an arch little half smile.

"No, poor man," she murmured. "It gives me almost a sense of the romantic. Perhaps he is dreaming of home—of some one dear to him. Corporals do have their romances, you know, as well as—"

"As well as colonels," the staff officer playfully finished the sentence for her. "Well, I congratulate him, if his is a thousandth part as joyful as mine."

"Oh, then, you have one!" pursued Miss Parmalee, allowing her eyes to sparkle for an instant before they were coyly raised again to the clouds. Darkness was gathering there rapidly.

"Why pretend that you don't understand?" pleaded Colonel Starbuck—and there seemed to be no answer forthcoming. The fan moved even more sedately now, with a tender flutter at the end of each downward sweep.

Presently the preoccupation of the couple—one might not call it silence in such an unbroken uproar as rose around them and smashed through the air above—was interrupted by the appearance of a young, sharp-faced man, who marched straight across the yard toward them and, halting, spoke hurriedly.

"I was asked specially to come here for a moment," he said, "but it can only be a minute. We're just over our heads in work. What is it?"

Miss Parmalee looked at the young man with a favorless eye.

He was unshaven, dishevelled, brusque of manner and speech. He was bare-headed, and his unimportant figure was almost hidden beneath a huge revoltingly stained apron.

"I asked for my friend, Dr. Willoughby," she said. "But if he could not come, I must insist upon immediate attention for Colonel Starbuck here—an officer of the headquarters staff."

While she spoke the young surgeon had thrown himself on one knee, adroitly though roughly lifted the Colonel's bandages, run an inquiring finger over his skull, and plumped the linen back again. He sprang to his feet with an impatient grunt. "Paltry scalp wound," he snorted. Then, turning on his heel, he almost knocked against Dwight Ransom, who had come slowly up behind him.

"You had no business to drag me off for foolishness of this sort," he said, in vexed tones. "Here are thousands of men waiting their turn who really need help, and I've been working twenty hours a day for a week, and couldn't keep up with the work if every day had two hundred hours. It's ridiculous!"

Dwight shrugged his unhurt shoulder. "I didn't ask you for myself," he replied. "I'm quite willing to wait my turn—but the lady here—she asked me to bring help—"

"It can't be that this gentleman understands," put in Miss Julia, "that his assistance was desired for an officer of the headquarters staff."

"Madam," said the young surgeon, "with your permission, damn the headquarters staff!" and, turning abruptly, he strode off.

"I will go and see the General myself," exclaimed Miss Parmalee, flushing with wrath. "I will see whether he will permit the Sanitary Commission to be affronted in this outrageous—"

She stopped short. Her indignant effort to rise to her feet had been checked by a hand on the ground, which held firmly in its grasp a fold of her skirt. She turned, pulled the cloth from the clutch of the tightened fingers, looked at the hand as it sprawled limply on the grass, and gave a little, shuddering, half-hysterical laugh. "Mercy me!" was what she said.

"You know who it is, don't you?" asked Dwight Ransom.

The meaning in his voice struck Miss Julia, and she bent a careful scrutiny through the dusk upon the face of the man stretched out beside her. His head had slipped sidewise on the knapsack, and his bearded chin was unnaturally sunk into his collar. Through the grime on his face could be discerned an unearthly pallor. His wide-opened eyes seemed staring fixedly, reproachfully, at the hand which had lost its hold upon Miss Julia's dress.

"It does seem as if I'd seen the face before somewhere," she remarked, "but I don't appear to place it. It is getting so dark, too. No, I can't imagine. Who is it?"

She had risen to her feet and was peering down at the dead man, her pretty brows knitted in perplexity.

"He recognized you!" said Dwight, with significant gravity. "It's Marsena Pulford."

"Oh, poor man!" exclaimed Julia. "If he'd only spoken to me I would gladly have fanned him, too. But I was so anxious about the Colonel here that I never took a fair look at him. I dare say I shouldn't have recognized him, even then. Beards do change one so, don't they!"

Then she turned to Colonel Starburk and made answer to the inquiry of his lifted eyebrows.

"The unfortunate man," she explained, "was our village photographer. I sat to him for my picture several times. I think I have one of them over at the Commission tent now."

"I'll go this minute and seize it!" the gallant Colonel vowed, getting to his feet.

"Take care! We unprotected females have a man trap there!" Julia warned him; but fear did not deter the staff officer from taking her arm and leaning on it as they walked away in the twilight.

Then the night fell, and Dwight buried Marsena.

A Day in the Wilderness

I

The Valley of Death

The rising sun lifted its first curved rim of dazzling light above the dark line of distant tree-tops just as the brigade band began a new tune—"The Faded Coat of Blue." The musicians themselves, huddled together under the shelter of a mound of rocks where the road descended into the ravine, did not get their share of this early morning radiance, but remained in the shadows.

Only a yard or two away from the outermost drummer-boy these shadows ended, and a picture began that was full of action and color, and flooded with golden sunshine.

The bandsmen, as they played, observed this picture, and thanked their stars they were no part of it. Better a whole life spent in the shade, than sunlight at such a price as was being paid for it out there in the road!

This road had never before been anything but a narrow, grass-grown, out-of-the-way track for mule-carts. Now it had become the bed of a broad, endless, moving human flood—filling it compactly from side to side, with ever a fresh wave of blue-coated men entering at the rear, where the scrub-oak opening began, and ever a front wave gliding off downward from view with that sinister slipperiness which arches the brow of a cataract.

The sense of motion conveyed by these thousands of passing men was at its perfection of rhythm just opposite the band. They were marching in eights, so close together that they trod continually on any lagging heel.

The ranks, when they first came in view, seemed pressing forward without much order. Then, as they drew close to the musicians, they fell into step instinctively, swung along in

229

swaying unison for a few rods, and again lapsed into jagged irregularity as they swept downward behind the rock.

It was indeed only this shifting section of the dozen nearest ranks that could catch the strains of the band. The others, whether in van or rear, moved on with their hearing numbed by a ceaseless and terrible uproar which came from the ravine in front, and, mounting upward, seemed to shake the earth on which they trod.

The musicians might blow themselves red in the face, the drummers beat the strained sheepskins to bursting, and make no headway against this din of cannon.

The men of Boyce's brigade, as they came into the little space where they could hear the music above the artillery, and caught the step it was setting, hardly looked that way, but pushed forward with eyes straight ahead, and grave, drawn faces on which the cheerful sunlight seemed a mockery.

When the band had finished "The Faded Coat of Blue" the sky was still clear overhead, but from the gully below a dense cloud of smoke had spread upward to choke the morning light. While the bandsmen paused, blowing their instruments clear and breathing hard, this smoke began to thicken the air about the rock which sheltered them.

In a minute more the front figures of the endless moving chain before them seemed to be walking off into a fog, and the atmosphere was all at once heavy with the smell of gunpowder.

Curiously enough, the men's faces brightened at this. There came a block now somewhere on the road ahead, and the column halted. The regimental flags, with the color-guard, were just abreast of the band. The sergeant took out his knife to cut one of the furling strings that was in a hard knot, and untied the rest, shaking out the silken folds of the banners.

"I always untie 'em when we get into the smoke," he said, speaking at large.

The drummer-boy nearest the road moved over to study the flags. He held his head to one side and scrutinized them critically.

"No bullet holes in 'em yet, to speak of, I notice," he remarked to the sergeant, raising a clear, sharp young voice above the universal racket. "Guess you'll get enough to-day to make up!" he added.

The old sergeant nodded his head. "Something besides flags will get holes in 'em too," he returned, lifting his voice also, like a man talking in the teeth of a roaring gale.

"What are you? Michiganders?" shouted the boy.

"No—Ohio!" the sergeant bawled back. "When they changed the corps, they brigaded us all up fresh, so that we don't know our own mothers. We've got in with some New Yorkers that ain't got no more sense than to chew fine-cut tobacco. You can't raise a plug in a whole regiment of 'em. Regular pumpkin-heads!"

"They'll show you fellows the way, down below there, though!" retorted the boy, his injured state pride adding shrillness to his tone. "Ohio's no good, anyhow!"

He instinctively moved beyond reach of the sergeant's boot, as he passed this last remark. Some of the men in the crowded ranks close by laughed at his impudence, and he himself was grinning with a sense of successful repartee, when he felt a hand laid on his shoulder. He looked up, and found himself confronting a young, fair-faced officer, who was regarding him with gravely gentle eyes.

"Don't say that about any men who are going out to die," this officer said; and though he did not seem to be speaking loudly, the words fell very distinctly. "I've got a brother at home about your size. So have lots of the rest of us here. We want to carry down there with us a pleasant notion of the last boy we saw."

"I was only fooling!" the drummer-boy rejoined.

There was no time for further words, as the preparatory rattle on the drum-edge behind warned him. In another minute he was back in his place, and the band was hurling forth into the general uproar the strains of "The Red, White, and Blue."

The column had begun to move again. The flags, the color-guard, the young officer with the sad, gentle eyes, had passed downward out of sight, and company after company of their regiment came pressing onward now.

The boy, as he kept up with his part of the familiar work, watched these Ohio men swing past. They seemed young fellows, for the most part, and their uniforms were significantly new and clean. Everything about them showed that they were going under fire for the first time, though they pushed forward as stoutly as veterans. The boy found himself hoping that a good many of these Ohio men would come back all right—and most of all that young officer who had a brother about his size.

All this while a group of field officers had been standing on the ridge up above the rocky mound which sheltered the band. Their figures, with broad hats and big-cuffed gauntlets, had grown indistinct against the sky as the smoke thickened. Now they gave up trying to follow through their glasses the movements in the vale below, and turned to descend.

Their horses, which men had been holding near the musicians, were hastily brought forward, and the general and his staff sprang into the saddle and trotted over toward the road.

The end of the column was in view, with the disorder of servants, baggage-carriers, soldiers who had lost their places, and behind, the looming canvas covers of ambulance-wagons and the train. Into the thick of this straggling mass General Boyce, sitting splendidly erect and with a bold smile on his rosy-cheeked face, spurred his way, and the staff in turn clattered after him down out of sight. The brigade had passed, and the band stopped playing.

Files of mules, heavily laden with stacks of cartridge-boxes, were still pouring along the road and being whacked down the ravine path; but the big wagons, as they came, halted, and were drawn off into the field to the left. Tall poles were taken out and set up. Coils of rope were unwound, stakes driven, and huge cylinders of canvas unrolled on the grass.

Soon there arose the gray outlines of tents—one dominating structure fully thirty yards long, and around it, like little mushrooms about the parent stool, a number of smaller tents, some square, some conical. The drummer-boy, his task ended, sauntered over with his companions toward the tents.

He paused to watch the heavy folds of canvas being hauled up to the ridge-pole of the big one. In one way it recalled those preparations on the old circus-ground at home which he used to watch with such zest. But in another way it was strangely different.

While some men tugged at the ropes or drove in stakes for the guy-lines, others were busy bringing from the wagons rolls of blankets and huge trusses of straw. Even before the roof was secure scores of rude beds were being spread on the trampled grass underneath.

Bearded and spectacled men, dressed after the fashion of officers, yet clearly not soldiers at all, were directing everything now. Among them, here and there, flitted young women, clad also in a sort of uniform, who seemed busiest of all.

No, this was decidedly different from a circus tent. The thunder of the batteries on the other side of the ridge was alone enough to throw a solemn meaning over this long, barnlike house of ropes and cloths. It was the brigade hospital-tent, and the hundreds of active hands at work could hardly hope to have it ready before it was needed.

It was the morning of the second day of the Battle of the Wilderness. The men of Boyce's brigade knew only vaguely, by hearsay, of what had happened on that terrible yesterday. They themselves, forming the rear-guard of the great army, had been nearly the last to cross the Rapidan on the swinging pontoon bridge of Germania ford. They had had a night's forced march; a two hours' nap in the open starlight; a hasty bite of rations at half-past three in the morning, and now this plunge in the chilly twilight of sunrise down into the unknown.

There had been, just before the general advance across the Rapidan, a wholesale shaking-up of army organization. Two whole corps had been abolished, and their strength distributed among the three remaining corps. Regiments found themselves suddenly torn from their old associates, and brigaded with strangers. Their pet officers disappeared, and others took their places whom the men did not know and were disposed to dislike.

To add to this discontent, there was an understanding that their leaders had been entrapped into this Wilderness fighting. Certainly it was no place which an invading army would have chosen for battle.

It was a vast, sprawling forest district, densely covered with low timber, scrub-oak, dwarf junipers, and tangled cedars and pines, all knit together breast-high and upward with interlacing wild vines, and foul underfoot with swamp or thicket.

In this gloomy and sinister wilderness men did not know where they were, nor whom they were fighting. Whole commands were lost in the impenetrable woods. Mounted orderlies could not get about through the underbrush, and orders sent out were never delivered.

Though gulches and steep ravines abounded, cutting sharp gashes through the forest, there were no hills upon which a general and his keen-eyed staff might perch themselves and get an idea of how the land about them lay. The Confederates had plenty of this knowledge, and used it to terrible purpose. The invaders could only put their heads down, and strive to crush their way blindly through.

After a little, the drummer-boy put his snare-drum in the wagon where the other instruments were, and started off up the ridge, to see what the general and his staff had been observing earlier in the morning.

As he neared the summit, he noticed that the roar of the cannon directly in front seemed to have died down a good deal. There were still angry outbursts, but one had to wait for them now; and a new kind of noise, made up of peal after peal of crackling musketry fire, was rising from the gully farther to the left.

The boy had come now to the top of the ridge, only to find it crowned with a thick fringe of alders which completely shut out his view. From the roots of the farther bushes the hillside dropped precipitously. He worked his way along until, by a cleft in the rocks, an opening offered itself.

Here, stooping low and bending aside the alders, he could creep out upon a big, flat, moss-grown boulder, which overhung the ravine like a balcony. He had not thought he was so high up. The other side of the gulf spread out before him could not be seen for the smoke—but the tops of tall pines growing on its bottom were far below him.

The steepness of the descent made him dizzy. The rock on which he stood seemed to be suspended in mid-air. He drew back a little. Then curiosity got the upper hand. He laid himself face down on the boulder, and edged cautiously forward till he could peer over its front.

The fog-like smoke was so dense that at first he could see nothing. Even when the bearings of the land below, masked as it all was under forest, began to be apparent to him, his ears were still the best guide to what was going on. The confused sound of men's shouts and yells mingled now with the intermittent volleys of musketry to the left. The cannon-firing had stopped altogether.

He discovered all at once that a good many of the tree-tops in front of him seemed to have been broken off very recently. Some were hanging to the trunks by their bark; everywhere the splinters were white and fresh. Now that he listened more intently, there were weird whistling noises among these shattered boughs and an incessant dropping of leaves and twigs.

Suddenly a big branch not far away shook violently, then toppled downward. At the same moment a swift ringing buzz sounded just over his head, and a bunch of alder-blossoms fell upon one of his hands. He pulled himself back abruptly.

Crawling backward out through the alders, he did not venture to lift his head until there was a comfortable wall of rocks between him and that murderous ravine. Then, getting to his feet, he looked amazed down upon the brigade camp, which he had left an hour before. The big tent, and the little ones about it, only a while ago the scene of such bustling activity, were all deserted.

Some of the wagons could be seen rolling and bumping off toward the road to the left under drivers who stood up to lash their teams. The white, canvas-hooped tops were the centres of wild confusion.

Other drivers were scurrying off on horseback, leading with them in a frantic gallop groups of the team horses, pulled along by their bunched reins. The people on foot—doctors, nurses, camp-guards and the rest—were all racing pell-mell toward the road for dear life.

Thunderstruck at the spectacle, the boy turned to the right. A long, double line of men had come out through the woods in which the ridge lost itself, and were advancing upon the camp at a sharp run. They seemed dressed in a sort of mud-colored uniform, and they raised a sharp whoop of triumph as they came. At the farther end of the line, some of these men lifted their guns as they ran, and fired into the receding mass of fugitives.

Down in front, meantime, the foremost of the advancing line had reached the camp and entered upon possession. They had begun overhauling the captured wagons, and were tossing out loaves of bread and hardtack boxes, which their comrades fell upon eagerly. The boy reflected now that he himself was hungry, and he scratched his head with perplexity.

The sound of panting breath close beside him made him turn swiftly. A man had clambered up the side of the ridge, away from the camp, and had rushed up to him, his eyes starting from his head with excitement. He waved something like a short stick, with wild gestures, and tried to shout, but could only pant instead.

He stopped as he came up, stared at the boy, then shook his head dolefully as he gasped for breath.

"Is dot you, Lafe?" he managed to groan. "Oh, my jiminy priest!"

"Look out!" cried the boy. "Lie down!"

Some of the men below had caught sight of them and two or three sparks and jets of smoke told that they were being fired at. Though they were probably beyond range, it was safer behind the alders, so the two crawled out on the overhanging ledge.

"I say, Foldeen, have they scooped the old band wagon? I couldn't see from here," was the boy's first remark.

"Dey von't get 'em my flute, anyhow," the other responded, holding proudly forth the ebony stock with its silver keys, which he had been waving so vehemently. "I don't catch me putting him in de bant vagon."

Even as he spoke he clutched the boy fiercely by the arm, with a smothered exclamation of horror. The rock on which they crouched had stirred from its foundations, and as the two instinctively strove to turn themselves, it lurched outward, and went crashing down the steep declivity.

II

Lafe Reconnoitres the Valley

On the river road below the tannery, away back in New York State, there stood for many years a small house, always surrounded in summer by sunflowers and hollyhocks and peonies that enwrapped it as in a beautiful garment. It seemed that flowers grew nowhere else as they did for the Widow Hornbeck.

There was no other such show of lilacs in Juno Mills as that which early May brought for her front yard. The climbing roses which covered the whole front and side of the poor little house were only of the simple, old sorts,—the Baltimore Bell, the yellow Scotch and the ordinary pink briar,—but they bore thick clusters of delightful blossoms. And in the fall, when the frosts had nipped and blackened other people's flowers, the asters and nasturtiums and glodiolus in this wee patch appeared unhurt by the weather.

When there was to be a wedding in the village, or some celebration at the church or the school-house, the children always went to the Widow Hornbeck to beg for flowers. Often they found her sitting out in her yard among the plants she loved— a mild-faced, patient little woman, with thin, bent shoulders and hair whitened before its time; and she would be poring through her spectacles over the same big Book spread open on her knees.

The spectacle of Mrs. Hornbeck and her family Bible, framed like a picture in vines and flowering shrubs, grew pleasantly familiar to everyone in the district. Strangers driving past used to stop their buggies and admire the place; and they, too, seeing the white-haired owner sitting there, would feel that her presence added to the charm of the scene.

The widow died suddenly one day in the autumn of 1863. She was found quite lifeless, seated as of old in the garden, with the old patient, wistful half-smile on her face, and the old Book spread open in her lap.

The village was sad for a day or two, and gently touched for a fortnight. Then the widow had been forgotten, and the family Bible had vanished. The cottage was taken for the mortgage upon it, and its meager contents went the way of humble, ownerless things. Mrs. Hornbeck had been very poor, and nothing was left for her son.

In that family Bible had been written the names of some score of Hornbecks. Against all these names but two a date of death had also been inscribed. One of these two names, the last in the list, was that of the boy, now made an orphan, the Benjamin of the widow's flock. He was described on the yellowed page, in his mother's scrawling hand, as "Washington Lafayette Hornbeck, born April 30, 1850." In real life he had always been known as "Lafe."

He grew up a brown-skinned, hardy sort of ordinary boy,

whose face might suggest some acuteness and more resolution, but whom nobody thought of calling good-looking.

He turned out to be the best wrestler among the village lads of his age, and he was also the strongest swimmer of all the lot who used to go down, of a summer evening, to dive off the spring-board into the deep pool below the mill-dam. This raised him a good deal in the esteem of the boys, but somehow their elders were not so much impressed by "Lafe's" qualities.

He had to work, and he did work, but always at some new job—now berry-picking, now stripping willows for the basket factory, now packing "heave-powders" for the local horse-doctor. He had been employed in the mills and in the tannery, and he had once travelled for a month as the assistant of a tin-peddler, not to mention various experiments in general farm-work.

People hardly blamed Lafe for this lack of steadiness in employment. They said it was in his blood. All the Hornbecks since any one could remember had been musicians—playing the fiddle or whatever else you liked at country dances, and some of them even journeying to distant parts as members of circus or minstrel bands.

It was felt that a boy from such a roving stock could scarcely be expected to tie himself down to regular work.

Doubtless Lafe felt this, too, for as soon as he began thinking what he should do, after the shock of his mother's death, he found himself wishing to be a drummer-boy. The notion struck all the neighbors as quite appropriate. Lafe was a capital drummer. Kind old Doctor Peabody went with him to Tecumseh, saw the head recruiting officer at the big barracks there, and arranged matters for him.

Lafe was sent forward to New York, and thence to head-quarters at the front. Men liked him, and his lifelong familiarity with instruments made him a handy boy to have about. Before long he was taken out of the little company drum-corps, and promoted to the big brigade band.

This very morning, when he went up from the hospital camp

to the ridge where he hoped to see the fighting beyond, he had been thinking whether his promotion had been what he wanted.

All his dreams had been of action—of brave drummer-boys who went into battle with fifes, and stood through it all by the side of the file-leader, valiantly pounding their sheep-skins as the shot and shell screamed past, and men pitched headlong, and officers were hurled from their horses, and the fight was lost or won.

Alas! a brigade band never got so much as a whiff of actual warfare, but tamely stayed about in camp, playing selections outside the general's headquarters while he ate his dinner, or contributing its quota to the ceremonial of a Sunday dress-parade.

Perhaps nothing more was to be looked for during the long winter in peaceful quarters at Brandy Station; but now that spring had come, and the grand advance was begun, and battles were in the air all about them—even now the bandsmen merely gave the warriors a tune or two to start them off, and then ingloriously loafed around the camp till they returned, or did not return, as the case might be. One might almost as well have stayed at home in Juno Mills!

The great rock on which Lafe and the German flute-player Foldeen had taken their station gave way beneath them, as was stated in the last chapter, and smashed its way down the steep hillside, crushing the brush and rooting up vines as it went, snapping saplings like pipestems, and bowling over even trees of a larger growth. It brought up almost at the bottom of the hill, in the heart of a clump of sturdy cedars.

A long gash of earth laid bare and of foliage ripped and strewn aside stretched up the incline to mark the track of the fallen boulder. Half-way up this pathway of devastation a boy presently appeared.

Lafe had crawled up out of the débris of saplings, boughs, and tangled creepers into which he had been hurled, and clambered over now to the open space. Then he stood looking up and down in a puzzled way, rubbing his head. His clothes were torn a good deal, he had lost his cap, and he was conscious of numerous bruises under these damaged clothes of his.

There was blood on the palm of his hand, which had come from his head. So far as feeling could guide him, this, however, was nothing but a scalp scratch. He cared more about the tremendous bark one of his shins had got, close up under his knee. When he took his first aimless steps, this had already stiffened, and was hurting him.

Suddenly he remembered that he had not been alone on the rock. Foldeen Schell had been with him, and had grabbed his arm just as everything gave way under them. His wits were still wool-gathering under the combined scare and tumble, and he began mechanically poking about among the underbrush at his feet, as if the missing flute-player might be hidden there. Or was he hunting for his cap? For a dazed minute or two he hardly knew.

Then the sense of bewilderment lifted itself, and was gone. Lafe straightened himself, and looked comprehensively about him.

"Foldeen!" he shouted shrilly, and then bent all his powers of hearing for a reply. There came no answering call.

The air was full of other sounds—the rattling echoes of musketry-firing and the boom of bigger guns, some far off, others seemingly near, all mingling here among the thicket recesses in a subdued, continuous clamor. Perhaps shouting was of no use.

Lafe climbed up the hill a dozen yards or so, to a point where he could go no farther, and scrutinized his surroundings carefully. The impenetrable wall of foliage shut out the valley from him even more completely than when he was on the ridge. He called again and again, and explored the bushes on either side, to no purpose.

Limping slowly down the track cleared by the passing rock, he continued his search to the right and left. He knew so little of how he himself had escaped death that there was nothing to help him guess how it had fared with his companion.

He had not known much about this missing bandsman heretofore, save that he seemed to be the best fellow among the three or four German musicians which the band contained. The boy, like the rest, spoke and thought of all these alien comrades as "Dutchmen," and he was far from comprehending that the outlandish name "Foldeen" was only a corruption of "Valentine." But a common misfortune binds swift ties, and Lafe, as he kept up his quest, began to think of Schell quite affectionately.

He recalled how good-tempered he had always been; how he alone had made jokes on the long march, when the cold and driving rain had soured every one else, and empty stomachs grumbled to keep company with aching bones.

Reflecting upon this, Lafe realized that he was very fond of the "Dutchman," and would be in despair if he had come to grief.

"Foldeen!" he yelled out again.

"Sh! Sh! geeb guiet!" came a guttural reply, from somewhere near by.

The boy's heart lightened on the instant. He looked hastily about him with a cheerful eye, trying to trace the direction of the voice. "Where are you?" he demanded, in a lower tone.

For answer, the blue-coated German rose from a cover of brush, away down the hill, and beckoned him, enforcing at the same time by emphatic gestures the importance of coming noiselessly.

Lafe stole down furtively, and in a minute was bending close beside Foldeen in shrubby shelter.

"Get hurt any?" Lafe asked, subduing his voice almost to a whisper in deference to the other's visible anxiety.

Foldeen shook his head. "It is much worse," he murmured back. "I have my flute lost."

The boy could not but smile. "We can thank our stars we weren't both smashed to atoms," he observed.

"Sh-h! don't talk!" Foldeen adjured him, and indicated with

a sidewise nod of the head that special reasons for silence lay in that direction.

Lafe edged himself forward, and looked out through the bushes. They were on the crest of a little mound which jutted out slightly from the descending face of the hillside. The bottom of the ravine lay only thirty feet or so below them.

Save for the scattered clumps of dwarf firs, hardly higher than the mullein stalks about them, the ground was clear, and the short grass told Lafe's practised eye that it was pasture land. Beyond, there was the gravelled bed of a stream, along which a small rivulet wandered from side to side.

At the first glance his eye had taken in various splashes of color dotting the grass, which suggested bluebells. He saw now that these were made by the uniforms of men, who lay sprawled in various unnatural postures, flat on the green earth. Most of them were on their faces, and not one of them stirred. Lafe moved his head about among the screening bushes, and was able to count twenty-six of these motionless figures.

The boy had seen such sights before, and had even helped bring in the wounded from the field of Payne's Farm during the most of a long, cold night in the previous November. This experience guided him now to remark a curious thing. No muskets, knapsacks, or canteens were scattered about beside these fallen men. And another odd detail—they were all barefooted.

"Some one's been along, after the fighting was over, and skinned everything clean," he muttered to his companion.

Foldeen nodded again, and once more held up a warning hand. He himself was intently watching something beneath, from his side of the leafy cover. The boy shifted his position, and craning his neck over the other's shoulder, saw that just below them, where the ascent began, there stretched a rough, newly made ridge of sods, fence rails and tree-tops, which had evidently been used as a breastwork.

Behind this there were other human forms, also lying prone,

but clad in gray or butternut instead of blue. Here, too, there was no sign of life, but only that fixed absence of motion to which the remote thunder of gun-fire gave such a bitter meaning.

"Anybody there?" whispered the boy.

"I dink so," returned Foldeen, under his breath. "Dere is some, what you call it, hanky-banky, goes on here. Look yourself!"

He moved aside, and Lafe crowded into his place, and put his head out cautiously through the bushes. In one corner of the breastwork there was to be seen a big pile of accoutrements— knapsacks, muskets, swords, water-bottles, and the like, as well as a heap of old boots and miscellaneous foot-gear.

"Vell, how you make it out?" asked Foldeen.

Lafe drew in his head. "The way I figure it," he whispered, "is first, that they held this place against our men, and drove 'em off. Then they went out, and gathered up these traps, and brought 'em in there. Then some more of our men came along, and chased them out. That's what it looks like."

"Well, den, vare is gone dem second men of ours?" the German demanded.

"They've gone after 'em, up the valley, there."

Foldeen shook his head. "Dey don't do such foolishness," he objected. "Ven dey take some place like dis, den dey shtick to him. I know so much, if I do blay mid the band."

"There'd be rations in the knapsacks," mused Lafe, after a pause. He had never been so hungry before in his life.

"What do you say to sneaking down there, and trying to find something to eat?" he suggested. "Come on!" he added persuasively. "There's nobody down there that—nobody that we need be afraid of."

"Vell, I am afraid, dot's all," responded Foldeen.

"They can't do more than make us prisoners," urged the boy, "and that's better than starving to death. Come on! I'm going to make a try."

The German took his companion by the arm. "See here," he

explained; "ven dey catch you, dot's all right. You are prisoner; dot's all. Ven dey catch me, den it goes one, two, dree—
bang, und den Foldeen Schell addends his own funeral. Dot's
the difference by you und me."

"Nonsense!" said Lafe. "They don't shoot anybody in the
band."

"Anyhow, dey shoot me out of de band," persisted Foldeen,
gloomily. "I was in dot oder army myself, sometimes."

The boy drew a long breath of enlightened surprise, which
was almost a whistle.

"Well, then, you stay here," he said, after a little, "and I'll
take a look at the thing by myself."

Suiting the action to the word, Lafe laid hold of the stoutest
saplings, and lowered himself down by his arms to the ledge
below. The footing was not quite easy; but by hanging to the
vines he managed to work his way obliquely across the face of
the declivity, and yet keep pretty well under cover of the
bushes.

Suddenly, emerging from the thicket, he found himself quite
inside the breastwork, which he had entered from the open
rear. The more terrible signs of the conflict which had been
waged here a few hours before forced themselves upon his
attention, first of all.

He braced himself to walk past them, and to go straight to
the heap of knapsacks piled up among the branches in the
corner.

Lifting one of the haversacks, he opened it. There was a tin
cup on top, and some woolen things which might be socks.
Pushing his hand under these, he came upon some bread, and
paused to express his content by a smile.

"Drop it—you!"

A loud, peremptory voice close at his shoulder caused the
boy to turn with alarmed abruptness. A burly man, with a
rough, sandy stuble of beard about his face, had come into the
breastwork—or perhaps had been hidden there all the while.

Lafe's first impulse was one of satisfaction at noting that the stranger wore the blue Union uniform.

Then he looked into the man's face, and the instinct of pleasure died suddenly away.

III

The Bounty-Jumper

When Lafe Hornbeck looked into the countenance of the strange man who appeared thus unexpectedly before him in the deserted breastwork, it needed no second glance to tell him that he had to deal with a scoundrel. A threatening and formidable scoundrel he seemed, too, with his heavy, slouching shoulders, his long arms ending in huge, hairy hands, and the surly scowl on his low-browed, frowzy face.

He wore the dark-blue jacket and light-blue trousers of the Federal infantry, and their relative newness showed that he was a fresh recruit. His badge was the Maltese cross of the Fifth Corps, and its color, red, indicated the First Division. This was the corps and division of Boyce's brigade.

Even in the first minute of surprised scrutiny of the fellow Lafe found himself thinking that he probably belonged to that Ohio regiment which he had seen bringing up the rear of the line forming for battle.

"Drop it, I say!" the man repeated, harshly.

Lafe drew his hand from the haversack slowly and reluctantly.

"There's enough more of 'em here," he protested, nodding at the pile in the corner of the earthwork. "I haven't had a mouthful since before sunrise, and I'm hungry."

"Where'd you come from, anyway, and what business have you got here?" the other demanded, with an oath and a forward step.

"I'm Fifth Corps, same as you are," replied Lafe, making an effort to keep his voice bold and firm, "and I came here by tumbling head over heels down that hill there, right spang from top to bottom." He took courage from the indecision apparent in the man's eyes to add, "And that's why I'm going to have something to eat."

The stranger gave a grunt, which, bad-tempered though it was, did not seem to forbid action, and Lafe drew forth the bread again. It was dry and tasteless enough, but he almost forgot to look at his unwelcome companion in the satisfaction which he had in gulping down the food.

The man lounged over to the pile of haversacks, muskets, and clothing, and seemed to be trying to make out whether anything was missing. He grunted again, and turned to Lafe just as the last crust was disappearing.

"You're a drummer, ain't you?" he said roughly. "Where do you belong?"

Lafe held up his hand to signify that his mouth was too full to talk. "Boyce's brigade," he explained after a little.

"That ain't what I asked. What's your regiment?"

"Haven't got any regiment," replied Lafe. "I'm in the brigade band."

"Oh!" growled the man, and turned on his heel. The information seemed to relieve his mind, for when he had taken a few loitering steps about the enclosure, and confronted Lafe again, his tone was less quarrelsome. "Left the hospital camp up there, eh?" he asked, with a sidelong nod of his head toward the top of the hill.

"Well, yes—and no," responded the boy. "It was there when I left it, but it ain't there now. Or rather, it *is* there, but *we* ain't there."

"What are you driving at?" the man demanded, once more in a rougher voice.

"The rebs have gobbled it," said Lafe. "Our folks were skedaddling and the rebs were coming in the last I saw."

The man gave a low whistle of surprise and interest. He

began walking about again, bending his ugly brows in thought meanwhile. From time to time he paused to ask other questions, as to which way the people of the brigade camp had fled, how large was the force which had captured the camp, and the like.

The news evidently impressed him a good deal. Lafe got the idea that somehow it changed his plans. What were these plans? the boy wondered. The whole thing was very hard to make out. More than once he had had it in mind to say that he had left another member of the band, a very nice fellow indeed, up on the side-hill above them, who must also be hungry, and to suggest that he should call him down.

But every time, when this rose to his tongue, a glance at the evil face of the man restrained him. He could not but remember what Foldeen had hinted, that there was some "deviltry" going on down below here. What was it?

"There must have been some pretty tough fighting right here," he ventured to remark, after a while.

"You bet there was!" the other assented. He seemed not averse to a little talk, though his mind was still on other things.

"I don't quite figure it out," the boy went on, cautiously. "Of course, wrastling around in the woods like this, you can't make head nor tail of how things go, or who's on top, or where —but how does it stand—right here, I mean? We're in our own lines here, ain't we?"

The stranger fixed a long, inquiring glance upon the boy's face. Lafe returned the gaze with all the calmness he could muster. He could not help feeling that there was a good deal of stupidity in the stare under which he bore up. The man was not quickminded; that was clear enough. But it was also plain that he was both a stubborn and a brutal creature.

"Yes," he growled, after he had stared Lafe out of countenance, "yes, these are our own lines."

The phrase seemed to tickle his fancy, for something like the beginning of a grin stirred on the stubbly surface about his mouth. "Yes—our own lines," he repeated. How strange it was! All at once, like a flash, Lafe remembered having seen this man before. That slow, sulky wavering of a grimace on his lips betrayed him. Swiftly pursuing the clue, the boy reconstructed in his mind a scene in which this man had played the chief part.

It must have been in the early part of the previous December—just after the army went into winter quarters behind the line of the Orange railroad, cooped up in its earth-huts all the way from Culpeper Court House to Brandy Station. Lafe had gone over on leave one afternoon to the corps headquarters—it must have been of a Thursday, because there was to be a military execution the next day, and these were always fixed for Friday.

The army was then receiving almost weekly large batches of raw recruits, sent from the big cities, some the product of the draft, others forwarded by the enlistment bureaus. Among these newcomers were a great many good citizens and patriots; but there were also a great many cowards and a considerable number of scoundrels who made a business of enlisting to get the bounty, deserting as soon as they could, and enlisting again from some other point.

To prevent wholesale desertions, both of the cowards and the "bounty-jumpers," the utmost vigilance was needed. Their best chance to run away was offered by picket duty, when they found themselves posted out in comparative solitude, in the dark, on the very outskirts of the army line.

To checkmate this, a cordon of cavalry had to be drawn still farther out than the pickets—cavalry-men who slept all day, and at night patrolled the uttermost confines of the great camp, watching with all their eyes and ears, ready on the instant to clap spurs and ride down any skulking wretch who could be discovered attempting his escape.

Even in the teeth of this precaution, the attempts were continually made, and it was the rarest event for a Friday to pass without the spectacle of summary punishment being meted out to some captured deserter on the corps' shooting-ground. Often there were more than one of these victims to martial law.

Lafe now remembered how, with a boy's curiosity, he had

prowled about the provost marshal's guard quarters, fascinated
by the idea that inside the log shanty, where the two sentinels
with fixed bayonets walked constantly up and down, there were
men condemned to be shot at six the following morning.

Standing around, and gossiping amiably with these sentinels,
who shared the common feeling of the army in making pets of
the drummer-boys, he had managed at last to get a glimpse at
one of these fated prisoners.

A face had appeared at the little window, square-cut in the
logs. It was a bad, unkempt face, with a reddish stubble of
beard on jaws and cheek. There may have been some rough
jest passed by the other prisoners inside the hut, for as the boy
watched this face, a grim, mean sort of smile flickered momentarily over it.

Then the face itself disappeared, and left the boy marvelling
that a man could grin in presence of the fact that he was to be
shot on the morrow.

The smile, and the countenance it played upon for that instant of time, burned themselves into his memory. Lafe racked
his brain now for some recollection of having heard that these
particular prisoners were reprieved, or had succeeded in escaping from their log jail. His memory was a blank on the subject.
Yet he felt sure that the face he had seen at that window was the
identical face he now saw before him.

For the life of him, he could not resist the temptation to venture upon this dangerous topic.

"You're one of the new regiments brought over to us from
the old First Corps, ain't you?" he asked, with an effort at an
ingratiating tone.

The man nodded his head in indifferent assent. He seemed to
be listening intently to the sounds of battle in the air. These
were reduced now to faint, far-away cracklings of rifle-firing, as
if only distant sharp-shooters were engaged.

"Suppose this is about the first time you've been under fire,
then," Lafe remarked. He added, with a bragging air: "I was

all through the Payne's Farm and Mine Run racket last November! That was hot enough, I tell you!"

The man made that inarticulate grunt of contempt which we try to convey by the word humph! "So was I," he growled, "and plenty more fights worse than them."

"Oh, got your discharge and 'listed again?" commented the boy.

Again the stranger turned upon him that steady, dull stare of inquiry—like the gaze of a vicious ox. He seemed satisfied at length with the artlessness of Lafe's countenance, but did not trouble himself to answer his suggestion.

"What do you figure on doin' with yourself?" he abruptly asked the boy after a pause.

"How do I know?" retorted Lafe. "I'd try and join brigade headquarters if I knew where they were, but I don't. The next best thing is to try and find some other brigade's headquarters. It's all clear enough outside here now. I guess I'll take some bread with me, and make a break through the woods down the run there. I'll fetch up somewhere, all right."

He bent over the pile of knapsacks, as if to pick one of them up.

"No," the man called out. "Leave 'em alone! You can't take no more of them rations, and you can't go down the run. You can't go anywhere."

Lafe straightened himself. "Why not?" he asked, with an assumption of boldness.

"Because you can't," the other retorted curtly.

"What can I do, then?" Lafe inquired defiantly.

The man looked him over. "You can turn up your toes to the daisies in about another minute, if you don't mind your own business. That's what you can do," he remarked, with an ugly frown.

"What's the use of talking that way?" said Lafe. "I haven't done you any harm, have I?"

"No—and you ain't going to, either," was the reply.

The stranger, as he spoke, took a two-barrelled pistol from his inside jacket-pocket. It was a beautiful weapon, ornamented with a good deal of chased silver. Lafe had seen pistols like this before, in the possession of officers, and knew that they were called Derringers. Private soldiers were not likely to carry weapons of that sort.

He was sure that this man must have stolen the pistol, and the conviction did not assist Lafe to calmness, as he observed the man push one of the hammers back with his thumb to full-cock. It is as bad to be shot by stolen firearms as by those which have been bought and paid for.

The stranger drew from another pocket a gold watch, with a long loop of broad black silk braid hanging from its ring. He held it in the palm of his free hand and glanced at its open face.

"It must be getting along toward noon," Lafe had the temerity to remark. There were cold shivers through his veins, but he managed to keep his tongue steady. If "cheek" could not help him, nothing could.

"About as nigh noon as you're ever likely to git," said the other, making a pretense of again consulting the watch.

Instinct told the lad with a flashlight swiftness that this looking at the watch was buncombe. Men who really meant to kill did not parade timepieces like that.

"I haven't got anything on me that would be of any use to you," he said, with an immense effort at unconcern. "Even if I had, you wouldn't need a gun to take it away from me."

"You've got a mouth on you," said the man, eying him, "and it'll be of use to me to shut it up."

He lifted the pistol as he spoke, and Lafe instinctively closed his eyes, with a confused rush of thoughts in which he seemed to see his old mother sitting in the garden with the Book on her knees, and also the young Ohio officer, who somehow came in among the tall flowers beside her, and these flowers themselves were the regimental flags which the color-sergeant was unfurling.

Then, as nothing happened, the boy opened his eyes again, and found himself able to look into the two black disks of the Derringer's muzzle without flinching.

He could even look beyond the muzzle, as the barrels sloped downward toward him, and he now saw distinctly that the two little upright steel nipples bore no caps. The discovery made him annoyed at his own cowardice. It was easier now to be bold.

"What's your idea, anyway?" he asked the man, with an added effrontery in his tone. "If you'd been going to shoot, you'd have done it long ago. This thing doesn't scare me at all, and I don't see how it does you any good. What are you getting at, anyhow?"

"I'd as soon shoot you as look at you!" the other declared with angry emphasis, but lowering the weapon.

"Yes, but seeing you ain't going to shoot, what are you going to do?" Lafe put in.

The ruffian eyed him again. "If I agree not to hurt you, will you do what I tell you?" he demanded.

"Well, maybe I will," replied the boy. His spirits rose as his contempt for this slow and shilly-shallying sort of scoundrel increased. "What is it you want me to do?"

"I want you to help me carry some things I've got together over there, on the other side of the creek. We'll go over now, and bring 'em back here."

"I'll take another bite of bread, first," it occurred to the boy to say. He lifted a haversack, and shoved in one hand to burrow among its contents, while with his foot, as if by accident, he pushed one of the muskets lengthwise so that he might grab it the more readily if occasion required.

Biting in leisurely fashion on the new crust he had found, Lafe felt emboldened to make the conversation personal. "That's a mighty fine watch you've got there," he remarked, affably. "I suppose it went with the pistol—sort o' thrown in, like."

The man put the watch back into his trousers pocket. He

seemed for a moment disposed to annoyance. Then the furtive, mean grin curled over the lower part of his face. "Yes—it was thrown in," he replied, almost with a chuckle. "Come on" he added. "You can chew that bread as you go along."

"But what am I to get?" the boy queried, slowly turning the crust over to select a place for the next bite. "Do I come in for any watches and silver-mounted Derringers, too?"

"You jest help me for all you're worth," replied the man, after a moment's pause, "and I'll see to it you git something worth your while."

"It's got to be something pretty good," said Lafe, meditatively chewing on the hard bread. "A fellow can't be expected to risk the chance of being shot for nothing."

"There ain't no danger of gittin' shot," the other replied.

"Well, hung, then," Lafe said impudently.

"What's that you say?" the man growled, with reawakened suspicion. "Who said anything about hangin'? What kind o' nonsense are you talkin', anyway?"

It might be a desperately foolish thing to do, but Lafe could not hold himself from doing it—and for that matter didn't try.

"Why, they hang men caught robbing the dead on battle-fields, don't they—especially when they're bounty-jumpers to begin with?"

He had called this out as swiftly as he could, holding himself in readiness as he spoke, and now he pounced downward, and clutching the musket, lifted it for defence.

The man sprang forward with a quicker motion than the boy had counted upon, and before Lafe had got erect he felt the stifling grasp of big, hard fingers around his throat.

IV

Red Pete in Captivity

Things grew black before Lafe's eyes as the iron clutch about his throat tightened. He strove desperately to twist himself loose, using in a frantic way the wrestling tricks he knew; but the grip of the bounty-jumper was to powerful. Lafe's head seemed swelling in the effort to burst, and feeling in all his body below that fatal circlet became numb. There was room for but a single thought—this was what being choked to death meant!

Afterward it never seemed to the boy that he entirely lost consciousness. He could remember that there was a violent sidewise jerk at his neck, and then the sense of intolerable squeezing there ceased.

But there was still an awful buzzing inside his head, and midnight blackness, shot with interlacing lines of crazy light, spread itself definitely about him.

Gradually he perceived that he was breathing again, and that he could feel his arms and legs once more to be parts of him. He knew that he was exceedingly tired and sleepy, and felt only that the one desirable thing was to lie still, just as he was. He mentally resolved that he would not stir or open his eyes for anybody.

"How vas it mit you, Lafe?"

The words were undoubtedly in the air. He realized that, and lay very still, lazily confident that he would hear them again.

Things began to assort themselves in his brain. Foldeen and he had been on a big, overhanging rock, which had tumbled with them, and by some chance they hadn't both been killed, and now Foldeen was looking for him. But he would lie still and rest.

"Vake up! Lafe! Vake up!"

The boy heard these words, too. The heavy drowsiness upon him seemed to be lifting, and he felt some one fumbling at his breast, inside his shirt. On the instant he was awake and sitting up, wonderingly staring.

A tall figure had risen away from him as he opened his eyes. The sun had come out, and was falling warm and full upon the mass of young green which covered the hillside. This erect standing figure was for a moment or two very indistinct against the dazzling light. Then Lafe made out that this was Foldeen.

Almost in the same glance he saw that he was sitting among the heap of knapsacks and battle-field débris in the corner of the breastwork. Close beside him—so near that he felt he must have been lying upon him when he recovered consciousness—sprawled the burly figure of the bounty-jumper, face downward, and quite still.

Lafe was so contented with the spectacle on which his eyes rested that it did not occur to him to ask what had happened.

It was pleasanter to look at Foldeen's honest face, beaming satisfaction back into the boy's slow and inquiring regard. The German said nothing, but just smiled at Lafe.

As the boy's memory cleared itself, the fact that Foldeen had had no breakfast, and that he had left him in his covert on the hillside with very little compunction, rose above everything else.

Lafe pointed to the knapsacks, and attempted to speak. His throat and windpipe, the roots of his tongue, and everything else involved in vocal sounds, seemed at the effort to shrivel up in pain. At first he thought he could not manage to utter a syllable. Then, at the cost of some suffering, he forced out the words, "Bread—there." They sounded quite strange in his ears.

Foldeen nodded his head, still with the jubilant grin on his round, kindly face. "Ya vole," he said, in a matter-of-fact way. "But first I fix me up dis fellow dight."

He sorted out of the pile of stolen property two officers'

sashes of knitted crimson silk, and kneeling down beside the outstretched form of the bounty-jumper, proceeded calmly to bind his legs together at the ankles with one of them.

Then, with some roughness, he dragged the prostrate man's arms together till their wrists met on the small of his back, and there tied them securely.

"He ain't dead, then?" commented Lafe, his throat feeling easier.

"Vell, maybe he is," said Foldeen. "I hit him shtraight by the top of his head mit dot gun-barrel, und he vent down like if he vas a tousand bricks. But it makes nodding. Ven he is dead, den he is good tied up. Ven he is alife, den he is much better tied up. Now ve eat us our breakfast in kviet. Bread, you say? Show me dot bread."

Foldeen needed no showing, but was on the instant wolfing huge mouthfuls from the half-loaf which the nearest haversack furnished. Lafe leaned back and watched him, his mind filled with formless emotions of thanksgiving.

In such intervals as he could spare from the bread, Foldeen lightly told what had happened. From his perch up on the hillside he had seen everything, and though beyond earshot, had been able to follow pretty well what was going on.

When the rascal drew the pistol, Foldeen slipped out from his hiding-place, and began letting himself noiselessly down the hill. He had entered the breastwork just at the critical moment, and had dealt Lafe's assailant a crushing blow on the skull with a gun he picked up. That was all. It was very simple.

"And mighty lucky for me, too!" was the boy's heartfelt comment. "Foldeen, do you know what this fellow here's been doing?"

"I haf some brains on my head. I haf seen his business. He is a dief."

"He got these things together here," said Lafe, "and he told me there was a lot more over on the other side of the creek. He was going to make me help him bring them here. That was what he had the pistol out for. But what beats me is, what did he expect to do with them? A man can't get out of the lines with a load of traps like this, even if he could carry 'em."

For answer Foldeen rose, and turned the sprawling, inert form of his captive over on its back. The pallor of the thief's face, contrasted with the coarse, sandy hair and stubble of beard, made it seem more repellent than ever.

The German bent over to examine this countenance more carefully.

"By jiminy priest! I bet me anydings I know dot man!" he exclaimed staring downward intently. "Vake up dere, you!" he called out, pushing the recumbent figure with his foot. "I know you, Red Pete! Dot's no use, your making out you vas asleep! Vake up, kvick now!" and he stirred him with his boot again.

"I bet he's dead," said Lafe.

No! The man half opened his eyes and moved his head restlessly. The color came back into his face, the muscles of which were drawn now into an angry scowl by pain. He fell back helpless after an instinctive effort to lift himself to a sitting posture. Then, shifting his head, he discovered the two friends, and fixed upon them a stolid, half-stupefied stare.

"How you like him, dot Red Pete, eh?" Foldeen burst forth, with exultation, never taking his jubilant glance from the face of the wretch on the ground. "Dot's a beauty, ain'd it? Dot's a first-glass Ghristmas bresent, eh, to find in your shtocking! Or no, he is too big. Ve hang him on a dree, eh? A nize Ghristmass-dree, all by ourselves, eh? O Red Pete, you vas git the best place by dot dree, right in front, on the biggest branch!"

The man on the ground had been staring upward at the speaker in a puzzled fashion. He had slowly taken in the situation that he was disabled, bound hand and foot, and at the German's mercy. At last he seemed to recall who was talking to him.

"I never done you no harm!" he growled.

"So-o!" ejaculated Foldeen, with loud sarcasm. "Dot vas no harm, eh, dot vas only some little fun, eh, to make me on fire und burn me up mit the rest in dot shteamboat? Just some funny joke, eh? Vell, den, now I will haf me *my* funny liddle jokes mit you."

Speaking with such swift volubility that Lafe followed with difficulty the thread of his narrative, Foldeen unfolded a curious tale. Before the war he had drifted about in the South a good deal, playing in orchestras in New Orleans some of the time, and then for whole seasons travelling up and down the Mississippi in the bands of the old passenger steamers.

This man, Red Pete, was a well-known character on the river, too well known all the way from Cairo to the last levee. Sometimes he was in charge of a squad of slaves, sometimes travelling on his own account as a gambler, slave-buyer, or even for a trip as minor boat officer—but always an evil-minded scoundrel.

One night when they were lying at the wharf under the bluff at Natchez, the cabins of the steamer had been robbed, and fire set to the boat in several places. Those on board barely escaped with their lives, and when they found that Red Pete was missing, every one knew well enough that he was the thief and would-be murderer.

Foldeen believed there had been some search for him, but those were rough times, and he was never tracked down. Then the war came, and Foldeen perforce went into the band of an Arkansas regiment—until the opportunity of making his escape to the Union lines occurred. During that period of reluctant service with the band which played "Dixie" and "The Bonnie Blue Flag," he had more than once heard of Red Pete as a sort of unattached guerilla, who, like many other river ruffians, played for his own hand between the lines.

"Und now it looks like dot game of his vas pretty near blayed out, eh?" Foldeen concluded with a chuckle.

Lafe gazed down with loathing upon this burly and powerful

desperado, lying in such utter helplessness. He told Foldeen in turn how he had seen this very man in the Fifth Corps "quod" only last winter, condemned to death.

"So-o!" exclaimed the German. "I remember dot. All five deserters und bounty-jumpers dug deir vay out, und gilled a sentinel, und skipped in the night. So-o! Ve don't have us dot private Ghristmas-dree after all. Ve make Red Pete a bresent to Cheneral Boyce, instead."

"Yes, but where shall we find General Boyce?" Lafe put in.

Moved by a common impulse, the two turned their backs on their prisoner, and went outside the earthwork.

The sky was overcast with shifting clouds again, and gave no hint as to the points of compass. The little valley, strewn with motionless, blue-clad figures, lay wrapped in such silence that they could hear the murmur of the rivulet beyond. On both sides the hills rose steeply, covered with thick, tangled verdure.

Behind and before them the valley lost itself a hundred yards away in dense thickets. A sharp wind had risen, under which the tree-tops moaned. Above the noises of the gathering gale, faint sounds of distant firing could be heard.

"We'd better stay where we are," the boy suggested. "There's been rough-and-tumble fighting all around here, and there's no way of figuring out where our people are. I guess they don't know themselves. If we go hunting around, we're as likely as not to walk into a hornets' nest. I tell you what we'll do. If we can find a piece of white cloth, we'll put it up on a pole out here, and we'll bury these men of ours. Nobody'll touch us, if they come along and find us doing that. Besides, it's the right thing to do."

They turned back into the breastwork, and Lafe, rummaging among the knapsacks, speedily found a roll of bandage-linen which would serve his purpose. He got out more bread as well, and found a scrap of fried bacon. The two ate standing; now that they had a plan, they were all eagerness to put it into operation.

Red Pete had closed his eyes again, and was lying perfectly still. The excitement of his capture having died away, they now scarcely gave him a glance.

"I wonder what time it's got to be," Lafe remarked, as they were finishing the last mouthful. "Oh, I forgot—he's got a gold watch in his pocket, and I think it's going."

Foldeen knelt, and feeling about for it, drew the watch from Red Pete's trousers pocket. "By jiminy priest! it's near four o'clock!" he exclaimed. Then rising, he looked more attentively at the watch, turning it over in his hand admiringly, and prying open the back of the case with his nail.

There seemed to be an inscription on the inside of the cover, and Foldeen held the watch sidewise to decipher this more readily, while Lafe peered over his shoulder to look.

"It's in writing," he said; "let me take it. I can make it out easier, perhaps."

The legend inside the gold case was delicately engraved in small running script. Lafe, reading with increasing surprise, discovered it to be this:—

Presented to

Lieut. Lyman Hornbeck,

January 22, 1864,

by his friends and admirers

of St. Mark's Church,

Cleveland.

"Say, Foldeen," Lafe burst forth, "I bet that's a relation of mine. I've got an uncle—"

"So everybody has got some ungles," put in the musician.

"No, but look here," the boy insisted. "That say's 'Lyman Hornbeck.' Well, my father's brother was Lyman Hornbeck. I've heard talk about my Uncle Lymie ever since I could remember. He left home years ago, before I was born. They always said he was out West, somewhere. I bet it's the same man. At any rate, I'm going to take a look around. You fix up the pole and the white flag outside here, and bring out the shovels. I'll be back again and help."

Lafe's eyes sparkled with a new excitement as he made his way across the pasture to the bank of the creek, noting as he strode along that all the lifeless forms on the grass wore the uniforms of privates.

He walked along the shelving edge of his bank from one end of the clearing to the other, to make sure that the winding bed of the stream below did not hold what he sought for. There was no sign, anywhere in the open, of an officer.

He remembered now that Red Pete had spoken of the other side of the creek, which lay so much lower than the bank on which he stood that it could not have been raked by the fire from the breastwork. It was swampy ground, covered heavily with high, bushing willows and rank growths of tall marsh grass. No path leading into it was discernible, perhaps because the wind blew the reeds and flags so stiffly sidewise.

With a running jump Lafe cleared the bed of the stream and pushed his way into the morass. It was not so wet underfoot as he had expected, but the tangle of vines and undergrowth made his progress slow and troublesome. It was easy enough to see that no portion of the brigade had passed this way; there were no indications that wild nature here had ever been disturbed. The boy pressed on until, finding the swamp-jungle getting worse with every yard, and the shadows deepening about him, it was clearly useless to go farther.

Turning, he fancied he knew from which direction he had advanced into this maze. There was no use in merely retracing his steps. He settled his bearings as well as might be, and struck off to the left, to work his way diagonally out to the clearing.

When he had floundered on over what seemed twice the distance of his first direct line, and halted, hot, tired, and out of breath, he could detect no open space ahead. The wind was blowing hard from up above, and the noise of its impact upon the wilderness was in itself enough to confuse the senses. It was undoubtedly growing dark.

"Hello—Hornbeck!" Lafe shouted.

The wind seized the shrill cry and scattered it into fragmentary echoes. It was worse than useless to call out. He must push doggedly on. Lafe turned a little to the right, and crushed his way forward through the brush and bracken, with a step to which dawning fears of being lost lent added vigor.

He was traversing slightly higher ground now. The willows and marsh grass had given place to a more orderly second growth of firs, with dry moss underfoot and open spaces overhead. In one of these breathing-places of the thicket, he came suddenly upon the blue-clad figure of a man sitting propped up against a stump, his head hanging on his breast.

He was young and fair-haired, and Lafe's glance took in the glint of gilt straps on his shoulders as he hurried toward him. Almost in the same instant the boy, kneeling at his side, saw that this was the young Ohio officer he had spoken with at sunrise and that he was alive.

As he sought to waken the wounded man, and make out how badly he had been hurt, it grew suddenly, strangely dark. Looking upward, Lafe saw above the tree-tops nearest him, piling skyward on the wind, a great writhing wall of black smoke.

It mounted in huge, waving coils as he looked, and came nearer, bending forward in a sinister arch across the heavens. His startled ears dimly heard a sullen, roaring sound, newly engrafted upon the whistling of the wind.

The woods were on fire!

V

Lafe Rescues an Officer, and Finds His Cousin

Lafe had seen forest fires near Juno Mills, and there was nothing in his recollection of them to suggest great danger in this one. He was more interested for the moment in the young Ohio officer propped against the stump. This lieutenant was barefooted. A thief had evidently taken also his sash, sword, and belt.

He was probably one of Red Pete's victims. The others could not be far away, among them Lafe's problematical kinsman with the presentation watch.

But finding a possible uncle was just now of less importance than finding a safe way out of the thicket. The smoke grew visibly thicker, and Lafe could detect, off to the left, the distinct crackling noise of flames. He dropped on one knee again, and patted the officer's shoulder with decision.

The young man moved his head restlessly, then opened his eyes and stared dully at Lafe.

"Which way is the creek?" the drummer-boy shouted.

The lieutenant, as if dazed, looked half wonderingly into the boy's face. Then he blinked, shook himself, and made a move to sit upright. He sank back with his mouth drawn awry by the severity of his pain, and forced the semblance of a laugh upon these pale lips.

"I thought at first I was home, and you were my brother," he said.

"How bad are you hurt? Can you walk?" Lafe demanded. "We've got to get out of this. The woods are on fire and the wind is blowing it dead this way. Where are you hit?"

"Minie ball here—between the shoulders and the lung, I hope," replied the other, indicating his left side. "It's stiffened and I can't lift myself. Help me on my feet, and I guess I can walk away."

Lafe put an arm under him and gave him his hand. The lieutenant, with a groan, set his teeth and scrambled up on his feet. He looked about him for an instant, and then hastily seated himself on the stump.

"I'm dizzy for the minute," he murmured. "I must have lost so much blood. It's afternoon, isn't it?"

"Past five. You'd better brace up now, and try to come on. Which way is it?"

The officer looked vaguely around. "I hardly know," he confessed. "I can just remember dragging myself off into the swamp. I thought I should find some water, and I guess my strength gave out about here. Somebody came along and pulled off my boots and stockings, and went through my pockets, but I was too near dead to resist, and I kept my eyes shut."

"Well, you want to keep 'em open now. This must be the way out, according to the wind. That's it; get your arm over my shoulder, and we'll make a break."

They walked thus for a dozen steps or so, the officer leaning a little on Lafe's right shoulder. Then the wounded man stopped.

"I'd rather you went ahead," he called into the boy's ear. "The branches knock against my game side, this way. I'll keep behind you"; and so they went on again, Lafe pushing the saplings and boughs aside for the other.

The smoke had become almost blinding now, as it sifted through the motionless air of the thicket. The noises had risen now into a pandemonium of uproar—on the left the furious bellowing of the tempest and the flames, to the right a series of outbursts that shook the earth like mine explosions. It sometimes seemed to Lafe as if he distinguished the cheers and vague cries of men, off on the other side—and then back would come the chaotic din.

Awed and deafened, the two pushed doggedly on, Lafe stealing glances over his shoulder, to see if the officer was following.

He came, holding to the branches with his right hand for support, and striving to pick soft places for his bare feet among the stones and prickly ground vines.

It had suddenly grown very hot. The heat began to sting Lafe's forehead and eyes. They were advancing into the temperature of a veritable furnace. The crackling noises to the left had swollen all at once to an angry tumult close at hand.

Looking up with smarting eyes through the pungent smoke, the boy beheld scattered flashes of flame dotting the murky shadows of the forest beyond, and even as he looked these tongues of fire ran forward under the wind with darting swiftness. An imperative outcry behind Lafe called a halt. He turned as his companion reeled, clutched wildly at an ash sapling, and fell against it, his head hanging helplessly forward on his breast.

"It's no use," he gasped, as the boy strode back. "I'm choking, and I'm played out. I can't go another step."

He falteringly lifted one of his torn and bleeding feet, and put it down again. His arm slipped from around the sapling, and he would have fallen if Lafe had not caught him.

"Why don't you be a man!" the boy screamed shrilly through the tumult.

A sort of angry desperation seized upon Lafe. He would drag this Ohio tenderfoot out of the fire in spite of himself. With rough energy he fitted his shoulder under the officer's armpit, and drew his right arm forward in the determined clutch of both his hands.

"Come on now, the best way you can. Never mind your feet or your shoulder either!" he yelled, and then, stiffening his back under the burden, he staggered forward.

He could never afterward recall anything definitely of how he did it, or how long it took. But through the shrivelling heat, through the murderous swoop of fire and smoke, somehow he came. All at once there was the play of cooler air upon his face. Instead of the choking smoke and darkness he was wrapped about by a clean wind. It had grown suddenly daylight again.

Bent almost double under his burden, he strove in vain to

fill his lungs with this fresh air. It was dimly in his mind to straighten himself, and breathe in all he could hold. But the load on his back seemed to be pressing him further down and whirling him round as well.

Then he was lying face downward, on the dry, soft earth with the sharp edges of stiff marsh grass in his hair. Something heavy lay across him. He rolled himself from the encumbrance and stretched himself out luxuriously on his back. The wind soughed pleasantly through the reeds about his head.

He went to sleep, dreaming placidly as he dropped off that ordered swarms of men were passing through the tall grass close beside him, firing volleys and cheering as they fired.

Four red points of light, at regular distances apart, and shining faintly against a broad canopy of blackness, was what Lafe, still lying on his back, beheld when he woke. He looked at them lazily for what seemed a long time, and did not care in the least what they signified. Then, quite without any effort he knew they were lanterns hung on a rope.

There were sinuous lines of motion in the darkness above the lanterns, and these revealed themselves to him as the sides of canvas-strips stirring in the wind. This, too, did not seem important, and he indolently closed his eyes again.

A sharp cry, ringing abruptly out close at hand, awoke him more thoroughly. He even lifted his head a little, and saw many more lights—lanterns, kerosene lamps, and tallow-dips stuck in bottles. They stretched out irregularly in all directions, illumining little patches of space, which seemed all the smaller by comparison with the vast blocks of deep shadows surrounding them.

The radiance of many of these lights centred upon a broad table, about which several men were standing in their shirt sleeves, and with aprons like butchers. There seemed to be another man lying on this table, and one of his legs was bared to the thigh. Some of these shadowy figures moved, and another cry arose. Lafe shut his eyes, and turned away from the spectacle.

There was now a rustle of straw under him, and he noted

that his head was resting on a canvas pillow filled with straw. A strong smell, as of arnica, attracted his attention. Now he understood that he was in a hospital tent.

He wondered where he himself had been hurt. Except for a general, dull aching of the muscles, he was conscious of no special pain. He tried opening and closing his fingers, and moving his toes.

Each member seemed in working order. He passed his hands along his sides, and still found nothing amiss. But his head certainly did ache.

Vague recollection of the events of the day began to stir in his memory, but not at all in their right order. It seemed as if it was Foldeen Schell whom he had carried out of the burning woods, and nearer still in point of time seemed to be Red Pete's stifling grip upon his neck. Then, somehow, his thoughts drifted to the watch and its inscription.

He drowsily tried to think what this Lyman Hornbeck must be like—a gray-bearded old man and a church-member, and yet only a lieutenant. So his vagrant fancy drifted about on the border-land of sleep.

Suddenly there were voices close about him. Half opening his eyes, Lafe blinked at three or four torches which some soldiers were holding up at the foot of his bed. A half-dozen officers were there as well, and the foremost one was General Boyce.

The light hurt Lafe's eyes, and he closed them. The general's cheery voice remained in his ears, though, and conveyed so true a notion of the man that Lafe seemed to continue to behold him, the red torchlight heightening the glow of health on his round cheeks and shining in his brave, kindly eyes.

"Oh, you'll be up and about in a day or two," the general was saying, in a hearty, encouraging way. "Won't he, surgeon-major?"

"Well, inside a week," answered another voice. "The wound in itself wasn't much. It's the loss of blood that's worst."

"Lieutenant," the general went on, "if I don't call you captain when you get back from your furlough, it won't be my fault. You've been mentioned in the despatches. Your company's tussle with the breastwork under the hill was as plucky a thing as has been done to-day. Well, good luck to you!"

There was a rattle of spurs and swords as if the group were moving, and then Lafe was conscious that the young Ohio officer spoke, as if from the very next bed.

"O general," he called out, "I'll save my own thanks for some other time! But I want you to take notice of this boy here. *He's* one who ought to be mentioned in despatches. I'd have been roasted alive if it hadn't been for him. He came into the woods and found me, and routed me up, and made me walk, and when I gave out he actually carried me right through the blaze. Talk about charging the breastwork! What he did was worth fifty of it."

Lafe felt through his closed eyelids that the torches were being held so as to cover him with their light. Oddly enough, he seemed without desire to look.

"I won't forget," said the general. "How badly off is he?"

"He was brought in with the lieutenant here," returned the surgeon-major. "I didn't see him myself. You were here, nurse?"

"Poor little fellow, he doesn't seem to have been shot, but his head was laid open to the bone somehow. Doctor Alvord thought it must have been a horse's hoof."

"We were both on the ground in the way when the big charge down the run was made," explained the lieutenant. "He must have got trampled on. I think he's a drummer in the brigade band. I noticed him when we went into line this morning."

"I wonder if it can be our Juno Mills boy," broke in the general. Lafe felt that the great man was bending over close to him. "Some Dutchman in the band was telling a tremendous yarn about a youngster who went down alone into the breastwork after it was deserted, and had a fight, single-handed, with a baggage-thief, and played the deuce generally. Does anybody know whether he's the same one?"

Lafe could never understand afterward what ailed him to behave so, but at this he kept his breathing down to its gentlest possible form. The general and his attendants moved off down the aisles, halting with the torches at other bedsides to give cheer. Their going gave Lafe leisure for the thought which interested him most.

The news that his head had been laid open to the bone had fascinated him. He put up a hand now and felt of his skull. It was covered all over with interlaced strips of stiff plaster encased in a soft linen bandage drawn tight.

"Are you feeling all right?"

It was the voice of the lieutenant. Lafe, proud of his plasters, opened his eyes and made out the young officer, propped up with a couple of straw pillows on the bed next his.

"My head aches a little, that's all," said Lafe. "Say, we had a squeak for it, didn't we?"

"I sha'n't forget it—nor you," responded the other.

"Cleveland's in Ohio, ain't it?" the boy asked, all at once pursuing a subject which had kept dodging in and out of his mind. "Perhaps you know an old man in one of the Ohio regiments—he must be getting along toward sixty—he's a lieutenant, and his name's Lyman Hornbeck. I was looking for him this afternoon when—when I lighted on you."

The young officer, quite heedless of his bandages, sat bolt upright and stared at Lafe as if too much amazed for words.

"I don't know what you're driving at," he said at last. "*My* name is Lyman Hornbeck, and I'm a Cleveland man and a lieutenant—but I'm a long way off from sixty. You can't mean my father? He's been dead two years. His name was Lyman. Why, hold on! General Boyce said something about Juno Mills —my father came from near there—you don't mean to say you're a Hornbeck?"

An irresistible impulse moved Lafe to crawl out of his bed and totter across to the other's pallet. He sat down on the edge of it, and leaned his head back on the officer's two pillows.

"Say, I'm Steve Hornbeck's son," he said, "and your father

was my Uncle Lyme. Do you know, I kind of felt like takin' a shine to you when you spoke to me early this morning."

The officer had put his arm affectionately round the boy's neck. "Why, don't you remember," he cried, with pleased interest, "how I said I had a brother like you at home?"

And so the two lay close together in a delighted gossip until the surgeon came, and laughingly but peremptorily drove them apart. They told him something of the strange story, and an attendant went out and found Foldeen, and brought him in, and he added many striking variations to the legend which now, by midnight, had become the talk of the brigade.

General Boyce came back to the hospital tent purposely to see the boy from his own Dearborn County whom men were talking about. He nodded his head approvingly as he stood by the bedside and listened to Foldeen's excited narrative of the lad's fight with Red Pete.

"I remember hearing about that fellow before," he said. "We'll hang him in the morning, if we have to go without breakfast to do it."

Foldeen shook his head. "He is no good for hanging, dot Red Pete," he explained. "When the fire is gone out by dot breastwork where he vas, maybe you find some chargoals from him—und maybe two, dree buttons—dot's all."

The beautiful city by the lake wore its most velvety, green robes of June when Lieutenant Hornbeck, who had been home invalided for some weeks, was able at last to accept the reception which the good people of St. Mark's Church wished to hold in his honor.

It seemed as if all Cleveland sought for admission to this festival of welcome to the brave young officer. Yet when he came in, leaning on his wife's arm, and with the flush of honest pride mantling upon the pallor of his face, it turned out that the real hero of the evening was the wiry, brown-faced boy he brought with him.

Lafe's story had been told in many other places. They knew it by heart here in his new home, where henceforth he was to live with his cousin. He blushed many times that evening at the things admiring people said to his face about him, and he still says if folks *will* insist on discussing it, that the only interesting thing of the whole day was his taking a shine to his cousin before he knew who he was.

The War Widow

I

Although we had been one man short all day, and there was a plain threat of rain in the hot air, everybody left the hay-field long before sundown. It was too much to ask of human nature to stay off in the remote meadows when such remarkable things were happening down around the house.

Marcellus Jones and I were in the pasture, watching the dog get the cows together for the homeward march. He did it so well and, withal, so willingly, that there was no call for us to trouble ourselves in keeping up with him. We waited instead at the open bars until the hay-wagon had passed through, rocking so heavily in the ancient pitch-hole, as it did so, that the driver was nearly thrown off his perch on the top of the high load. Then we put up the bars, and fell in close behind the hay-makers. A rich cloud of dust, far ahead on the road, suggested that the dog was doing his work even too willingly, but for the once we feared no rebuke. Almost anything might be condoned that day.

Five grown-up men walked abreast down the highway, in the shadow of the towering wagon mow, clad much alike in battered straw hats, gray woollen shirts open at the neck, and rough old trousers bulging over the swollen, creased ankles of thick boots. One had a scythe on his arm; two others bore forks over their shoulders. By request, Hi Tuckerman allowed me to carry his sickle.

Although my present visit to the farm had been of only a few days' duration—and those days of strenuous activity darkened by a terrible grief—I had come to be very friendly with Mr. Tuckerman. He took a good deal more notice of me than the others did; and, when chance and leisure afforded, addressed the bulk of his remarks to me. This favoritism, though it fascinated me, was not without its embarrassing side. Hi Tuckerman had taken part in the battle of Gaines's Mill two years before, and had been shot straight through the tongue. One could still see the deep scar on each of his cheeks, a sunken and hairless pit in among his sandy beard. His heroism in the war and his good qualities as a citizen had earned for him the esteem of his neighbors, and they saw to it that he never wanted for work. But their present respect for him stopped short of the pretence that they enjoyed hearing him talk. Whenever he attempted conversation, people moved away, or began boisterous dialogues with one another to drown him out. Being a sensitive man, he had come to prefer silence to these rebuffs among those he knew. But he still had a try at the occasional polite stranger —and I suppose it was in this capacity that I won his heart. Though I never of my own initiative understood a word he said, Marcellus sometimes interpreted a sentence or so for me, and I listened to all the rest with a fraudulently wise face. To give only a solitary illustration of the tax thus levied on our friendship, I may mention that when Hi Tuckerman said "*Aah!*-ah-*aah!*-uh," he meant "Rappahannock," and he did this rather better than a good many words.

"Rappahannock," alas! was a word we heard often enough in those days, along with Chickahominy and Rapidan, and that odd Chattahoochee, the sound of which raised always in my boyish mind the notion that the geography-makers must have achieved it in their baby-talk period. These strange Southern river names and many more were as familiar to the ears of these four other untravelled Dearborn County farmers as the noise of their own shallow Nedahma rattling over its pebbles in the valley yonder. Only when their slow fancy fitted substance to these names they saw in mind's eye dark, sinister, swampy currents, deep and silent, and discolored with human blood.

Two of these men who strode along behind the wagon were young half-uncles of mine, Myron and Warren Turnbull, stout, thick-shouldered, honest fellows not much out of their teens, who worked hard, said little, and were always lumped together in speech, by their family, the hired help, and the neighbors, as "the boys." They asserted themselves so rarely, and took everything as it came with such docility, that I myself, being in my eleventh year, thought of them as very young indeed. Next them walked a man, hired just for the haying, named Philleo, and then, scuffling along over the uneven humps and hollows on the outer edge of the road, came Si Hummaston, with the empty gingerbeer pail knocking against his knees.

As Tuckerman's "Hi" stood for Hiram, so I assume the other's "Si" meant Silas, or possibly Cyrus. I dare say no one, not even his mother, had ever called him by his full name. I know that my companion, Marcellus Jones, who wouldn't be thirteen until after Thanksgiving, habitually addressed him as Si, and almost daily I resolved that I would do so myself. He was a man of more than fifty, I should think, tall, lean, and what Marcellus called "bible-backed." He had a short iron-gray beard and long hair. Whenever there was any very hard or steady work going, he generally gave out and went to sit in the shade, holding a hand flat over his heart, and shaking his head dolefully. This kept a good many from hiring him, and even in haying-time, when everybody on two legs is of some use, I fancy he would often have been left out if it hadn't been for my grandparents. They respected him on account of his piety and his moral character, and always had him down when extra work began. He was said to be the only hired man in the township who could not be goaded in some way into swearing. He looked at one slowly, with the mild expression of a heifer calf.

We had come to the crown of the hill, and the wagon started down the steeper incline, with a great groaning of the brake. The men, by some tacit understanding, halted and overlooked the scene.

The big old stone farm-house—part of which is said to date almost to the Revolutionary times—was just below us, so near, indeed, that Marcellus said he had once skipped a scaling-stone from where we stood to its roof. The dense, big-leafed foliage of a sap-bush, sheltered in the basin which dipped from our feet, pretty well hid this roof now from view. Farther on, heavy patches of a paler, brighter green marked the orchard, and framed one side of a cluster of barns and stables, at the end of which three or four belated cows were loitering by the trough. It was so still that we could hear the clatter of the stanchions as the rest of the herd sought their places inside the milking-barn.

The men, though, had no eyes for all this, but bent their gaze fixedly on the road, down at the bottom. For a long way this thoroughfare was bordered by a row of tall poplars, which, as we were placed, receded from the vision in so straight a line that they seemed one high, fat tree. Beyond these one saw only a line of richer green, where the vine-wrapped rail-fences cleft their way between the ripening fields.

"I'd 'a' took my oath it was them," said Philleo. "I can spot them grays as fur's I can see 'em. They turned by the school-house there, or I'll eat it, school-ma'am 'n' all. And the buggy was follerin' 'em, too."

"Yes, I thought it was them," said Myron, shading his eyes with his brown hand.

"But they ought to got past the poplars by this time, then," remarked Warren.

"Why, they'll be drivin' as slow as molasses in January," put in Si Hummaston. "When you come to think of it, it *is* pretty nigh the same as a regular funeral. You mark my words, your father'll have walked them grays every step of the road. I s'pose he'll drive himself—he wouldn't trust bringin' Alvy home to nobody else, would he? I know I wouldn't, if the Lord had given *me* such a son; but then *He* didn't!"

"No, He didn't!" commented the first speaker, in an unnaturally loud tone of voice, to break in upon the chance that Hi Tuckerman was going to try to talk. But Hi only stretched out his arm, pointing the forefinger toward the poplars.

Sure enough, something was in motion down at the base of the shadows on the road. Then it crept forward, out in the sunlight, and separated itself into two vehicles. A farm wagon came first, drawn by a team of gray horses. Close after it came a buggy, with its black top raised. Both advanced so slowly that they seemed scarcely to be moving at all.

"Well, I swan!" exclaimed Si Hummaston, after a minute, "it's Dana Pillsbury drivin' the wagon after all! Well—I dunno—yes, I guess that's prob'ly what I'd 'a' done too, if I'd b'n your father. Yes, it does look more correct, his follerin' on behind, like that. I s'pose that's Alvy's widder in the buggy there with him."

"Yes, that's Serena—it looks like her little girl with her," said Myron, gravely.

"I s'pose we might's well be movin' along down," observed his brother, and at that we all started.

We walked more slowly now, matching our gait to the snail-like progress of those coming toward us. As we drew near to the gate, the three hired men instinctively fell behind the brothers, and in that position the group halted on the grass, facing the driveway where it left the main road. Not a word was uttered by any one. When at last the wagon came up, Myron and Warren took off their hats, and the others followed suit, all holding them poised at the level of their shoulders.

Dana Pillsbury, carrying himself rigidly upright on the box-seat, drove past us with eyes fixed straight ahead, and a face as coldly expressionless as that of a wooden Indian. The wagon was covered all over with rubber blankets, so that whatever it bore was hidden. Only a few paces behind came the buggy, and my grandfather, old Arphaxed Turnbull, went by in his turn with the same averted, far-away gaze, and the same resolutely stolid countenance. He held the restive young carriage horse down to a decorous walk, a single firm hand on the tight reins, without so much as looking at it. The strong yellow light of the declining sun poured full upon his long gray beard, his shaven upper lip, his dark-skinned, lean, domineering face—and made me think of some hard and gloomy old prophet seeing a vision, in the back part of the Old Testament. If that woman beside him, swathed in heavy black raiment, and holding a child up against her arm, was my Aunt Serena, I should never have guessed it.

We put on our hats again, and walked up the driveway with measured step behind the carriage till it stopped at the side-piazza stoop. The wagon had passed on toward the big new red barn—and crossing its course I saw my Aunt Em, bareheaded and with her sleeves rolled up, going to the cow-barn with a milking-pail in her hand. She was walking quickly, as if in a great hurry.

"There's your Ma," I whispered to Marcellus, assuming that he would share my surprise at her rushing off like this, instead of waiting to say "How-d'-do" to Serena. He only nodded knowingly, and said nothing.

No one else said much of anything. Myron and Warren shook hands in stiff solemnity with the veiled and craped sister-in-law, when their father had helped her and her daughter from the buggy, and one of them remarked in a constrained way that the hot spell seemed to keep up right along. The newcomers ascended the steps to the open door, and the woman and the child went inside. Old Arphaxed turned on the threshold, and seemed to behold us for the first time.

"After you've put out the horse," he said, "I want the most of yeh to come up to the new barn. Si Hummaston and Marcellus can do the milkin'."

"I kind o' rinched my wrist this forenoon," put in Si, with a note of entreaty in his voice. He wanted sorely to be one of the party at the red barn.

"Mebbe milkin' 'll be good for it," said Arphaxed, curtly. "You and Marcellus do what I say, and keep Sidney with you." With this he, too, went into the house.

II

It wasn't an easy matter for even a member of the family like myself to keep clearly and untangled in his head all the relationships which existed under this partriarchal Turnbull roof.

Old Arphaxed had been married twice. His first wife was the mother of two children, who grew up, and the older of these was my father, Wilbur Turnbull. He never liked farm-life, and left home early, not without some hard feeling, which neither father nor son ever quite forgot. My father made a certain success of it as a business man in Albany until, in the thirties, his health broke down. He died when I was seven and, although he left some property, my mother was forced to supplement this help by herself going to work as forewoman in a large store. She was too busy to have much time for visiting, and I don't think there was any great love lost between her and the people on the farm; but it was a good healthy place for me to be sent to when the summer vacation came, and withal inexpensive, and so the first of July each year generally found me out at the homestead, where, indeed, nobody pretended to be heatedly fond of me, but where I was still treated well and enjoyed myself. This year it was understood that my mother was coming out to bring me home later on.

The other child of that first marriage was a girl who was spoken of in youth as Emmeline, but whom I knew now as Aunt Em. She was a silent, tough-fibred, hard-working creature, not at all good-looking, but relentlessly neat, and the best cook I ever knew. Even when the house was filled with extra hired men, no one ever thought of getting in any female help, so tireless and so resourceful was Em. She did all the housework there was to do, from cellar to garret, was continually lending a hand in the men's chores, made more butter than the household could eat up, managed a large kitchen-garden, and still had a good deal of spare time, which she spent in sitting out in the piazza in a starched pink calico gown, knitting the while she watched who went up and down the road. When you knew her, you understood how it was that the original Turnbulls had come into that part of the country just after the Revolution, and in a few years chopped down all the forests, dug up all the stumps, drained the swale-lands, and turned the entire place from a wilderness into a flourishing and fertile home for civilized people. I used to feel, when I looked at her, that she would have been quite equal to doing the whole thing herself.

All at once, when she was something over thirty, Em had up and married a mowing-machine agent named Abel Jones, whom no one knew anything about, and who, indeed, had only been in the neighborhood for a week or so. The family was struck dumb with amazement. The idea of Em's dallying with the notion of matrimony had never crossed anybody's mind. As a girl she had never had any patience with husking-bees or dances or sleigh-ride parties. No young man had ever seen her home from anywhere, or had had the remotest encouragement to hang around the house. She had never been pretty—so my mother told me—and as she got along in years grew dumpy and thick in figure, with a plain, fat face, a rather scowling brow, and an abrupt, ungracious manner. She had no conversational gifts whatever, and, through years of increasing taciturnity and confirmed unsociability, built up in everybody's mind the conviction that, if there could be a man so wild and unsettled in intellect as to suggest a tender thought to Em, he would get his ears cuffed off his head for his pains.

Judge, then, how like a thunderbolt the episode of the mowing-machine agent fell upon the family. To bewildered astonishment there soon enough succeeded rage. This Jones was a curly-headed man, with a crinkly black beard like those of Joseph's brethren in the Bible picture. He had no home and no property, and didn't seem to amount to much even as a salesman of other people's goods. His machine was quite the worst then in the market, and it could not be learned that he had sold a single one in the county. But he had married Em, and it was calmly proposed that he should henceforth regard the farm as his home. After this point had been sullenly conceded, it turned out that Jones was a widower, and had a boy nine or ten years old, named Marcellus, who was in a sort of orphan asylum in Vermont. There were more angry scenes between father and daughter, and a good deal more bad blood, before it was finally agreed that the boy also should come and live on the farm.

All this had happened in 1860 or 1861. Jones had somewhat improved on acquaintance. He knew about lightning-rods, and had been able to fit out all the farm buildings with them at cost price. He had turned a little money now and again in trades with hop-poles, butter-firkins, shingles, and the like, and he was very ingenious in mending and fixing up odds and ends. He made shelves and painted the woodwork, and put a tar roof on the summer kitchen. Even Martha, the second Mrs. Turnbull, came finally to admit that he was handy about a house.

This Martha became the head of the household while Em was still a little girl. She was a heavy woman, mentally as well as bodily, rather prone to a peevish view of things, and greatly given to pride in herself and her position, but honest, charitable in her way, and not unkindly at heart. On the whole she was a good stepmother, and Em probably got on quite as well with her as she would have done with her own mother—even in the matter of the mowing-machine agent.

To Martha three sons were born. The two younger ones, Myron and Warren, have already been seen. The eldest boy, Alva, was the pride of the family, and, for that matter, of the whole section.

Alva was the first Turnbull to go to college. From his smallest boyhood it had been manifest that he had great things before him, so handsome and clever and winning a lad was he. Through each of his schooling years he was the honor man of his class, and he finished in a blaze of glory by taking the Clark Prize, and practically everything else within reach in the way of academic distinctions. He studied law at Octavius, in the office of Judge Schermerhorn, and in a little time was not only that distinguished man's partner, but distinctly the more important figure in the firm. At the age of twenty-five he was sent to the Assembly. The next year they made him District Attorney, and it was quite understood that it rested with him whether he should be sent to Congress later on, or be presented by the Dearborn County bar for the next vacancy on the Supreme Court bench.

At this point in his brilliant career he married Miss Serena Wadsworth of Wadsworth's Falls. The wedding was one of the most imposing social events the county had known, so it was said, since the visit of Lafayette. The Wadsworths were an older family, even, than the Fairchilds, and infinitely more fastidious and refined. The daughters of the household, indeed, carried their refinement to such a pitch that they lived an almost solitary life, and grew to the parlous verge of old-maidhood simply because there was nobody good enough to marry them. Alva Turnbull was, however, up to the standard. It could not be said, of course, that his home surroundings quite matched those of his bride; but, on the other hand, she was nearly two years his senior, and this was held to make matters about even.

In a year or so came the war, and nowhere in the North did patriotic excitement run higher than in this old abolition stronghold of upper Dearborn. Public meetings were held, and nearly a whole regiment was raised in Octavius and the surrounding towns alone. Alva Turnbull made the most stirring and important speech at the first big gathering, and sent a thrill through the whole country-side by claiming the privilege of heading the list of volunteers. He was made a captain by general acclaim, and went off with his company in time to get chased from the field of Bull Run. When he came home on a furlough in 1863 he was a major, and later on he rose to be lieutenant-colonel.

We understood vaguely that he might have climbed vastly higher in promotion but for the fact that he was too moral and conscientious to get on very well with his immediate superior, General Boyce, of Thessaly, who was notoriously a drinking man.

It was glory enough to have him at the farm, on that visit of his, even as a major. His old parents literally abased themselves at his feet, quite tremulous in their awed pride at his greatness. It made it almost too much to have Serena there also, this fair, thin-faced, prim-spoken daughter of the Wadsworths, and actually to call her by her first name. It was haying time, I remember, but the hired men that year did not eat their meals with the family, and there was even a question whether Marcellus and I were socially advanced enough to come to the table, where Serena and her husband were feeding themselves in state with a novel kind of silver implement called a four-tined fork. If Em hadn't put her foot down, out to the kitchen we should both have gone, I fancy. As it was, we sat decorously at the far end of the table, and asked with great politeness to have things passed to us, which by standing up we could have reached as well as not. It was slow, but it made us feel immensely respectable, almost as if we had been born Wadsworths ourselves.

We agreed that Serena was "stuck up," and Marcellus reported Aunt Em as feeling that her bringing along with her a nursemaid to be waited on hand and foot, just to take care of a baby, was an imposition bordering upon the intolerable. He said that that was the sort of thing the English did until George Washington rose and drove them out. But we both felt that Alva was splendid.

He was a fine creature physically—taller even than old Arphaxed, with huge square shoulders and a mighty frame. I could recall him as without whiskers, but now he had a waving lustrous brown beard, the longest and biggest I ever saw. He didn't pay much attention to us boys, it was true; but he was affable when we came in his way, and he gave Myron and Warren each a dollar bill when they went to Octavius to see the Fourth of July doings. In the evening some of the more important neighbors would drop in, and then Alva would talk about the war, and patriotism, and saving the Union, till it was like listening to Congress itself. He had a rich, big voice which filled the whole room, so that the hired men could hear every word out in the kitchen; but it was even more affecting to see him walking with his father down under the poplars, with his hands making orator's gestures as he spoke, and old Arphaxed looking at him and listening with shining eyes.

Well, then, he and his wife went away to visit her folks, and then we heard he had left to join his regiment. From time to time he wrote to his father—letters full of high and loyal sentiments, which were printed next week in the Octavius *Transcript,* and the week after in the Thessaly *Banner of Liberty.* Whenever any of us thought about the war—and who thought much of anything else?—it was always with Alva as the predominant figure in every picture.

Sometimes the arrival of a letter for Aunt Em, or a chance remark about a broken chair or a clock hopelessly out of kilter, would recall for the moment the fact that Abel Jones was also at the seat of war. He had enlisted on that very night when Alva headed the roll of honor, and he marched away in Alva's company. Somehow he got no promotion, but remained in the ranks. Not even the members of the family were shown the letters Aunt Em received, much less the printers of the newspapers. They were indeed poor misspelled scrawls, about which no one displayed any interest or questioned Aunt Em. Even Marcellus rarely spoke of his father, and seemed to share to the full the family's concentration of thought upon Alva.

Thus matters stood when spring began to play at being summer in the year of '64. The birds came and the trees burst forth into green, the sun grew hotter and the days longer, the strawberries hidden under the big leaves in our yard started into shape, where the blossoms had been, quite in the ordinary, annual way, with us up North. But down where that dread thing they called "The War" was going on, this coming of warm weather meant more awful massacre, more tortured hearts, and desolated homes, than ever before. I can't be at all sure how much later reading and associations have helped out and patched up what seem to be my boyish recollections of this period; but it is, at all events, much clearer in my mind than are the occurrences of the week before last.

We heard a good deal about how deep the mud was in Virginia that spring. All the photographs and tin-types of officers which found their way to relatives at home, now, showed them in boots that came up to their thighs. Everybody understood that as soon as this mud dried up a little, there was to be most terrific doings. The two great lines of armies lay scowling at each other, still on that blood-soaked fighting ground between Washington and Richmond where they were three years before. Only now things were to go differently. A new general was at the head of affairs, and he was going in, with jaws set and nerves of steel, to smash, kill, burn, annihilate, sparing nothing, looking not to right or left, till the red road had been hewed through to Richmond. In the first week of May this thing began —a push forward all along the line—and the North, with scared eyes and fluttering heart, held its breath.

My chief personal recollection of these historic forty days is that one morning I was awakened early by a noise in my bedroom, and saw my mother looking over the contents of the big chest of drawers which stood against the wall. She was getting out some black articles of apparel. When she discovered that I was awake, she told me in a low voice that my uncle Alva had been killed. Then a few weeks later my school closed, and I was packed off to the farm for the vacation. It will be better to tell what had happened as I learned it there from Marcellus and the others.

Along about the middle of May, the weekly paper came up from Octavius, and old Arphaxed Turnbull, as was his wont, read it over out on the piazza before supper. Presently he called his wife to him, and showed her something in it. Martha went out into the kitchen, where Aunt Em was getting the meal ready, and told her, as gently as she could, that there was very bad news for her; in fact, her husband, Abel Jones, had been killed in the first day's battle in the Wilderness, something like a week before. Aunt Em said she didn't believe it, and Martha brought in the paper and pointed out the fatal line to her. It was not quite clear whether this convinced Aunt Em or not. She finished getting supper, and sat silently through the meal, afterwards, but she went upstairs to her room before family prayers. The next day she was about as usual, doing the work and saying nothing. Marcellus told me that to the best of his belief no one had said anything to her on the subject. The old people were a shade more ceremonious in their manner toward her, and "the boys" and the hired men were on the lookout to bring in water for her from the well, and to spare her as much as possible in the routine of chores, but no one talked about Jones. Aunt Em did not put on mourning. She made a black necktie for Marcellus to wear to church, but stayed away from meeting herself.

A little more than a fortnight afterwards, Myron was walking down the road from the meadows one afternoon, when he saw a man on horseback coming up from the poplars, galloping like mad in a cloud of dust. The two met at the gate. The man was one of the hired helps of the Wadsworths, and he had ridden as hard as he could pelt from the Falls, fifteen miles away, with a message, which now he gave Myron to read. Both man and beast dripped sweat, and trembled with fatigued excitement. The youngster eyed them, and then gazed meditatively at the sealed envelope in his hand.

"I s'pose you know what's inside?" he asked, looking up at last.

The man in the saddle nodded, with a tell-tale look on his face, and breathing heavily.

Myron handed the letter back, and pushed the gate open. "You'd better go up and give it to father yourself," he said. "I ain't got the heart to face him—jest now, at any rate."

Marcellus was fishing that afternoon, over in the creek which ran through the woods. Just as at last he was making up his mind that it must be about time to go after the cows, he saw Myron sitting on a log beside the forest path, whittling mechanically and staring at the foliage before him, in an obvious brown study. Marcellus went up to him, and had to speak twice before Myron turned his head and looked up.

"Oh! it's you, eh, Bubb?" he remarked dreamily, and began gazing once more into the thicket.

"What's the matter?" asked the puzzled boy.

"I guess Alvy's dead," replied Myron. To the lad's comments and questions he made small answer. "No," he said at last, "I don't feel much like goin' home jest now. Lea' me alone here; I'll prob'ly turn up later on." And Marcellus went alone to the pasture, and thence, at the tail of his bovine procession, home.

When he arrived he regretted not having remained with Myron in the woods. It was like coming into something which was prison, hospital, and tomb in one. The household was paralyzed with horror and fright. Martha had gone to bed, or rather had been put there by Em, and all through the night, when he woke up, he heard her broken and hysterical voice in moans and screams. The men had hitched up the grays, and Arphaxed Turnbull was getting into the buggy to drive to Octavius for news when the boy came up. He looked twenty years older than he had at noon—all at once turned into a chalk-faced, trembling, infirm old man—and could hardly see to put his foot on the carriage-step. His son Warren had offered to go with him, and had been rebuffed almost with fierceness. Warren and the others silently bowed their heads before this mood; instinct told them that nothing but Arphaxed's show of temper held him from collapse—from falling at their feet and grovelling on the grass with cries and sobs of anguish, perhaps even dying in a fit. After he had driven off they forbore to talk to one another, but went about noiselessly with drooping chins and knotted brows.

"It jest took the tuck out of everything," said Marcellus,

relating these tragic events to me. There was not much else to
tell. Martha had had what they call brain fever, and had
emerged from this some weeks afterward a pallid and dim-eyed
ghost of her former self, sitting for hours together in her rocking-chair in the unused parlor, her hands idly in her lap, her
poor thoughts glued ceaselessly to that vague, far-off Virginia
which folks told about as hot and sunny, but which her mind's
eye saw under the gloom of an endless and dreadful night.
Arphaxed had gone South, still defiantly alone, to bring back
the body of his boy. An acquaintance wrote to them of his being down sick in Washington, prostrated by the heat and
strange water; but even from his sick-bed he had sent on orders
to an undertaking firm out at the front, along with a hundred
dollars, their price in advance for embalming. Then, recover-
ing, he had himself pushed down to headquarters, or as near
them as civilians might approach, only to learn that he had
passed the precious freight on the way. He posted back again,
besieging the railroad officials at every point with inquiries,
scolding, arguing, beseeching in turn, until at last he overtook
his quest at Juno Mills Junction, only a score of miles from
home.

Then only he wrote, telling people his plans. He came first
to Octavius, where a funeral service was held in the forenoon,
with military honors, the Wadsworths as the principal mourn-
ers, and a memorable turnout of distinguished citizens. The
town-hall was draped with mourning, and so was Alva's pew
in the Episcopal Church, which he had deserted his ancestral
Methodism to join after his marriage. Old Arphaxed listened
to the novel burial service of his son's communion, and watched
the clergyman in his curious white and black vestments, with
sombre pride. He himself needed and desired only a plain and
homely religion, but it was fitting that his boy should have
organ music and flowers and a ritual.

Dana Pillsbury had arrived in town early in the morning
with the grays, and a neighbor's boy had brought in the buggy.
Immediately after dinner Arphaxed had gathered up Alva's

widow and little daughter, and started the funeral cortège upon its final homeward stage.

And so I saw them arrive on that July afternoon.

III

For so good and patient a man, Si Hummaston bore himself rather vehemently during the milking. It was hotter in the barn than it was outside in the sun, and the stifling air swarmed with flies, which seemed to follow Si perversely from stall to stall and settle on his cow. One beast put her hoof square in his pail, and another refused altogether to "give down," while the rest kept up a tireless slapping and swishing of their tails very hard to bear, even if one had the help of profanity. Marcellus and I listened carefully to hear him at last provoked to an oath, but the worst thing he uttered, even when the cow stepped in the milk, was "Dum your buttons!" which Marcellus said might conceivably be investigated by a church committee, but was hardly out-and-out swearing.

I remember Si's groans and objurgations, his querulous "Hyst there, will ye!" his hypocritical "So-boss! So-boss!" his despondent "They never will give down for me!" because presently there was crossed upon this woof of peevish impatience the web of a curious conversation.

Si had been so slow in his headway against flapping tails and restive hoofs that, before he had got up to the end of the row, Aunt Em had finished her side. She brought over her stool and pail, and seated herself at the next cow to Hummaston's. For a little, one heard only the resonant din of the stout streams against the tin; then, as the bottom was covered, there came the ploughing plash of milk on milk, and Si could hear himself talk.

"S'pose you know S'reny's come, 'long with your father," he remarked, ingratiatingly.

"I saw 'em drive in," replied Em.

"Whoa! Hyst there! Hole still, can't ye? I didn't know if you quite made out who she was, you was scootin' 'long so fast. They ain't—*Whoa there!*—they ain't nothin' the matter 'twixt you and her, is they?"

"I don't know as there is," said Em, curtly. "The world's big enough for both of us—we ain't no call to bunk into each other."

"No, of course—*Now you stop it!*—but it looked kind o' curious to me, your pikin' off like that, without waitin' to say 'How-d'-do?' Of course, I never had no relation by marriage that was stuck-up at all, or looked down on me—*Stiddy there now!*—but I guess I can reelize pretty much how you feel about it. I'm a good deal of a hand at that. It's what they call imagination. It's a gift, you know, like good looks, or preachin', or the knack o' makin' money. But you can't help what you're born with, can you? I'd been a heap better off if my gift 'd be'n in some other direction; but, as I tell 'em, it ain't my fault. And my imagination—*Hi, there! git over, will ye?*—it's downright cur'ous sometimes, how it works. Now I could tell, you see, that you 'n' S'reny didn't pull together. I s'pose she never writ a line to you, when your husband was killed?"

"Why should she?" demanded Em. "We never did correspond. What'd be the sense of beginning then? She minds her affairs, 'n' I mind mine. Who wanted her to write?"

"Oh, of course not," said Si lightly. "Prob'ly you'll get along better together, though, now that you'll see more of one another. I s'pose S'reny's figurin' on stayin' here right along now, her 'n' her little girl. Well, it'll be nice for the old folks to have somebody they're fond of. They jest worshipped the ground Alvy walked on—and I s'pose they won't be anything in this wide world too good for that little girl of his. Le's see, she must be comin' on three now, ain't she?"

"I don't know anything about her!" snapped Aunt Em with emphasis.

"Of course, it's natural the old folks should feel so—she bein'

Alvy's child. I hain't noticed anything special, but does it—
Well, I swan! Hyst there!—does it seem to you that they're
as good to Marcellus, quite, as they used to be? I don't hear
'em sayin' nothin' about his goin' to school next winter."

Aunt Em said nothing, too, but milked doggedly on. Si told
her about the thickness and profusion of Serena's mourning,
guardedly hinting at the injustice done him by not allowing him
to go to the red barn with the others, speculated on the likelihood of the Wadsworths' contributing to their daughter's support and generally exhibited his interest in the family through
a monologue which finished only with the milking; but Aunt
Em made no response whatever.

When the last pails had been emptied into the big cans at the
door—Marcellus and I had let the cows out one by one into the
yard, as their individual share in the milking ended—Si and Em
saw old Arphaxed wending his way across from the house to the
red barn. He appeared more bent than ever, but he walked
with a slowness which seemed born of reluctance even more
than of infirmity.

"Well, now," mused Si, aloud, "Brother Turnbull an' me's
be'n friends for a good long spell. I don't believe he'd be mad
if I cut over now to the red barn too, seein' the milkin's all out
of the way. Of course I don't want to do what ain't right—
what d'you think now, Em, honest? Think it 'ud rile him?"

"I don't know anything about it!" my aunt replied, with
increased vigor of emphasis. "But for the land sake go somewhere! Don't hang around botherin' me. I got enough else to
think of besides your everlasting cackle."

Thus rebuffed, Si meandered sadly into the cow-yard, shaking his head as he came. Seeing us seated on an upturned
plough, over by the fence, from which point we had a perfect
view of the red barn, he sauntered toward us, and, halting at
our side, looked to see if there was room enough for him to sit
also. But Marcellus, in quite a casual way, remarked, "Oh!
wheeled the milk over to the house, already, Si?" and at this
the doleful man lounged off again in new despondency, got out

the wheelbarrow, and, with ostentatious groans of travail hoisted a can upon it and started off.

"He's takin' advantage of Arphaxed's being so worked up to play 'ole soldier' on him," said Marcellus. "All of us have to stir him up the whole time to keep him from takin' root somewhere. I told him this afternoon 't if there had to be any settin' around under the bushes an' cryin', the fam'ly 'ud do it."

We talked in hushed tones as we sat there watching the shut doors of the red barn, in boyish conjecture about what was going on behind them. I recall much of this talk with curious distinctness, but candidly it jars now upon my maturer nerves. The individual man looks back upon his boyhood with much the same amused amazement that the race feels in contemplating the memorials of its own cave-dwelling or bronze period. What strange savages we were! In those days Marcellus and I used to find our very highest delight in getting off on Thursdays, and going over to Dave Bushnell's slaughter-house, to witness with stony hearts, and from as close a coign of vantage as might be, the slaying of some score of barnyard animals— the very thought of which now revolts our grown-up minds. In the same way we sat there on the plough, and criticised old Arphaxed's meanness in excluding us from the red barn, where the men-folks were coming in final contact with the "pride of the family." Some of the cows wandering toward us began to "moo" with impatience for the pasture, but Marcellus said there was no hurry.

All at once we discovered that Aunt Em was standing a few yards away from us, on the other side of the fence. We could see her from where we sat by only turning a little—a motionless, stout, upright figure, with a pail in her hand, and a sternly impassive look on her face. She, too, had her gaze fixed upon the red barn, and, though the declining sun was full in her eyes, seemed incapable of blinking, but just stared coldly, straight ahead.

Suddenly an unaccustomed voice fell upon our ears. Turning, we saw that a black-robed woman, with a black wrap of

some sort about her head, had come up to where Aunt Em
stood, and was at her shoulder. Marcellus nudged me, and
whispered, "It's S'reny. Look out for squalls!" And then we
listened in silence.

"Won't you speak to me at all, Emmeline?" we heard this
new voice say.

Aunt Em's face, sharply outlined in profile against the sky,
never moved. Her lips were pressed into a single line, and she
kept her eyes on the barn.

"If there's anything I've done, tell me," pursued the other.
"In such an hour as this—when both our hearts are bleeding
so, and—and every breath we draw is like a curse upon us—
it doesn't seem a fit time for us—for us to—" The voice fal-
tered and broke, leaving the speech unfinished.

Aunt Em kept silence so long that we fancied this appeal,
too, had failed. Then abruptly, and without moving her head,
she dropped a few ungracious words as it were over her
shoulder. "If I had anything special to say, most likely I'd say
it," she remarked.

We could hear the sigh that Serena drew. She lifted her
shawled head, and for a moment seemed as if about to turn.
Then she changed her mind, apparently, for she took a step
nearer to the other.

"See here, Emmeline," she said, in a more confident tone.
"Nobody in the world knows better than I do how thoroughly
good a woman you are, how you have done your duty, and more
than your duty, by your parents and your brothers, and your
little step-son. You have never spared yourself for them, day
or night. I have said often to—to him who has gone—that I
didn't believe there was anywhere on earth a worthier or more
devoted woman than you, his sister. And—now that he is gone
—and we are both more sisters than ever in affliction—why in
Heaven's name should you behave like this to me?"

Aunt Em spoke more readily this time. "I don't know as I've
done anything to you," she said in defence. "I've just let you
alone, that's all. An' that's doin' as I'd like to be done by."

Still she did not turn her head, or lift her steady gaze from those closed doors.

"Don't let us split words!" entreated the other, venturing a thin, white hand upon Aunt Em's shoulder. "That isn't the way we two ought to stand to each other. Why, you were friendly enough when I was here before. Can't it be the same again? What happened to change it? Only to-day, on our way up here, I was speaking to your father about you, and my deep sympathy for you, and—"

Aunt Em wheeled like a flash. "Yes, 'n' what did *he* say? Come, don't make up anything! Out with it! What did he say?" She shook off the hand on her shoulder as she spoke.

Gesture and voice and frowning vigor of mien were all so imperative and rough that they seemed to bewilder Serena. She, too, had turned now, so that I could see her wan and delicate face, framed in the laced festoons of black, like the fabulous countenance of "The Lady Iñez" in my mother's "Album of Beauty." She bent her brows in hurried thought, and began stammering, "Well, he said—Let's see—he said—"

"Oh, yes!" broke in Aunt Em, with raucous irony, "I know well enough what he said! He said I was a good worker—that they'd never had to have a hired girl since I was big enough to wag a churn dash, an' they wouldn't known what to do without me. I know all that; I've heard it on an' off for twenty years. What I'd like to hear is, did he tell you that he went down South to bring back *your* husband, an' that he never so much as give a thought to fetchin' *my* husband, who was just as good a soldier and died just as bravely as yours did? I'd like to know —did he tell you that?"

What could Serena do but shake her head, and bow it in silence before this bitter gale of words?

"An' tell me this, too," Aunt Em went on, lifting her harsh voice mercilessly, "when you was settin' there in church this forenoon, with the soldiers out, an' the bells tollin' and all that —did he say, 'This is some for Alvy, an' some for Abel, who went to the war together, an' was killed together, or within a

month o' one another?' Did he say that, or look for one solitary
minute as if he thought it? I'll bet he didn't!"

Serena's head sank lower still, and she put up, in a blinded
sort of way, a little white handkerchief to her eyes. "But why
blame *me?*" she asked.

Aunt Em heard her own voice so seldom that the sound of it
now seemed to intoxicate her. "No!" she shouted. "It's like
the Bible. One was taken an' the other left. It was always Alvy
this, an' Alvy that, nothin' for anyone but Alvy. That was all
right; nobody complained: prob'ly he deserved it all; at any
rate, we didn't begrudge him any of it, while he was livin'. But
there ought to be a limit somewhere. When a man's dead, he's
pretty much about on an equality with other dead men, one
would think. But it ain't so. One man gets hunted after when
he's shot, an' there's a hundred dollars for embalmin' him an'
a journey after him, an' bringin' him home, an' two big funerals,
an' crape for his widow that'd stand by itself. The *other* man
—he can lay where he fell! Them that's lookin' for the first one
are right close by—it ain't more'n a few miles from the Wilderness to Cold Harbor, so Hi Tuckerman tells me, an' he was all
over the ground two years ago—but nobody looks for this other
man! Oh, no! Nobody so much as remembers to think of him!
They ain't no hundred dollars, no, not so much as fifty cents,
for embalmin' *him!* No—*he* could be shovelled in anywhere,
or maybe burned up when the woods got on fire that night, the
night of the sixth. They ain't no funeral for him—no bells
tolled—unless it may be a cowbell up in the pasture that he
hammered out himself. An' *his* widow can go around, week days
an' Sundays, in her old calico dresses. Nobody ever mentions
the word 'mournin' crape' to her, or asks her if she'd like to
put on black. I s'pose they thought if they gave me the money
for some mournin' I'd buy *candy* with it instead!"

With this climax of flaming sarcasm Aunt Em stopped, her
eyes aglow, her thick breast heaving in a flurry of breathless-
ness. She had never talked so much or so fast before in her
life. She swung the empty tin-pail now defiantly at her side to

hide the fact that her arms were shaking with excitement. Every instant it looked as if she was going to begin again.

Serena had taken the handkerchief down from her eyes and held her arms stiff and straight by her side. Her chin seemed to have grown longer or to be thrust forward more. When she spoke it was in a colder voice—almost mincing in the way it cut off the words.

"All this is not my doing," she said. "I am to blame for nothing of it. As I tried to tell you, I sympathize deeply with your grief. But grief ought to make people at least fair, even if it cannot make them gentle and soften their hearts. I shall trouble you with no more offers of friendship. I—I think I will go back to the house now—to my little girl."

Even as she spoke, there came from the direction of the red barn a shrill, creaking noise which we all knew. At the sound Marcellus and I stood up, and Serena forgot her intention to go away. The barn doors, yelping as they moved on their dry rollers, had been pushed wide open.

IV

The first one to emerge from the barn was Hi Tuckerman. He started to make for the house, but, when he caught sight of our group, came running toward us at the top of his speed, uttering incoherent shouts as he advanced, and waving his arms excitedly. It was apparent that something out of the ordinary had happened.

We were but little the wiser as to this something when Hi had come to a halt before us, and was pouring out a volley of explanations, accompanied by earnest grimaces and strenuous gestures. Even Marcellus could make next to nothing of what he was trying to convey; but Aunt Em, strangely enough, seemed to understand him. Still slightly trembling, and with a little occasional catch in her breath, she bent an intent scrutiny upon Hi, and nodded comprehendingly from time to time, with encouraging exclamations, "He did, eh!" "Is that so?" and "I expected as much." Listening and watching, I formed the uncharitable conviction that she did not really understand Hi at all, but was only pretending to do so in order further to harrow Serena's feelings.

Doubtless I was wrong, for presently she turned with an effort, to her sister-in-law, and remarked, "P'rhaps you don't quite follow what he's saying?"

"Not a word!" said Serena, eagerly. "Tell me, please, Emmeline!"

Aunt Em seemed to hesitate. "He was shot through the mouth at Gaines's Mills, you know—that's right near Cold Harbor and—the Wilderness," she said, obviously making talk.

"That isn't what he's saying," broke in Serena. "What *is* it, Emmeline?"

"Well," rejoined the other, after an instant's pause, "if you want to know—he says that it ain't Alvy at all that they've got there in the barn."

Serena turned swiftly, so that we could not see her face.

"He says it's some strange man," continued Em, "a yaller-headed man, all packed and stuffed with charcoal, so't his own mother wouldn't know him. Who it is nobody knows, but it ain't Alvy."

"They're a pack of robbers 'n' swindlers!" cried old Arphaxed, shaking his long gray beard with wrath.

He had come up without our noticing his approach, so rapt had been our absorption in the strange discovery reported by Hi Tuckerman. Behind him straggled the boys and the hired men, whom Si Hummaston had scurried across from the house to join. No one said anything now, but tacitly deferred to the old man's principal right to speak. It was a relief to hear that terrible silence of his broken at all.

"They ought to all be hung!" he cried, in a voice to which the excess of passion over physical strength gave a melancholy quaver. "I paid 'em what they asked—they took a hundred dollars o' my money—an' they ain't sent me *him* at all! There I went, at my age, all through the Wilderness, almost clear to Cold Harbor, an' that, too, gittin' up from a sick bed in Washington, and then huntin' for the box at New York an' Albany, an' all the way back, an' holdin' a funeral over it only this very day—an' here it ain't *him* at all! I'll have the law on 'em though, if it costs the last cent I've got in the world!"

Poor old man! These weeks of crushing grief and strain had fairly broken him down. We listened to his fierce outpourings with sympathetic silence, almost thankful that he had left strength and vitality enough still to get angry and shout. He had been always a hard and gusty man; we felt by instinct, I suppose, that his best chance of weathering this terrible month of calamity was to batter his way furiously through it, in a rage with everything and everybody.

. "If there's any justice in the land," put in Si Hummaston, "you'd ought to get your hundred dollars back. I shouldn't wonder if you could, too, if you sued 'em afore a Jestice that was a friend of yours."

"Why, the man's a fool!" burst forth Arphaxed, turning toward him with a snort. "I don't want the hundred dollars— I wouldn't 'a' begrudged a thousand—if only they'd dealt honestly by me. I paid 'em their own figure, without beatin' 'em down a penny. If it'd be'n double, I'd 'a' paid it. What *I* wanted was *my boy!* It ain't so much their cheatin' *me* I mind, either, if it'd be'n about anything else. But to think of Alvy— *my boy*—after all the trouble I took, an' the journey, an' my sickness there among strangers—to think that after it all he's buried down there, no one know where, p'raps in some trench with private soldiers, shovelled in anyhow—oh-h! they ought to be hung!"

The two women had stood motionless, with their gaze on the grass; Aunt Em lifted her head at this.

"If a place is good enough for private soldiers to be buried in," she said, vehemently, "it's good enough for the best man in the army. On Resurrection Day, do you think them with shoulder-straps 'll be called fust an' given all the front places? I reckon the men that carried a musket are every whit as good, there in the trench, as them that wore swords. They gave their lives as much as the others did, an' the best man that ever stepped couldn't do no more."

Old Arphaxed bent upon her a long look, which had in it much surprise and some elements of menace. Reflection seemed, however, to make him think better of an attack on Aunt Em. He went on, instead, with rambling exclamations to his auditors at large.

"Makin' me the butt of the whole county!" he cried. "There was that funeral to-day—with a parade an' a choir of music an' so on: an' now it'll come out in the papers that it wasn't Alvy at all I brought back with me, but only some perfect stranger —by what you can make out from his clothes, not even an offi-cer at all. I tell you the war's a jedgment on this country for its wickedness, for its cheatin' an' robbin' of honest men! They wa'n't no sense in that battle at Cold Harbor anyway—every-body admits that! It was murder an' massacre in cold blood —fifty thousand men mowed down, an' nothin' gained by it! An' then not even to git my boy's dead body back! I say hang-in's too good for 'em!"

"Yes, father," said Myron, soothingly; "but do you stick to what you said about the—the box? Wouldn't it look better—"

"No!" shouted Arphaxed, with emphasis. "Let Dana do what I told him—take it down this very night to the poor-master, an' let him bury it where he likes. It's no affair of mine. I wash my hands of it. There won't be no funeral held here!"

It was then that Serena spoke. Strangely enough, old Arph-axed had not seemed to notice her presence in our group, and his jaw visibly dropped as he beheld her now standing before him. He made a gesture signifying his disturbance at finding her among his hearers, and would have spoken, but she held up her hand.

"Yes, I heard it all," she said, in answer to his deprecatory movement. "I am glad I did. It has given me time to get over the shock of learning—our mistake—and it gives me the chance now to say something which I—I feel keenly. The poor man you have brought home was, you say, a private soldier. Well, isn't this a good time to remember that there was a private soldier who went out from this farm—belonging right to this family—and who, as a private, laid down his life as nobly as General Sedgwick or General Wadsworth, or even our dear Alva, or any one else? I never met Emmeline's husband, but Alva liked him, and spoke to me often of him. Men who fall in the ranks don't get identified, or brought home, but they deserve funerals as much as the others—just as much. Now, this is my idea: let us feel that the mistake which has brought this poor stranger to us is God's way of giving us a chance to remember and do honor to Abel Jones. Let him be buried in the family lot up yonder, where we had thought to lay Alva, and let us do it reverently, in the name of Emmeline's husband, and of all others who have fought and died for our country, and with sympathy in our hearts for the women who, somewhere in the North, are mourning, just as we mourn here, for the stranger there in the red barn."

Arphaxed had watched her intently. He nodded now, and blinked at the moisture gathering in his old eyes. "I could e'en a'most 'a' thought it was Alvy talkin'," was what he said. Then he turned abruptly, but we all knew, without further words, that what Serena had suggested was to be done.

The men-folk, wondering doubtless much among themselves, moved slowly off toward the house or the cow-barns, leaving the two women alone. A minute of silence passed before we saw Serena creep gently up to Aunt Em's side, and lay the thin white hand again upon her shoulder. This time it was not shaken off, but stretched itself forward little by little, until its palm rested against Aunt Em's further cheek. We heard the tin-pail fall resonantly against the stones under the rail-fence, and there was a confused movement as if the two women were somehow melting into one.

"Come on, Sid!" said Marcellus Jones to me; "let's start them cows along. If there's anything I hate to see it's women cryin' on each other's necks."

The Eve of the Fourth

It was well on toward evening before this Third of July all at once made itself gloriously different from other days in my mind.

There was a very long afternoon, I remember, hot and overcast, with continual threats of rain, which never came to anything. The other boys were too excited about the morrow to care for present play. They sat instead along the edge of the broad platform-stoop in front of Delos Ingersoll's grocery-store, their brown feet swinging at varying heights above the sidewalk, and bragged about the manner in which they contemplated celebrating the anniversary of their Independence. Most of the elder lads were very independent indeed; they were already secure in the parental permission to stay up all night, so that the Fourth might be ushered in with its full quota of ceremonial. The smaller urchins pretended that they also had this permission, or were sure of getting it. Little Denny Cregan attracted admiring attention by vowing that he should remain out, even if his father chased him with a policeman all around the ward, and he had to go and live in a cave in the gulf until he was grown up.

My inferiority to these companions of mine depressed me. They were allowed to go without shoes and stockings; they wore loose and comfortable old clothes, and were under no responsibility to keep them dry or clean or whole; they had their pockets literally bulging now with all sorts of portentous engines of noise and racket—huge brown "double-enders," bound with waxed cord; long, slim, vicious-looking "nigger-chasers;" big "Union torpedoes," covered with clay, which made a report like a horse-pistol, and were invaluable for

305

frightening farmers' horses; and so on through an extended catalogue of recondite and sinister explosives upon which I looked with awe, as their owners from time to time exhibited them with the proud simplicity of those accustomed to greatness. Several of these boys also possessed toy cannons, which would be brought forth at twilight. They spoke firmly of ramming them to the muzzle with grass, to produce a greater noise —even if it burst them and killed everybody.

By comparison, my lot was one of abasement. I was a solitary child, and a victim to conventions. A blue necktie was daily pinned under my Byron collar, and there were gilt buttons on my zouave jacket. When we were away in the pasture playground near the gulf, and I ventured to take off my foot-gear, every dry old thistle-point in the whole territory seemed to arrange itself to be stepped upon by my whitened and tender soles. I could not swim; so, while my lithe bold comrades dived out of sight under the deep water, and darted about chasing one another far beyond their depth, I paddled ignobly around the "baby-hole" close to the bank, in the warm and muddy shallows.

Especially apparent was my state of humiliation on this July afternoon. I had no "double-enders," nor might hope for any. The mere thought of a private cannon seemed monstrous and unnatural to me. By some unknown process of reasoning my mother had years before reached the theory that a good boy ought to have two ten-cent packs of small fire-crackers on the Fourth of July. Four or five succeeding anniversaries had hardened this theory into an orthodox tenet of faith, with all its observances rigidly fixed. The fire-crackers were bought for me overnight, and placed on the hall table. Beside them lay a long rod of punk. When I hastened down and out in the morning, with these ceremonial implements in my hands, the hired girl would give me, in an old kettle, some embers from the wood fire in the summer kitchen. Thus furnished, I went into the front yard, and in solemn solitude fired off these crackers one by one. Those which, by reason of having lost their tails, were only fit for "fizzes," I saved till after breakfast. With the exhaustion of these, I fell reluctantly back upon the public for entertainment. I could see the soldiers, hear the band and the oration, and in the evening, if it didn't rain, enjoy the fireworks; but my own contribution to the patriotic noise was always over before the breakfast dishes had been washed.

My mother scorned the little paper torpedoes as flippant and wasteful things. You merely threw one of them, and it went off, she said, and there you were. I don't know that I ever grasped this objection in its entirety, but it impressed my whole childhood with its unanswerableness. Years and years afterward, when my own children asked for torpedoes, I found myself unconsciously advising against them on quite the maternal lines. Nor was it easy to budge the good lady from her position on the great two-packs issue. I seem to recall having successfully undermined it once or twice, but two was the rule. When I called her attention to the fact that our neighbor, Tom Hemingway, thought nothing of exploding a whole pack at a time inside their wash-boiler, she was not dazzled, but only replied: "Wilful waste makes woful want."

Of course the idea of the Hemingways ever knowing what want meant was absurd. They lived a dozen doors or so from us, in a big white house with stately white columns rising from veranda to gable across the whole front, and a large garden, flowers and shrubs in front, fruit-trees and vegetables behind. Squire Hemingway was the most important man in our part of the town. I know now that he was never anything more than United States Commissioner of Deeds, but in those days, when he walked down the street with his gold-headed cane, his blanket-shawl folded over his arm, and his severe, dignified, close-shaven face held well up in the air, I seemed to behold a companion of Presidents.

This great man had two sons. The elder of them, De Witt Hemingway, was a man grown, and was at the front. I had seen him march away, over a year before, with a bright drawn sword, at the side of his company. The other son, Tom, was my senior by only a twelvemonth. He was by nature proud, but often consented to consort with me when the selection of other available associates was at low ebb.

It was to this Tom that I listened with most envious eagerness, in front of the grocery-store, on the afternoon of which I speak. He did not sit on the stoop with the others—no one expected quite that degree of condescension—but leaned nonchalantly against a post, whittling out a new ramrod for his cannon. He said that this year he was not going to have any ordinary fire-crackers at all; they, he added with a meaning glance at me, were only fit for girls. He might do a little in "double-enders," but his real point would be in "ringers"—an incredible giant variety of cracker, Turkey-red like the other, but in size almost a rolling-pin. Some of these he would fire off singly, between volleys from his cannon. But a good many he intended to explode, in bunches say of six, inside the tin washboiler, brought out into the middle of the road for that purpose. It would doubtless blow the old thing sky-high, but that didn't matter. They could get a new one.

Even as he spoke, the big bell in the tower of the town-hall burst forth in a loud clangor of swift-repeated strokes. It was half a mile away, but the moist air brought the urgent, clamorous sounds to our ears as if the belfry had stood close above us. We sprang off the stoop and stood poised, waiting to hear the number of the ward struck, and ready to scamper off on the instant if the fire was anywhere in our part of the town. But the excited peal went on and on without a pause. It became obvious that this meant something besides a fire. Perhaps some of us wondered vaguely what that something might be, but as a body our interest had lapsed. Billy Norris, who was the son of poor parents, but could whip even Tom Hemingway, said he had been told that the German boys on the other side of the gulf were coming over to "rush" us on the following day, and that we ought all to collect nails to fire at them from our cannon. This we pledged ourselves to do—the bell keeping up its throbbing tumult ceaselessly.

Suddenly we saw the familiar figure of Johnson running up the street toward us. What his first name was I never knew. To every one, little or big, he was just Johnson. He and his family had moved into our town after the war began; I fancy they moved away again before it ended. I do not even know what he did for a living. But he seemed always drunk, always turbulently good-natured, and always shouting out the news at the top of his lungs. I cannot pretend to guess how he found out everything as he did, or why, having found it out, he straightway rushed homeward, scattering the intelligence as he ran. Most probably Johnson was moulded by Nature as a town-crier, but was born by accident some generations after the race of bellmen had disappeared. Our neighborhood did not like him; our mothers did not know Mrs. Johnson, and we boys behaved with snobbish roughness to his children. He seemed not to mind this at all, but came up unwearyingly to shout out the tidings of the day for our benefit.

"Vicksburg's fell! Vicksburg's fell!" was what we heard him yelling as he approached.

Delos Ingersoll and his hired boy ran out of the grocery. Doors opened along the street and heads were thrust inquiringly out.

"Vicksburg's fell!" he kept hoarsely proclaiming, his arms waving in the air, as he staggered along at a dog-trot past us, and went into the saloon next to the grocery.

I cannot say how definite an idea these tidings conveyed to our boyish minds. I have a notion that at the time I assumed that Vicksburg had something to do with Gettysburg, where I knew, from the talk of my elders, that an awful fight had been proceeding since the middle of the week. Doubtless this confusion was aided by the fact that an hour or so later, on that same wonderful day, the wire brought us word that this terrible battle on Pennsylvanian soil had at last taken the form of a Union victory. It is difficult now to see how we could have known both these things on the Third of July—that is to say, before the people actually concerned seemed to have been sure of them.

Perhaps it was only inspired guesswork, but I know that my town went wild over the news, and that the clouds overhead cleared away as if by magic.

The sun did well to spread that summer sky at eventide with all the pageantry of color the spectrum knows. It would have been preposterous that such a day should slink off in dull, Quaker drabs. Men were shouting in the streets now. The old cannon left over from the Mexican war had been dragged out on to the rickety covered river-bridge, and was frightening the fishes, and shaking the dry worm-eaten rafters, as fast as the swab and rammer could work. Our town bandsmen were playing as they had never played before, down in the square in front of the post-office. The management of the Universe could not hurl enough wild fireworks into the exultant sunset to fit our mood.

The very air was filled with the scent of triumph—the spirit of conquest. It seemed only natural that I should march off to my mother and quite collectedly tell her that I desired to stay out all night with the other boys. I had never dreamed of daring to prefer such a request in other years. Now I was scarcely conscious of surprise when she gave her permission, adding with a smile that I would be glad enough to come in and go to bed before half the night was over.

I steeled my heart after supper with the proud resolve that if the night turned out to be as protracted as one of those Lapland winter nights we read about in geography, I still would not surrender.

The boys outside were not so excited over the tidings of my unlooked-for victory as I had expected them to be. They received the news, in fact, with a rather mortifying stoicism. Tom Hemingway, however, took enough interest in the affair to suggest that, instead of spending my twenty cents in paltry firecrackers, I might go downtown and buy another can of powder for his cannon. By doing so, he pointed out, I would be a part-proprietor, as it were, of the night's performance, and would be entitled to occasionally touch the cannon off. This generosity affected me, and I hastened down the long hill-street to show myself worthy of it, repeating the instruction of "Kentucky Bear-Hunter-coarse-grain" over and over again to myself as I went.

Half-way on my journey I overtook a person whom, even in the gathering twilight, I recognized as Miss Stratford, the school-teacher. She also was walking down the hill and rapidly. It did not need the sight of a letter in her hand to tell me that she was going to the post office. In those cruel war-days everybody went to the post-office. I myself went regularly to get our mail, and to exchange shin-plasters for one-cent stamps with which to buy yeast and other commodities that called for minute fractional currency.

Although I was very fond of Miss Stratford—I still recall her gentle eyes, and pretty, rounded, dark face, in its frame of long, black curls, with tender liking—I now coldly resolved to hurry past, pretending not to know her. It was a mean thing to do; Miss Stratford had always been good to me, shining in that respect in brilliant contrast to my other teachers, whom I hated bitterly. Still, the "Kentucky Bear-Hunter-coarse-grain" was too important a matter to wait upon any mere female friendships, and I quickened my pace into a trot, hoping to scurry by unrecognized.

"Oh, Andrew! is that you?" I heard her call out as I ran past. For the instant I thought of rushing on, quite as if I had not heard. Then I stopped and walked beside her.

"I am going to stay up all night: mother says I may; and I am going to fire off Tom Hemingway's big cannon every fourth time, straight through till breakfast time," I announced to her loftily.

"Dear me! I ought to be proud to be seen walking with such an important citizen," she answered, with kindly playfulness. She added more gravely, after a moment's pause: "Then Tom is out playing with the other boys, is he?"

"Why, of course!" I responded. "He always lets us stand around when he fires off his cannon. He's got some 'ringers' this year too."

I heard Miss Stratford murmur an impulsive "Thank God!" under her breath.

Full as the day had been of surprises, I could not help wondering that the fact of Tom's ringers should stir up such profound emotions in the teacher's breast. Since the subject so interested her, I went on with a long catalogue of Tom's other pyrotechnic possessions, and from that to an account of his almost supernatural collection of postage-stamps. In a few minutes more I am sure I should have revealed to her the great secret of my life, which was my determination, in case I came to assume the victorious rôle and rank of Napoleon, to immediately make Tom a Marshall of the Empire.

But we had reached the post-office square. I had never before seen it so full of people.

Even to my boyish eyes the tragic line of division which cleft this crowd in twain was apparent. On one side, over by the Seminary, the youngsters had lighted a bonfire, and were running about it—some of the bolder ones jumping through it in frolicsome recklessness. Close by stood the band, now valiantly thumping out "John Brown's Body" upon the noisy night air. It was quite dark by this time, but the musicians knew the tune by heart. So did the throng about them, and sang it with lusty fervor. The doors of the saloon toward the corner of the square were flung wide open. Two black streams of men kept in motion under the radiance of the big reflector-lamp over these doors— one going in, one coming out. They slapped one another on the back as they passed, with exultant screams and shouts. Every once in a while, when movement was for the instant blocked, some voice lifted above the others would begin "Hip-hip-hip-hip—" and then would come a roar that fairly drowned the music.

On the post-office side of the square there was no bonfire. No one raised a cheer. A densely packed mass of men and women

stood in front of the big square stone building, with its closed
doors, and curtained windows upon which, from time to time,
the shadow of some passing clerk, bareheaded and hurried,
would be momentarily thrown. They waited in silence for the
night mail to be sorted. If they spoke to one another, it was in
whispers—as if they had been standing with uncovered heads
at a funeral service in a graveyard. The dim light reflected over
from the bonfire, or down from the shaded windows of the post-
office, showed solemn, hard-lined, anxious faces. Their lips
scarcely moved when they muttered little low-toned remarks to
their neighbors. They spoke from the side of the mouth, and
only on one subject.

"He went all through Fredericksburg without a scratch—"

"He looks so much like me—General Palmer told my brother
he'd have known his hide in a tanyard—"

"He's been gone—let's see—it was a year some time last
April—"

"He was counting on a furlough the first of this month. I
suppose nobody got one as things turned out—"

"He said, 'No; it ain't my style. I'll fight as much as you like,
but I won't be nigger-waiter for no man, captain or no captain'
—"

Thus I heard the scattered murmurs among the grown-up
heads above me, as we pushed into the outskirts of the throng,
and stood there, waiting for the rest. There was no sentence
without a "he" in it. A stranger might have fancied that they
were all talking of one man. I knew better. They were the
fathers and mothers, the sisters, brothers, wives of the men
whose regiments had been in that horrible three days' fight
at Gettysburg. Each was thinking and speaking of his own, and
took it for granted the others would understand. For that matter, they all did understand. The town knew the name and
family of every one of the twelve-score sons she had in this
battle.

It is not very clear to me now why people all went to the
post-office to wait for the evening papers that came in from the

nearest big city. Nowadays they would be brought in bulk and sold on the street before the mail-bags had reached the post-office. Apparently that had not yet been thought of in our slow old town.

The band across the square had started up afresh with "Annie Lisle"—the sweet old refrain of "Wave willows, murmur waters," comes back to me now after a quarter-century of forgetfulness—when all at once there was a sharp forward movement of the crowd. The doors had been thrown open, and the hallway was on the instant filled with a swarming multitude. The band had stopped as suddenly as it began, and no more cheering was heard. We could see whole troops of dark forms scudding toward us from the other side of the square.

"Run in for me—that's a good boy—ask for Dr. Stratford's mail," the teacher whispered, bending over me.

It seemed an age before I finally got back to her, with the paper in its postmarked wrapper buttoned up inside my jacket. I had never been in so fierce and determined a crowd before, and I emerged from it at last, confused in wits and panting for breath. I was still looking about through the gloom in a foolish way for Miss Stratford, when I felt her hand laid sharply on my shoulder.

"Well—where is it?—did nothing come?" she asked, her voice trembling with eagerness, and the eyes which I had thought so soft and dove-like flashing down upon me as if she were Miss Pritchard, and I had been caught chewing gum in school.

I drew the paper out from under my roundabout, and gave it to her. She grasped it, and thrust a finger under the cover to tear it off. Then she hesitated for a moment, and looked about her. "Come where there is some light," she said, and started up the street. Although she seemed to have spoken more to herself than to me, I followed her in silence, close to her side.

For a long way the sidewalk in front of every lighted store-window was thronged with a group of people clustered tight about some one who had a paper, and was reading from it aloud.

Besides broken snatches of this monologue, we caught, now groans of sorrow and horror, now exclamations of proud approval, and even the beginnings of cheers, broken in upon by a general " 'Sh-h!" as we hurried past outside the curb.

It was under a lamp in the little park nearly half-way up the hill that Miss Stratford stopped, and spread the paper open. I see her still, white-faced, under the flickering gaslight, her black curls making a strange dark bar between the pale-straw hat and the white of her shoulder shawl and muslin dress, her hands trembling as they held up the extended sheet. She scanned the columns swiftly, skimmingly for a time, as I could see by the way she moved her round chin up and down. Then she came to a part which called for closer reading. The paper shook perceptibly now, as she bent her eyes upon it. Then all at once it fell from her hands, and without a sound she walked away.

I picked the paper up and followed her along the gravelled path. It was like pursuing a ghost, so weirdly white did her summer attire now look to my frightened eyes, with such a swift and deathly silence did she move. The path upon which we were described a circle touching the four sides of the square. She did not quit it when the intersection with our street was reached, but followed straight round again toward the point where we had entered the park. This, too, in turn, she passed, gliding noiselessly forward under the black arches of the overhanging elms. The suggestion that she did not know she was going round and round in a ring startled my brain. I would have run up to her now if I had dared.

Suddenly she turned, and saw that I was behind her. She sank slowly into one of the garden-seats, by the path, and held out for a moment a hesitating hand toward me. I went up at this and looked into her face. Shadowed as it was, the change I saw there chilled my blood. It was like the face of some one I had never seen before, with fixed, wide-open, staring eyes which seemed to look beyond me through the darkness, upon some terrible sight no other could see.

"Go—run and tell—Tom—to go home! His brother—his

brother has been killed," she said to me, choking over the words as if they hurt her throat, and still with the same strange dry-eyed, far-away gaze covering yet not seeing me.

I held out the paper for her to take, but she made no sign, and I gingerly laid it on the seat beside her. I hung about for a minute or two longer, imagining that she might have something else to say—but no word came. Then, with a feebly inopportune "Well, good-by," I started off alone up the hill.

It was a distinct relief to find that my companions were congregated at the lower end of the common, instead of their accustomed haunt farther up near my home, for the walk had been a lonely one, and I was deeply depressed by what had happened. Tom, it seems, had been called away some quarter of an hour before. All the boys knew of the calamity which had befallen the Hemingways. We talked about it, from time to time, as we loaded and fired the cannon which Tom had obligingly turned over to my friends. It had been out of deference to the feelings of the stricken household that they had betaken themselves and their racket off to the remote corner of the common. The solemnity of the occasion silenced criticism upon my conduct in forgetting to buy the powder. "There would be enough as long as it lasted," Billy Norris said, with philosophic decision.

We speculated upon the likelihood of De Witt Hemingway's being given a military funeral. These mournful pageants had by this time become such familiar things to us that the prospect of one more had no element of excitement in it, save as it involved a gloomy sort of distinction for Tom. He would ride in the first mourning-carriage with his parents, and this would associate us, as we walked along ahead of the band, with the most intimate aspects of the demonstration. We regretted now that the soldier company which we had so long projected remained still unorganized. Had it been otherwise we would probably have been awarded the right of the line in the procession. Some one suggested that it was not too late—and we promptly bound ourselves to meet after breakfast next day to organize and begin drilling. If we worked at this night and day, and our parents instantaneously provided us with uniforms and guns, we should be in time. It was also arranged that we should be called the De Witt C. Hemingway Fire Zouaves, and that Billy Norris should be side captain. The chief command would, of course, be reserved for Tom. We would specially salute him as he rode past in the closed carriage, and then fall in behind, forming his honorary escort.

None of us had known the dead officer closely, owing to his advanced age. He was seven or eight years older than even Tom. But the more elderly among our group had seen him play baseball in the academy nine, and our neighborhood was still alive with legends of his early audacity and skill in collecting barrels and dry-goods boxes at night for election bonfires. It was remembered that once he carried away a whole front-stoop from the house of a little German tailor on one of the back streets. As we stood around the heated cannon, in the great black solitude of the common, our fancies pictured this redoubtable young man once more among us—not in his blue uniform, with crimson sash and sword laid by his side, and the gauntlets drawn over his lifeless hands, but as a taller and glorified Tom, in a roundabout jacket and copper-toed boots, giving the law on this his playground. The very cannon at our feet had once been his. The night air became peopled with ghosts of his contemporaries—handsome boys who had grown up before us, and had gone away to lay down their lives in far-off Virginia or Tennessee.

These heroic shades brought drowsiness in their train. We lapsed into long silences, punctuated by yawns, when it was not our turn to ram and touch off the cannon. Finally some of us stretched ourselves out on the grass, in the warm darkness, to wait comfortably for this turn to come.

What did come instead was daybreak—finding Billy and myself alone constant to our all-night vow. We sat up and shivered as we rubbed our eyes. The morning air had a chilling freshness that went to my bones—and these, moreover, were filled with those novel aches and stiffnesses which beds were invented to prevent. We stood up, stretching out our arms, and gaping at the pearl-and-rose beginnings of the sunrise in the eastern sky. The other boys had all gone home, and taken the cannon with them. Only scraps of torn paper and tiny patches of burnt grass marked the site of our celebration.

My first weak impulse was to march home without delay, and get into bed as quickly as might be. But Billy Norris looked so finely resolute and resourceful that I hesitated to suggest this, and said nothing, leaving the initiative to him. One could see, by the most casual glance, that he was superior to mere considerations of unseasonableness in hours. I remembered now that he was one of that remarkable body of boys, the paper-carriers, who rose when all others were asleep in their warm nests, and trudged about long before breakfast distributing the *Clarion* among the well-to-do households. This fact had given him his position in our neighborhood as quite the next in leadership to Tom Hemingway.

He presently outlined his plans to me, after having tried the centre of light on the horizon, where soon the sun would be, by an old brass compass he had in his pocket—a process which enabled him, he said, to tell pretty well what time it was. The paper wouldn't be out for nearly two hours yet—and if it were not for the fact of a great battle, there would have been no paper at all on this glorious anniversary—but he thought we would go downtown and see what was going on around about the newspaper office. Forthwith we started. He cheered my faint spirits by assuring me that I would soon cease to be sleepy, and would, in fact, feel better than usual. I dragged my feet along at his side, waiting for this revival to come, and meantime furtively yawning against my sleeve.

Billy seemed to have dreamed a good deal, during our nap on the common, about the De Witt C. Hemingway Fire Zouaves. At least he had now in his head a marvellously elaborated system of organization, which he unfolded as we went along. I felt that I had never before realized his greatness, his born genius for command. His scheme halted nowhere. He allotted offices

with discriminating firmness; he treated the question of uniforms and guns as a trivial detail which would settle itself; he
spoke with calm confidence of our offering our services to the
Republic in the autumn; his clear vision saw even the materials
for a fife-and-drum corps among the German boys in the back
streets. It was true that I appeared personally to play a meagre
part in these great projects; the most that was said about me
was that I might make a fair third-corporal. But Fate had
thrown in my way such a wonderful chance of becoming intimate with Billy that I made sure I should swiftly advance in
rank—the more so as I discerned in the background of his
thoughts, as it were, a grim determination to make short work
of Tom Hemingway's aristocratic pretensions, once the funeral
was over.

We were forced to make a detour of the park on our way
down, because Billy observed some half-dozen Irish boys at
play with a cannon inside, whom he knew to be hostile. If there
had been only four, he said, he would have gone in and routed
them. He could whip any two of them, he added, with one hand
tied behind his back. I listened with admiration. Billy was not
tall, but he possessed great thickness of chest and length of arm.
His skin was so dark that we canvassed the theory from time
to time of his having Indian blood. He did not discourage this,
and he admitted himself that he was double-jointed.

The streets of the business part of the town, into which we
now made our way, were quite deserted. We went around into
the yard behind the printing-office, where the carrier-boys were
wont to wait for the press to get to work; and Billy displayed
some impatience at discovering that here too there was no one.
It was now broad daylight, but through the windows of the
composing-room we could see some of the printers still setting
type by kerosene lamps.

We seated ourselves at the end of the yard on a big, flat,
smooth-faced stone, and Billy produced from his pocket a
number of "em" quads, so he called them, and with which the
carriers had learned from the printers' boys to play a very

beautiful game. You shook the pieces of metal in your hands and threw them on the stone; your score depended upon the number of nicked sides that were turned uppermost. We played this game in the interest of good-fellowship for a little. Then Billy told me that the carriers always played it for pennies, and that it was unmanly for us to do otherwise. He had no pennies at that precise moment, but would pay at the end of the week what he had lost; in the meantime there was my twenty cents to go on with. After this Billy threw so many nicks uppermost that my courage gave way, and I made an attempt to stop the game; but a single remark from him as to the military destiny which he was reserving for me, if I only displayed true soldierly nerve and grit, sufficed to quiet me once more, and the play went on. I had now only five cents left.

Suddenly a shadow interposed itself between the sunlight and the stone. I looked up, to behold a small boy with bare arms and a blackened apron standing over me, watching our game. There was a great deal of ink on his face and hands, and a hardened, not to say rakish expression in his eye.

"Why don't you 'jeff' with somebody of your own size?" he demanded of Billy after having looked me over critically.

He was not nearly so big as Billy, and I expected to see the latter instantly rise and crush him, but Billy only laughed and said we were playing for fun; he was going to give me all my money back. I was rejoiced to hear this, but still felt surprised at the propitiatory manner Billy adopted toward this diminutive inky boy. It was not the demeanor befitting a side-captain —and what made it worse was that the strange boy loftily declined to be cajoled by it. He sniffed when Billy told him about the military company we were forming; he coldly shook his head, with a curt "Nixie!" when invited to join it; and he laughed aloud at hearing the name our organization was to bear.

"He ain't dead at all—that De Witt Hemingway," he said, with jeering contempt.

"Hain't he though!" exclaimed Billy. "The news come last

night. Tom had to go home—his mother sent for him—on account of it!"

"I'll bet you a quarter he ain't dead," responded the practical inky boy. "Money up, though!"

"I've only got fifteen cents. I'll bet you that, though," rejoined Billy, producing my torn and dishevelled shin-plasters.

"All right! Wait here!" said the boy, running off to the building and disappearing through the door. There was barely time for me to learn from my companion that this printer's apprentice was called "the devil," and could not only whistle between his teeth and crack his fingers, but chew tobacco, when he reappeared, with a long narrow strip of paper in his hand. This he held out for us to see, indicating with an ebon forefinger the special paragraph we were to read. Billy looked at it sharply, for several moments in silence. Then he said to me: "What does it say there? I must 'a' got some powder in my eyes last night."

I read this paragraph aloud, not without an unworthy feeling that the inky boy would now respect me deeply:

"CORRECTION. Lieutenant De Witt C. Hemingway, of Company A, —th New York, reported in earlier despatches among the killed, is uninjured. The officer killed is Lieutenant Carl Heinninge, Company F, same regiment."

Billy's face visibly lengthened as I read this out, and he felt us both looking at him. He made a pretence of examining the slip of paper again, but in a half-hearted way. Then he ruefully handed over the fifteen cents and, rising from the stone, shook himself.

"Them Dutchmen never was no good!" was what he said.

The inky boy had put the money in the pocket under his apron, and grinned now with as much enjoyment as dignity would permit him to show. He did not seem to mind any longer the original source of his winnings, and it was apparent that I could not with decency recall it to him. Some odd impulse prompted me, however, to ask him if I might have the paper he had in his hand. He was magnanimous enough to present me with the proof-sheet on the spot. Then with another grin he turned and left us.

Billy stood sullenly kicking with his bare toes into a sand-heap by the stone. He would not answer me when I spoke to him. It flashed across my perceptive faculties that he was not such a great man, after all, as I had imagined. In another instant or two it became quite clear to me that I had no admiration for him whatever. Without a word I turned on my heel and walked determinedly out of the yard and into the street, homeward bent.

All at once I quickened my pace; something had occurred to me. The purpose thus conceived grew so swiftly that soon I found myself running. Up the hill I sped, and straight through the park. If the Irish boys shouted after me I knew it not, but dashed on heedless of all else save the one idea. I only halted, breathless and panting, when I stood on Dr. Stratford's doorstep, and heard the night-bell inside jangling shrilly in response to my excited pull.

As I waited, I pictured to myself the old doctor as he would presently come down, half-dressed and pulling on his coat as he advanced. He would ask, eagerly, "Who is sick? Where am I to go?" and I would calmly reply that he unduly alarmed himself, and that I had a message for his daughter. He would, of course, ask me what it was, and I, politely but firmly, would decline to explain to any one but the lady in person. Just what might ensue was not clear—but I beheld myself throughout commanding the situation, at once benevolent, polished, and inexorable.

The door opened with unlooked-for promptness, while my self-complacent vision still hung in mid-air. Instead of the bald and spectacled old doctor, there confronted me a white-faced, solemn-eyed lady in a black dress, whom I did not seem to know. I stared at her, tongue-tied, till she said, in a low grave voice, "Well, Andrew, what is it?"

Then of course I saw that it was Miss Stratford, my teacher, the person whom I had come to see. Some vague sense of what the sleepless night had meant in this house came to me as I gazed confusedly at her mourning, and heard the echo of her sad tones in my ears.

"Is some one ill?" she asked again.

"No; some one—some one is very well!" I managed to reply, lifting my eyes again to her wan face. The spectacle of its drawn lines and pallor all at once assailed my wearied and over-taxed nerves with crushing weight. I felt myself beginning to whimper, and rushing tears scalded my eyes. Something inside my breast seemed to be dragging me down through the stoop.

I have now only the recollection of Miss Stratford's kneeling by my side, with a supporting arm around me, and of her thus unrolling and reading the proof-paper I had in my hand. We were in the hall now, instead of on the stoop, and there was a long silence. Then she put her head on my shoulder and wept. I could hear and feel her sobs as if they were my own.

"I—I didn't think you'd cry—that you'd be so sorry," I heard myself saying, at last, in despondent self-defence.

Miss Stratford lifted her head and, still kneeling as she was, put a finger under my chin to make me look in her face. Lo! the eyes were laughing through their tears; the whole counte-nance was radiant once more with the light of happy youth and with that other glory which youth knows only once.

"Why, Andrew, boy," she said, trembling, smiling, sobbing, beaming all at once, "didn't you know that people cry for very joy sometimes?"

And as I shook my head she bent down and kissed me.

My Aunt Susan

I held the lamp, while Aunt Susan cut up the pig.

The whole day had been devoted, I remember, to preparations for this great event. Early in the morning I had been to the butcher's to set in train the annual negotiations for a loan of cleaver and meat-saw; and hours afterward had borne these implements proudly homeward through the village street. In the interval I had turned the grindstone, over at the Four Corners, while the grocer's hired man obligingly sharpened our carving-knife. Then there had been the even more back-aching task of clearing away the hard snow from the accustomed site of our wood-pile in the yard, and scraping together a frosted heap of chips and bark for the smudge in the smoke-barrel.

From time to time I sweetened this toil, and helped the laggard hours to a swifter pace, by paying visits to the wood-shed to have still another look at the pig. He was frozen very stiff, and there were small icicles in the crevices whence his eyes had altogether disappeared. My emotions as I viewed his big, cold, pink carcass, with its extended legs, its bland and pasty countenance, and that awful emptiness underneath, were much mixed. Although I was his elder by seven or eight years, we had been close friends during all his life—or all except a very few weeks of his earliest sucking pighood, spent on his native farm. I had fed him daily; I had watched him grow week by week; more than once I had poked him with a stick as he ran around in his sty, to make him squeal for the edification of neighbors' boys who had come into our yard, and would now be sharply ordered out again by Aunt Susan.

As these kindly memories surged over me I could not but

feel like a traitor to my old companion, as he lay thus hairless and pallid before my eyes. But then I would remember how good he was going to be to eat—and straightway return with a light heart to the work of kicking up more chips from the ice.

From the living-room in the rear of our little house came the monotonous incessant clatter of Aunt Susan's carpet loom. Through the window I could see the outlines of her figure and the back of her head as she sat on her high bench. It was to me the most familiar of all spectacles, this tireless woman bending resolutely over her work. She was there when I first cautiously ventured my nose out from under the warm blanket of a winter's morning. Very, very often I fell asleep at night in my bed in the recess, lulled off by the murmur of the diligent loom.

Presently I went in to warm myself, and stood with my red fingers over the stove top. She cast but one vague glance at me, through the open frame of the loom between us, and went on with her work. It was not our habit to talk much in that house. She was too busy a woman, for one thing, to have much time for conversation. The impression that she preferred not to talk was always present in my boyish mind. I call up the picture of her still as I saw her then under the top bar of the cumbrous old machine, sitting with lips tight together, and resolute, masterful eyes bent upon the twining intricacy of warp and woof before her. At her side were piled a dozen or more big balls of carpet rags, which the village wives and daughters cut up, sewed together and wound in the long winter evenings, while the men-folks sat with their stockinged feet on the stove hearth, and read out the latest "news from the front" in their *Weekly Tribune*.

I knew all these rag balls by the names of their owners. Not only did I often go to their houses for them, upon the strength of the general village rumor that they were ready, and always carry back the finished lengths of carpet; but I had long since unconsciously grown to watch all the varying garments and shifts of fashion in the raiment of our neighbors, with an eye single to the likelihood of their eventually turning up at Aunt

Susan's loom. When Hiram Mabie's checkered butternut coat was cut down for his son Roswell, I noted the fact merely as a stage of its progress toward carpet rags. If Mrs. Wilkins concluded to turn her flowered delaine dress a third year, or Sarah Northrup had her bright saffron shawl dyed black, I was sensible of a wrong having been done our little household. I felt like crossing the street whenever I saw approaching the portly figure of Cyrus Husted's mother, the woman who dragged everybody into her house to show them the ingrain carpet she had bought at Tecumseh, and assured them that it was much cheaper in the long run than the products of my Aunt's industry. I tingled with indignation as she passed me on the sidewalk, puffing for breath and stepping mincingly because her shoes were too tight for her.

Nearly all the knowledge of our neighbors' sayings and doings which reached Aunt Susan came to her from me. She kept herself to herself with a vengeance, toiling early and late, rarely going beyond the confines of her yard save on Sunday mornings, when we went to church, and treating with frosty curtness the few people who ventured to come to our house on business or from social curiosity. For one thing, this Juno Mills in which we lived was not really our home. We had only been there for four or five years—a space which indeed spanned all my recollections of life—but left my Aunt more or less a stranger and a newcomer. She spared no pains to maintain that condition. I can see now that there were good reasons for this stern aloofness. At the time I thought it was altogether due to the proud and unsociable nature of my Aunt.

In my child's mind I regarded her as distinctly an elderly person. People outside, I know, spoke of her as an old maid, sometimes winking furtively over my head as they did so. But she was not really old at all—was in truth just barely in the thirties. Doubtless the fact that she was tall and dark, with very black hair, and that years of steady concentration of sight, upon the strings and threads of the loom, had scored a scowling vertical wrinkle between her near-sighted eyes gave me my notion of her advanced maturity. And in all her ways and words, too, she was so far removed from any idea of youthful softness! I could not remember her having ever kissed me. My imagination never evolved the conceit of her kissing anybody. I had always had at her hands uniformly good treatment, good food, good clothes; after I had learned my letters from the old maroon plush label on the Babbitt's soap box which held the wood behind the stove, and expanded this knowledge by a study of street signs, she had herself taught me how to read, and later provided me with books for the village school. She was my only known relative—the only person in the world who had ever done anything for me. Yet it could not be said that I loved her. Indeed she no more raised the suggestion of tenderness in my mind than did the loom at which she spent her waking hours.

"The Perkinses asked me why you didn't get the butcher to cut up the pig," I remarked at last, rubbing my hands together over the hot stove griddles.

"It's none of their business!" said Aunt Susan, with laconic promptness.

"And Devillo Pollard's got a new overcoat," I added. "He hasn't worn the old army one now for upward of a week."

"If this war goes on much longer," commented my Aunt, "every carpet in Dearborn County'll be as blue as a whetstone."

I think that must have been the entire conversation of the afternoon. I especially recall the remark about the overcoat. For two years now the balls of rags had contained an increasing proportion of pale blue woollen strips, as the men of the country round about came home from the South, or bought cheap garments from the second-hand dealers in Tecumseh. All other colors had died out. There was only this light blue, and the black of bombazine or worsted mourning into which the news in each week's papers forced one or another of the neighboring families. To obviate this monotony, some of the women dyed their white rags with butternut or even cochineal, but this was a mere drop in the bucket, so to speak. The loom spun out only long, depressing rolls of black and blue.

My memory leaps lightly forward now to the early evening, when I held the lamp in the woodshed, and Aunt Susan cut up the pig.

How joyfully I watched her every operation! Every now and again my interest grew so beyond proper bounds that I held the lamp sidewise, and the flame smoked the chimney. I was in mortal terror over this lamp, even when it was standing on the table quite by itself. We often read in the paper of explosions from this new kerosene by which people were instantly killed and houses wrapped in an unquenchable fire. Aunt Susan had stood out against the strange invention, long after most of the other homes of Juno Mills were familiar with the idea of the lamp. Even after she had yielded, and I went to the grocery for more oil and fresh chimneys and wicks, like other boys, she refused to believe that this inflammable fluid was really squeezed out of hard coal, as they said. And for years we lived in momentary belief that our lamp was about to explode.

My fears of sudden death could not, however, for a moment stand up against the delighted excitement with which I viewed the dismemberment of the pig. It was very cold in the shed, but neither of us noticed that. My Aunt attacked the job with skilful resolution and energy, as was her way, chopping small bones, sawing vehemently through big ones, hacking and slicing with the knife, like a strong man in a hurry.

For a long time no word was spoken. I gazed in silence as the head was detached, and then resolved itself slowly into souse— always tacitly set aside as my special portion. In prophecy I saw the big pan, filled with ears, cheeks, snout, feet, and tail, all boiled and allowed to grow cold in their own jelly—that pan to which I was free to repair any time of day until everything was gone. I thought of myself, too, with apron tied round my neck and the chopping-bowl on my knees, reducing what remained of the head into small bits, to be seasoned by my Aunt, and then fill other pans as head-cheese. The sage and summer savory hung in paper flour-bags from the rafters overhead. I looked up at them with rapture. It seemed as if my mouth already tasted them in head-cheese and sausage and in the hot gravy which basted the succulent sparerib. Only the abiding menace of the lamp kept me from dancing with delight.

Gradually, however, as my Aunt passed from the tid-bits to the more substantial portions of her task, getting out the shoulders, the hams for smoking, the pieces for salting down in the brine-barrel, my enthusiasm languished a trifle. The lamp grew heavy as I changed it from hand to hand, holding the free fingers at a respectful distance over the chimney-top for warmth, and shuffling my feet about. It was truly very cold. I strove to divert myself by smiling at the big shadow my bustling Aunt cast against the house side of the shed, and by moving the lamp to affect its proportions, but broke out into yawns instead. A mouse ran swiftly across the scantling just under the lean-to roof. At the same time I thought I caught the muffled sound of distant rapping, as if at our own rarely used front door. I was too sleepy to decide whether I had really heard a noise or not.

All at once I roused myself with a start. The lamp had nearly slipped from my hands, and the horror of what might have happened frightened me into wakefulness.

"The Perkins girls keep on calling me 'Wise child.' They yell it after me all the while," I said, desperately clutching at a subject which I hoped would interest my Aunt. I had spoken to her about it a week or so before, and it had stirred her quite out of her wonted stern calm. If anything would induce her to talk now, it would be this.

"They do, eh?" she said, with an alert sharpness of voice, which dwindled away into a sigh. Then, after a moment, she added, "Well, never you mind. You just keep right on, tending to your own affairs, and studying your lessons, and in time it'll be you who can laugh at them and all their low-down lot. They only do it to make you feel bad. Just don't you humor them."

"But I don't see," I went on, "why—what do they call me 'wise child' *for?* I asked Hi Budd, up at the Corners, but he only just chuckled and chuckled to himself, and wouldn't say a word."

My Aunt suspended work for the moment, and looked severely down upon me. "Well! Ira Clarence Blodgett!" she said, with grim emphasis, "I am ashamed of you! I thought you had more pride! The idea of talking about things like that with a coarse, rough, hired man—in a barn!"

To hear my full name thus pronounced, syllable by syllable, sent me fairly weltering, as it were, under Aunt Susan's utmost condemnation. It was the punishment reserved for my gravest crimes. I hung my head, and felt the lamp wagging nervelessly in my hands. I could not deny even her speculative impeachment as to the barn; it was blankly apparent in my mind that the fact of the barn made matters much worse.

"I was helping him wash their two-seated sleigh," I submitted, weakly. "He asked me to."

"What does that matter?" she asked, peremptorily. "What business have you got going around talking with men about me?"

"Why, it wasn't about you at all, Aunt Susan," I put in more confidently. "I said the Perkins girls kept calling me 'wise child,' and I asked Hi—"

Aunt Susan sighed once more, and interrupted me to inspect the wick of the lamp. Then she turned again to her work, but less spiritedly now. She took up the cleaver with almost an air of sadness.

"You don't understand—yet," she said. "But don't make it any harder for me by talking. Just go along and say nothing to nobody. People will think more of you."

My mind strove in vain to grapple with this suggested picture of myself, moving about in perpetual dumbness, followed everywhere by universal admiration. The lamp would *not* hold itself straight.

All at once we both distinctly heard the sound of footsteps

close outside. The noise of crunching on the dry, frozen snow came through the thin clapboards with sharp resonance. Aunt Susan ceased cutting and listened.

"I heard somebody rapping at the front door a spell ago," I ventured to whisper. My Aunt looked at me, and probably realized that I was too sleepy to be accountable for my actions. At all events she said nothing, but moved toward the low door of the shed, cleaver in hand.

"Who's there?" she called out in shrill, belligerent tones; and this demand she repeated, after an interval of silence, when an irresolute knocking was heard on the door.

We heard a man coughing immediately outside the door. I saw Aunt Susan start at the sound—almost as if she recognized it. A moment later this man, whoever he was, mastered his cough sufficiently to call out, in a hesitating way:

"Is that you, Susan?"

Aunt Susan raised her chin on the instant, her nostrils drawn in, her eyes flashing like those of a pointer when he sees a gun lifted. I had never seen her so excited. She wheeled round once, and covered me with a swift, penetrating, comprehensive glance, under which my knees smote together, and the lamp lurched perilously. Then she turned again, glided toward the door, halted, moved backward two or three steps—looked again at me, and this time spoke.

"Well, I *swan!*" was what she said, and I felt that she looked it.

"Susan! Is that you?" came the voice again, hoarsely appealing. It was not the voice of any neighbor. I made sure I had never heard it before. I could have smiled to myself at the presumption of any man calling my Aunt by her first name, if I had not been too deeply mystified.

"I've been directed here to find Miss Susan Pike," the man outside explained, between fresh coughings.

"Well, then, mog your boots out of this as quick as ever you can!" my Aunt replied, with great promptitude. "You won't find her here!"

"But I *have* found her!" the stranger protested, with an accent of wearied deprecation. "Don't you know me, Susan? I am not strong, this cold air is very bad for me."

"I say 'get out!'" my Aunt replied, sharply. Her tone was unrelenting enough, but I noted that she had tipped her head a little to one side, a clear sign to me that she was opening her mind to argument. I felt certain that presently I should see this man.

And, sure enough, after some further parley, Susan went to the door, and with a half-defiant gesture, knocked the hook up out of the staple.

"Come along then, if you must!" she said, in scornful tones. Then she marched back till she stood beside me, angry resolution written all over her face and the cleaver in her hand.

A tall, dark figure, opaque against a gleaming background of moonlight and snow light, was what I for a moment saw in the frame of the open doorway. Then, as he entered, shut and hooked the door behind him, and stood looking in a dazed way over at our lamplit group, I saw that he was a slender, delicately featured man, with a long beard of yellowish brown, and gentle eyes. He was clad as a soldier, heavy azure-hued caped overcoat and all, and I already knew enough of uniforms—cruel familiarity of my war-time infancy—to tell by his cap that he was an officer. He coughed again before a word was spoken. He looked the last man in the world to go about routing up peaceful households of a winter's night.

"Well, now—what is your business?" demanded Aunt Susan. She put her hand on my shoulder as she spoke, something I had never known her to do before. I felt confused under this novel caress, and it seemed only natural that the stranger, having studied my Aunt's face in a wistful way for a moment, should turn his gaze upon me. I was truly a remarkable object, with Aunt Susan's hand on my shoulder.

"I could make no one hear at the other door. I saw the light through the window here, and came around," the stranger explained. He sent little straying glances at the remains of the pig and at the weapon my Aunt held at her side, but for the most part looked steadily at me.

"That doesn't matter," said Aunt Susan, coldly. "What do you want, now that you *are* here? Why did you come at all? What business had you to think that I ever wanted to lay eyes on you again? How could you have the courage to show your face here—in *my* house?"

The man's shoulders shivered under their cape, and a wan smile curled in his beard. "You keep your house at a very low temperature," he said with grave pleasantry. He did not seem to mind Aunt Susan's hostile demeanor at all.

"I was badly wounded last September," he went on, quite as if that was what she had asked him, "and lay at the point of death for weeks. Then they sent me North, and I have been in the hospital at Albany ever since. One of the nurses there, struck by my name, asked me if I had any relatives in her village—that is, Juno Mills. In that way I learned where you were living. I suppose I ought not to have come—against doctor's orders—the journey has been too much—I have suffered a good deal these last two hours."

I felt my Aunt's hand shake a little on my shoulder. Her voice, though, was as implacable as ever.

"There is a much better reason than that why you should not have come," she said, bitterly.

The stranger was talking to her, but looking at me. He took a step toward me now, with a softened sparkle in his eyes and an outstretched hand. "This—this then is the boy, is it?" he asked.

With a gesture of amazing swiftness Aunt Susan threw her arm about me, and drew me close to her side, lamp and all. With her other hand she lifted and almost brandished the cleaver.

"No, you don't!" she cried. "You don't touch him! He's mine! I've worked for him day and night ever since I took him from his dying mother's breast. I closed her eyes. I forgave her. Blood is thicker'n water after all. She was my sister. Yes, I forgave poor Emmeline, and I kissed her before she died. She gave the boy to me, and he's mine! Mine, do you hear?— *mine!*"

"My dear Susan—" our visitor began.

"Don't 'dear Susan' me! I heard it once—once too often. Oh, never again! You left me to run away with her. I don't speak of that. I forgave that when I forgave her. But that was the least of it. You left her to herself for months before she died. You've left the boy to himself ever since. You can't begin now. I've worked my fingers to the bone for him—you can't make me stop now."

"I went to California," he went on in a low voice, speaking with difficulty. "We didn't get on together as smoothly as we might, perhaps, but I had no earthly notion of deserting her. I was ill myself, lying in yellow-fever quarantine off Key West, at the very time she died. When I finally got back you and the child were both gone. I could not trace you. I went to the war. I had made money in California. It is trebled now. I rose to be Colonel- -I have a Brigadier's brevet in my pocket now. Yet I give you my word I never have desired anything so much, all the time, as to find you again—you and the boy."

My Aunt nodded her head comprehendingly. I felt from the tremor of her hand that she was forcing herself against her own desires to be disagreeable.

"Yes, that war," was what she said. "I know about that war! The honest men that go get killed. But you—*you* come back."

The man frowned wearily, and gave a little groan of discouragement. "Then this is final, is it? You don't wish to speak with me; you really desire to keep the boy—you are set against my ever seeing him—touching him. Why, then, of course—of course—excuse my—"

And then for the first time I saw a human being tumble in a dead swoon. My little brain, dazed and bewildered by the strange new things I was hearing, lagged behind my eyes in following the sudden pallor on the man's face—lagged behind my ears in noting the tell-tale quaver and gasp in his voice. Before I comprehended what was toward—lo! there was no man standing in front of me at all.

Like a flash Aunt Susan snatched the lamp from my grasp and flung herself upon her knees beside the limp and huddled figure. After a momentary inspection of the white, bearded face, she set the lamp down on the frozen earth floor and took his head upon her lap.

"Take the lamp, run to the buttery, and bring the bottle of hartshorn!" she commanded me, hurriedly. "Or, no—wait— open the door—that's it—walk ahead with the light!"

The strong woman stood upright as she spoke, her shoulders braced against the burden she bore in her arms. Unaided, with slow steps, she carried the senseless form of the soldier into the living-room, and held it without rest of any sort, the while I, under her direction, wildly tore off quilts, blankets, sheets, and feather-tick from my bed and heaped them up on the floor beside the stove. Then, when I had spread them to her liking, she bent and gently laid him down.

"*Now* get the hartshorn," she said. I heard her putting more wood on the fire, but when I returned with the phial she sat once again with the stranger's head upon her knee. She was softly stroking the fine, waving brown hair upon his brow, but her eyes were lifted, looking dreamily at far-away things. I could have sworn to the beginnings of a smile about her parted lips. It was not like my Aunt Susan at all.

"Come here, Ira," I heard her say at last, after a long time had been spent in silence. I walked over and stood at her shoulder, looking down upon the pale face upturned against the black of her worn dress. The blue veins just discernible in temples and closed eyelids, the delicately turned features, the way his brown beard curled, the fact that his breathing was gently regular once more—these are what I saw. But my Aunt seemed to demand that I should see more.

"Well?" she asked, in a tone mellowed beyond all recognition. "Don't you—don't you see who it is?"

I suppose I really must have had an idea by this time. But I remember that I shook my head.

My Aunt positively did smile this time. "The Perkins girls were wrong," she said; "there isn't the least smitch of a 'wise child' about *you!*"

There was another pause. Emboldened by consciousness of a change in the emotional atmosphere, I was moved to lay my hand upon my Aunt's shoulder. The action did not seem to displease her, and we remained thus for some minutes, watching together this strange addition to our family party.

Finally she told me to get on my cap, comforter, and mittens, and run over to Dr. Peabody's and fetch him back with me. The purport of my mission oppressed me.

"Is he going to die then?" I asked.

Aunt Susan laughed outright. "You little goose," she said; "do you think the doctors kill people *every* time?"

And, laughing again, with a trembling softness in her voice and tears upon her black eyelashes, she lifted her face to mine —and kissed me!

No fatality dogged good old Doctor Peabody's big footsteps through the snow that night. I fell asleep while he was still at my Aunt's house, but not before the stranger had recovered consciousness, and was sitting up in the large rocking-chair, and it was clearly understood that he was soon to be well again.

The kindly, garrulous doctor did more than reassure our little household. He must have spent most of the night going about reassuring the other households of Juno Mills. At all events, when I first went out next morning—while our neighbors were still eating their buckwheat cakes and pork fat by lamplight—everybody seemed to know that my father, the distinguished Colonel Blodgett, had returned from the war on sick-leave, and was lying ill at the house of his sister-in-law. I felt at once the altered attitude of the village toward me. Important citizens who had never spoken to me before—dignified and portly men in blue cutaway coats with brass buttons, and high stiff hats of shaggy white silk—stopped now to lay their hands on the top of my head and ask me how my father, the Colonel, was getting along. The grocer's hired man gave me a Jackson ball and two molasses cookies the very first time I saw him. Even the Perkins girls, during the course of the afternoon, strolled over to our front gate, and instead of hurling enigmatic objurgations at me, invited me to come out and play. The butcher of his own accord came and finished cutting up the pig.

These changes came back to me as one part of the great metamorphosis which the night's events had wrought. Another part was the definite disappearance of the stern-faced, tirelessly toiling old maid I had known all my life as Aunt Susan. In her place there was now a much younger woman, with pleasant lines about her pretty mouth, and eyes that twinkled when they looked at me, and who paid no attention to the loom whatever, but bustled cheerily about the house instead, thinking only of good things for us to eat.

I remember that I marked my sense of the difference by abandoning the old name of Aunt Susan, and calling her now just "Auntie." And one day, in the mid-spring, after she and her convalescent patient had returned from their first drive together in the country round about, she told me, as she took off her new bonnet in an absent-minded way, and looked meditatively at the old disused loom, and then bent down to brush my forehead with her warm lips—she told me that henceforth I was to call her Mother.